THE LEAFLESS FOREST

Book Two of the Apotheosis Trilogy

'The impressive thing about *The Lightless Dome* is that it
operates both as a rousing piece of high fantasy and a mild
satire on same. Good-natured fun is had from both the
fantasy genre and the film business. It is swiftly paced and
well told . . . It is a fitting milestone in a productive career.'
— Stan Nicholls, *Darkside*

Also by Douglas Hill in Pan Books

THE LIGHTLESS DOME

DOUGLAS HILL

The Leafless Forest

THE APOTHEOSIS TRILOGY

BOOK TWO

PAN BOOKS

LONDON, SYDNEY AND AUCKLAND

First published 1994 by Pan Books Limited

a division of Pan Macmillan Publishers Limited
Cavaye Place London SW10 9PG
and Basingstoke

Associated companies throughout the world

ISBN 0 330 32960 X

1 3 5 7 9 8 6 4 2

A CIP catalogue record for this book is available from
the British Library

Phototypeset by Intype, London
Printed by Mackays of Chatham PLC, Chatham, Kent

For

DENNIS AND FIONA

now may the best man win

A young actor named Red Cordell, having come upon an unusual sword with a glowing blade, is plucked from his familiar world into a land of barbaric violence and magical powers. Upon arrival he finds himself defending a beautiful blonde against an assassin; befriending an immensely strong man named Krost; and having a wound miraculously healed by a small stranger called Hallifort. Afterwards, he learns that the blonde woman, Aurilia, is one of the Circle of Nine that rules a community of enchantresses known as the Sisterhood. It was Aurilia who summoned the luminous sword to her aid and caught Red up in her summoning. For the sword, which cannot be broken or blunted, was made by the Sisterhood for a hero of that land, now dead, named Corodel. And Red Cordell has a strange, timeless correlation with his near-namesake.

He also learns that his bulky new friend, Krost, is a dwarf-giant, born of a race of beings twice as tall as normal humans. And finally, he is told that Krost and Aurilia have both been called to the city by the ruler of the Four-Cornered Continent, Prince Phaedran, whose daughter, Evelane, now a lovely young woman, has been mysteriously abducted.

Later, restlessly exploring with Krost, Red sees and pursues the assassin Vanticor, who had earlier attacked Aurilia. Red finds that Vanticor's henchmen are inhuman beings from distant swamps, the Barachi, and he is saved from the Barachi by, again, the strange healer Hallifort. His news about the Barachi confirms for Phaedran that his daughter's abductor must be his old enemy, Talonimal – a power-hungry and sexually insatiable sorcerer whom Phaedran had banished years before. Soon the prince's wizards discover an impenetrable magical barrier on the coast of the Western Woodlands, where the Barachi come from and to which Talonimal is thought to have fled.

The prince puts together a mobile force to travel westward and rescue the princess. Aurilia and Krost go along, as does Red. But when the force is attacked by the Barachi, on the river, only six survive, thanks to Aurilia's magic: Red, Aurilia herself, Krost, the prince and two others. Before long, deep in the Woodlands, more Barachi attack, led by Vanticor, and capture the prince. Red, Krost and Aurilia survive, mysteriously aided by demonic creatures called Zhraike – and the three pursue Vanticor and his Barachi, hoping to free the prince.

They are led to the coast, where they find an immense, shiny-black Dome – the protection raised by Talonimal. With Aurilia's veiling, they enter unseen. But within the uncanny darkness of the interior, Red is separated from his friends. Alone and prowling, he comes upon a young woman who is Princess Evelane herself, not the sorcerer's captive, but his accomplice and lover. After that Red overhears a long-range magical confrontation between Talonimal and an immensely powerful mage named Lebarran Magister, apparently the one who sent the Zhraike to attack the Barachi. But then Talonimal becomes aware of Red, and flings him into a magical dungeon where he finds Aurilia, Krost and the prince.

Soon they are visited by the sorcerer and the princess, where they learn the truth about Evelane's betrayal of her father – how she was seduced by Talonimal's promise to confer on her the gift of magic she has always yearned for. Aurilia tells her it cannot be done, but Evelane maniacally asserts that Talonimal will achieve it when he has enhanced his own powers to the utmost, which can be done by the dire evil of *sacrifice*. And Red and the others are about to become the next offerings.

At the appointed time, while the captives are guarded by Vanticor and some Barachi, Talonimal reveals what is to happen. He relates how Lebarran Magister first made contact with a monstrous, supernaturally powerful entity known only as the Unformed, which dwells in the Void Beyond. Lebarran then recruited others, including Talonimal, to help find a means to control the Unformed and to give it the true life-force and stable form that it craves. Thereby it and they together would achieve the powers of gods – an Apotheosis. But Talonimal broke away from Lebarran's Order of the Apotheosis, seeking to gain supremacy on his own behind his protective Dome, by sacrificing to the Unformed.

He then begins to prepare for that further offering, invoking a tall misty threshold and the equally ethereal image of an endless bridge, on which the immense and horrifying being, the Unformed, appears. But when Aurilia is chosen to be first into the sacrificial flame, she uses all her beauty and her magic to entrap Talonimal with his own lusts. Like a mindless rutting beast, blind to all else, Talonimal struggles with Aurilia while Red and Krost do battle with their guards, aided by a destructive poltergeist outburst from Evelane. Though severely wounded, Red kills Vanticor while the prince flings Talonimal into his own sacrificial fire, to be destroyed by the Unformed.

Fleeing the Dome, trying to keep Red alive, the survivors are astonishingly met by Hallifort the Healer, who instantly restores Red and tries also to ease the damaged mind of the princess. And although he claims sadly to have no real powers beyond healing, Hallifort also warns them that the fall of Talonimal has not put an end to the great peril that menaces the land.

PART ONE

THE MUSTERING

All that day, as during nearly all the days preceding it, a thin weak drizzle – more mist than rain – had fallen steadily upon the valley. With the arrival of twilight, the permanent cloud cover that mantled the valley seemed to settle lower, thickening the rain-mist into something approaching the density of fog. As it collected, it drifted in floating banks just above the ground, leaving the gleam of its moisture on the boles of the trees that loomed like ghostly pillars in the dimness.

They were ancient and massive, those trees, their tangled branches reaching high to disappear in the descending clouds. They stood rank upon irregular rank to form a mighty forest that covered most of the valley floor. Yet in that forest the trees drew no sustenance from the near-endless fall of moisture. They were beyond all natural processes of nutrition and growth, beyond life itself. No leaves grew on the trees' uplifted branches, no leaves lay on the bare earth at their feet, no leaves had sprouted in that forest for centuries. Every one of the trees was dead. And in death, through all that time, they had slowly undergone petrification, trunk and root and branch inexorably altering into hard grey stone. Amid the enveloping mist and descending darkness, they stood like crude misshapen statuary, eerie mockeries of life and nature.

None the less, some life did exist in that place of stony tree-trunks and empty ground. Here and there on the trees or on rock outcrops grew sickly yellow smears of lichen, patches of pale moss, puffs of corpse-white fungus, all looking like the outward symptoms of some unknown pestilence. And also among the trees lived other things – beings that moved, upon two legs.

The beings were not beasts, yet neither were they human. Just as the petrified trees looked like sculpted images, so those

3

beings resembled badly carved but mobile statues. They were squat, heavily built, with small heads sunk deep between mounded shoulders. Their hairless skin, a sickly grey, looked as creased and weathered – and as solid – as the trunks of the petrified trees, as if the flesh of the beings had somehow also turned to stone.

Roaming the forest in their hundreds, the creatures were foraging among the trees, moving in a shuffling lurch as they tore up handfuls of fungus and moss and stolidly ate it. At the same time they all seemed to be making their slow ways towards various dips and hollows in the ground that would serve them as lairs for the night. But though their wanderings seemed mostly aimless and random, it was clear that they all kept themselves well away from the heart of the petrified forest. There, at the centre of an expanse of ground that was entirely free of trees, stood a structure that was itself more grotesque than anything else in that unnatural valley.

It was enormous, containing more than half a hundred chambers of varying size, with linking corridors. And all of it had been formed from the petrified trees of the forest. Yet those trees had not been felled and shaped for the purpose. They still stood upright, still rooted. But somehow they had been *rearranged*, by an unimaginable force – gathered into straight ranks and rows, pressed tightly together side by side, to form the walls, outer and inner, of the structure. Above the walls the branches of the trees were interwoven and overarched to form the semblance of a ceiling, while the bare earth served as floor. But higher above it all, almost hidden in the clouded darkness, loomed something that was neither stone nor earth nor cloud. It was an immense canopy, shaped like a flattened cone, made of darkly shiny metal. High above the topmost branches of the trees, it reached out over the entire breadth of the huge structure, as its uppermost covering. Yet despite the canopy's size and incalculable weight, it hung motionless above the structure without apparent support of any kind.

The structure's interior lay mostly in darkness and also mostly empty, save for the mist that drifted in unopposed through the outer doorways. Only one chamber was occupied, one of the largest, at the centre, bright with the glow of a strange pale light that seemed to have no visible source. There the structure's only inhabitant, and its creator, sat in a hard high-backed chair and stared down into a large stone bowl at his feet.

He was a short, stocky man wearing a robe of thick fur. His head and his blunt-featured face were entirely hairless, though thick black hair sprouted on his wrists and at the base of his throat exposed by the robe. Indifferent to the dank fog or the darkness that were trying to seep in at the door, he sat with his gaze riveted on to the glimmer of light from within the bowl, like a reflection of the almost phosphorescent glow that flickered around the man's fingers. The bowl was filled to the brim with a shiny black liquid, its unmoving surface offering a darkly perfect mirror. Staring into the bowl as if peering through a window, the fur-robed man was watching a scene like a portion of a drama, depicted in miniature on the shiny surface. A scene of six people together on an empty beach, by the edge of a glistening sea.

It was not the first time that the fur-robed man had watched that scene in his scrying bowl, for its events had taken place in the fairly recent past. Yet he studied the six moving figures with intensity, as if hoping that in this viewing something new might be revealed. And his deep-set eyes seemed to shine with a light of their own, bright and yellow and feral, as they stared at the six people on that faraway shore.

Two of them were women, one of them beautiful and full-bodied with a mass of tawny blonde hair, the other one younger, slim and dark and strangely vacant-eyed. From them the fur-robed man's gaze shifted to two of the other figures – a tall man with grey hair and a lined, grim face and another man only slightly shorter but disproportionately large in breadth and girth, vast muscles rolling with his every movement. Again the man's glowing eyes shifted, to fix unblinkingly on the last two of the six people on that shore. One was a rangy young man, lean and athletic-looking, with a tangle of russet-red hair, carrying a sword whose blade shone as if the metal contained its own source of multicoloured light. And

5

the other, the sixth of the group, was small, round-faced, with receding white hair, dressed all in blue with a tall hat, who would have looked quite harmless and almost comical if not for his eyes, with their irises of startling purple and pupils of a pure, inhuman white.

The fur-robed man raised a finger, with its phosphorescent glow, and the image of the small man in the bowl was held still. 'Hallifort,' the fur-robed man muttered, his eyes flaring. 'Hallifort the Healer. What are you, Hallifort? Where have you come from? And, in all the Realms and Spheres, *where are you now?*'

The muttering became an angry roar in the last four words, and the man's hand gestured sharply. At once the images in the bowl blurred, shifting from one scene to another in a sequence of dizzying speed. Rigid with concentration, he stared as the images passed before him, as his scrying sight swept across great distance and through passing time – over woodlands, plains and mountain ranges, into farmsteads, villages and city streets. And throughout it all, wherever his sight ranged, not once did its focus stop and settle again on the image of the little man with the weird eyes.

The fur-robed man's eyes blazed as he ground his teeth with rising anger. 'Where *are* you, Hallifort?' he rasped. '*What* are you? What manner of *healer* is it who can hide himself from a Magister's scrying?'

Then he paused, becoming as still and rigid as one of his petrified trees, struck by a sudden thought. 'Can that be it?' he snarled, staring up at the blackness above him. 'Is *that* what you are? Could it be . . . ?'

For a long moment he remained unmoving. Then another gesture cleared the surface of the scrying bowl, and placed upon it the still image of the young red-headed man holding the luminous sword.

'Three times,' the fur-robed man growled to himself. 'Three times Hallifort the Healer has come unbidden to the aid of the outlander who now bears the sword of Corodel. Does it mean that the outlander is fated to play a central role in events to come, as he has played in events just past?' A mirthless smile formed on his thick lips. 'If so, he might be prevented. While at the same time he might provide a means to lure Hallifort from his hiding-place, so his mystery may be plumbed.'

He lunged to his feet, the high-backed chair vanishing abruptly behind him. As he stalked away from the scrying bowl, shaping complex gestures with his glowing hands, a bright circle of energy materialized, like a large golden hoop, suspended horizontally some feet from the floor near the centre of the chamber. The fur-robed man spoke a few harsh syllables, and within the hovering golden circle a darkness began to gather, deeper than any of the shadows that had descended on the forest around that dwelling.

In a few moments, as the man spoke more of the ugly phrases, the darkness within the circle began to take on solidity and shape – the hideous shape of embodied horror. It was a monstrous creature, rearing taller than the fur-robed man though it stood on all fours. Its forelegs or arms were long and powerfully muscled, its massive shoulders and upper back tapered to narrow hindquarters and short, thick hind legs. Huge talons sprouted from its paws, huge fangs glinted in its gaping mouth. The matted black fur that covered it stank like a mass of nameless corruption, and in the sockets where its eyes should have been things like tendrils of red smoke ceaselessly twisted and writhed.

The monster turned its head this way and that, as if listening rather than looking, baring its fangs in an evil, croaking growl.

'Be still,' the fur-robed man ordered, seeming quite undaunted. 'I have invoked you, demon . . .'

But the eyeless monster growled more loudly, drowning his words, and lunged forward – until its snarling face almost touched the glowing circle that enclosed it. Then it jerked back, its growl altering to an eerie, pain-filled howl.

'Be silent!' the man snapped. 'Do you not know me, demon? I am Lebarran, the Magister, and you will not overcome *my* constraints!'

The monster cowered in the centre of the bright circle, its howl diminishing to a choked whine.

'Take note, there,' the man named Lebarran went on harshly,

indicating the scrying bowl that still presented the image of the red-haired man. 'There is the task to which I have invoked you. Find this man, this outlander who bears another's sword, and bring him to me – alive.'

The demon, still whining, seemed to stare at the bowl with the writhing red tendrils of its eyes.

'The outlander is presently with the witches of the Sisterhood,' Lebarran continued, 'in their northern Fastness. You would have no hope of entering there, but you can wait near by until he emerges, and then take him. Do you understand?' At the demon's muted croak that seemed to signify assent, he nodded sharply. 'Afterwards you will be returned to your own Realm. But first, I will *ensure* obedience.'

He gestured, and the glowing circle surrounding the demon began to shrink. Within a moment it had contracted to a small golden circlet fitting neatly around the demon's thick neck, gleaming amid the black fur. The demon moaned and whined, baring its teeth in a grimace that seemed filled with pain. And again Lebarran smiled his mirthless smile.

'Perform your task swiftly, and the collar will be more swiftly removed.' He raised a glowing hand. 'Now begone! Bring me the one who bears the sword of Corodel!'

In the afternoon of the following day, no one was actively bearing the sword of Corodel. In its leather sheath with attached belt it had been irreverently slung around the slender neck of a nude female statue that graced one corner of a stone-flagged courtyard. Near by, the sword's usual bearer, Red Cordell, was instead wielding a light fencing sabre with un-guarded blade and point, trying to defend himself against an opponent who was measurably more skilled.

The courtyard was in the midst of a complex of low, solid buildings that formed part of the enclave known as the Fast-ness, built by the enchantresses of the Sisterhood as their princi-pal base. The Fastness stood on the sheltered side of a ridge among broad open moorlands that formed the northern sector of the Four-Cornered Continent. More or less the size of a small village, its buildings and outer protective wall were made of thick and solid hardwood reinforced with stone, often also faced or decorated with varicoloured clay, so that the Fastness looked almost as if it had grown organically out of the land around it, its subdued earth-colours as rich and warm as those of the moors themselves.

They looked particularly warm on that sunlit afternoon, when the year was striding on towards high summer. The pale sky could not produce the tiniest cloud to filter the sun's relentless glare, so that within the first moments of swordplay Red had flung his shirt off, while wishing that he could exchange his trousers and boots for the shorts and running shoes that he would have worn in his own world. His opponent had been enviably more able to cast aside outer garments – although it was not only envy that Red was feeling. The other fencer, also wielding a light sabre, was a leggy dark-haired woman named Brennia, with skin the colour of cinnamon and a knowing grin that was all too evident in the course of their mock-battle. Almost as tall and wide-shouldered as Red, and perhaps in her early thirties, a year or two older than him, she seemed to be at least his equal athletically and certainly his superior with a blade. Although, in fairness, he had lost some portion of his concentration since she had partially disrobed. Her light sleeveless undershirt was skimpy enough to display the circular mark of the Sisterhood like a brand between the upper slopes of her unrestrained breasts. And he was certain, from a tantalizing half-glimpse or two, that she wore nothing at all under the kirtle that reached only halfway down her thighs.

He was also aware that she was grinning as much because she knew what he was looking at as because he was having a hard time with the sabre against her. In fact, at that very moment she gave a supple twitch of her hips that caused the hem of her kirtle to flutter. And as Red inevitably looked down, she attacked. Red fell back against the onslaught of her blade as it wove its patterns with eye-baffling speed. Somehow, by reflex, he managed a jerky, desperate defence, but he was being steadily forced to give way, unable to hold her off or to offer any riposte or counterattack. Subtly then she altered the rhythm and the pattern, and at the same time managed to accelerate her sabre's speed. It flickered around Red's blade in a complex curve, until the curve incredibly twisted back on itself in a movement that ended with Red's blade flying from his hand.

With that she halted, her grin widening. And in that moment of hesitation Red struck out, his left hand moving in a blur. The extended knuckle of his middle finger drove into the nerve centre of her upper arm, and her own sabre fell from her suddenly numbed hand.

Her grin vanishing, she jumped back with a small pained exclamation, while a burst of deep, hoarse laughter came from the far side of the courtyard. Red and Brennia looked around, towards the massive form of Krost il Hak taking his ease in the shade of one of the buildings. Seated on a heavy stone bench – which looked almost frail compared to its occupant's bulk – gripping a pottery jug of frothing ale and laughing immoderately, Krost was clearly having a fine time in his role as spectator.

'You must watch him, Brennia!' he roared. 'When he thinks he might lose, he cheats!'

Brennia nodded, rubbing her arm to restore its feeling. 'They teach strange ways of swordsmanship in your Sphere, Red.'

Going to pick up his sword, Red looked contrite. 'Sorry. You left the opening, and I couldn't help myself.'

Brennia's grin reappeared. 'I wouldn't have left the opening in battle. I stopped my blade before it completed the movement.'

'Which probably would have cut my throat,' Red said.

'No, skewered your liver.' She laughed cheerfully, reaching down for her sabre, her arm restored. 'You might show me that stroke of yours, someday.'

'Any time,' Red said, 'though I don't think I have much to teach you about combat, unarmed or otherwise.'

Again Krost's laughter rolled out from his shady bench. 'Let him stay your pupil, Brennia. A man who carries a famous sword should try to gain *some* skill with it.'

'He's not so bad, Krost,' Brennia said, smiling.

Red gave her a half-bow. 'High praise,' he said lightly. 'Ready to go on?'

She raised her sabre. 'We can try that last pattern again. Watch for the change of tempo, and see if you can find a counter. With your *blade*.'

At once she began the attack, barely giving Red time enough to bring his own sabre into position. Again he was driven back, trying to keep his weight properly balanced as he retreated, trying to concentrate on the movement of Brennia's sabre rather than that of her body. Halfway across the courtyard in his retreat he sensed the change of tempo, but even as he glimpsed a partial opening for a parry the chance was lost. As her blade completed its coiling return sweep, Red's sabre flew once more from his hand.

Brennia's blade flashed onwards, and sliced a line of bright scarlet across the flat muscle of Red's belly.

At once they both moved back, Brennia's eyes and mouth opening wide with horror, Red grimacing at the sudden flare of pain. He looked down at the blood dripping over his lower abdomen and pawed vaguely at the sweat that was also trick-

11

ling over his torso, adding its salt sting to the pain of the wound.

'Red, I'm *sorry*!' Brennia gasped.

He gave her a lopsided grin. 'I guess I left the opening this time and you couldn't help yourself.' He touched a finger to the edge of the cut. 'It's nothing much. I'll get something to stop the bleeding . . .'

'I can do that.' Brennia moved close to him, reaching out to the wound, the knotted gold ring of the Sisterhood gleaming on one finger. 'This may sting a little.'

'It stings already,' Red told her, watching as her hand touched his skin, slowly and delicately trailing two fingers along the seeping wound. Red tried not to flinch as the slashed flesh grew suddenly hot – but it lasted for only an instant. And in the wake of Brennia's touch, the flow of blood from the wound slowed and stopped.

'Good trick,' he said, impressed. 'Handy for a battlefield.'

He lifted his gaze to her face – and was suddenly, powerfully aware of how close she was standing, how her hand rested almost caressingly on his midriff, how her skin smelled like flowers, how her mouth was slowly softening . . .

Then she abruptly removed her hand and stepped back, shattering the moment. Just as Krost ambled up, jug in hand, to peer with interest at the angry red weal of the wound.

'Healer as well as warrior,' he remarked. 'Very useful.'

Brennia made a vague gesture. 'The Earth-magic doesn't do true, complete healing. It just stops bleeding and speeds up the body's natural mending. But there will be a scar . . .'

'There are worse places for scars,' Krost said with a grin.

Red cleared his throat, pulling his gaze away from her. 'You have any beer left, Krost?'

'Not a drop,' Krost told him cheerfully.

'Just as well,' Brennia said. 'You should bathe the wound now, Red. With water, not ale.'

'You need to bathe more than the wound,' Krost commented, indicating the smeared blood and sweat on Red's torso. 'Time enough for ale this evening.'

He turned away, going to reclaim his heavy iron quarterstaff that he had left leaning against the bench. Red and Brennia went in the other direction, gathering up Red's sword and the items of clothing that they had removed.

'I'll send someone with a salve for your wound,' Brennia said, pulling on the short gauzy tunic that was her outer garment. 'You'll certainly be able to fence again tomorrow – if you wish.'

'Bring the salve to me yourself,' Red said quietly.

She looked at him for a long moment, then heaved a sigh. 'Red, I have no doubt that I would enjoy what you have in mind. But I can't, and won't. I know you are pledged to Aurilia, and she to you.'

Red's mouth twisted. 'That's as may be, as they say. Does it make such a difference?'

'It does,' Brennia insisted. 'Out of courtesy and respect for Aurilia. Mine because she is my friend and also one of my leaders in the Circle of Nine. Yours . . . for obvious reasons.'

'Not all that obvious, these days,' Red said dourly. 'But I get the message.' He forced a jaunty smile. 'Come and have a drink with Krost and me tonight, anyway.'

She smiled. 'I'll try.'

'And I'll try,' he added, 'to keep you from cutting me open again, in tomorrow's fencing lesson.'

Alone in his quarters – a suite of small airy rooms high in a building near the outer wall of the Fastness – Red flung off his clothing and lay awhile in a bath of cool water. It should have been a delight, after the heat and exertion of the courtyard, but his mood had taken him past such small pleasures. At last he climbed out of the bath and carelessly dried himself, then flung himself naked on to a settee by a window. Staring blankly out, he scarcely noticed the glorious view – over a rolling expanse of the Northern Moorlands, where in the distance a flock of woolly beasts grazed peacefully, tended by a bronze-skinned herdsman. Instead, his gaze was turned almost entirely inwards, to examine a far less pleasurable view.

He knew, because he had been told often enough, that he was by nature a restless, edgy and impatient person. He had little time for the more serene, contemplative processes of living. All his life he had craved action and excitement, always seeking to release his energies and test his nerve, hopelessly addicted to the rush of adrenalin, ready for nearly anything that would end inactivity and relieve boredom. Yet there in the Fastness of the Sisterhood, for him, inactivity and boredom seemed the order of the day – as they had for almost every day since his arrival. The only real breaks to the dullness had been the fencing sessions with Brennia, when she had the time, and a few well-behaved drinks with Krost most evenings. But even those recreations were growing repetitive and stale for Red, as his volatile nature asserted itself.

That, he knew with his usual self-awareness, was why he had made his impulsive overture to Brennia. Trying for something to break the monotony. And that wasn't much of a reason, he thought with a grimace. Not much regard there for Brennia herself – nor for Aurilia, whom he would have been betraying. He glowered darkly at the landscape, thinking about Aurilia, seeing the images that always arose unbidden when he turned his thoughts to her. Images of Aurilia in her younger form – in vivid conversation, in thoughtful stillness, in supple and graceful movement, or in wanton invitation with her long blonde hair swirling around her as if it had a life of its own . . .

He knew very well that it was not her fault, in any direct way, that he was feeling restless, bored and caged. And yet, illogically, he did blame her. He was there in the Fastness because of her, his wish to be with her. He had anticipated a sweet and untroubled time when they could relax together, enjoy themselves, get to know each other even more intimately, away from all the violence and danger that had beset them ever since they had met. Indeed, it had been more or less just such a time during their slow, uneventful journey from the west, with Krost and Phaedran and Evelane, back to the capital city, Quamarr. But the idyll had started to come to an end, he recalled, during their brief stay then in the prince's palace. Aurilia was one of many important folk who were regularly closeted with Phaedran, considering what had been learned from the terror of the Lightless Dome, and what new terrors

14

might be visited upon the Continent by another mysterious and powerful enemy.

And later, after their swift journey to the Fastness – where they had been staying for little more than a fortnight – Aurilia had been even more caught up with whatever was occupying the Circle of Nine. That, indeed, had been *why* she had had to travel to the Fastness: so that the Nine could be complete, united, in whatever complex, magical and of course *secret* business they were involved with. So she had little time to spare for Red, even choosing to have her own separate apartments as if fearing that extended intimacy might disrupt her concentration. And whenever they had managed some time together, she had usually been tense, distracted and deeply weary.

Yes, I *know* she's powerful and important, he snarled at himself, I *know* they're all worried about what Lebarran Magister might be plotting, I *know* I'm being selfish and inconsiderate . . . But I feel like a prisoner, like a bored zoo beast pacing an empty cage, and it's the feeling I hate most of all.

So, he told himself emptily, maybe it's time to move on. But – *where*? He could go back to Quamarr, where he would be welcome again in the palace. Krost might go with him, though the dwarf-giant seemed quite untroubled by their time of placid indolence in the north. But what was there to do in Quamarr? Spend money, with which Phaedran had been amply generous after the Dome – eat and drink too much – get bored and restless all over again. Where was the point in that?

Maybe, he thought, it's time to go *home*.

The thought jolted him upright. He knew the translocation could be done – by a conclave of wizards, by the Named Nine in their unity. He thought briefly of how Aurilia might react if he made the request. But even as he considered how he might be returned to his own world, another part of his mind was drawing sharply back from the idea. Go back to being just one more struggling actor in an indifferent city? Leave a woman he loved and friends he prized for a collection of idle acquaintances and strangers? Abandon a world where he bore the name, the sword and now something of the reputation of a

15

hero – a world that had already provided him with the most exhilarating, tumultuous antidotes to boredom that he could imagine, with perhaps the promise of more to come?

No chance, he thought, and smiled to himself, feeling his dark mood begin to lift. It's just time to move *around*, not away. Go find some excitement, he told himself, somewhere else, while Aurilia's busy. Before you get into trouble with Brennia or someone, here. Maybe Krost would come, too, and we could explore other parts of the Continent . . .

A sudden tap on his door startled him. Springing up, he pulled on a light robe, remembering that Brennia had said she would send him a salve for his small wound, wondering as he went to the door if she had relented and brought it herself. But it was not Brennia who stood in the narrow passage, bearing a small ceramic jar. It was Aurilia, in her alternate form, that of a skinny, wrinkled old woman with luxuriant white hair.

'Brennia said you'd been hurt,' she said, handing him the jar as he stepped back to let her in.

'It's not much,' he said, following her as she hobbled wearily towards a chair. 'She mostly healed it.' He pulled his robe open to show her the weal on his belly, before scooping out a fingerful of salve from the jar, gluey and faintly warm, and smearing it on the wound. 'Though she said it would leave a scar,' he added with a half-smile. 'Maybe I should go find Hallifort, to fix it.'

She looked at him strangely, then lowered her gaze to those areas on his half-bared body where other blades had not merely nicked the skin but had stabbed deep to open up life-threatening wounds. Yet not even the tiniest hairline traces remained from those injuries – thanks to the astonishing power of Hallifort the Healer.

'It's odd that you should mention Hallifort,' Aurilia said. 'The Nine have been giving some thought to him.'

He raised his eyebrows. 'Friendly thought, I hope. He *is* on our side.'

'Of course,' she replied. 'But . . .' She paused, as if to collect her thoughts. 'You've probably gathered,' she went on, 'that the Nine have been working hard . . .'

16

'I'd noticed,' he said drily.

A sharp look flashed from her green eyes, which remained the same in either of her forms. 'Working hard,' she continued firmly, 'to look carefully at everything even remotely connected with the danger that the Continent now faces. Just as Phaedran has a contingent of high adepts doing, in Quamarr.'

Red nodded. It needed no great deductive powers for him to realize that the Sisterhood's leadership would have been urgently weighing up the threat of the Continent's enemies, Lebarran Magister and his so-called Order of the Apotheosis. I wonder what they've found, he thought, feeling a tinge of excitement as well as curiosity arise within him.

'The trouble is,' Aurilia said, almost as if he had spoken his thought aloud, 'we haven't seemed able to learn much, directly. Lebarran remains in his valley in the Southern Highlands, surrounded by some sort of barrier against magical intrusion that's at least as effective as Talonimal's Dome. I'm told that Phaedran's mages have been exerting themselves trying to penetrate or by-pass the barrier, but also with little success. We haven't even been able to locate and study other members of the Order of the Apotheosis – because those that have been identified have all *vanished*, fairly recently. Presumably gone to join Lebarran in his protected valley.'

'Sounds frustrating,' Red commented.

She sighed tiredly. 'It is. Not that it would ever be easy to spy on the land's most powerful sorcerer. So the Nine have started to look in different directions. To see what might be learned from other elements that featured prominently in the events just past.' Her green gaze regarded him steadily. 'Other elements, Red, that include you – and Hallifort.'

'Me?' he asked, startled. 'What do you expect to learn about Lebarran from *me*?'

'Perhaps nothing from yourself, exactly,' she told him, 'but from the mere fact of your presence. Red, it's plain that ever since my summoning brought you to this Sphere, you've played a crucial part in things. You and Corodel's sword. You've been in the right place at the right time, picking up vital pieces of information and so on. It's as if you've been a kind of *catalyst*, at the centre of events, sometimes *causing* those events.'

'By accident, mostly,' Red said.

'No matter. By accident or fate or what you will, the fact is that you've become deeply and often pivotally involved with the destiny of the Continent.'

'Hallifort said much the same thing,' Red recalled with a frown. 'Back at the Dome. Though the same could be said for you and Krost . . .'.

She shrugged bony shoulders. 'In some ways, yes. But remember, as the most important instance, it was *you* who discovered the presence of Lebarran at the centre of all this evil.'

'True,' he replied, 'for what it's worth. But what's your point?'

'The point,' she said intently, 'is that your role, your catalys-ing involvement, seems somehow to be bound up with a per-sistent mystery – which is Hallifort.' A shadow of memory darkened her eyes. 'He has seemed to come from nowhere when you needed him. You would not *be* here without him. And yet, most oddly, hardly anyone has heard much about Hallifort before now. A few older Sisters recall encountering him once or twice in the past, usually when he was healing someone. Otherwise, he has been an unknown quantity, per-haps a recluse, certainly an enigma. Yet he has readily and magically been on hand, three times, just when you needed him.'

Red was still frowning, remembering those three occasions of pain and terror when the little healer had miraculously appeared at the crucial moment. Even though he always insisted that he had no real magical power beyond the gift of healing.

'So we've been wondering about Hallifort,' Aurilia was con-tinuing. 'Wondering where he comes from, where he has been, how and why he has come to emerge *now* from obscurity.' She leaned stiffly forward, her gaze solemn. 'Some of the Nine are unsure of him, Red. They're unsure of *why* he does what he does. They're unsure of who or what he *is*, or of the true extent

18

of his powers, or what purpose those powers may ultimately serve.'

'He has never shown anything but kindness, as far as I know,' Red said doubtfully.

'That's so. But he seems both powerful and mysterious – which is enough to make some of the Nine mistrust what he might *yet* show.'

'But can't you . . .' Red waved a hand vaguely. 'Don't you have magic ways to find out?'

'That's what we've been trying to do,' she agreed. 'But without success. All our seeking and scrying has found no trace of him. As far as we can tell, Red, at this moment, Hallifort is no longer anywhere in this Sphere.'

'You mean he's *dead*?' Red asked, shocked.

'Possibly – but we don't think so. He may somehow have crossed into another Sphere or Realm. Or perhaps he can balk our searching vision with a defence that remains completely undetectable.'

Red shook his head. 'He always said he had no other magic.'

'So he *said*. Though he has seemed able to travel – to wherever you are, Red – in fairly remarkable ways.'

'I suppose,' Red agreed. 'Not that it matters now. If he's gone somewhere, you're at a dead end.'

'Not entirely.' She leaned back, studying him thoughtfully. 'You probably know that the Earth-magic gives some Sisters different psychic gifts as well. Among the Nine, the lady Inghilla is one of the more gifted in that way – able to send her mind ranging widely over distances and deeply beneath surfaces. And, with some of the others, Inghilla has recently stopped searching for Hallifort directly, with their mental powers, and instead began looking for what you could call his psychic *trail*. Traces and impressions that his presence has left behind on the world.'

'Neat trick,' Red said edgily. 'What did she find?'

'Again, weirdly, almost nothing. As if Hallifort can move through this Sphere without leaving a mark, psychic or astral or physical. All that they picked up were a few very recent hints and glimpses – which in Inghilla's view only serve to deepen the mystery. Especially when those glimpses gave her a clear sense of Hallifort somehow moving in parallel with *you*. As if he has been keeping pace with you, watching you.'

Red stirred uneasily, his skin prickling. 'I'd say that's just as well, considering what he's done for me.'

'Of course,' she replied. 'I think Inghilla may be too quick to see something sinister in Hallifort's mystery, his near-invisibility. But still, she is right to say that this is no time to be ignoring *any* mysteries.' She peered at him, her green eyes intense. 'So I've come now with a request, Red, from the Nine. They would like you to come to a gathering, in the Hall of the Nine, so we can learn what you know about Hallifort.'

'I've told you everything,' Red said, looking puzzled. 'You were *there*, Aurilia, two of the times I saw him.'

She nodded her white head. 'I know. But the human memory is a strange place. It's known to retain the images of *all* experience, in the finest detail, even though the conscious mind may not be able to remember. And Sisters with mental powers, like Inghilla, can reach into the depths of memory and unlock those images.'

'They want to use those powers on *my* memory?' Red asked warily.

'If you'll allow it. It won't harm you. But we need to *see*, Red. To examine for ourselves what your memory may reveal, about Hallifort and his links with you.' She paused, her eyes shadowed. 'I don't want to alarm you . . . But Inghilla had one very clear intimation, when she sought Hallifort's psychic trail. She sensed other presences somehow gathered around him or connected to him, in this world. Presences that she could not see or identify – but that she felt were terrible and fearsome, inhuman and monstrous.'

TWO

Red remained silent while the two of them made their way across the Fastness, in the extending shadows of early twilight, towards the large central building that housed the Hall of the Nine. He had taken his time preparing himself, choosing his most respectable clothes from the enlarged wardrobe that he had acquired thanks to Phaedran's generosity. Also, since Aurilia had not objected, he had buckled on the sword of Corodel, since he had begun to feel incomplete and uneasy without it. But he was uneasy anyway, as he followed Aurilia's stooped figure, because magic of any sort – the Sisterhood's Earth-magic or the 'higher' magic of wizards and sorcerers – still sometimes had that effect on him. He could think calmly enough about magic in the abstract, or even about the marshalling of huge magical forces to investigate an also hugely powerful mage like Lebarran. But when some of those forces were aimed *his* way, his nerve-ends started sounding alarms.

Especially when it gets really personal, he thought unhappily as they entered the central building. When they're going to open up my head like a clamshell and scoop out my memories.

At the end of a shadowy passageway near the heart of the building, they came to an ordinary-looking pair of double doors made of reddish wood that had been left its natural colour, glowing from much rubbing. Pausing there, Aurilia turned to him with a small smile on her lined face.

'You do understand what a rare event this is,' she told him. 'A man entering the Hall of the Nine. It's quite a privilege.'

'Meaning I should be on my best behaviour?' Red managed a smile in response. 'Don't worry. I won't disgrace you.'

Her smile widened. 'You might also like to know that the last man to walk through these doors was Corodel.'

I might have known, Red thought, as he stepped through

21

the doorway and paused on the threshold, looking around. The Hall, he saw with interest, was far from being an overpowering or forbidding place. It was big enough, with a high domed ceiling, but its large windows, the rich colours of the décor, the glowing wood of the floor, all combined to make it seem attractive, welcoming, even comfortable. One of its dominant features was a series of large murals around the walls, presumably depicting important occasions in the Sisterhood's history. And he noticed that while the pictures showed many women who were fully armed and even armoured, there was not a single scene of the kind of violence that might have dominated such a historical record in a similarly grand chamber designed for men. No battle, no torture, no carnage – almost no bloodshed, except in two graphically detailed images of births.

At the Hall's centre stood a huge, gleaming wooden table, not quite circular, more of a rounded oval. And around it, on plain but firmly cushioned chairs, sat eight women who became nine as Aurilia took her place among them. The Circle of Nine, Red thought, feeling slightly awed. Although just then they were not a literal circle. Clearly they had rearranged themselves for his sake, moving their chairs closer together in a semicircle that faced a single chair. At Aurilia's gesture he bowed slightly to the others with respect and acknowledgment, then took his seat in the empty chair, studying the group of women with interest, just as they were studying him.

The Nine looked remarkably unremarkable, he thought. A group of reasonably well-dressed women, each wearing an identical gold ring with the distinctive knot. He had seen some of them before, around the Fastness, all seeming quite ordinary. But there in the Hall, aware of what they were, he could see more easily that they all had one quality in common. However plain and unaffected they all appeared, they exuded – as he had noticed with Aurilia so often – a sense of controlled *power*, like an invisible aura around them.

That sense of power could even be detected, unexpectedly, in the woman who held the central position at the table. She appeared to be by far the oldest of all – tiny, hunched, wizened, frail, with a cloud of thin white hair, and pale wrinkled skin hanging on her fragile bones. Her head and hands trembled ceaselessly with the palsy of great age, and she seemed barely strong enough to maintain a sitting position. Yet her blue eyes were bright and clear, some remaining inner strength still glowing within them. She was called Naemony – Red had earlier been told her name, though not of course her secret Name – and she was the principal figure of the Nine, the chosen leader of the Sisterhood. In another society, she might have held the status of a queen, an empress. Among the Sisters, who had little interest in rank or titles or insignia, she was sometimes respectfully called 'Mother' and otherwise just called by name.

Aurilia began the formal introductions, presenting Red to Naemony first before moving on to the woman on her left – middle-aged and formidable, with a strong-boned face and severely cut grey hair. She was Inghilla, whose vision had so ominously featured Hallifort, and who stared at Red expressionlessly as he was presented.

Then, in turn, Aurilia introduced him to the others, who all looked at him just as closely, though sometimes less coolly. Jhoranna, plump and matronly, who smiled. Prelisse, tall and greying-blonde, who frowned. Malavie, small and birdlike, who fluttered. Ulaminelle, bulky and brown-haired, who nodded. Queminda, pale with white-streaked black hair, who also nodded. Wybrette, dark-skinned and white-haired, who grinned.

Settling himself at last in the lone chair, using his actor's training to hide his tension, Red laboured to fix the names in his memory – feeling grateful that he did not also have to learn their *Names*. Then Inghilla leaned forward, still with the same forbidding absence of expression.

'Thank you for coming, Red Cordell,' she said formally. 'The Nine had hoped to find a time to meet you sooner, but . . . I hope you have not thought us discourteous.'

Red smiled, still striving to appear at ease. 'Not at all. I know you've been busy with important matters. I'm honoured to have been invited into your Fastness, and your Hall.'

Inghilla inclined her head. 'We too are honoured. We know

23

very well what you accomplished, in the Lightless Dome. Without you, the Continent might never have had advance warning of the evil that is threatening us.'

Before Red could think of a suitably modest reply, he was surprised by a small mewing giggle from the ancient Naemony. 'Never thought we'd see that sword here again,' she said in a quavery voice, 'in the hands of a new Corodel. Better-looking than the old one, too.'

The women all laughed, and Red gave them an uncomfortable grin. But the easing of the tension was all too short-lived.

'I've told him what will happen,' Aurilia said to the others as the laughter faded. She was seated next to Inghilla, although there seemed to be no implications of rank in their positions. 'He may be a little apprehensive, so perhaps we should begin.'

More than a little, Red said silently. But he maintained an expression of relaxed interest as Inghilla spoke again.

'It's only a mental process,' she reassured him. 'We will put a light waking sleep on you, a kind of trance. Then we will draw out your specific memories to do with Hallifort – and display them so we may all see and consider them.'

Sounds a bit like hypnosis, Red thought. 'What do you mean by *display*?' he asked carefully.

'Just what the word implies,' Inghilla said. 'But I promise' – she glanced knowingly in Aurilia's direction – 'we will expose nothing that would embarrass you.'

He lifted a sardonic eyebrow. 'I'm not all that easily embarrassed. So – let's do it.'

As he spoke, Inghilla's eyes seemed weirdly to enlarge, to become wide clear silvery spaces. Somehow Red felt himself being drawn into those spaces, enveloped by them, calm and untroubled. He could still see the women, the table, the Hall around them – but at the same time he had the most peculiar feeling deep within his mind, as if something small and gentle and unthreatening was moving through those mental depths on tiny feet, searching, sniffing. He noticed without concern that Prelisse and Queminda were also staring at him with uncannily bright eyes, and that a small dew of sweat had appeared on their and Inghilla's brows.

In the next moment, without warning, at the centre of the

great oval table, small perfect three-dimensional images began to form – and move, as if alive.

Red recognized the images at once – because they re-created moments in his life that he could never forget. Moments of high drama and violence and horror, in which he had been a central figure. As had Hallifort the Healer.

Watching from the unruffled calm of the trance-state, Red saw again the time at the very start of things, when Hallifort had healed a knife-wound in his arm and had also stilled the turmoil in his mind caused by his sudden arrival in a place where magic was a reality. As that scene ended, with an almost cinematic fade, another formed – and he watched himself being stalked again through a slum alley by inhuman, murderous Barachi. Until Hallifort had appeared, in the shape somehow of a giant dragon, to frighten the killers away.

That scene in turn gave way to another, at the start of Red's most recent and most prolonged encounter with Hallifort. When the little healer had astoundingly turned up on the desolate western shore where the five of them – Red, Aurilia, Krost, Phaedran and the princess Evelane – had halted after fleeing the Lightless Dome. Then Hallifort had brought Red back from the threshold of death, and had tried also to help Evelane out of her near-catatonic withdrawal. After which, Red recalled, watching the tiny moving figures on the table, Hallifort had quietly turned and walked away along the beach . . .

By the time the five of them were mounted, with Phaedran cradling Evelane before him on his saddle, they discovered to their surprise that Hallifort was on a horse of his own – a nondescript, bony, splay-footed nag. Yet it kept up quite effortlessly as they all set off together, heading more or less northeast, planning to move along the fringes of the Western Woodlands so as eventually to reach the River Tenebris. And at first Red and Krost positioned themselves watchfully on either side of the little cavalcade, until Hallifort reassured them.

'There is no danger,' he told them. 'The Barachi have all fled into the deepest heart of their swamps – perhaps fearing retribution now that their master has fallen.'

'Let them stay fearful,' Phaedran said bleakly. 'We will have other matters to confront, and other scores to settle, on our return.'

So they rode steadily on, unimpeded. And it soon became clear that Hallifort had remained with them mainly for the sake of Evelane – for though he had partly lifted the terrible empty blankness that had cloaked her mind, she still remained silent and unresponsive, seeming only half-aware of what was happening. When they halted that first evening, Hallifort sat for some time beside her, with one small hand resting gently on her head, looking deeply into her eyes.

Until at last he arose with a sigh and a mournful expression, and turned to Phaedran. 'I regret that I can do no more for her,' he said sadly.

The prince looked appalled. 'But you said you could heal her!'

'I *hoped* I could,' Hallifort replied. 'I also said that in cases of mental damage the patient must be willing to be healed and must participate in the healing. But that is not happening. I am meeting enormous, unexpected *resistance* within the depths of her mind, so that I cannot reach or act upon the embedded roots of her illness.'

'I don't understand,' Aurilia intervened. 'What kind of resistance is it that can thwart *your* healing power?'

Hallifort shook his head slowly. 'I cannot say, for I cannot reach deeply enough into the princess's mind to identify it. It may be that other powers – aspects of the higher magic – could *force* their way deeper into her mind, to the roots of her trouble. But I . . . lack those powers. And indeed I would be concerned that such an intrusion, such an *invasion*, could damage her even more.'

As he spoke of 'other powers', an expression had briefly shown on the healer's face that Red had seen before – a look of unutterable loss and desolation. But Phaedran and the others seemed aware of nothing but their own overriding distress concerning Evelane.

'Hallifort, please,' Phaedran said desperately. 'I beg you – continue with her. Perhaps you will find a way. I will give you anything . . .'

'With respect, prince,' Hallifort said softly, 'there is nothing you can give me that I want. I would help her if I could, but I fear I cannot. She will possibly show some slight improvement, in time, with care and nurturing, but she must receive those things from people who know and love her, not from a stranger. I'm most deeply sorry.'

He turned away then, with another shadow of torment flickering across his face, and said no more. And the next morning, when Red and the others awoke from their troubled rest, they found that Hallifort and his strange bony horse were no longer there.

Nor did they see any sign of him along the rest of their journey back to Quamarr and the prince's palace. Nor had Red – or any of them – seen him since.

The tiny figures faded from sight on the table, and Inghilla and the others leaned back with weary sighs. Red emerged from the trance with a small jolt, feeling a heaviness like a headache behind his eyes, feeling also strangely wrung out and unaccountably disturbed.

'Are you all right?' Aurilia asked him concernedly.

'Yes, fine,' he said with a half-shrug, then looked at Inghilla. 'Did you get what you wanted from all that?'

She pursed her mouth. 'Little we didn't already know.'

'But did you notice that horse?' Queminda said. 'It seemed to appear and disappear just as he did.'

'Though he claims to have no magic,' Ulaminelle remarked.

Inghilla sniffed. 'He's a shape-shifter, certainly. That dragon-shape he took was no illusion. As far as I could tell, it had real substance.'

'Dragons . . .' Jhoranna mused. 'You don't think he has a *demonic* origin?'

'He has shown too much benevolence,' Aurilia said firmly. 'Anyway, I would have sensed a demonic nature.'

'But did you notice the look on his face,' said Prelisse, 'whenever he spoke about magical powers? That seemed to be a look of suffering – the look perhaps of someone who has *lost* something irreplaceable. Is it possible that he could be a mage,

27

a high adept, who has lost some portion of his magical gift?'

'Or renounced it,' Aurilia said thoughtfully, as Red nodded, having had the same idea himself.

But Inghilla looked doubtful. 'If he is a mage, his name is quite unknown among other adepts. And I can't recall ever hearing of a mage losing or rejecting his power – though I suppose it's possible in theory.'

'Yet why would he,' Wybrette asked, 'if it pains him so?'

Inghilla shook her head, turning again to Red. 'It seems, Master Cordell, that we have troubled you needlessly. Your memories have left us with as many questions as before. And yet . . . I feel no less certain that my vision was a true one, and that there is some dark and perhaps threatening mystery lurking in the shadows around Hallifort.'

With a chill gathering along his spine, Red could find no reply. And the chill deepened as the ancient Naemony, who had seemed mostly asleep, opened her eyes to make a startling suggestion.

'Invite the man Hallifort before us,' she croaked. 'Ask him your questions directly.'

'We can't, Mother,' Aurilia said gently. 'Remember, we haven't been able to locate him, anywhere.'

'I know that,' the old woman said. Slowly, unnervingly, she then raised a palsied hand, one arthritic finger like a claw pointing at Red. 'Send another, then, to seek him,' she quavered. 'One to whom Hallifort seems strangely bound. Send the new Corodel to seek him, and invite him!'

The effort seemed to drain the old woman's energy, so that her arm fell and she drooped sideways in her chair. That seemed to put an end to the proceedings, with the women either gathering around Naemony or collecting in small groups to murmur together, leaving Aurilia to accompany Red back to his quarters.

Again they went in silence across the Fastness, by then in deep twilight. But back in his rooms Red turned on Aurilia, disquiet and anger mingling in his pale eyes.

'I don't like *any* of this,' he snapped. 'I get the strong feeling of a set-up – as if the dice are being loaded against me.'

'Don't be silly,' Aurilia said, looking startled. 'No one knew Naemony would say that.'

'Maybe not,' he said, glowering. 'But it's all too neat. I get *sent* away, off on some fairly hopeless quest, which very usefully keeps me busy and at some distance so you can get on with things without wasting any more valuable time and energy on me.'

She stared at him. 'Do you really think the Named Nine would bring you to their Hall just for such a petty purpose?'

He turned away from her, suddenly less sure of his ground. 'I don't know. But everyone seems anxious enough to get rid of me. Sending me off to look for some mystery man who's able to hide himself from the full power of the Nine . . .' He swung back to her with a scowl. 'Hell, I don't even know my way around this place yet! And what anyone thinks I could do about all the inhuman monsters or whatever that might be hanging around Hallifort . . .'

'You needn't go if you don't want to,' she said tiredly. 'It wasn't an order, or even a decision. Though I would have thought you'd welcome the activity.'

That stopped him. Because, he discovered, beyond his annoyance, he did welcome it, he did want to go. The whole idea of searching for Hallifort, plunging into new excitements, solving the mystery, attracted him enormously. Even while he was mulishly, contrarily, objecting to being *sent*.

'No one wants to get rid of you,' Aurilia was continuing. 'Or to put you into danger. Though I doubt if Hallifort is likely to harm you, after twice saving your life. As for your travels, I was going to suggest you ask Krost to go with you.'

He was silent for a moment, still unwilling to give up feeling aggrieved. 'How long do you suggest I spend on this search?' he asked acidly. 'Or should I just stay away indefinitely?'

She shook her head wearily, her face clouding. 'Red, please. I know you've been restless and fretful – but it's a troubled time, can't you see? I came here to do my *work*, within the unity of the Nine, trying to learn more about the most dangerous enemy the Continent has ever had. It's *hard* work, Red, exhausting and time-consuming, possibly even dangerous.

And it has necessarily left me very little time for . . . for . . .'

'For me,' Red said bluntly.

'Yes, all right, for you. But I thought you'd understand.'

'Oh, I understand,' he snapped. 'I know you and the Nine have been busy, and what you've been busy at. But I also know you haven't really been *with* me even when we're together. In fact, most of the time when I do see you, you're in that body' – he gestured at her aged form – 'as if you're determined to keep me at a distance.'

She glanced down at herself, and at once her whole form began to ripple and shimmer. In the next instant the younger Aurilia was there, shapely and graceful in a sea-green gown, tawny hair piled high.

'Is this better?' she asked, her eyes flashing. 'The truth is that I sometimes simply *forget*. I take my other form most of the time when I'm with the Nine, because then many of my powers are slightly stronger.'

'If you say so,' he replied sourly, turning away from her magnetic beauty to stare moodily out of the window at the Moorlands evening.

'Red,' she said, moving towards him, 'please don't do this. We're just going through a difficult time, you and I. Things were bound to be different, here. This is my whole *life*. Being one of the Circle of Nine carries a huge load of duties and responsibilities. I can't shirk them or ignore them – not for you or anyone.'

Red began to turn towards her, feeling a little subdued and regretful. But before he could speak, he was interrupted. From some night-veiled Moorland ridge beyond the Fastness, a howl arose. Its drawn-out notes lifted and fell, full of desolation – but also like the howl of a hunting predator, freezing the blood with the sound of remorseless hunger.

The hairs on Red's neck lifted as he peered through the window. 'What in hell was *that*?'

'I have no idea,' Aurilia said uneasily. 'There's no wildlife on the Moorlands that makes such a sound.'

They turned away from the window, towards one another, suddenly aware that they were standing very close. Almost hesitantly he lifted a hand to rest it on the honey-bronze skin of her cheek, while her mouth began to soften and curve in a smile. Until the moment was shattered – by a heavy thump on the door that made them both start.

At the door, Red found Krost grinning merrily, though the grin faltered a little when he saw that Aurilia was there and that the room's atmosphere seemed highly charged. 'Sorry to burst in,' he said gruffly. 'I just heard something about you going off to look for Hallifort. And I wanted to tell you not to leave without me.'

Red smiled. 'I wouldn't dream of it.'

'Then you'll go?' Aurilia asked, sounding amazed.

'Of course,' Red said drily. 'That's what you want, isn't it? What the Nine want?'

Krost glanced from one to the other, then cleared his throat uncomfortably. 'It will be good to have something useful to do. Though I have no idea where to start looking for the man.'

'Start in Quamarr,' Aurilia suggested. 'You've found him there before. Maybe some of Phaedran's adepts will have some ideas.'

Red smiled crookedly. 'As a last resort, I could always arrange to get seriously stabbed. In the hope that old Hallifort would reappear and fix me up again.'

As Aurilia gave him a horrified look, Krost cleared his throat again. 'When are we setting off, then?'

'Let's say tomorrow morning,' Red told him. 'I never liked dragging out a goodbye.'

'Wolle and I will be ready to leave after breakfast,' Krost said. 'We can meet at the stables.' And, with an awkward nod to Aurilia, he hurried away.

In silence Red and Aurilia looked at each other, aware again of the tensions that had existed between them before they had heard the eerie howl. After a moment, Aurilia raised a hand in a helpless gesture.

'I'm sorry. I really have to get back . . .'

His mouth tightened. 'Right. You go and tend to your duties and responsibilities, and I'll get ready to go and do what I'm supposed to do in the wonderful city of Quamarr.'

31

Again she made the small helpless gesture. 'I'm sorry, Red. I'll come and see you off in the morning, if I can.'

'Fine,' he said emptily, as she turned towards the door. 'If you can.'

As the door closed behind her, Red wheeled away with an angry snarl that was partly aimed at Aurilia and at their circumstances but mostly at himself. And from beyond the Fastness he heard again the distant, uncanny howl from the moors, sounding no less full of hunger and loneliness than before – seeming to Red to be giving voice to the sudden sense of dire foreboding that was rising within him to supplant the annoyance and unease.

THREE

They had been travelling for most of the morning in almost unbroken silence, mainly because Red had been sunk in a self-absorbed gloom since leaving the Fastness. Aurilia had indeed come to the stables to see them off – but she had been visibly as preoccupied as ever, and again in her older form, so that the farewell had become slightly perfunctory on her part, slightly acidulous on Red's. He and Krost had then ridden off in silence, while Red veered within his thoughts from rehearsing all the pointed, unanswerable remarks he might have made to a growing suspicion that he had not behaved at all well. In the mean time Krost tried to avoid saying anything, in the hope that his young friend might eventually find his own way out of his self-imposed melancholy.

In fact, when Red did show signs of emerging from his gloom, around midday, it was largely due to another blonde female – his beautiful golden mare, Grilena. Given the close rapport of horse and rider, Grilena might well have been affected by Red's mood and have grown upset and skittish. But she had been so delighted at the prospect of travelling, and she was visibly so happy on the open rolling turf of the Moorlands, that instead her joy communicated itself to Red, breaking through his shadows. Responding to her, Red's naturally mercurial nature reassembled itself, so that gradually he began to find that he was enjoying himself.

They were following a narrow winding road, not much more than a trail, which led southward through the more eastern fringes of the Moorlands. In the end the trail would lead on to better roads which would finally intersect with a much broader highway that ran all the way to Quamarr. But that northerly trail was a rarely travelled route, giving Red a sense that he and Krost and their horses were the only living beings under the entire, gigantic Moorlands sky. Even more unsettlingly, the weather was growing steadily hotter as they moved closer to the Central Grasslands. The sky wore a pale cloud cover that screened them from the blistering summer sun but also seemed to lie over the land like a sheet of insulation. All morning there had been no hint of a breeze on the usually windswept moors, so that the motionless air became steadily more humid and oppressive. An occasional faraway rumble of thunder suggested that the pressure might give way to a storm, and an atmosphere of tension and menace seemed to build as the Moorlands braced themselves for the assault from the sky.

Yet, perversely, Red's mood lightened even further in that ominous atmosphere, as if he was eagerly awaiting the release of a storm's violent outburst. Noting that improvement, Krost began breaking into the silence, pointing out a feature or some phenomenon of the landscape. Before long they were chatting normally, with Red even managing a wry joke or two. So the day wore on, the horses moved willingly along, and the storm seemed content to hover far to the south and growl to itself.

By mid-afternoon, the trail was leading them around the base of some fairly steep slopes, with the sharply defined edge of a flat-topped promontory looming above them. On impulse, Krost urged Wolle off the trail and up a slope, calling to Red to follow. At the top, he halted on the lip of the promontory and gestured sweepingly at the very different landscape spread before them in the near distance.

'The Eastern Wastelands,' he announced. 'Their margins are always eating into the Moorlands, but here much faster than elsewhere. See that small vale, there?' he added, pointing. 'Only a few years ago it was still part of the moors, with healthy turf, small flowering bushes, everything. Now look at it.'

Red looked, deeply interested to see another, unfamiliar sector of the Four-Cornered Continent. The vale that Krost was indicating, a small shallow basin of land not far from where they had stopped, held only powdery grey sand rippled like water by previous winds, its emptiness interrupted by scattered outcrops of rock and a few withered stems of long-dead brush.

And beyond the vale lay the Wastelands themselves.

34

Staring out over that bleakness, which stretched to the horizon, Red felt that he could almost see its slow inexorable advance, its deadly gnawing at the edges of the moors. The wastes were flat and grey and desolate, with almost nothing to relieve the eye except more upthrusts and heaps of rock. And, away to the south-east, the dimly visible beginnings of some steep dunes or low hills.

'I've been on some deserts, back where I come from,' Red told Krost. 'But that's one of the *deadest*-looking deserts I've ever seen.'

'It is not quite as dead as it looks,' Krost said. 'Not everywhere. You can find water in some places – and in those places you might also find a few sparse plants, with perhaps insects and small serpents, all hardy and fierce to match their land.'

'Any people?' Red asked.

'No settlements. One or two religious cults tried to live in the Wastelands, but did not stay. And there are some men, the more unsociable sort, who wander there now and then, prospecting for the precious stones that can be found in some places.'

'Wasn't there supposed to be some mysterious lost tribe? That Corodel went looking for?'

Krost shrugged. 'There are many tales of secret things hidden in the Wastelands. Strange creatures, lost treasures, the ruins of fabulous cities ... Many have sought those things – and many have died in the seeking, including Corodel. Yet no real proof of their existence has yet been found.'

'Couldn't have been a pleasant death out there,' Red mused, 'for my namesake.'

'The Sisters who went to seek him said that he appeared to have died of a seizure. Yet his sword was in his hand, as if he was facing some enemy when life left him.'

'Probably wasn't going to let death take him without a fight,' Red said, still staring out across the desert.

Krost glanced at him oddly. 'You gauge the man well, for one who never knew him.'

'Oh, I'm getting to know him,' Red replied, with one of his crooked smiles.

35

'So it seems,' Krost said. 'In which case, you should also know that Corodel apparently set off on the adventure that killed him, to seek some legendary tribe on the Wastelands, because he had been plunged into unhappiness by parting from a woman he cared for.'

Red gave him a sharp look, but Krost offered only the blandest of smiles. 'All right, I get the point,' Red said. 'Don't worry. I'm not about to go and die in a desert.'

They slid back down to the trail, after that, and rode steadily on. For the rest of the day their route continued to wind along the very edge of the Moorlands, so that other vantage points frequently gave them other sweeping vistas over the grey emptiness to the east. Red gazed into the wastes with tireless interest, and just as tirelessly prodded Krost for more details about Corodel's last exploit, until finally the encroaching dusk set them to finding a place to camp for the night.

With the arrival of evening, the cloud cover seemed to droop even lower, making the air even more dense and moist and weighty. Still the land seemed poised for the storm's onslaught, the deepening darkness charged and ominous as sheet lightning flared in the southern sky like warning signals and the thunder muttered wordless threats. After seeing to the horses, Red and Krost put together a light meal from their supplies before searching out acceptable places on the turf for their beds. Red lay awake for a while, his thoughts drifting, short-lived and fragmented as the glimmers of lightning. Images of Aurilia and the Circle of Nine, of Hallifort and Inghilla's dire vision, mingled in his mind with the thought of Corodel, always an unknown, and yet increasingly familiar. And when at last he slid into a fitful sleep, troubled by the constant rumbles of thunder, his thoughts were transformed into dreams across his sleeping vision.

He dreamed of a part of the Wastelands he had never seen, a rock-strewn stretch of desert in the almost solid blackness of a starless night. But the darkness then was broken by the glow of a luminous sword, held by a heavy-shouldered man whose face was in shadow – as were the shapeless, menacing forms creeping through the darkness around him. For a moment the man seemed about to turn, to reveal his face. But then the dream-scene shifted. Red found himself in another landscape, where another darkness was deepened by clinging mist. There, different half-seen figures moved, circling around the form of a man whom Red could clearly see, and recognize: Lebarran Magister, fixing his yellow raptor eyes on Red, with a knowing, almost triumphant smile on his brutal face. Suddenly then that smiling mouth opened, impossibly wide, and from it came a high, eerie, inhuman howl so filled with hate and horror that it brought Red joltingly awake, sweat-drenched, reaching for the sword that lay next to him.

And still, fully awake, he could hear the last quivering notes of that ghastly howl as it echoed in actuality over the darkened land around him.

Getting to his feet, shaken to find that the sound was real, he saw Krost – a solid bulk of darkness against the night's shadows – moving to the horses, calming them, his iron quarterstaff held ready. Red went to join him, beginning to draw the sword from its sheath for the sake of the blade's light, but Krost stopped him with a hoarse whisper.

'No light, Red. Whatever that was, we need not bring it to us.'

Red stared around at the darkness, feeling chilled despite the night's humid heat. We need a searchlight, he thought. Or a flare. 'I heard something like that last night,' he said quietly. 'Outside the Fastness. Is it some wild thing?'

Krost stirred uneasily. 'No creature that I know of. But it may be something out of the Wastelands, unknown to me.'

'I'm in no hurry to make its acquaintance,' Red muttered.

For the rest of the night they remained awake and watchful, but the howl was not repeated, and nothing untoward had shown itself by the time the darkness began to give way to a dawn as grey and forbidding as the Wastelands over which it formed. Before long, as the sun was rising, Red and Krost had saddled up and were riding away, still keeping a careful eye on the terrain around them.

'I wonder if that *was* the same creature that I heard before,' Red mused as they rode on. 'Or just another of the same kind, whatever it may be.'

Krost scowled. 'What the thing may be is mystery enough.

37

If it is just one creature, perhaps following us from the Fastness, that is a darker mystery.'

'Following us?' Red echoed. 'I hadn't thought of that. Maybe it's just wandering in the same direction, by chance.' He paused, remembering. 'You want a spooky thought, Krost, try this. Just before the howl woke me up, I was dreaming. About Corodel, at first. But then the dream changed – and I was looking at Lebarran.'

Krost stiffened. 'For anyone who believed in soothsaying by dreams,' he growled, 'that would be a very ill omen.'

'Wouldn't it,' Red agreed, as lightly as he could.

But no more omens or eerie cries afflicted them as they rode on through the day. And by the time midday had come and gone, it seemed that the long-awaited storm had finally decided to make its move northwards, to where the dense atmosphere still weighed on the land like a depressant. The thunder's rumbles drew nearer, flares of lightning showed more often among the thickening clouds, and the hot breath of a breeze began to push its way through the heavy air.

'Any rainproof shelter around here?' Red asked idly, looking up at the bulging clouds.

Krost shrugged. 'Not really – but it probably will not rain. Not this close to the Wastelands. The storm will fill the sky with bangs and flashes, but any water in those clouds will fall on higher ground to the north.'

As he spoke he was peering into the distance, not to the south from where the storm was advancing but eastwards, into the desert. Following his gaze, with a ripple of tension along his spine, Red could see only the usual distant expanse of dusty grey sand and craggy interruptions of dark rock.

'What're you looking at?' he asked. 'Have you spotted that howler from last night?'

'No, no,' Krost replied. 'But we should be near something that will interest you . . . ah. There. Do you see that rock formation in the distance, almost due east? With part of it reaching up high, like a chimney? That is not a natural formation, Red. It is a cairn, a grave marker. Raised by the Sisterhood to mark the place where Corodel is buried.'

'Is it,' Red said softly. For a long moment he sat motionless in his saddle, gazing across the emptiness at the final resting place of the hero with whom he had such a strange connection. 'Krost,' he said at last, 'let's make a detour. I'd like a closer look at that cairn.'

'Why?' Krost asked, frowning. 'It is a heap of rocks piled upon one another, nothing more. Nothing to indicate whose grave it is, or even that it *is* a grave. What do you expect to see?'

'I don't know,' Red said, still gazing at the distant marker. 'I just want to look at it. Maybe . . . pay my respects.'

'It is some hours' ride,' Krost pointed out, 'and the going will not be easy when we enter the desert. Could you not pay your respects from here?'

Red shook his head slowly. 'We're not in a race – a few hours won't matter. Come on, Krost. Even if we have to camp out there, where's the harm?' He grinned. 'That close to Corodel, I might have dreams full of *good* omens.'

Krost sighed. 'Come along, then. But I hope you think the ride was worth it when we get there.'

Krost's description of the journey they faced, to the cairn, turned out to be an understatement. And its difficulty was made worse by the weather. Once they were fully out on to the Wastelands, the humid heat seemed to be reflected and magnified by the bare sand and rock, while the swirling breeze that had arisen lifted into the air all the powdery grey dust stirred by the horses' hoofs. As the two riders sweated in the heat, the hazy dust settled clinging on their damp skin, inside their clothing and out, finding its gritty way also into eyes, mouths, throats. While above them the storm continued to draw nearer, thunder and lightning ever more in bright and noisy evidence, making the horses – especially Grilena – increasingly nervous.

But the terrain would have been difficult even without the heat or the storm. The desert was unexpectedly rough and uneven, with almost no level areas extending more than a few paces. From sloping patches of treacherous gravel to heaps of great boulders like the ruins of crude fortifications, rock barred their way and threatened the horses' footing. Nor was all of the threat visible, for the outcrops that jutted up from the sand were only the topmost portions of more rock lying just below the thin dusty covering. All too often the horses would stumble as the sand under their hoofs skidded on an unseen stony surface, so that everyone's misery worsened with every step.

After two hours or more, when the cairn that was their goal seemed to be only slightly closer, they halted briefly to give the horses some water and to rinse the grit from their own mouths. 'Thanks for not saying "I told you so",' Red said to Krost as they returned the leather water-bottles to their saddlebags.

Krost grinned. 'I think you have been saying it to yourself. But no matter. I can understand why you want to do this. And perhaps the Wastelands themselves are interesting to you. I sometimes forget that you are a stranger to the Continent.'

'I'm not sure that I'm all that overwhelmed by the Wastelands,' Red said. 'But, yes, I suppose I'm glad to have had a look. And now that leaves just one Corner of the Continent I haven't seen. The one you come from.'

'Ah, the Highlands,' Krost said dreamily as they moved on. 'The most beautiful of the Four Corners. Especially the high plateaux where my people live – cool and clean and healthy, with air so fresh it bubbles within you like a sparkling wine.'

'In other words, freezing cold with a bitter wind. Not to mention craggy, icy and inhospitable.'

Krost laughed. 'What else do you expect from mountains? Still, you would like it there, Red.' His smile twisted into a grimace. 'I cannot say you would like my people, the Highland giants, or some of their attitudes . . . But you would like the mountains.'

'They'd make a change from this desert,' Red replied. But he said no more, letting the subject go, knowing Krost's love for his homeland but also his painful memories of his life there.

So they rode on, silent again awhile. In any case, the wind-whipped dust and the rolling thunder were making conversation increasingly difficult. And as more time passed, only stubbornness on Red's part and a near-saintly patience on Krost's kept them going. The storm's continuing advance provided only a troublesome backdrop to the increasingly rugged hardships of the landscape. Where they had at first faced shallow cuts and depressions or low ridges and knolls, they were having then to find their way around deeper trenches and gullies, steeper slopes and rises where often the sand had been scraped away to leave naked and forbidding stone.

Yet, finally, they reached their goal, the cairn of Corodel. Though it was less of a cairn, Red found, than a substantial monument. Huge dark masses of rock, slabs and boulders, still in their rough natural shapes, had been piled upon one another and fixed permanently together – by some cementing power of the Earth-magic – into a mighty, looming mound. From its summit, smaller slabs had been joined and raised to make a tall shape like a crude spire, stretching high towards the thundery sky. The overall effect was deeply impressive, Red thought, as harsh and stark as any of the desert's rock formations yet imbued by the Sisters' art with a special grandeur.

'Quite a memorial,' Red said solemnly. 'Even if it's in a sort of unlikely spot.'

'It was Corodel's wish, I believe,' Krost said. 'His greatest fear was of growing old and feeble and dying pathetically in bed. He declared that he intended to die adventuring – and to remind the world that he had done so, he wished to be buried somewhere near where he fell.'

As Red gazed up at the spire, it was suddenly, startlingly silhouetted against an immense double flash of lightning, with an attendant roar of thunder, like a sort of elemental salute. For a chilled moment then Red wondered what form his own memorial might take, shivering slightly at the reminder of the brevity of life. Especially in that world of dark mysteries and eerie powers.

Krost was staring past the monument, assessing the advance of the storm, eyes slitted against the whirling dust. 'Come,' he said. 'The Sisters are ever practical, even when they are constructing a memorial. They built in a small cavern on the far side of the cairn, where travellers may shelter.'

It was a very small cavern, barely room enough for two, but Red breathed silent thanks to the thoughtfulness that had put it there. It kept out almost all of the wind and flying dust, and muffled much of the thunder that was by then almost incessant. The storm was also combining with the advancing afternoon to bring a gloomy semi-darkness to the desert, so Red was quite willing when Krost suggested that they make their night's camp in the cave, hoping that the storm would have blown itself out by morning.

But the horses seemed decidedly less than glad to be stopping there, and to be remaining outside. Of course they both hated the blizzard of dust that surrounded them, even on the lee side of the memorial where Red and Krost tethered them to metal rods embedded in the stone for that purpose. Yet at the same time both horses seemed unduly upset, and not entirely by the assault of the storm. Even Krost's immensely powerful dappled grey, Wolle, was tossing his head and rolling his eyes, staring through the swirling dust with ears pricked. And Red's Grilena seemed inexplicably close to panic, showing no interest in the food he offered her, snorting and twitching as he tried to comfort her, stamping and shivering as she too stared out into the deepening darkness.

'I think Grilena wants to spend the night in here with us,' Red remarked to Krost as they took their saddles back into the cave. 'Even Wolle seems a bit spooked.'

'Perhaps it is this place, as well as the storm,' Krost suggested. 'There is an atmosphere here, like you would find in a graveyard.'

'You'll get *me* spooked if you go on,' Red told him.

Krost grinned. 'What is there to fear in this place but the ghost of Corodel? And he would not harm us.'

'He might come looking for his sword,' Red said with a half-smile. 'Maybe I'll make it easy for him, and give us some light.'

He drew the sword, leaning it against the rear wall of the cave so that the blade's glow filled the space with its warm, shifting colours. 'Better than a chandelier,' he said. 'Now, what's to eat?'

It was another simple traveller's meal, hard bread with dried meat and fruit and a sparing mouthful of water. And before long Red was re-sheathing the sword, to let full darkness envelop them as they sought reasonably smooth places to sleep on the sandy floor. But again despite his weariness Red found sleep elusive. Again his mind filled with whirling thoughts and images, disjointed memories and anticipations. And through it all, as well, the storm imposed itself – sounding as if it had settled directly above them, thunder booming and crashing like cannonades, lightning flaring constantly like a giant neon sign flashing on and off outside the cave. And the horses were contributing their own distress to the level of noise, stamping and snorting, with Grilena whinnying in fright at every furious blaze of lightning.

Until, after some while, in the midst of all that sleep-inhibiting din, Red was startled by a totally unexpected phenomenon. When a small eddy of wind swept in through the cave's mouth and brought with it an appalling stink. As if some maggoty, decomposing heap of vileness had been dumped outside, where before there was only empty, sterile sand.

'Krost . . .' Red hissed.

'Yes,' he heard Krost mutter hoarsely from the darkness. 'Be careful.'

As Red got to his feet, reaching for the sheathed sword, he heard the tiny clink of Krost's iron quarterstaff being lifted from where it had leaned against stone. Together, silently, they crept forward a few paces to the cave-mouth, gripped by a greater tension.

As the stench continued to assail them from the darkness, they could see a glowing light some distance from the cave. Weirdly, it appeared to hover some way above the ground as it moved towards them – a small strip of brightness, glowing gold, unwavering, uncanny. Another time Red might have called out, believing it to be a light borne by some traveller. But not on that night, with the thunder bellowing above him, the horses squealing and plunging in what sounded like abject terror, the abominable stink wafting around him like a breath from a grave.

Then a giant fork of lightning leaped across the sky from cloud to cloud, and in its stark white light Red and Krost saw what was advancing towards their cave.

43

Even when darkness reclaimed the land, as the lightning faded, Red could see the after-image in dreadful clarity. The image of the monster that was loping towards them – its huge shoulders and long powerful arms, its gaping fanged jaws, the matted black hair that covered it, the weird glow of something like a golden collar around its immense neck. It looked like some giant baboon or gorilla, Red thought numbly, with its sloping back and short bowed hind legs. But no primate of any sort had ever possessed such eyes, the sockets filled with things like tendrils of red smoke that glowed and writhed.

And in that instant, as the accompanying eruption of thunder died away, the horror outside the cavern lifted its ghastly face to the sky and howled. A hollow, piercing, echoing sound, filled with hatred and malevolent hungers, like a cry from some unthinkable abyss.

FOUR

'Outside!' Krost yelled. 'It must not trap us in here!'

As he spoke he gripped Red's arm in one mighty hand and almost threw him out of the cave, leaping out after him. The lightning flared again, showing the monster even nearer, though seeming to slow its advance as they emerged to face it. And – was Red imagining it? Did the creature seem to flinch from that vivid blast of brightness?

Flinging the sheath aside, he stood with the glowing sword held before him, fixing his gaze on the narrow golden gleam at the monster's throat that revealed its position even in the blinding darkness between lightning flashes. On the far side of the cairn the horses were still crying out in terror, and somehow as their frenzy reached him even through the non-stop thunder it began to turn Red's own fear into fuel for his anger. Taking a firmer grip on the sword's hilt, he began to drift away to one side, wondering where Krost had got to in the darkness.

When the lightning blazed again, he saw that the dwarf-giant had also begun moving aside, so that they would not present a single target. But the creature did not even glance Krost's way. With frightening speed it charged straight at Red, huge jaws agape.

Ignoring the icy sweat that burst out on his body as the darkness returned, Red took a half-step forward to find his balance and slashed furiously at the golden collar that was all he could see of the black-furred horror. The foul stench of the thing surrounded him like a noxious cloud as he heard it snarl – and saw, in the next burst of lightning, that it had dodged back, away from his bright blade.

In the same motion it wheeled and bounded towards Krost. Another fork of lightning showed Krost swinging the iron staff in a blow that might have felled a healthy tree. But the monster avoided it with blurring quickness, at the same time grabbing at the staff and wrenching it from Krost's grip. And as Krost stumbled, off-balance and shocked after being so suddenly and powerfully disarmed, the creature swung a long arm with a mighty taloned paw that slammed into the side of Krost's head with battering-ram force.

The blow would have flung an ordinary man some distance away, perhaps with a broken neck or crushed skull. But Krost's strength and inhuman weight could absorb even that unnatural power. He merely staggered back a few steps before falling dazed on to one knee, blood pouring from claw-wounds on scalp and cheekbone.

The lightning flared again, by then almost a continuous stream of light, to show the monster seeming to hesitate as if confused by the limited effect of its blow on Krost. And in that instant, his fighting anger turned nearly berserk by the attack on his friend, Red leaped towards the monster, yelling, swinging the sword like a smaller lightning flash of his own.

As before, the creature tried to dodge the blow, so that the blade bit only into the heavy muscle on the black-furred shoulder. But it bit deep, and the creature sprang back with a howl of pain, the blade enlarging the wound as it was torn free. Still howling, the thing hesitated once more, the red tendrils of its eyes seething, and again it appeared to flinch from the endless bursts of lightning as Red pursued it, brandishing the glowing sword. Unexpectedly, then, the monster turned away, to charge in another direction. Not at the half-kneeling Krost but at the shrieking horses, battling with their tethers in their extremity of terror. As the hideous figure sprang towards them, the frantic animals somehow found an extra, manic strength. Their tethers snapped like threads, and they fled in a wild frenzied gallop into the desert night.

And the monster, without looking again towards Red or Krost, bared its teeth and bounded after them.

Within seconds the sound of hoofbeats on the powdery sand were fading from earshot. But another second later Red heard the ghastly howl of the beast, as if in triumph, and the piercing, desperate scream of a horse.

46

'Grilena!' Red yelled. And instinctively, reflexively, still in the mindless grip of a battle fury, he dashed away in a headlong sprint, eastwards, in the direction taken by the horses, heedless of Krost's hoarse shout behind him.

At that furious pace Red covered a considerable amount of ground before exhaustion forced him to slow down. Even so, he had come upon no sign of horses or monster, and near-panic began to grip him as he feared he had gone the wrong way. The wind that still whipped across the desert had too quickly dispersed any dust raised by the fleeing horses, as well as any sand that might have retained hoofprints. Worse, the storm was falling away from its stupendous peak, the lightning growing less frequent, so that the blackness between each burst of light left Red dazzled and mostly blind despite the glow of his sword.

At last, gasping for breath, he stumbled to the top of a knoll and stared wildly around, hoping to glimpse the horses or some sign of them in the next flash of the departing lightning. For several moments he waited there, catching his breath, growing more desperate with each second as the flares of light showed him nothing at all but shadowed, empty sand on every side.

But then he was rewarded. An erratic swerve of the wind bore with it the distant, falling notes of a monstrous howl – mingled with the faint but piercing sound of a horse's squeal. That might be Wolle, Red thought, for the sound seemed to have as much anger as fear in it, and he knew all about the bulky horse's temper. He listened intently, but heard nothing more except the wind's moan and the receding thunder's sullen rumble. Even so, he refused to consider a possible grisly reason why he had heard Wolle's voice but not Grilena's. All that he cared about was that the sounds definitely seemed to come from almost due east, deeper into the desert.

Don't give up, my love, he called silently to Grilena. I'm coming . . .

Yet some judgement had returned to him by then, so he did not again hurtle away in a wild sprint. Instead, he set off in a loping trot, the stride of a long-distance runner, as smooth and

47

steady as he could manage. But of course he was running over very uneven ground, often having to detour around hidden ditches or heaped rocks, the strength of his legs being further taxed by the thick drifts of sand underfoot. Before long his stride slowed, became more ragged, declined into a heavy-footed jog. Yet still he would not stop. Still he forced himself on towards the east, jaw clenched and sword half-lifted.

If any thought of halting and turning back might have come to enter his mind, it was pushed away when once more, still ahead of him in the east, he heard the howl of the monster carried on the wind. It seemed also that the sound might have again overlaid another terrified shriek from a horse, but the distance was too great for him to be sure. None the less, it confirmed his direction and strengthened his resolve. And as he jogged leadenly on, with the storm grumbling and flashing away towards the far northern horizon, the wind began to shred the clouds in the night sky, allowing a half-moon to spread its wan light over the Wastelands.

He took that as a good sign and ran on, forcing himself to ignore the clenching ache in his legs, the burning in his lungs. More and more often he stumbled over hidden teeth of rock, nearly falling, a hair's-breadth away from a wrenched knee or a sprained ankle. Sometimes, after such near-accidents, he would grudgingly pause to give his legs a moment's respite, gulping for air like a drowning man, wiping a sleeve across his sweaty, dust-smeared face, staring longingly across the desert's expanse. As time went on and the moon sank towards the west his jog-trot slowed to a lurching walk, yet still he kept on – although he had heard no more cries from the east for some time. He kept on because every time he felt that it was hopeless, that he should turn back, his mind produced the image of his beautiful horse, he saw her large intelligent eyes looking at him with love and trust, he heard in his mind the anguish of her screams as she fled the monster. And every time, in the face of that image, he hefted his sword again and decided that he might go on just a little farther.

So the night wound on, with only the occasional whisper of the dying breeze and the scrape of his boots on sand to break the moonlit silence. He had no idea of how much time had passed or how much ground he had covered since he left the cairn. Occasionally he felt twinges of guilt at having left Krost alone, but he had seen that the dwarf-giant had not been dangerously injured. And he still clung to the idea, the slender hope, that he might find his Grilena somewhere in the desert, unharmed, and ride her back to rejoin his friend. Yet his unsteady walk was slowing even more, as the landscape went on growing more difficult – the gullies becoming as deep as small canyons, the rises developing into near-vertical inclines topped by sharp-edged ridges. And the moon had slid down nearly to the horizon, so that the shadows cast by its light were longer and more impenetrably black, especially on the eastern side of the slopes that Red confronted. So it was a combination of darkness and weariness that kept him from noticing, as he struggled to the top of another ridge, that the ground did not simply slope downwards again but fell suddenly away, straight down from a crumbling overhang.

Red fell, as well, with a choked cry. And though a thick layer of sand at the bottom of the drop cushioned some of his fall, he also had his hands extended to break the impact. When the heel of his right hand that still held the sword struck against a hidden edge of stone, he heard as well as felt the muffled *snap* of a bone cracking in his wrist.

The agony that flared along his forearm overwhelmed any other pain from his crash-landing. The sword fell from his limp right hand as he involuntarily cried out, coming to his knees, gasping as his left hand reached to support the damaged wrist. For some moments he remained kneeling, teeth gritted, cradling his right forearm against his chest.

Until he heard the faint grinding sound of sand crushed on to stone, and was surrounded by the charnel-house stink of the monster.

He jerked his head up. He had fallen into a fairly sizeable trench, like a small ravine, its steep sides reaching up more than his own height. In the uncertain light he could see the black-furred horror poised on the edge, staring down at him with its writhing, red-smoke eyes.

49

As Red looked up, the beast bared its fangs and leaped into the ravine, landing lightly in a puff of dust. It began to edge forward with a rolling gait, on all fours, and by the sword's light Red saw that one of its taloned forepaws was smeared with a gluey mess that looked partly reddish-brown – which had to be blood, mingled with the desert's dust. And sick horror swept through Red at the near-certainty that the monster had injured or killed at least one of the horses, before turning back to deal with him.

He forced himself to his feet, the sword in his left hand, grunting with pain as he thrust his broken right wrist into the front of his shirt to give it at least some support. The monster seemed to hold back briefly, as if watching those movements with suspicion. Then it edged forward again, circling around to come at Red from his right, avoiding the sword. Red swung around as well so that the bright blade followed the creature's movement while also illuminating their narrow battlefield. For a few more strides the creature still circled. But then without warning it changed direction, lunging at Red with huge ape-arms outstretched.

Red slashed wildly at its reaching claws, stumbling backwards. The beast dodged away from the blade, then resumed its stalking circle. Again it attacked, and again, each time thwarted by the desperate flailing of the sword, clumsy in Red's left hand. Yet while it seemed tireless in its unnatural strength, Red's movements were growing slower and shakier as he grew more weakened by fatigue, fear, pain and shock.

Oddly, though, he was sure that once or twice in his growing weakness he had left a sizeable gap in his defence, left himself open to a killing blow from the monster. Yet the blows had not been delivered – as if for some unguessable reason the creature was not seeking to take his life. The idea briefly heartened Red, spurring him to a few more vigorous strokes and lunges with the sword. But the monster evaded those attacks, while for Red the short burst of strength soon ebbed away. His feet were almost dragging, the sword felt awkward and heavy in his hand, the choking dust kicked up by the fight was blinding him even more than sweat and exhaustion. So he was dangerously slow to turn with the sword when the beast came hurtling in once more, on the attack.

But the monster was as swift as ever. One huge clawed paw lashed out at Red's left arm, clearly aiming to make him drop the sword. Some remnant of his reflexes drove Red to try to spin away from the blow, but the talons sliced like knives across his torso, carving diagonal trails of sudden anguish. Though only a glancing blow, its force hurled Red back and down, sending him crashing to the ground in a welter of dust and blood. Stunned and dazed with pain, vision dimmed, Red still dredged from somewhere enough strength and will to bring himself up to a kneeling position, scrabbling with his left hand to regain the fallen sword. And as he swayed there, fighting to clear his head and keep his balance, he grimly lifted the bright blade to present its point to the advancing monster, watching its terrible red-tendrilled eyes coil and squirm more rapidly. Then it crouched, poising itself for a final leap.

But instead, it halted, as if it had become rooted. Slowly it lifted its head, turning its ghastly eyes towards the east, its body stiffening and shuddering, rippling the thickly matted hair. It remained like that for a longer moment, before again turning its fearsome gaze back to Red, and the shining obstacle of the sword. Again it seemed to crouch, then again turned its face towards the east. And finally, incredibly, with a strangled moan like a muted echo of its howl, it turned away – bounding off at speed towards the shadowy farther end of the ravine.

Staring after it with disbelief, Red let his sword-arm fall. Some nameless urge drove him then to try to get to his feet, but the effort was too great. The sword fell from his limp hand as he crumpled to the ground and lay still, eyes closed, blood streaming from his wounds, unaware that to the east where the sky had cleared of all traces of the night's storm, dawn was breaking over the desert.

Consciousness returned slowly to Red, bringing with it an awareness of pain that made him groan aloud, yearning for a return to insensibility. The groan emerged only as a grating croak, for his throat and mouth were gritty with dust and

51

seared by thirst. Yet that was one of his lesser afflictions, along with the deep-rooted ache in his legs or the bruises from his two falls. Far worse was the torment from the gashes across his torso, matched by the throbbing from his cracked wrist.

It took an almost impossible effort to lift himself even partly from the ground, since his torn chest muscles and his hugely swollen right wrist screamed at every movement. But he finally managed a wobbly kneeling position, looking down at himself to assess the damage. The claw-wounds by then had mostly stopped bleeding – staunched partly by the fine dust blown over him by the breeze as he lay on the ravine floor – and as far as he could tell they had not slashed deeply enough to damage bone or internal organs. Still, that was a very small mercy. By the look of the sand around him, he had lost a great deal of blood, which combined with pain and shock to make his head swim ominously as he fought his way to his feet.

Yet he did not give up the fight, and eventually achieved some kind of uprightness, swaying unsteadily. Only then did his awareness reach out beyond his own tortured being to notice that the sun had risen while he had lain unconscious, though not yet high enough to light up the whole of the ravine floor. Vaguely remembering how the monster had shrunk away from the lightning and from his sword, he wondered if the arrival of daylight explained why he was still alive and why the monster had fled. Though he also remembered feeling at the last that the creature was not trying to kill him ... But he was too hurt and dazed to persist with the effort of thinking about it. Instead, he applied himself to the task of stooping, just managing not to fall over, to pick up the sword with his left hand. Finding that all his various efforts had started his chest wounds oozing again, he peeled off what was left of his slashed and blood-soaked shirt, hissing with pain when the sleeve dragged at his broken wrist and when the cloth had to be pulled away from the crusted edges of the claw-wounds. Finally he fumbled to wad up the ruined shirt into something like a pad, then crossed his arms awkwardly in front of him, pressing the filthy cloth against his seeping cuts to stop the bleeding, using his left forearm to support his right. After all

52

that, with the sword still dangling limply from his left hand, he began to walk.

The early morning sun was already bearing down upon the desert, and he had no doubt that its impact would grow steadily worse. Just then, however, he was more concerned with its position. It had of course risen in the east, so to set a westward course he needed only to start off with his back to the sun, to find his way back to the cairn and Krost. Unfortunately, though, the ravine ran roughly north–south, and he had little hope of clambering out, injured and one-handed, over its sheer and crumbly sides. He was forced to walk along it, hoping that it would eventually peter out and bring him back up on to the level of the desert by means of a manageable slope.

He chose to move southward along the ravine, simply because he happened to be facing that way. From the outset his movement was an erratic, wavering stagger, almost overbalancing once or twice in the first few strides. He could feel blood still dripping from some of his wounds, could feel the threat of cramp in his aching legs, could feel sweat bursting out on his skin to be dried instantly in the moistureless air. He had a sudden image of himself stumbling along the ravine for hours without finding an escape, with the sun's scorching heat being magnified by the ravine's confining walls, with pain and thirst and loss of blood threatening to bring him down at every step. And from somewhere, almost dream-like, a comparable image came to his mind – of another half-naked, red-haired man staggering over the same desert, assaulted by pain and thirst and fiery sun, grimly clinging to the same sword . . .

I'm going to *die* here, he thought. Just like Corodel.

His mind seemed quite unperturbed as it considered that likelihood, as if dying like his namesake was an acceptable part of all their other resemblances. Dimly he wondered if Corodel might also have encountered some monster akin to the beast of the previous night. Numbly he thought of Aurilia and Krost, and bade them a silent farewell – wondering with the ghost of a half-smile if anyone would raise a memorial to *him*, in the Wastelands. Remotely it occurred to him that even if heat, thirst and injury failed to finish him off during the day, the monster might well return to stalk him again when darkness fell.

Yet even that prospect could not stir him from the strange blank detachment that was stealing over him as he stumbled on, distancing himself from his torments, while at the same time some wilfulness at the centre of his being refused to let him lie down where he was and accept the end. On he staggered, along the ravine that might have been a stream-bed long before when the Wastelands were still fertile. His stagger became a dragging shuffle, his head drooped, his awareness contracted to a blurred focus only on the ground before his feet. But even that focus did not save him when he lurched into a patch of gravel and loose rock, and tripped, and fell in a heap.

A fragment of his martial-arts training reacted as he fell, twisting him reflexively so that his left hip and shoulder struck the ground first. He cried out as the impact sent new agony flaming through broken wrist and torn flesh. Then he rolled on his back and stared helplessly up at the unforgiving sky, not sure he had the strength to rise again, willing his death to come quickly if that was its time.

He took it to be a hallucination when he heard the sound above him. Something between a rustling and a rattling, perhaps the skeletal bones of Death moving within the folds of his hooded cloak. He listened vaguely, no longer much caring if the sound was real or not, simply lying still with pain rushing through him in a torrent, his vision beginning to film over. So he saw them only indistinctly when they came, the sources of the strange noise, appearing suddenly in a row on the lip of the ravine above him. Their arrival made him blink with failing strength, trying to see them more clearly though he had no doubt that they were a vision of delirium. There were about twelve of them, standing silently looking down at him. As far as he could tell they were man-sized, and certainly upright on two legs like men – but they were not human.

They had small heads, hairless and almost featureless save for round eyes, shiny and blank, and small slits of mouths. Their bodies were long and narrow, shiny-smooth as if encased in armour. Their legs were stumpy and hairy, as far as he could see from his supine position, and their arms were equally short and hairy, with small three-fingered hands. But there any even slight resemblance to humanity came shockingly to an end.

They had *four* arms. Two pairs, neatly arranged one above the other. And, just as inhumanly, from the head of each of them rose a pair of long, insectile antennae, feathery and flexible, in constant motion with the soft rustling rattle that Red had heard before.

Slowly, as he stared up at them, a corner of Red's mouth curved up. What a way to go, he thought. With visions of giant bugs. So death is just a bad trip, after all . . .

Then his vision began to blur again, as weakness rolled over him in a final wave – bringing with it like a drawn curtain a sweep of pain-free darkness, so that his smile widened slightly with relief as he sank down into it.

FIVE

Krost paused on the broken crest of a ridge, leaning on his quarterstaff to catch his breath, noting with relief that dawn was at last brightening the eastern horizon. He had been in pursuit of Red and the horses throughout the night, from the moment when he had regained his wits and his balance after the monster's ferocious blow. Along the way the gashes left by the beast's claws along the side of his head had stopped bleeding, and he had simply refused to acknowledge the pain, focusing himself entirely on the search. From the cairn to that moment's pause on the ridge, Krost had moved steadily at a lumbering, tireless trot. Yet it had been a slow progress, especially when he had been casting back and forth like a hunting dog, trying in the lightning flashes to catch some distant glimpse of man or beast, hoping that some patch of sand might hold a hoofmark despite the sweeping wind.

But he had had no luck. And when in time the departing storm took away the lightning that was his only source of illumination, he could do no more but continue on – his pace slowing further over the rough terrain in darkness – in the eastward direction that Red and the horses had taken, hoping that chance would favour him. He knew that they could have changed direction at any point, just as he also knew that he might at any time be attacked again by the fearsome, uncannily strong monster, which he had come to believe might be some sort of demon. But he thrust away those thoughts as firmly as he shut off his awareness of his wound.

Once, during those dark empty hours, he thought he heard the cry of a horse, faint and far away. As far as he could tell in the uncertain shifts of a desert wind, the sound – if it was in fact a horse – did seem to come from more or less due east. But he would not let himself feel hope any more than he would let himself feel despair, knowing how such feelings could be uselessly debilitating – along with his frustration at the feebleness of the moonlight that did not speed his search, and his fierce yearning for daylight. Silencing all those inner clamourings with unwavering mental strength, Krost had simply gone on, ever deeper into the Wastelands, because it was the only thing that he could do.

But pausing there on that ridge, watching the land around him slowly emerge from shadow as the dawn developed, he allowed himself to savour the relief. Which lasted only until the shapes and planes of the landscape grew more clearly defined. Then he had to fight against a wave of heart-sinking disappointment. Not because there was no sign of Red or the horses – he had not expected it to be that easy – but because of the change in the terrain.

Behind him the desert's irregularities had been comparatively manageable, fairly low dunes and rises, reasonably shallow dips and hollows. But the eastward landscape ahead of him was far more disrupted and contorted, heaved up into an expanse of starkly bare, rock-slabbed hills, scarred with fissures and crevices, criss-crossed by countless deep, steep-sided troughs and ravines that were half-choked with rubble and drifted sand.

The Devil's Rifts, Krost thought with a grimace. The beginnings of one of the most trackless, pitiless regions of the Wastelands, where not even the boldest or the craziest of prospectors would willingly spend any length of time. A good place for a demon, Krost said dourly to himself, briefly wondering if the creature might be native to the Rifts. But then he dragged his thoughts back to the immediate matter of the dire prospect facing him. He would do no more running, even at his slow trot, in that terrain. He would instead be scrambling up slopes, climbing into and out of ravines, backtracking and detouring to avoid the more impassable obstacles. And though he knew that those he was pursuing would also be slowed and obstructed, the knowledge offered little hope. Travelling through the Rifts would be hardship enough, but *searching* them – for perhaps a wounded man or horse who might be

57

hidden in any shadowed ravine or under any hilltop's over-hang – would be impossible. An army might fail in such a search. So what chance had he, alone? Especially when he was without water, with the sun about to rise into another desert-summer day. More especially when he had found nothing at all to indicate that Red and the horses had even come in that direction, or that far.

Slowly, reluctantly, he brought himself to consider the fact that continuing on would be fruitless, foolish and probably fatal. The odds against success had lengthened beyond all possibility, in the Rifts. It was time to turn back – retrace his steps to the cairn of Corodel, where a leather water-bottle waited in his saddlebags to soothe his dry cracked lips . . .

And yet he hesitated, and did not turn. The thought of the saddlebags with their supplies summoned also the thought of his bulky dappled horse – which brought with it the sure and shaming knowledge that in other circumstances Wolle would never give up the search for *him*. The powerful, dauntless horse would keep on, scouring the Rifts, as long as he had the strength to move. For that matter, Krost thought, if their situations were reversed, Red too might do just the same, with no thought for his own welfare.

'*No*, by the gods' beards,' he growled to himself aloud. 'There is still some hope. Go on a while yet, and see what the fates may bring.'

Over the next hours of the morning, the fates seemed to bring only heat, dust, pain, thirst and uncommonly obstructive terrain. In that time Krost felt that he had plodded along a hundred ravines, detoured around a thousand cliffs, struggled up ten thousand precarious, gravelly slopes. The sun's rays beat down on his unprotected head like clubs, the iron of his quarterstaff grew hot enough to sear his hand, his mouth and throat felt as if they were silting up with the suffocating dust. Yet he called on every scrap of his inhuman strength and boundless determination and forced himself forward, doggedly examining the depths of every trench or hollow in his path, surveying the land with sand-inflamed eyes from every hill-crest along his way.

He seemed to have forgotten his idea of going on for only a while. Though he paused to rest more and more often, at those times he simply let himself slump into a kind of half-stupor, thinking about almost nothing at all, before rousing himself after a few moments and struggling on again. Yet if his mind was more or less shut down during that morning, his experienced wilderness instincts were not.

So he did not fail to see, from the top of yet another ridge, the small blurred movement and faint plume of dust near the foot of a stony slope some distance to his right, to the southeast.

It had not just been a trick of shadow on the rock, a swirl of sand stirred by the breeze. He was sure of that. And since it was the first thing he had seen in the Rifts all morning besides sand and stone, he trudged away towards it for a closer look.

He was only slightly more than halfway to the slope – which, as he drew nearer, appeared to be one of two slopes with a broad shadowed cleft between them – when the cry burst out that almost stopped his heart.

But it was no demonic howl or fearsome shriek. It was the ringing, carrying call of a horse, full of the same astonishment and joy that surged up within Krost.

As he gave a croaking yell and began to run in a lurching shamble, needing the quarterstaff to keep his balance, he saw the huge grey bulk of his Wolle step out from the cleft, ears pricked, raising his head to call again. In the next moment the powerful horse galloped across the intervening space to be reunited with Krost, whickering deep in its throat with joy, nudging Krost with his nose in happy thumps that might have splintered the ribs of an ordinary man. And Krost laughed, and embraced Wolle's neck, stroking and patting him, wiping moisture from his own eyes that was not all sweat. At which point he realized with a start that the wetness on Wolle's broad muzzle was also not sweat, but was as if Wolle had dipped his nose into water.

'What a friend you are,' Krost rumbled, caressing the horse's damp nose. 'To find water and to find me, both.'

Wolle snorted with apparent eagerness as Krost gripped his

mane, preparing to hoist himself up on to the broad back. But he paused, staring at Wolle's massively muscled hindquarters. Across that expanse of dappled grey skin he saw and recognized four long deep gashes, which had obviously bled profusely before crusting over.

Krost ground his teeth in anger, then pulled himself carefully up on to Wolle's back. But the horse seemed untroubled by the wound, and by carrying Krost bareback. As they set off, back in the direction of the cleft and the water source, Krost looked around again at the clawmarks.

'Not many horses could escape a demon's attack,' he mused. 'But then, my Wolle, I wonder what you did to the demon.'

The water source turned out to be a tiny, murky pool oozing up out of the ground at the centre of a patch of thorny brush, deep in the cleft where it was shaded from the blaze of the sun. The water was warm, gritty and slightly sour, but it slid down Krost's throat as wonderfully as the finest ale in the Continent. It also was what he needed to cleanse his wound and Wolle's, and to wash away some of the dried blood from their skin and hair. And shortly, refreshed by the water and even more uplifted by the joy of finding his friend, Krost unhesitatingly returned to his search of the Devil's Rifts.

But then, of course, he had the benefit not only of the horse's formidable strength but also its acute senses. In the next while, the two of them steadily and unswervingly ascended every ridge, peered into every jumble of heaped boulders, inspected the depths of every ravine, over a startlingly wide sweep of the desert. The sun reached its midday zenith, its heat reached its most murderous peak, the water that they had drunk became only a distant memory – but they kept on, swinging back and forth, clambering up and down, covering the ground with scarcely a halt. Yet it was painfully obvious that they were still searching only a small fraction of the Rifts. And it was more painful, for Krost, when they paused for one of their infrequent rests on another hilltop, to survey the land around.

At first sight it looked as if the Rifts were coming to a gradual end. Not too far ahead, the land swept down into a wide, shallow basin full of heavy sand rippled into small dunes by the wind. But beyond the basin rose another region of rocky

60

hills, which looked at least as extensive as the Rifts – and perhaps even more spikily ridged, more gouged and scarred by deep ravines. Krost had worked out that even with Wolle he would need several more days to scour the rest of the Rifts. But for those farther ranges, those even more hostile heights and depths, they would need weeks. And, he thought, as despair threatened to claim him, who knew what lay beyond there? Farther to the east he could see only a peculiar haze, rising from one spot, broad and high but blurred by the sun's glare and the shimmer of heatwaves. Perhaps a dust-storm, he thought uneasily, which was another good reason to think again about whether to continue in that direction. In any case, what real chance was there that Red could have come so far? No, he decided gloomily, if Red was even still alive he would be moving slowly, afoot, and would almost certainly be still somewhere in the Rifts. While if by some miracle he had found his own horse, he would surely have turned back at once towards the west, towards the cairn.

Oh, Red, my friend, Krost thought wretchedly, I should never have agreed to turn this way. I should never have let you enter the desert.

Then, slowly, with weariness and regret settling upon him like a mountainous weight, Krost turned Wolle away, back into the Rifts. To continue the dismal search along paths they had not yet trodden, fighting to maintain alertness as the land threw up more obstacles and the sun struck down at them remorselessly.

Some time later, when Wolle unexpectedly snorted and half-reared, pricking his ears and flaring his nostrils, Krost jerked and snarled with the surprise of it before peering quickly around for any sign of danger. At first he saw only the usual expanse of sun-bright sand and jagged stone. But then, following Wolle's fixed stare, he saw something utterly and shockingly out of place.

A patch of bright colour, lying among broken chunks of stone on a fairly level patch of sand near the edge of a ravine. Moving slightly, as if it was light enough to be rippled by the breeze.

Krost urged Wolle forward. But when they reached the patch

of colour, when Krost leaned over to prod at it with the quarter-staff, he almost wished he had not found it. It was a torn, stained and filthy piece of cloth, which he recognized at once. The shirt Red had been wearing, when he had gone dashing into the desert night.

And it was not just torn but almost shredded, as if by several blades. And drenched in blood as well, so that the cloth seemed to have been dyed a crusty reddish-brown.

Slowly, his great shoulders drooping, Krost lifted the ruined garment, looking more closely at the damage left by the demon's claws. Then he spoke to Wolle, and for another hour or more they swung back and forth over every step of ground around the spot where the shirt had lain, for some distance in every direction, without finding the smallest further sign of Red's presence.

At last Krost pulled Wolle up, staring emptily out across the desert, confronting the fact that the dreaded possibility had become a near-certainty. The damage to the shirt, and the amount of blood on it, indicated severe injury at the least. Even if Red had then somehow, improbably, overcome the demon or escaped from it, a man with such wounds – without water or food or shelter or help – would be unlikely to have survived for long in the Wastelands.

There could no longer be any doubt. Red was gone. Just how he had fallen, and what had happened to his body, was unguessable. But those were unimportant details, compared to the unbearable fact of his death.

His face contorted, his eyes squeezed shut, Krost flung back his head as if to bellow in fury at the arid, indifferent wastes where his friend had died. But he made no sound. Slowly he lowered his head, eased his grip on the quarterstaff, rested his other hand on Wolle's neck as the horse shifted uneasily beneath him. Staring unseeingly eastwards, he considered and weighed how he might accomplish what he knew remained still to do.

For him to continue the search for Red, for his body, alone and without supplies in that brutal landscape, would probably be pointless and certainly risky. For him to seek the demon-monster and try to avenge Red, alone, would surely be just as futile and dangerous. Yet every fibre of his being cried out that Red should be sought – for proper burial if nothing else – and that he should be avenged.

His sigh was almost a groan as he recognized the only possible conclusion. 'We cannot do it ourselves, Wolle,' he rumbled aloud. 'It would do no service to Red's memory if we die out here as well. We will return to the cairn, for food and water. And then we will seek *help*, to find our friend and his killer.'

He raised the gory relic of Red's shirt to stare at it once more, before crumpling it furiously in his huge hand. 'Oh, *gods*,' he roared, his voice cracking, 'what will I say to Aurilia?'

Some time later, in an overcast valley lying deep in the heart of the Southern Highlands, the man named Lebarran Magister stood in his spell-chamber at the centre of his unnatural dwelling, leafing through the pages of an immense, cracklingly ancient manuscript bound in stained metal. The manuscript rested on nothing but empty air, hovering motionless as Lebarran's fierce eyes scanned it, his face darkening with disappointment and irritation.

'Drivel!' he snarled at last, flicking over the final few pages. 'Borrowed lore and worthless generalities!' His face twisted as he slammed the great volume shut and with the twitch of a glowing finger sent it hurtling across the chamber, to disappear just before it struck the ridged stony tree-trunks of the far wall. With an equally minimal gesture he summoned from nowhere a high-backed chair into which he sank, staring broodingly at one of the wafts of thin mist that floated here and there around the walls.

'There *must* be a way to control it!' he said to himself, his voice taut and hollow. 'Some force, some pattern of spells, must exist to constrain even the power of the Unformed!' He rested his chin on his hands, pondering, his yellow eyes hooded. 'Such a force might be sought in the barrier that I raise at the threshold – but *where*? How is it that I can halt it, bar its path, yet I can't control and *direct* it? Muscles leaped in his jaw as his eyes smouldered. 'Yes, certainly, look for the answer in the

63

threshold and its barrier. Perhaps if the force could be altered by some means into a *yoke* . . . Oh, yes, if that could be done, *then* I would master it!'

He subsided, irritation and frustration showing on his face as he sat awhile in silence, still pondering. Finally, with an exasperated snarl, he turned away as if seeking diversion from an insoluble problem and glared into the corner of the chamber at the great scrying bowl with its shiny-black liquid surface. Another small gesture brought the bowl across to him without the smallest ripple on the liquid.

'Let me see, then,' he muttered, 'how my foul emissary is progressing.'

He gestured, and an image instantly formed on the dark surface. An image of the huge demon-monster, which at that moment was cowering in the semi-darkness of a shallow cavity that it had seemingly clawed out from the sandy wall of a deep gully, shaded from the blaze of an afternoon desert sun.

'The Wastelands?' Lebarran glowered. 'Has the outlander left the witches? Or is the demon inept enough to lose its way?' He raised a hand as if to alter the image in the bowl, but then slowly let it drop again, shaking his head. 'No, I have no time to waste on scrying through the Continent for the outlander.' He scowled again at the image of the demon huddled in its poor burrow. 'That may have been careless,' he mused, 'to choose a creature that shuns the light. Perhaps another, from the Realm of—'

He broke off suddenly, his eyes widening as if a new thought had struck him. Ignoring the bowl and the demon's image, he stared again into emptiness, lost in thought. After many moments, he twitched one hand almost absently, to erase the image and send the great bowl skidding away.

'*Yes*,' he hissed, his eyes alight. 'The Unspeakable Texts, from the Realm of Ancient Frost! *There* I might find a spell-sequence to serve as a constraint! One that I might take to the Void itself, to harness the Unformed!'

His hands opened, and between them a book appeared, its covers formed of thin black ice that gave off a vapour with a vile odour. Untroubled, Lebarran left the book hovering in mid-air before him, gestured to open it, and began intently to read the unpleasantly shaped characters etched upon its pages.

SIX

By the time dusk had settled to relieve some of the desert starkness, Krost was riding steadily south-west across the much less forbidding terrain on the outer fringes of the Wastelands. Some hours earlier, he and Wolle had swiftly and directly retraced their steps to the Corodel memorial, where Krost had relievedly eased his and Wolle's hunger and thirst, and with equal relief had buckled his saddle on to the horse's broad back. With sadness he had set Red's saddle aside, to be collected when he returned to the Wastelands, as he unfailingly intended to do before too long.

Yet despite that intention he did not force Wolle into a pointlessly tiring pace, when they set off again. Though he knew the immense reserves of strength that his horse could call on, he had no wish to plunder them needlessly. He was sure that he would need all of Wolle's stamina over the days and nights to come. So he let the horse maintain a steady, undemanding trot, while the comparative coolness of night settled gently upon them. He also let Wolle pick his own path over the darkening land, as long as he held to the south-westerly course. If anyone had seen, Krost as he rode would have seemed lost in some deep meditative thought. But then a closer look would have shown the scowl on the heavy brows, the muscles bunching in the broad jaw. For despite his outward calm, Krost was inwardly suffering a roaring turbulence of emotion.

Its largest portion was the pain of bereavement, the loss of the young stranger from another world who had become Krost's comrade-in-arms and close friend. But allied to that pain was the knife-stab of self-blame, guilt at having condoned and indeed guided Red's detour on to the Wastelands and then having failed to prevent his wild dash into the night where a demon lurked. And with the guilt as well there was a sharp

66

edge of unease, as Krost's mind considered a selection of the more probable reactions from Aurilia and the Sisterhood, few of which would be forgiving. But rivalling all those feelings was another powerful strand, a colossal fury, fuelled by loathing and impelled by vengefulness. Yet even that fury remained mostly buried within Krost. He had always experienced emotions as large and powerful as the rest of him, but he had learned early in his troubled youth not to let himself be their victim. Just as he had learned, among men, that his vast strength required him to impose more restraints on his feelings, especially anger, to ensure that others did not become their victims.

So he remained outwardly calm, save for the clench of facial muscles with each onrushing wave of sorrow and rage. And Wolle, perfectly at ease in the darkness, trotted tirelessly on over a landscape that was by then gradually giving way to the softer, turf-clad sweep of the lower Moorlands.

In time the moon rose to make their progress easier, and eventually Krost roused himself from his inner turmoil, becoming aware that Wolle was moving up a gentle slope towards a cluster of mounded rises or knolls. As Krost well knew, those knolls stood like earthworks, a kind of natural fortification, very near to the southernmost frontiers of the moors. In daylight, a traveller on the higher points of the knolls could see in the distance the expanse of the Central Grasslands, or at least their rolling upper steppes that would lead by gradual stages down to the lower and more level stretches.

But in that darkness Krost turned Wolle slightly to approach the knolls at an angle, seeking a particular gully that wound along and through them. He found it mostly by sound rather than sight, for it contained a small stream, no more than a rivulet, chuckling its way down from the higher spring that was its source. There Krost paused briefly to sip some water, to rinse away the last Wasteland dust from his face, to top up his water-bottle and to let Wolle drink as well. Then they continued, following the little stream as it descended through and beyond the bastion of the knolls, out on to more open land. At that point they were entering settled farmland, still mostly pasturage but some tillage as well – and somewhere ahead, the rivulet would meet another waterway and become a good-sized creek. Beyond which, Krost was fairly sure, he would shortly come to a cluster of small farm dwellings that the owners called a village, which was his goal.

Wolle continued willingly down the slope, following the rivulet, alert and sure-footed. As they went on, it became increasingly obvious how alive the land was around them, how unlike the barren Wastelands that they had left behind. At every step Krost could hear small creatures rustling in dark patches of brush, could see the wings of nightbirds flitting across the stars. Even the small insects that came to whine around the dried blood of his and Wolle's wounds were almost welcome, after the lifelessness of the Devil's Rifts. Though that notion only reminded Krost afresh of a particular life that had been lost in the desert, some special blood that had been spilled, which plunged him into misery again.

Yet still he remained watchful, especially when they reached the junction of the two streams. There, almost at once, he heard another sound echoing through the night that filled him with glum relief. The throaty barking of a dog, which had to come from a place where people lived. And in fact the place, and the dog, were just over the next rolling crest of farmland – where the so-called village, no more than a half-dozen cottages, nestled in a gentle vale beside the creek. The cottages were all in darkness, save for one, but the moonlight showed them to be solid and well-kept, built with a mingling of timber and stone with high-peaked thatched roofs.

Krost headed at once for the cottage showing a light in one narrow, deep-set window. From a byre behind the cottage the dog barked again, nervously, as he dismounted and approached the cottage door, seeing that its stoutness matched that of the thick walls around it – a door made of heavy planks bound and reinforced with iron, so solid that it barely quivered when he lifted his fist and knocked.

He heard a flurry of muttering and scuffling within the cottage, before one of the occupants called out with a man's rough voice, made rougher by tension and suspicion. 'Who's there? What do you want?'

'I am a traveller, alone,' Krost said. 'I mean you no harm. I need your help, if you—'

He broke off as the door rattled on the inside and was then jerked partway open. In the doorway, with a fitful light flickering behind him, stood a very tall narrow-bodied man, leathery and raw-boned, gripping a short-hafted axe in one knuckly hand. Behind him clustered two other men, armed with clubs, all three bearing the close resemblance of brothers, all three glaring at Krost.

'I am sorry to disturb you,' Krost said politely, 'but I would ask your help. I am seeking . . .'

He got no further. The man with the axe, staring down his long nose at the bulky, shadowy figure outside his door, curled his lip to reveal a few brown teeth. 'We have nothing here for a fat vagabond,' he snarled. 'Begone.'

And he slammed the door shut, its crash followed at once by the rattle of a heavy inner bar being dropped into brackets across the doorway.

For a short-lived moment Krost remained still, his face blank. But the muscles of his massive shoulders and arms were swelling to threaten his tunic's seams, and the tendons of his right hand crackled as his grip tightened on the quarterstaff. Until finally the rage that had been building within him throughout his ride from the Wastelands found an outlet past all restraints.

With a bellow to rival the thunder of the night before, he lifted one booted foot and smashed it furiously against the door.

The door did not just fly open. It exploded. Its iron lock and hinges and stout reinforcing bar shrieked as they were ripped from their moorings, the door-frame split as it was wrenched away from the wall in a shower of broken stone. The door itself flew into the cottage in fragments, in splintered kindling, as Krost surged in through the opening. Stumbling slightly over the wreckage of the door, he caught his balance in time to see the three brothers on the far side of the cottage, wildly trying to squeeze through an open window all at the same time in a flailing tangle of bony limbs. But Krost remained still, merely watching their panicky scrambling escape, then

69

listening with a small smile to the frantic running footsteps receding into the night.

On a nearby table he noticed that one of the two candles that dimly lit the room had toppled over, its flame threatening to ignite some cloths heaped next to it. Calmly he stepped over to set the candle upright, brushing out the small flame that had begun to nibble at one edge of cloth. As he did so, he heard a muffled whimper, and turned to see a scrawny, chinless youth, barely into his teens, huddled with panicky eyes in the shadow of the far corner.

'Come,' Krost said, feeling slightly abashed at the terror on the boy's face. 'I mean you no harm. Truly.'

The boy gulped, huge Adam's apple bobbing. 'Please don't kill me,' he whimpered, his voice cracking.

'Of course not,' Krost assured him. 'I came seeking help, and when the door was closed in my face I grew angry. I am sorry for that, and for frightening you.'

The boy said nothing to that, but merely stared and gulped.

'I came to ask,' Krost went on patiently, 'if this village has a wise-woman or anyone at all of the Sisterhood. Or if there is one such anywhere near by.'

The boy still merely stared, bony knees trembling.

Krost sighed. 'I need a Sister's help *urgently*,' he rumbled. 'Before I grow angry again.'

The boy twitched, pressing back against the wall. 'If I tell you,' he quavered, 'will you leave and not kill me?'

'Most certainly,' Krost promised.

The boy gulped again. 'Then you must seek the witch Silgid. She lives beyond the village, that way.' He pointed, finger trembling.

'Thank you,' Krost said. Reaching into a small pouch at his belt, he drew out some coins and placed them on the table. 'That will pay for the door. And you might tell those three' – he gestured at the open window – 'that showing kindness to needy strangers can be not only virtuous but *safer* than turning them away.'

Some moments later, remounted again, he was urging Wolle at a canter in the direction of the woman named Silgid. Her house, when he reached it, was slightly smaller than those of the village, and showed a light at a small window, as well as from the wide-open door. Dismounting, Krost approached the door carefully and peered in. He could see portions of a small, cosy room with home-made furnishings, lit by an ornate lamp. But his view was obstructed, for in the doorway stood a strongly built, fair-skinned woman wearing a plain blue gown like a nightdress. She had thick brown hair with a white streak across the crown, fearless brown eyes and sinewy, graceful hands – which at that moment were holding an armed crossbow aimed unwaveringly at Krost's chest.

'I heard your noise from the village,' the woman said evenly. 'If you are here now to harm *me*, you will die where you stand.'

Remaining quite still, Krost sighed. 'Why does everyone in this place think the worst of strangers?' he asked wearily. 'I have no wish at all to harm you. My name is Krost il Hak, and if you are Silgid of the Sisterhood I need your help in an urgent matter.'

'What matter?' asked the woman, the crossbow unmoving.

'I need you, or someone like you, to send a message to the Fastness. To the lady Aurilia or any other of the Circle of Nine.'

Silgid's eyes widened slightly. 'You speak of them as if you know them.'

'I do know them,' Krost said. 'I was recently a guest in the Fastness, and I have known Aurilia for years.'

'And what message would you send her?' Silgid asked.

'That a man who has been her friend, and mine, has been slain, perhaps by a demon. That I need magical assistance to find his body – and to pursue his killer.'

He had spoken in a flat tone, yet even so the intensity and depth of his emotion was clearly audible. Peering at him, Silgid slowly lowered the crossbow. 'Yes – I see that is so. My apologies, and my sympathies.'

'Can you help me?' Krost asked.

She shrugged broad shoulders, setting the bow aside. 'My share of the Earth-magic does not enable me to speak over distance, mind to mind. But I can try a small song of calling,

71

in the hope that it will be heard by one of the Nine whose mind *can* reach this far.'

'Will it take long?' Krost asked.

'I have no idea. I have never done it before. But I'll do my best for you, Krost il Hak. Be seated, rest while I proceed. There is a cordial on the table that you will find refreshing.'

She moved to a clear space in the room, sinking down to a seated position on the floor, face raised, eyes closed, hands held slightly to the side. Moving to the table, Krost poured the cordial – a clear golden liquid in a tall pitcher – into a ceramic mug, then settled into a chair that looked strong enough to take his weight and watched with interest as she began to sing.

It was a pure melodic line, not loud yet oddly resonating in the room. As it rose and built, the air in the room seemed to stir and move, though the flame of the lamp remained steady. The movement somehow ruffled Silgid's thick hair, rippled her nightdress around her body, and Krost saw the mark of the Sisterhood glowing bright in the deep cleft between her breasts. Enraptured, Krost continued to watch, sipping his drink, as the soft breeze circled around him and the rising song filled the room. Somehow it seemed also to be filling his mind with its resonant music, oddly restful and comforting, so that the pain and weariness that had tried for so long to assert itself against his will-power began to fade and float away. As he too seemed to float, his eyes drooping shut . . .

A small stab of pain at the side of his head brought him awake with a jerk and a growl, reaching for his quarterstaff. Only to find that he was still in the sturdy chair, with Silgid next to him, her fingertips gently dabbing cool ointment on to the claw-wounds left by the demon.

'I hoped I could do this without waking you,' she said softly. 'I hadn't seen that you were hurt, before.'

Krost blinked, trying to gather his wits. 'Did you reach the Nine?'

'After some while my song was heard,' she told him. 'By the lady Inghilla, whom you will know.' As Krost nodded, she continued. 'When she plucked my message from my mind, she seemed greatly distressed. And in that thought-exchange I learned some things – about your friend, Red Cordell, and about you also, Krost of the giants.'

Krost grimaced, then nodded again. 'I am grateful to you. Did she say I would get the help I need?'

'You will.' Silgid's eyes darkened. 'But there is something else. Afterwards, while you slept, Inghilla spoke to me again. Krost – the Nine sent a magical seeking across the Wastelands, and also the Moorlands and some of the Grasslands, trying to locate your friend. They found no trace of his life-force, any-where – but also, they could find no indication even of his *body's* whereabouts, or that of the sword he carried.'

A half-stifled groan rumbled in Krost's chest. 'The demon must have taken him,' he growled. 'To whatever dark Realm it crept out of.'

Surprisingly, Silgid shook her head. 'It seems not. Or if it *did* take your friend to another Realm, it itself has since returned. The Nine's seeking found it still prowling the Wastelands.'

Krost got to his feet, fury in his eyes. 'Then I will return as well, and put an end to its prowling, with the Sisterhood's help.' He reached up to touch the side of his head, realizing that the claw-wounds and bruises had become free of pain under the light covering of ointment. 'I owe you thanks, Silgid, and more. What is your fee for this work?'

She shook her head. 'Let it be my gift, to you and the Nine and the memory of your friend. But perhaps . . . perhaps one day when your task is done, you might visit me sometime, and tell me the tale of these events over another glass of cordial.'

'Gladly,' he replied with a half-smile. 'If I live through them. But tell me – what sort of force will the Nine send to help me?'

'The message,' Silgid replied, 'was that Aurilia will meet you at the cairn of Corodel, as soon as she can get there.'

'Aurilia?' Krost repeated with astonishment. 'Alone?'

Silgid's level gaze met his and held it. 'You did not tell me that she and your friend were lovers. While I was mentally linked with Inghilla, she relayed your message to the rest of the Nine. And I was shaken even at this distance by the storm of Aurilia's grief. When that grief turns to anger, Krost, you will need no other power to help you avenge your friend.'

'I hope so,' Krost rumbled doubtfully, turning to the door.

'One other thing,' Silgid said, reaching out to stop him. 'I must tell you . . . My own powers do include some portion of what is called the "sight". It can give me small fragmentary glimpses of what is to come.'

'The future?' Krost asked. 'I thought that could not be done.'

'Not with certainty. Prophecy can only perceive a range of possibility. But my glimpses often prove accurate, Krost. And when my mind-link with Inghilla ended, when my mind was briefly open and adrift from the calling, I had such a glimpse. Concerning you.'

'Me?' Krost asked uneasily.

'I saw a shadowed place,' she went on tensely, 'full of terrors that were not clear. But I also saw, high above that place, a shape like a warrior's shield, yet so enormous that it would stretch from here almost to the village.' She clutched his arm. 'If you ever see such a thing, Krost, beware it. Because I saw the immensity of it come crashing down, with all its crushing weight – *upon you*.'

Only a few candles guttered smokily in the chandeliers, forming misshapen shadows in the main room of Aurilia's quarters where she was assembling the things she would take on her journey. By then her first tidal wave of grief and horror at Krost's message had passed, or had been thrust aside, sealed off in a corner of her mind to await a later solitary time when she could release those emotions and confront them. Meanwhile, there in that shadowy room, in her younger form, she might have seemed almost emotionless as she made her preparations. But those in the room with her who knew her well could see that while her face was set like stone and her eyes were like green ice, a volcanic flame was stirring beneath that surface so that the very air was charged with the force of her.

Some of those in the room, younger Sisters who were her friends or aides or both, found themselves almost quailing from that force whenever Aurilia passed near them. Otherwise they watched her in silence, having diffidently tried to turn her from her dangerous intentions or to offer their help, only to be flintily refused. None of those Sisters wished to risk stirring the volcano by continuing to press her. Only those of the Nine who had come to join the group seemed determined to do so.

'You aren't listening to us!' said the matronly Jhoranna, her plump face taut with compassion and concern. 'Aurilia, you must see that you are putting yourself at terrible risk at a time when grief is clouding your mind!'

'My mind is perfectly clear,' Aurilia said tonelessly, refastening the buckles on a bulging satchel.

Several of the others sighed unhappily. 'My dear,' pleaded Malavie, almost twittering with agitation, 'please stop and *think*. How can you say your mind is clear when you're about to ride into the Wastelands alone, to face a murderous demon—'

'—which you know almost nothing about,' put in the tall Prelisse, 'from that skimpy message.'

'I expect I'll find out,' Aurilia said in the same flat voice, peering into an also bulging saddlebag.

But then on the far side of the room, Inghilla rose slowly to her feet, looking drawn and weary, yet as she straightened up looking also as forceful and purposeful as Aurilia herself.

'If you refuse to consider your own danger, Aurilia,' Inghilla said sharply, 'consider this. We of the Nine have been exerting ourselves without respite to learn more about perhaps the greatest danger that has ever faced the Continent. We have not done with that task, which needs *all* of us, in unity, to be effective. And more importantly, if that danger does develop as we fear – if Lebarran does move to fulfil his evil ambition – our power will then especially be needed as never before. *All* of our power, Aurilia – the united power of the *Nine*.' She took a step forward, stern and intense. 'You know that without you the Nine would be weakened. You know how long it would take to prepare one to replace you, with the full and proper ceremony. If you are so self-absorbed and irrational as to risk your life for empty vengeance at such a time, it may be that you should be *restrained*, for your own good and that of all of us.'

Again some of the younger Sisters in the room quailed – from the authority of Inghilla, but even more from Aurilia. Without visibly altering her posture or expression, she seemed to gather power around her, condensed and heightened by her anger, almost appearing to tower in the room, her hair loosening itself from its coiffure, crackling with force.

'*Restrained?*' she repeated. 'As if I were a madwoman, to be chained?'

'No, no,' Inghilla said hastily. 'I meant only that you should not set off while you're still— '

'Irrational?' Aurilia spat the word. 'Is that your diagnosis? Have you looked into my mind and found lunacy?' She held up a hand, silencing Inghilla's reply. 'No, Inghilla, my mind is clear and sane, and quite made up.' She glanced around at all the other women, staring breathlessly at her. 'I will say this

76

once more, as plainly as I can. And then, if there are any of you who still cannot accept or understand, I recommend that you simply stay out of my way.'

The others watched her in silence, even Inghilla, held by the ferocity of her eyes.

'According to Krost's message,' she went on, her voice hardening as she refused to let it tremble, 'Red Cordell was slain by a demon. We have since found no trace of his body, or his sword, though the demon remains in this Sphere. So, whoever *invoked* the demon seems also to have moved Red's body to another Sphere or Realm, or perhaps . . . to have annihilated him.' Her voice shook slightly over that phrase, but she recovered. 'Whatever is the case, I intend to find out what happened and who did it. Inghilla speaks of my seeking needless vengeance, but it isn't so. If there is someone wielding dark magic on the Wastelands, we need urgently to know about it. And to know why the demon remains there. And then, if possible, to stop it.'

She paused, fighting back the emotions that threatened again to engulf her, before continuing. 'It may be selfish on my part, as Inghilla suggests, to do this. But it is not irrational. I'll go to the Wastelands, not alone, but in the company of Krost il Hak, whose formidable prowess is known to many of you. And indeed my own powers are not . . . negligible.' She looked challengingly around, her gaze finally resting on Inghilla. 'Nor will I put myself unnecessarily at risk. If the evil on the desert is as strong as I expect, I will of course seek the help of the Nine. But I want you finally to understand this. If any attempt is made to stop me, to "restrain" me, *I will flatten the walls of the Fastness to clear my path!*'

The others quailed again, and even Inghilla took a step back as the volcano within Aurilia spilled some of its fury into her eyes and voice. But as her words rang around the room, another voice was heard – small, delicate, tremulous and yet authoritative.

'No one will try to stop you, my child,' the voice said. 'Instead, we shall do what we can to help you, and give you our blessing.'

Aurilia and the others turned to the doorway to see the

tiny frail figure of Naemony, half-reclining on a cushioned framework like a couch without legs, borne by four sturdy young Sisters.

'Thank you for coming, Mother,' Aurilia said quietly. 'I'll be grateful for your blessing.'

'Then you have it, daughter.' The ancient woman smiled. 'There was a time when I would have done the same as you, for one I loved.'

'I wish I was going with the same range of powers as you would take,' Aurilia said.

Naemony shook her head slowly. 'My portion of the Earth-magic is weakened by age and feebleness. Your own gifts of transformation, Aurilia, are quite considerable enough.'

Inghilla sniffed. 'I still think,' she said tersely, 'that her gifts would be best employed here, against a more dangerous enemy.'

Aurilia swung around, glaring, but was forestalled by a gesture from Naemony's almost translucent hand. 'Inghilla,' she quavered, 'your concern does you credit, but I believe that at this time Aurilia's presence would serve us best elsewhere.' She paused to gather her strength. 'We have laboured long and hard to study the enemy, Lebarran, yet we have learned little. We have located no apparent weaknesses that would benefit us, and we know little more about the evil entity that he seeks to use in his Apotheosis. Hence I have been forced to conclude that even if we go on striving without cease, we have small chance of achieving more.'

A murmur of dismay swept through the listening Sisters.

'Yet one thing does seem clear,' Naemony went on. 'Lebarran is *poising* himself and his Order, on the brink of launching their bid for ultimate power. As the adepts in Prince Phaedran's employ have also begun to confirm, the moment that the enemy has chosen, when he plans to strike, is drawing near.'

'We don't *know* that,' Inghilla said doubtfully.

'We know it by intuition, if not deduction,' Naemony told her. 'For one thing, surely, Lebarran will have advanced his plans simply because he knows they have been *discovered*.' She turned her bright gaze on to Aurilia. 'Lebarran must also know that Phaedran is assembling forces, magical and otherwise. For those who can sense it, my dears, the whole of the Continent is in ferment, the very *air* is turbulent with the powers being gathered and honed for the conflict to come.'

As she spoke, in her urgency, her tiny body seemed to lift from the cushions. Not merely as someone might raise their upper body from a prone position, but an uplifting of her entire person, head to foot, so that she floated without support some hand's breadths above the couch where she had lain.

'Mother,' Inghilla said firmly, while the others looked on with mild alarm, 'please don't overtax yourself.'

With a small sigh Naemony sank slowly back on to the couch. 'Once I might have rested on empty air for hours,' she murmured, as if to herself. Then she peered around at them all again. 'No matter. The point is that I believe we have reached a time when we must abandon investigation for the sake of preparation – when we must see to our own mustering, to stand in readiness. And when we must send our standard-bearer, our Auriflamme, to represent us among the councils of the prince.'

The air of the room seemed to throb at the speaking of Aurilia's secret Name. And Aurilia herself stood stiffly, her expression unreadable, as the ancient woman continued.

'Take our blessing, then, Aurilia,' Naemony quavered. 'From the others of the Nine and all your Sisters. Seek the evil on the Wastelands if you must – but then, when you can, make your way to Quamarr.'

Aurilia bowed her head. 'Thank you, Mother.'

'Yet do not abandon wisdom in your anger,' Naemony added. 'When you confront the demon, call to us. We shall stand ready to send what aid we can. As we could not do, once before.'

The memory of distress was evident in the frail old voice, and Aurilia gazed into Naemony's eyes, both of them thinking of the time when Aurilia faced a horror against which even her powers were helpless, yet when no aid could possibly have been sent to her through the barrier of the Lightless Dome.

'I will call,' Aurilia promised. 'And afterwards, I'll go to

79

Phaedran and do what is to be done.' She gazed steadily around at them all. 'I pledge to you, I won't fail you. But equally – I won't fail to avenge Red Cordell.'

Retracing their path to the Wastelands, much restored by the brief rest, Krost and the tireless Wolle maintained much the same pace as before. Yet it was not long before all thought of that peaceful interlude had been set aside in Krost's mind – just as he put aside the thought of Silgid's appealing invitation to him to return, and of her disturbing vision. As he rode again into the fringes of the Wasteland, he firmly refocused his mind and energies on nothing but the prospect of the grim search and fearful struggle that lay ahead. As before, to any observer, he would have seemed lost within himself, oblivious to his surroundings. Yet he was fully aware of everything around him all through what remained of the night, and of every detail of the desert landscape as the sun eventually rose to illuminate it. Both he and Wolle sustained their alertness and the pace throughout the morning, without suffering much visible effect beyond dustiness. And Krost allowed himself no more than a small moment of satisfaction, as well as relief, when not too long after midday he drew Wolle to a halt in front of the cairn of Corodel.

But he felt a stab of shock when Aurilia, who had had farther to come, stepped calmly out of the cavern within the cairn to greet him.

'Did you *fly*?' Krost asked with a half-smile as he dismounted.

Aurilia offered only the ghost of a smile in return. 'I wish I had that power. No, the rest of the Nine helped to smooth my path and enhance my speed for a while. After that – I just rode very hard.'

By then Krost had seen that for himself. She looked pale and weary, even in her younger form, her doeskin tunic and leggings and her tawny hair powdered with dust. And there were *two* horses, her favourite white gelding and an equally leggy sorrel, tethered in the shade of the cairn. She had obviously been changing from one to the other along the way, and just as obviously had not stopped at all, for both horses stood with heads drooping exhaustedly.

'There was no need for such haste,' Krost remarked.

'For me there was,' she told him. 'I wanted . . . I had the idea that being here would make me feel closer to him.' Her eyes were filling with tears as she spoke, but she made no movement to brush them away. 'This has become Red's memorial, now, as it is Corodel's. And I wanted a time here by myself, hoping to find some sense of his presence . . .' She fought to control her voice. 'But, Krost, there is nothing. Just an emptiness. And, oh, may the gods forgive me, I let our last moments together be marred by a foolish quarrel!'

As the tears spilled she turned away, rigid with self-recrimination, and Krost put a tentatively comforting arm around her shoulders.

'Red regretted the quarrel too,' he said gently. 'And no doubt blamed himself just as you blame yourself.'

'It wouldn't have happened,' she said through her tears, 'if I hadn't seemed so neglectful and indifferent, in his eyes . . .'

Krost gently patted her shoulder. 'You are not at fault, Aurilia. No one is. You were preoccupied with important matters because of what you are. Red became restless and impatient because of what *he* was. It would not have been important at all, if that vile creature had not intervened.'

'Yes,' she said almost inaudibly. 'The demon. Its destruction will ease some of this pain . . .' She lifted her head, tears fading, her expression again stony with determination. 'Come out of the sun, Krost, and tell me exactly what happened, every detail that you can remember about the demon and the attack. And then, when the horses are rested – we can go hunting.'

Since Krost was convinced that the demon was nocturnal, they felt no need to move too swiftly when they finally set off. But even riding easily and steadily, they arrived before too long at the broken, hostile terrain of the Devil's Rifts. And by the time the sun was setting, they had penetrated deep into the region's heart, near the spot where Krost had found the remnants of Red's bloodstained shirt.

81

'We're here in good time,' Aurilia commented, glancing back at the sunset.

'It is not a *good* time,' Krost rumbled. 'Or a good place.' He was staring intently eastwards, to where the horizon was darkest, and Aurilia turned curiously to follow his gaze.

'What do you see?' she asked warily.

'Just more Wasteland. But before, when I was farther east from here, I saw something strangely tall and hazy on the horizon. I thought then it might be a dust-storm, but if it was it seems not to have come this way, or to have already passed.'

'Good,' Aurilia said, studying the landscape immediately around them, which was looking more barren and brutal as the ravines grew black with shadow. 'What there is here is bad enough without dust-storms. These ravines have a million places where the creature could be hiding.'

Krost nodded. 'We will have to be on guard when we search for it.'

Aurilia frowned slightly with thought, still studying the terrain. 'On guard, yes. But we may not need to risk searching all these crevices and crannies. Not if it hates the light, as you say. When the darkness is complete and the moon is up, I'll see if I can *force* it from its hiding-place.'

She turned then to building a small fire, beside which the two of them ate a light meal, almost as if they were on a carefree holiday. Yet the fire was no ordinary campfire. It was made from small woven twigs and knotted grasses taken from Aurilia's saddlebags, over which she had breathed a few phrases of a song as she had lit it. And though it burned brightly, its fuel did not even slightly burn away.

Even so, Krost regarded the fire with doubt. 'Are you intending to hold the demon off with that little flame?'

'Not at all,' Aurilia said. 'This has another purpose. And it's dark enough now to make ready.'

She moved away from the fire, shimmering through her shape-shift to her older form in a long plain gown of silver-white. Glancing at Krost, she noted his continuing expression of doubt. 'Do you disapprove?'

Krost looked discomfited. 'It is only that the demon is very quick, agile, enormously strong . . .'

82

She smiled faintly. 'I don't plan to fight it hand-to-hand, Krost. My older self wields the Earth-magic a little more potently than the other.'

So Krost subsided, going to lead the horses away, out of danger. When he returned, Aurilia's hands were raised to the sky, her thick white hair had come loose to flow down past her thighs like a bright cape, and she had begun to sing a high floating song that sent a shiver along Krost's spine.

As the song grew, it acquired an eerie echo in the moan of a rising night wind, mingling its voice with Aurilia's. Dust stung Krost's face as the wind swept over him, yet he saw that the flame of the tiny fire did not waver at all, even though in the sky above the wind was whipping and slashing at the thin cloud cover, stripping its veils away from the face of the newly risen moon. It was little more than a half-moon, yet as the clouds were torn apart its magically enhanced light streamed down on to the desert with dazzling brilliance, to be reflected back by the pale sand. No part of the land, not the deepest cleft or most secret cranny, could escape that silvery glare. It probed and illumined every shadow, every edge or smear of darkness, making the Wastelands appear weirdly stark and flattened and alien, even more unnaturally threatening and hostile.

As the song's final notes drifted away on the wind, Krost was looking doubtful again. 'Aurilia,' he said carefully, 'surely all this light will only drive the demon deeper into hiding.'

She shook her white head, studying the bright desert around them. 'It will not easily find a hiding-place from *this* light. More likely it will attack, seeking to put an end to the magic that brought the light. Demons would always rather kill than run.'

'Still . . .' Krost began. But as he spoke, a sweep of wind brought to him the festering stench that he well remembered, and the monster erupted out of the desert, its howl mingling pain and hatred, its crimson eyes writhing, the moonlight glinting on the golden collar at its neck.

Aurilia straightened her aged body, facing the creature without fear. Her white hair lifted around her, seeming to absorb the moonlight, turning to bright silver, growing brighter as Krost watched. Her gown, too, was brightening, until she seemed to be entirely clothed in a light so fierce and stark that it made Krost blink and narrow his eyes. The demon's howl became a scream as it flinched away from that silver beacon. Still screaming, it circled Aurilia in a menacing lope, as if seeking some weak point in her armour of light. And through the demonic cries and the more distant squealing of the terrified horses, Krost heard Aurilia's voice lifting in a different song, high-pitched and strident.

Without warning the frenzied monster leaped at her, claws extended. But at once it jerked away again with a shriek as a tress of Aurilia's hair lifted as if it were alive, lashing out at the demon in a sweep of searing brightness. And before the beast could attack again, Krost lunged forward and swung the iron quarterstaff with ferocious power.

The demon tried to dodge and ward off the blow at the same time, but it was not quite quick enough. The mighty weapon crashed full into its raging face, hurling it away in a tumbling, flailing tangle towards the fire. It seemed unmarked and unhurt, howling with fury as it recovered itself, but then hesitating, flinching away from the bright little flame almost at its feet.

The instant was all that Aurilia needed. Her song faded to a whisper, her hands flexed and gestured. And eight tiny tongues of flame leaped from the fire, leaped on to the ground to form a slightly flattened circle, like an ellipse, all around the demon's feet. Then each small flame flared up, as if the very sand was as inflammable as tinder, rising higher and higher until the demon was caged within eight soaring, slender columns of brilliant light.

It screamed and cowered, covering its gruesome eyes. And Aurilia stepped forward, still robed in silver brightness.

'Demon, speak!' Her voice was high and toneless as she uttered the ritual command. 'Whence came you? Whose was the power that invoked you?'

The monster continued to howl, clawing at the sand as if hoping to dig its way out of the fiery cage. And Aurilia shook her head slowly, glancing around at Krost.

'I don't think it *can* speak,' she said. 'Not a high-level demon at all.'

Krost glowered at the cringing monster. 'Then you have no way to learn who sent it?'

'I haven't,' she said. 'But others may have. That sorcerous collar it wears may offer a clue to its maker.'

She turned away again, lifting her face and then her voice, crying out in a musical, lilting call.

'*Naemosyne!*'

Krost twitched with a sudden chill as he heard a sound like a gentle, whispering sigh floating on the night wind – as if part of the wind's own voice, yet also somehow shaping the syllables of a word. A Name.

'Auriflamme,' the wind sighed.

'Naemosyne,' Aurilia repeated, her voice grown raw with the strain of wielding her different magics. And Krost twitched again, almost shocked as he realized that he had been allowed to hear the secret Name of the leader of the Circle of Nine. 'Mother,' Aurilia went on. 'The demon is caged. Send the strength of the Nine to learn its master's identity – and then to aid me in what must be done.'

'Banishment,' breathed the eerie voice on the wind.

'But I would not banish it to its own Realm!' Aurilia cried. 'I would fling it into the undying fire that burns *between* the Realms!'

The strength of her fury seemed to fill the night, and the demon's howl became a hideous wail of terror. Wildly it flung itself at the fiery cage encircling it, only to stagger back with a shriek, its black fur singed. At that assault Aurilia also swayed and staggered, but held the magic firm – and once again began to sing. The new song rose in a rasping drone, while her whole being trembled with the force of it and her eyes grew distant and glassy. And the power of the song was taken up and amplified by a chorus of voices on the sweeping wind, mingling and swelling in an atonal clamour. The song heightened, becoming a sound that seemed no longer to issue from human throats. Shuddering, Krost clamped his hands over his ears as the song grew, while the demon fell to the ground and clawed at its own flesh in a transport of terror.

Above it, above where Aurilia stood with wide-stretched

hands reaching towards the sky, a portion of the moonlight seemed to coalesce, settling downwards, forming a glittering roof above the cage of flame where the demon cringed. The song's abrasive discords vibrated up to an even higher pitch, holding one intense note. And with that note the very ground beneath the demon fell away and vanished. In place of the pale sand, a pit of empty darkness appeared – where, far down in its depths, light rose from unnatural tongues of flame that burned a ghostly blue without sound or heat. The demon seemed to hover in the air above the opening, its howl rising beyond the range of human hearing as it saw its fate. And then it fell, down and down to where the blue flames burned, while the dark opening in the ground slowly closed.

The song then abruptly cut off, the eight tall flames that had caged the demon quivered and vanished, the wind whined and faded away. And Aurilia, the silver blaze of her hair and gown extinguished, sagged to the ground as night's blackness returned to the Wastelands.

Hurrying to her, Krost half-lifted her from the sand. Slowly she opened her eyes, darkened by fatigue and horror.

'I'm all right,' she said faintly. 'Such magics can be . . . wearying.'

Krost nodded shakily, swallowing to ease his throat's tightness. 'I did not expect it to be so terrible.'

'But it was fitting, and deserved.' Her voice was fierce again as she struggled to her feet with Krost's help. 'And now I must ride to Quamarr— '

'*We* will ride,' Krost interrupted.

She nodded, with a small grateful smile. 'I'd be glad of your company, my friend, as I have been tonight. And in the city I plan to find adepts to help me scan the dark Realms where Red may be, and to bring his body back here to rest. Before we go looking for the one who sent the demon – to complete our vengeance.'

EIGHT

He had been running for a long time, in desperation and near-panic. Yet the ravine where he was running showed no sign of coming to an end, offered no way out over its high sheer sides. It wound interminably on and on, never deeper or shallower, never wider or narrower, constantly curving back around on itself in a spiral and angling upwards in a continuous incline that made running all the more exhausting. Beneath his feet the pale sand was as smooth and hard as concrete, as were the featureless cliff-faces of the ravine's sides. His legs were aching, his breathing was agonized, his eyes burned from the sky's white glare, yet still he ran on – as one runs who fears for his life, though there was no sign of pursuit behind him, no other living thing visible anywhere around him.

He had no clear idea of where the ravine was or where it might lead, just as he had no sure recollection of how he had come into it or why he had begun to run. Beyond all such efforts of thought, his mind was filled almost entirely with the unfocused awareness of fear and the urgent need to escape. On he ran, steadily on for another measureless time, while his pace began to slow to a jolting trot and then at last to a leaden-footed stagger. Exhaustion came to blur his vision and threaten his balance, agony stabbed at his lungs like hot knives, a terrible deadly numbness seeped into the muscles of his legs, his blood threatened to burst its veins with every beat of his overtaxed heart. Until, just as he became dimly aware that within a few more shambling strides he would surely fall, the upward spiral of the ravine came to an abrupt end.

At the flint-sharp edge of an impossible precipice. Where he reeled and wavered, flailing his arms to keep from toppling forward into emptiness.

Below his feet, below the narrow ledge of rock where he

fought for his balance, rafts of thin cloud drifted slowly past. And far, far below them, the land that formed the floor of that dizzying abyss was too distant, too hazily indistinct, for any of its features to be discernible beyond wide blurred smears of brown or green. Vertigo struck him then as he stared fearfully down into those inestimable depths. Fighting again to keep his balance as his surroundings seemed to spin sickeningly around him, he dragged his gaze away, looking up, where he discovered at last why it was that the ravine had led upwards in its continuing spiral.

The ravine was in fact a deeply cut channel that wound around and around, up and up, on the sides of a colossal mountain – one immense, towering, symmetrical spire of dark bare stone. The ravine's end, the narrow ledge where he was precariously balancing, lay some distance below the topmost point of the spire. And when he had raised his eyes at last to look at that peak, he lost all awareness of his pain and exhaustion and vertigo, in the sudden total paralysis of uncomprehending shock.

The entire summit of the mountain had been *shaped*, by some gigantic hand, into a sculpture. An enormous, awesome statue of a person seated upon a throne. The throne was ornate and splendid, but the massive nude figure seated upon it was stark and plain, the features of its face and body only hinted at.

In the immobilizing grip of fear and awe he stood and stared for an unknowable time, not blinking, hardly breathing, although at times his overstrained legs would tremble or a sound like a small groan would escape his bloodless lips. But then at last his entire body began to quake and quiver and he groaned aloud again, more loudly, with an unbearable heightening of dread.

The blank stone sockets below the brows of the giant statue had begun, appallingly, to open.

Revealing huge, inhuman eyes with shocking purple irises and pupils of purest white.

The two points of whiteness began to enlarge and intensify, their light reaching out, twin beams of fierce energy that lanced down towards him. He moaned once more at the pain of that brightness, struggling against his paralysis, trying to turn away. And as he struggled and twisted, he felt his foot slip on the ledge, felt himself wavering and overbalancing and beginning to fall . . .

Red awoke with a jerk, his eyes still squeezed shut against that blast of brightness. But as the effects of the dream receded, he eased his slightly gummy eyelids open a little – only to shut them again by reflex, because a band of yellow sunlight was falling in a hot blaze across his face.

Rolling his head to one side, he opened his eyes again, rubbing at their stickiness, while his mind grudgingly struggled through the remaining processes of awakening. The foul taste in his mouth, the dryness of his throat, the faint throb of a headache behind his eyes, all suggested that he might be hungover. That notion seemed to be reinforced by his discovery that he was naked, lying uncovered on a hard, lumpy surface. But he had no recollection of a drinking party. No clear recollections at all, in fact, of what might have been happening before he fell asleep. Desultorily he pried at the interstices of his memory, while also managing to extend his awareness beyond his own being – and was shocked into breathless immobility when he saw where he was.

It was a small, bare, empty room, its walls and floor and low ceiling all crude and irregular in shape, made of a stony substance that had the colour of sand but the texture and uneven surface of rough concrete. The room made him think of a cell, or a dungeon, although there was a narrow ill-shaped doorway that lacked any barrier. Nor did the place appear to be a cave, for there was an even narrower slit in one wall, a window or ventilator, through which the sun flung its strip of light across where he lay. Levering himself up on an elbow, he found that he was lying on pale soft sand, heaped thickly on the floor as if to provide a primitive mattress. Otherwise, there was nothing else in the room, and no sounds from beyond the doorway to indicate who might have brought him there.

And then he sagged back down on to the sand, feeling all at once weak and shaken, as some of the doors of his memory finally creaked open. He saw again the Wastelands ravine where he had fallen, his blood oozing away, the morning sun fierce on his face. And he saw again the creatures appearing with eerie suddenness along the lip of the ravine – with their four arms, their long chitinous bodies, their rustling insectile antennae . . .

Maybe it was all part of that weird dream, he said to himself. But *somebody* brought me here, wherever here is. And in this world, it could just as well be oversized bugs as anyone . . .

The memory that came to him then galvanized him into a surge that brought him all the way up to his feet. My God, he thought, *Krost*! He had been there, in the desert – maybe *he* brought me here, somehow. But then where is he now? And how did he manage . . .

Then he halted, because with that question his mind had at last become consciously aware of a remarkable fact – that his upwards leap to his feet had been entirely effortless and pain-free. Heart hammering, thinking again of how the dream had ended, the eerie eyes of the statue, he looked down at his naked body and felt sure that he knew at least *one* person who was involved in his rescue. Because his right wrist that had been broken was solid and firm and normal, without any signs of damage or swelling. And the fearful gashes from the demon's claws across his body had also entirely vanished, without so much as a hairline blemish remaining on his skin. He even had no trace at all of sunburn on his upper body, though he had been shirtless for some while under a desert sun. For that matter, he saw – and the sight produced a shaky half-smile – that the small scar on his belly, left by Brennia's sabre not so long before, had also disappeared.

He stared tensely at the doorway, hoping that some explanation of the mystery might step through it. Such as Hallifort, he thought, since he had no doubt that he had once again been restored by the remarkable power of the little healer. Unless it had *all* been a dream, he thought – chasing and fighting the demon, being hurt, all of it. And maybe a dream still . . . But he couldn't believe it. The memory of that dire night and morning on the desert was too vivid, the details of his present condition and surroundings too solid and normal. Nothing like the surreal weirdness of the actual dream images now mostly faded from his mind, save for the final vision of the giant mountain-top statue with the living eyes of Hallifort.

But if this is real, he thought, where *is* it? And did the bug-people bring me here, or did Hallifort? It occurred to him then that the insectile beings might themselves be magical, that they and not Hallifort might have healed him. But either way, he told himself, I still need to know where I am, and why, and what happens next.

He stepped towards the door, wishing that he was dressed or at least had some trousers. I could do with the sword, too, he thought, but it's probably lost in the desert somewhere. And I could really use a drink of water . . .

Then he stiffened and half-crouched, backing slowly away as with a faint crackling rustle one of the armoured insect-beings stalked into the room. In its four arms it was carrying something like a large cask, apparently made of the same stony stuff as the walls and making interesting sloshing noises. Despite the cask's size and probable weight the creature carried it quite effortlessly, moving unhurriedly and impassively past Red.

'Um . . . hello?' Red said edgily. 'Could you . . . er . . . tell me what place this is?'

The creature did not pause or turn or react in any way. The shiny stare of its eyes remained fixed straight ahead as it set the cask on the floor. Then it turned, still without looking at Red, and left.

'Thanks a heap,' Red muttered sourly, leaning back against the rough wall as his tension faded a little. Nothing else moved in the doorway, no further sound reached him from beyond it. Going over to the cask, he peered in, sniffing, and his eyes brightened. Plain water. And surely good water, since his insectile hosts were unlikely to poison him after having rescued him from the desert. He bent farther down and plunged his face into the water to drink gratefully and luxuriously, then scooped handfuls of the cool liquid up over his head and body. Straightening up, dripping and feeling amazingly restored, he stepped over to the narrow window-slit. To his surprise he saw that he was a considerable distance from the ground, with a panoramic view across another forbidding expanse of the Wastelands. This region looked even more scarred and broken – steeper and more jagged hills, deeper and more shadowed ravines – than the area where he had finally collapsed. Unfriendly country, he thought. Not a place to go walking around bare-assed. But, he reminded himself, the first priority was to find out where he was, and why, and how he could get out – *if* he could. Time to worry about desert survival after that.

He had been reassured by the absence of hostility from the insect-being with the water, and by the gift of the water itself, not to mention his healing. But even so he moved warily towards the doorway, his hand yearning for the familiar feel of his sword-hilt. And then he halted at the door, nodding slightly as if he might have anticipated the astonishing sight that met his gaze. The door led to another small room or cell, nearly identical to the one he had awakened in except that it had another doorway on its far side, and except that the sunlight streamed through its ventilation slit to fall on a startling collection of objects.

His trousers, boots and all the other clothing that he had been wearing when he had fallen finally in the ravine. And with them the sword of Corodel, which had even been replaced in the sheath that he had discarded outside the cairn.

Not bad service in this hotel, he thought, feeling a little dazed by so much mysterious good fortune as he dressed and buckled on the sword. Now let's see if they can run to a new shirt, and some breakfast. But first of all, a few answers.

The second little room opened on to a narrow, low-ceilinged passage like a tunnel, formed of the same pale stone as the rest of the structure, its dimness relieved by light from a few doorways at irregular intervals along its length. Creeping watchfully along, Red glanced through the first of those doorways and saw not another small room but a branching passage, its floor angling slightly upwards like a ramp. The sight provoked a fragmentary memory, a flash of his weird dream with

92

the upward-spiralling ravine that had led him to the mountain-top. But I don't want to go *up*, he thought . . .

The thought broke off, as from another of the narrow doorways ahead of him four of the insect-beings stepped into the passage and began to move towards him.

Red stood still, trying not to let his tension show as they advanced. 'Hello,' he said, trying again. 'Can you tell me . . .'

Then he stopped, seeing that the four beings were ignoring him as thoroughly as had the one with the water-cask. They did not move their heads or eyes even slightly, they showed no sign of registering his presence in any way, just as if he were invisible.

Be like that, Red thought as they continued to approach. What would you say to a bug, anyway? It occurred to him then that they might lack the faculty of speech – but it didn't seem likely. They didn't seem to lack many faculties, not when they could build enormous buildings and save a human from the desert and everything. These aren't just outsize versions of ordinary bugs, he thought with sudden certainty. They have to be some sort of advanced, evolved form. Maybe so highly evolved that they see me as insignificant, and that's why they ignore me.

Thinking such thoughts, he could not bring himself to push through their group in that narrow space, unsure of how they might react. So, instead, he turned back to the opening that led to the upward-sloping passage, and stepped through.

The ramp did not turn out to be a spiral like the ravine in his dream, but it did curve partly back on itself as it swept up to the next level. That led Red into another chamber, larger than the one where he had awakened, with another of the narrow ventilator openings. There were three other doorways leading from that chamber – but Red's attention was fixed on the middle one of the three, where another small group of bug-people suddenly loomed. Dodging away through the nearest of the available exits, he found himself on another ascending ramp that led him upwards – reluctantly – to another twisting corridor.

It's like an enormous three-dimensional *maze*, he thought

numbly, not built for humans to find their way around. He had an unnerving vision of himself wandering the empty passages, being ignored by the insect-beings, until he died of starvation. Yet they brought me that water, he reminded himself. They must know I'm here, and awake, and on the move. Or *some-one* must know . . . Come on, Hallifort, or someone, he thought fervently – come and get me. At least bring me a *map*.

He moved on along the new passageway, where he began to use the sword's indestructible blade to scrape small marks on the walls – to show where he had been, he thought sourly, even if he didn't know where he was going. That passage too had a number of dim little rooms opening here and there along its length, but then it abruptly ended in a junction where it became three branching passages. Arbitrarily choosing the one on the right, because it seemed to slope downwards, he soon found that the slope was a short-lived aberration, more evidence of the generally weird and apparently patternless construction. In fact, before long, that passage began to slope upwards again, until it ended at a T-junction where the narrow left-hand passage took a downwards dip while the right-hand one continued upwards. Turning left, growing less wary and more irritated, Red increased his pace – until he nearly collided with another group of the beings coming around a curve towards him.

There were six of them, each carrying smallish, pale, shapeless objects that Red did not recognize. For once, as the group came to a sudden halt before him and remained quite still, he had no doubt that their shiny eyes were looking at him. Indeed, they seemed ready to stand there and simply look for the rest of the day. Until, belatedly, he realized that he was standing in the middle of the narrow space, sword in hand, blocking the way. He even automatically muttered 'sorry' as he stepped aside, pressing back against the side wall. But the group made no acknowledgment, no sound other than the usual soft rattling of antennae as they filed calmly past. While behind them, with more rattling, came an even larger group, also advancing towards the upward slope of the passage behind him.

This new group showed no sign of slowing or pausing as it

marched forward – and while Red still had no wish to keep going upwards, he grew uneasy as he considered their number and their steady, empty-eyed advance. Go up a bit more, he thought, and look for another way down. There's too much traffic on this route.

So he turned back to the T-junction and then continued along the other passage, sloping upwards fairly steeply. He could hear the larger group of bug-people coming along behind him – but soon a quite different level of sound brought him to a tense and wary halt. From somewhere ahead, unseen along the unevenly twisting length of the passageway, he heard the loudest noise that he had yet heard in those labyrinthine ways. As if an enormous number of the insect-beings were gathered, the usual sound of their rustling antennae swelling into a mighty clattering tumult. In that moment's hesitation he considered turning back, away from whatever throng was collected ahead of him. But he could still hear the other group of the creatures advancing steadily towards him. And also, his naturally reckless curiosity was impelling him to go on, to take at least a quick, stealthy look. In case the gathering, ahead, might offer some clue to the nature of the weird beings and their structure, some answers to the whole mystery in which he had found himself.

Sword still ready in his hand, he crept silently forward up the slope. Rounding a bend, he saw a fairly wide opening at the end of the passage, from which the volume of sound seemed even greater. He moved towards it, crouching, pressing himself against the wall, and peered through. And a low, choking sound escaped his lips as shock hit him like a body-blow.

He was looking into an enormous chamber, many times larger than the biggest room he had yet seen in that place. It was jammed, literally swarming, with the insect-beings – who were moving with busy purposefulness around the prone forms of two quite different beings. Different not in details of appearance but simply because they were *huge*, monstrously enlarged versions of the others, their vast bulbous bodies resting on what looked like pads or nests of thickly heaped sand, like the makeshift bed where Red had slept.

95

The normal-sized beings in the chamber seemed to be waiting on the two huge ones in various ways, mostly presenting heaps of the smallish, shapeless objects that Red had seen in the hands of some of the beings he had met in the passageways. And he dazedly realized then that the objects were *food*, for the two huge ones were examining, nibbling and then devouring all that they were given. Many other servitors were also gathered on the far side of the bigger of the two huge creatures, where they were carrying off, one at a time, a seemingly endless supply of smooth, pale, shiny-wet objects about the size and shape of a large loaf of bread. Those things were being taken to another part of the great chamber where the walls were honeycombed with thousands of small niches, many of which held the loaf-sized objects while many more contained instead small squirming things like oversized maggots. And Red's almost overwhelmed mind began to see a glimmer of the reality – that the things in the niches were very much like eggs, or else like newly hatched larvae. At the same time he realized, with equal amazement, that not one of the beings in that obviously important chamber had reacted in any way to his visible presence at the door, or had even looked in his direction.

Then he drew back, adrenalin surging, as the group of beings that had been coming up the sloping passageway behind him reached the door where he crouched. But they merely brushed past him indifferently, with only the faintest of unintentional nudges from the armoured bodies. As they pushed in among the rest of the swarm, the general swirl of the other insectile bodies moved and shifted in different directions. For the first time Red saw a narrow raised area in a corner, like a stony shelf or ledge jutting from the wall, though only one low step up from the floor. And on that ledge stood a quite different kind of figure, solitary and unmoving.

A statue – in a human shape. Small and slender, sculpted from pale stone with apparently the same texture as the wall behind it. A nude figure, unnaturally smooth, almost impressionistic in its absence of any distinct features save the suggestion of blank eye-sockets beneath a slight curve of brow. It stood with slim arms folded, its head slightly bent, giving a sense of a lordly presence gazing eyelessly down on the seething mass of insect-folk in the room.

As before, Red had a flash of memory from his dream, a recollection of the statue, vaguely similar though far more immense, that his dreaming self had seen enthroned upon the mountaintop. Maybe this *is* still a dream, he thought edgily. And in the next instant he became more disturbingly sure that it was so, that he was still dreaming or perhaps hallucinating.

For the statue moved. As easily and flexibly as flesh moves, it unfolded its arms, lifted its head. And opened its eyes.

To expose vivid purple irises and blinding white pupils, their inhuman gaze reaching across the chamber to fall upon Red where he crouched, frozen and aghast.

The moment of paralysis seemed to continue endlessly as Red felt himself pinned by that piercing stare. Until, without warning, the statue simply disappeared. And in its place stood the small, white-haired, blue-suited, reassuringly familiar figure of Hallifort the Healer.

NINE

With a warm and somewhat apologetic smile, Hallifort stepped carefully down from the ledge and hurried across the chamber towards Red. As ever, the little man looked entirely unthreatening and almost comical, except for his uncanny eyes, and for the fact that the insect-beings stepped quickly out of his way to clear a path for him as he crossed the room.

'I am very sorry, Red,' Hallifort said with the apologetic smile. 'I wanted to be there when you woke, but I was delayed, here. The queen had a complication in her ovipositor . . .

Red blinked slowly, finding that his mouth was open, and closing it. A large number of questions was gathering in his astonished mind, all clamouring insistently for answers like journalists around a celebrity. From them all, for no sensible reason, he found himself selecting just about the least important.

'Her what?'

'Her egg-laying organ,' Hallifort replied. 'She . . .' He paused, his smile widening. 'But I think that can wait. There are many things you will want to know before you come to learn about the reproductive processes of the Riodae.'

Red nodded vaguely, trying to gather himself, to impose something like orderly calm on the storm of mystification within his mind. He was surprised then to find that he had sheathed the sword, and that Hallifort's small hand was gently turning him, leading him back down the passageway.

'Come,' the healer said. 'We will find a quiet place to talk, and some food for you as well, and I will tell you what you need to know.'

'Tell me first,' Red said quickly as they started away, 'do you know what happened to my friend, Krost?'

'Your friend is safe and well,' Hallifort assured him. 'But

come. When we are settled I can tell you everything you need to know.'

'And this isn't all some kind of dream or delirium?' Red asked.

'Indeed, no,' Hallifort said with a chuckle. 'Of course you might get the same reply if it *were* a dream. But I promise you, it is not.'

They turned then into a side doorway leading to another of the tunnel-like passages, from which Hallifort led the way along a bewildering succession of further passages, ramps and small chambers, moving as unhesitatingly as if he were following a clearly marked path. Finally they reached a fairly large chamber where another of the stone water-casks stood, with beside it some shapeless lumps of the foodstuff that Red had seen in the hands of the insect beings.

Hallifort gestured. 'There is water, and some of the staple food of the Riodae. It is made from forms of vegetable matter, very bland but nutritious enough, and humans can eat it safely.'

Red peered doubtfully at the objects, wondering if he was really all that hungry. But he had no doubts about being mystified. 'Riodae,' he repeated. 'That's the name of these ... bug-people?'

Hallifort nodded. 'It is the name in an ancient language of this land for the insects that were their ... ancestors.' For an instant his small round face twisted in a spasm like those Red had seen in him before, a look of inexplicable pain and sorrow. Then his expression cleared, and became the warm smile once again. 'Eat something, while I explain.'

Squatting on his heels, for there was no seating, Red broke a crumbly bit from one of the lumpy objects and took a gingerly nibble. It was certainly bland, almost tasteless, though perhaps with a distant hint of sweetness. Encouraged, his hunger returning, he took a larger bite.

'Finding you here,' he said as he chewed, 'already explains a lot, including what happened to my wounds. And I'm grateful to you all over again, Hallifort, more than I can say.'

The little man gestured as if to brush the gratitude aside. 'I am glad to have been able to help.'

'Did you help Krost too?' Red asked. 'Or do anything about that monster?'

'There was no need,' Hallifort told him. 'Krost and the lady Aurilia are riding out of the Wastelands at this very moment, towards the main road to Quamarr, having banished the demon last night.'

Red stared at him, his mind whirling with new questions and puzzles. So the monster had been a *demon*, he thought dazedly. And Krost had been joined by . . .

'*Aurilia?*' he echoed. 'How did she get into the act?'

Hallifort looked distantly sad. 'I am sorry to say that she and Krost believe you to be dead. She came to find the demon and avenge you.'

Red looked appalled at his mental image of a grieving Aurilia doing battle with a demon on the desert's cruel landscape. 'I have to go after them!' he burst out, wheeling away.

'So you shall,' Hallifort agreed. 'Very soon. But calmly, Red. The desert is no place for reckless haste.'

Turning again, his urgency subsiding a little at the healer's quiet tone, Red shook his head as if trying to clear away its chaos of questions and doubts and fears. At least she and Krost were all right, he thought numbly. And he'd catch up with them soon enough . . .

Then he twitched violently as another thought struck him. 'If so much has been happening,' he asked shakily, 'how long have I *been* here?'

'Two days and two nights,' Hallifort told him, holding up a small hand as Red began to look appalled again. 'I placed you in a prolonged sleep,' he explained, 'to complete the healing. Battling a demon and being harmed by it can leave wounds on a man's psyche as well as on his flesh. Your friend the dwarf-giant, or an enchantress like Aurilia, may be able to recover more swiftly from such an encounter, but it is less easy for an ordinary man. Especially one from another Sphere.'

Red nodded slowly, trying to accept what he did not fully understand, remembering more of the horror of the demon's attack. 'What about the horses?' he asked, fearing the answer. 'Grilena?'

100

'Your beautiful mare is quite unharmed,' Hallifort assured him with a smile. 'And Krost is riding his own sturdy mount, which suffered only a minor wound.'

Red's face lit up with an astounded grin. 'Grilena survived . . .! Where is she?'

'Here, in a ground-level chamber,' Hallifort said. 'I have been tending her myself, since she is somewhat nervous of the Riodae.'

'I can understand that,' Red said wryly. 'I'd have been nervous myself, if I'd been awake when they brought me here. Which I suppose they did . . .?'

'Indeed,' Hallifort said. 'They are aware of most things that go on here in their homeland, and they had been keeping a careful watch on the demon, though it was never aware of them. I learned of your presence through them, then of your injuries. And they brought you here then, at my request.'

'Are you their ruler or something?' Red asked.

Again the small strange shadow of pain flitted across Hallifort's face. 'Not at all,' he said quietly. 'They rule themselves entirely. But I have known them a long time, and have often . . . helped them. So they are usually willing to do as I ask.'

Red frowned. 'Does that have something to do with your . . . with the way you looked, when I first saw you up there?'

'Not really,' Hallifort said, looking away with shadowed eyes. 'I can alter my own form, as you know, and they seem most comfortable with me in the form you saw, which is how they first saw me.' He sighed. 'But I can say no more about that. And I would be glad, Red, if you would not seek to probe too deeply into my relationship with the Riodae.'

'Of course,' Red said at once. 'That's your business. It's just . . . they're so remarkable, they make me curious.'

'Naturally,' Hallifort replied. 'And I can tell you more of *them*, at least, if you wish.' At Red's eager nod, he went on. 'They are beings with intelligence of a high order, and with communal bonds more powerful than you could imagine. They survive with great tenacity and skill in this barren land, searching out underground water, adapting various organisms to be their food. They are perceptive and sensitive, though virtually

101

without emotion as humans know it, and are incapable of delusion or falsehood. They are fearless, tireless, more than ten times stronger than their size would suggest. And with a comparable mental strength, although their form of intelligence is almost beyond the grasp of human understanding. Their minds work in alien ways, inconceivable patterns, while together in unity their intelligence is not only incomprehensible but gigantic. For they are *hive* beings, Red. Their minds are linked in a transcendent hive mentality. And though that unified intelligence is mostly focused with unwavering single-mindedness on the hive's survival, there are times when its separate individuals will briefly consider other matters and respond to other urgings, or requests.'

Red nodded again, listening silently, impressed beyond measure at the tones of admiration and respect – almost love – that suffused the little man's words.

'But enough,' Hallifort said. 'The fact is that I am in constant contact with them, so when they found you I was in a position to ask them to help you.'

'And I'm deeply thankful,' Red replied. 'But . . . I hope you won't be offended if I don't hang around too long.'

'Of course not.' Hallifort's warm smile reappeared. 'If we leave shortly, we should be at the memorial of Corodel by nightfall.'

'*We?*' Red repeated, startled.

'Indeed,' Hallifort said calmly. 'I shall ride with you that far – to ensure that you find your way, and to point you towards Quamarr, if that is your destination.'

'I'll be glad of the company, and the directions,' Red told him. 'Especially if there might be more demons wandering around the desert.'

'There are none,' Hallifort assured him. 'Demons are not native to the Wastelands. The one you encountered would have been *invoked*, from its own dark Realm, by a sorcerer in this land.'

'What for?' Red asked.

'I cannot tell, with certainty. Yet I sense an ominous shadow. I have said before, Red, that you seem destined to play some

102

crucial role in the transforming events that may soon beset this Continent. It may be that some other has foreseen your destiny as well, and sent the demon against you to avert it.'

Tension and anger glinted in Red's pale eyes. 'You mean some sorcerer sent a demon to kill me.' He paused, then smiled bitterly. 'Too bad he picked one that was afraid of lightning and daylight, and my sword as well.'

'Indeed, it seems a curious choice.' Hallifort glanced at the sword on Red's belt. 'The demon's fear of your sword is interesting. Did you strike at it, wound it?'

Red's smile grew wolfish. 'Oh, yes. A good deep cut on the shoulder. Should have been its neck.'

'No doubt,' Hallifort said. 'But an unusual blade, to wound a demon. The Sisterhood wove its magics well to make Corodel's sword. Perhaps better than they knew. More things even than demons might abhor that blade.'

The words were vaguely puzzling to Red, but he was still mostly focused on the memory of his confrontations with the monster. 'You know – a couple of times I had the feeling that the demon wasn't really trying to *kill* me. As if it was holding back.'

'Really?' Hallifort frowned. 'Demons are rarely reluctant to kill. Unless it was constrained, by the one who invoked it, for some reason.'

'And that one has to be Lebarran,' Red said tightly.

'Almost certainly,' the healer agreed.

'And there's probably a good chance that he'll try again.'

'A chance, yes,' Hallifort said. 'Though he is too well-shielded for anyone to probe his intentions. Still, you may take heart from the possibility that he may not have wanted you dead. And also from the likelihood – forgive me, Red – that he sees you as of only minor importance, worth only a *low-level* demon.'

Red laughed uneasily. 'For once, I'm glad to be a nobody.'

'You are not *that*,' Hallifort replied with a smile. 'In any case, all this provides another good reason why you should return now, swiftly, to your friends.'

Leaving the chamber, they descended through another lengthy succession of mazy passageways. Hallifort did not pause to collect any belongings, nor did he seem to feel the need to mention his departure or even to speak to any of the Riodae that they met along the way. And the passing Riodae, equally, moved past the two of them as if they were both invisible – which made Red begin to wonder if some other kind of communication was going on.

'Did you say,' he asked, 'that the Riodae are telepathic, or something like that?'

Hallifort nodded. 'In a way, yes. They are mentally linked with the overall *hive* mentality. Each individual is in constant contact, or *communion*, with the hive mind, even over some distance. As indeed am I. But the individuals can also communicate with one another, separately, through a complex code of signals, with their antennae.'

'If you're speaking to them, then,' Red said lightly, 'tell them thanks and goodbye from me.'

'I doubt if they would understand those courtesies,' Hallifort said with a smile.

'All right, then tell them . . . that their human guest wishes their hive an endless life of peace and plenty.'

Hallifort looked at him with surprised approval. 'Your instinct is accurate, Red. That is *exactly* the right thing to say to them.'

By then they seemed to be coming to the end of their long descent, moving from yet another passageway on to a much wider, flatter ramp that led them into a warren of small chambers. As they approached the doorway of one chamber, Red heard from within a horse's ecstatic whicker of joy. And the same joy filled him as he stepped through the door, to greet his golden Grilena. She looked to be in perfect health, standing next to a container of water like a small stone trough, with another next to it holding some dry grass and leaves. And she snorted and cavorted with delight, flourishing her blonde mane, nudging Red lovingly as he stroked her neck and muzzle and whispered affectionately into her ear.

Then he took hold of the broken strap that had been her

tether at the cairn and led her out, following Hallifort back out of the warren of chambers by another route. That brought them to an unusually large, high-ceilinged chamber with a considerable scattering of sand on the floor, and with an opening like an oversized doorway in one high wall – a doorway blocked and sealed by one immense slab of stone.

There one of the Riodae stood as if waiting for them, holding something that looked like a piece of grey-brown cloth, loose-woven like coarse burlap. Taking the cloth, Hallifort handed it to Red with a smile.

'I asked the Riodae to make this, from plant fibres,' he said, 'to protect you from the sun. I fear that weaving is still very new to them, though their hands are deft enough.'

'I'm glad to have it,' Red said gratefully, yearning for a mirror as he draped the cloth over his head and shoulders. Cordell of Arabia, he thought. Or do I need ashes to go with my sackcloth?

'They would have brought your own things, and your saddle,' Hallifort went on. 'But those items were all inside the Corodel memorial, and the Riodae will not enter a human structure. And now your friends have taken your things with them.'

'No matter,' Red said. 'Grilena won't mind me riding bare-back. And I'm grateful for this covering.'

He had included the silent Rioda in his thanks, and was startled to find the creature's shiny eyes fixed on him while its antennae rustled.

Hallifort nodded. 'This one is now expressing the hive's acknowledgment of your earlier good wishes, and extending the same to you.'

As he spoke the Rioda turned away towards the huge slab of stone that rose twice its height and extended twice its width, calmly picked up the immense mass in its four hands and moved it aside. Through the open doorway Red saw the Waste-lands stretching away before him, stark and glaring under a high sun. But his attention was drawn more to the massive slab that had been so effortlessly shifted. Going to look at it more closely, he pushed against it where it had been set leaning against the wall. It was like pushing against a mountainside.

'As I said,' Hallifort remarked, 'they are disproportionately strong for their size. As were their insect forebears.'

'Incredible,' Red said, deeply impressed. 'You should have sent a squad of them to deal with that demon.'

'They would not have gone,' Hallifort replied. 'The hive was willing to send Riodae out to find you, at my request, because the action posed no risk. But it would never endanger Riodae lives for anything less than defence of the hive itself. And the demon, which was never aware of the Riodae, offered no threat to them.'

As he spoke, they moved out through the doorway on to a level stretch of sun-baked sand. Red swung himself up on to Grilena's back, glanced around to watch the giant slab of rock being replaced, then lifted his gaze upwards in amazement and awe. The structure rose above him overpoweringly – a skyscraper of pale stone that looked more like a natural rock formation than a construction, despite the small scars of the ventilation slits. It might have risen of itself from the earth, random and haphazard, with no apparent guiding intelligence or plan. It bulged here and retracted there, thrust out humped shoulders in some places and fell away in aimless concavities in others. And to Red its misshapen ugliness was almost as impressive as its size.

'Interesting style of architecture,' he said lightly. 'Sort of Quasimodo Baroque.'

Hallifort looked faintly puzzled, but did not pursue it. 'The Riodae secrete a fluid that acts as an adhesive, binding loose sand into firm stone. With that they have made their home and their stoneware. But they are utilitarians, with no aesthetics. This structure has arisen in stages, slowly, its size and shape dictated solely by the needs of the population. Yet it has stood for many generations, and will stand for many more.'

By then Red was studying a faint haze that seemed to be hovering around the summit of the malformed tower. Turning to ask Hallifort about it, he was startled to see that the little man had also somehow become mounted on a bony, nondescript horse that Red had seen before.

'That's the horse you had in the west, at the Dome,' he said.

'Indeed,' Hallifort confirmed. 'It is my usual mount, which attracts little notice.'

'Not even when it appears and disappears?' Red asked idly. 'I didn't know you could do that.'

'That is not quite how it is. In fact the horse is a kind of . . . solid illusion. I have simply altered my own form, as I *can* do – from the shape of a man to the shape of a man-on-a-horse.'

Red blinked, unable to think of anything to say, not sure if Hallifort would welcome any further questions. And the healer, with a small nod, shook the reins of his bony horse and moved away. As he and Grilena followed, Red looked back again at the looming tower – and saw that the strange haziness at its top seemed to be spreading. Continuing to look back as they rode away, he was amazed to see that the farther they went from the building the more the haze extended over and around it, like a veil. In a very short time, after a limited distance, the tower could no longer be seen at all. Only the haze remained, swirling slightly, and if Red had not known otherwise he might have taken it for an oddly shaped cloud of fine dust, or a much more distant shimmer of heatwaves.

'Now that's an even better trick,' he managed to say. 'Another of your illusions, Hallifort?'

'No, neither illusion nor mine.' Again for an instant the spasm of nameless pain crossed the little man's face again. 'It is a deceptive spell of concealment, immeasurably powerful. It can resist any vision, including a high adept's spells of seeing or scrying. Even the Riodae, outside the tower, could not find it again if they were not guided by their link with the hive mind.'

'And it's there to keep the Riodae hidden?'

'Indeed. To keep their very existence unknown, so that they will remain unmolested.'

Red thought about that for a moment, and in that moment unexpectedly thought again of the unnerving vision of Inghilla, back in the Fastness. The vision of shadowy *presences*, inhuman and fearsome, that Inghilla's mental power had glimpsed around Hallifort – which was clearly some distorted paranormal perception of the Riodae. So, he thought, this veiling isn't

107

perfect. And then another possible breach of it occurred to him.

'What about the Riodae who go out?' he asked. 'Aren't they ever spotted?'

'They are skilled at staying unseen,' Hallifort said, 'so it is a small risk. Almost no one ventures into this more forbidding region of the Wastelands. And though a few have glimpsed the Riodae once or twice in the past, their stories have always been dismissed as mirages or hallucinations.'

'Not always,' Red demurred. 'Those stories brought Corodel out here, searching.'

'So they did,' Hallifort said sadly. 'Though he found only his death.'

'Was there no way to prevent that?' Red asked carefully.

'I tried to do so,' Hallifort told him. 'Corodel's search brought him close to the Riodae tower – and though he could not see it, he did by mischance see some foraging Riodae. He pursued them, and they fled, unwilling to confront him and his sword. In the end they eluded him, but by then Corodel was exhausted, his supply of water had run out and he had lost his way. Seeking to save him, I asked the Riodae to bring him to me as they brought you, Red. But they could not. Though he had grown weak by the time they reached him, he still tried to fight them – until a blood vessel burst within his brain, and he fell dead.'

Red was silent, thinking of the invincible heroic will that had impelled the man into that last unnecessary battle. 'That's something of a tragedy,' he said at last.

'Indeed. A tragic hero bringing about his own downfall.' Hallifort's eerie eyes peered at Red intently. 'You must seek to avoid emulating him in *that* way, Red.'

Red twitched, feeling slightly chilled. 'Count on it. I never was much for playing tragedy.' He looked back again at the featureless haze where the Riodae tower had been. 'You said all that back there isn't *your* spell. Whose, then?'

Hallifort turned away, his face haunted. 'I cannot tell you that, Red. But certainly it is not mine. I have told you before that I have no such powers.'

Red shook his head, confused. 'Sorry, but I don't get this.

108

You seem to have *lots* of powers, Hallifort. You can appear and disappear, as you did after the Dome – and you can change your shape in some impressive ways – and you seem to know everything that's happening all over the Continent . . .'

Hallifort held up a small hand, the expression of pain and sorrow again passing over his face. 'Red, I know it all puzzles you. And it is true that I can alter and affect and move my own being, and that I have some forms of extended perception. But outside of my own person, I can wield no power, I can achieve no alterations or effects, beyond the one limited area of healing. *Nothing* more. And I beg you, Red, not to question me further on these matters.'

'Sorry,' Red said again, contritely. 'I don't mean to be nosy. I just can't help being curious . . .' He took a deep breath. 'And I'm not the only one. I was sort of sent to *look* for you, Hallifort, by the Sisterhood. Because they're curious about you too. I think some of the Nine are worried that you might be a threat, while others are wondering if you might be able to help them against Lebarran.'

'I see,' Hallifort said, his voice hollow and dejected. 'I regret their suspicion, for I am certainly no threat. But I regret also that I must disappoint them, for I can offer no help.'

'Because you're unable,' Red asked, 'or unwilling?'

The little man sighed. 'Both, I expect. You must simply tell the Nine that it is *impossible* for me to participate or interfere directly in the events of this Sphere. Beyond offering my healing, when I can.'

Red felt a wave of sympathy as he watched another shadow of grief and loss pass across the healer's face. 'Whatever you say. I'll tell them in those exact words, and try to get them to leave you alone. I owe you that, at least, after all you've done for me.'

'I would be grateful.' Hallifort turned to fix him again with his compelling gaze. 'And if you feel that way, there is a more vital thing I would ask you to do for me.'

'Name it,' Red said at once.

'Swear an oath,' Hallifort replied. 'A vow, a sacred pledge, in the form most binding to you. Give me your promise that

109

you will not reveal what you know of the Riodae, or the location of their hive, or anything to do with them. Tell your friends only that *I* found you and restored you, if you must tell them anything. But *swear*, Red, I beg you, to keep the Riodae a secret.'

Red felt shaken by the urgency in the healer's voice, the almost desperate tone. 'Of course, yes, I will. I give you my word.' He cast about in his mind for a suitably solemn pledge. 'I swear it on my life – and on the sword of Corodel.'

'Thank you,' Hallifort said, looking relieved.

'But I still wonder,' Red added, 'how long you can hope to keep the Riodae safely hidden. Because if Lebarran puts his plans into action, and if nobody can stop him, it could be the end of everything for the whole Continent. Which would probably include you and the Riodae, Hallifort, in the end, no matter how strong that spell is around the tower.'

'That may well be so,' Hallifort said mournfully, staring out over the empty desert. 'But it is in the hands of the gods, and the fates, as the future always is.'

'There was a time,' Krost growled, 'when being a guest in the royal palace was a great pleasure. Now it is a grim duty, to be dreaded. I wonder if it will ever again be as it was.'

'Or if anything will,' Aurilia said gloomily.

They were in a narrow room on the main floor of the palace, which served as anteroom to one of the public reception chambers. Krost was standing, unwilling to entrust his weight to any of the elegant chairs, next to a sofa where Aurilia sat in her older form, looking hunched and strained. And somehow drained, Krost thought, as she had looked ever since that night on the Wastelands. The loss of Red and the banishment of the demon had taken a considerable toll on her, leaving her pale and weary and hollow-eyed in both her forms.

Krost forced a smile, to lighten the mood. 'Listen to us, Aurilia. We are like two ancient grumblers by a fireside, complaining of how the world has worsened.'

She lifted her head, the green eyes solemn. 'But it *has*, Krost. That's the truth, whoever voices it. As you say of the palace. We've just arrived and already I can hardly wait to leave. And the city, too, has become a place of tension and dread and dark rumour.'

Krost nodded. 'Perhaps because of Phaedran, and his present state of mind. He seems even worse than he was before, when we arrived to learn that Evelane had been taken.'

They both glanced towards the door to the royal reception room, behind which their prince was briefly occupied with some business of governance. The night before, when they had reached the palace, and had been settled into guest suites, Phaedran had spared them only a few moments – and had seemed remote even by the normal standards of his grim and chilly nature. Only twice during that brief interview did the prince's icy control seem to waver under the onslaught of emotion. The first occurred when Aurilia asked after his daughter, the princess Evelane. In some anguish Phaedran told her that Evelane was as unstable as ever, veering between the extremes of blank depression and frenzied hysteria, with short-lived periods of calm only now and then. And the second breach in Phaedran's cold rigidity occurred when Krost informed him of the death of Red Cordell.

The prince had wheeled abruptly away, stalking to one of the room's tall windows, peering unseeingly into the night. 'A bitter loss,' he had said, his voice harsh. 'And you say it was Lebarran who invoked the demon?'

'No doubt of it,' Aurilia had said. 'Before we banished it, Inghilla herself used her mental sight to study the creature's collar. The traces of Lebarran's sorcery were clear.'

'Though no one can be sure *why* the demon was sent,' Krost had said. 'It might have attacked Red by chance, while on some other evil business.'

'Yet perhaps not,' Phaedran had replied, turning back to scowl at them. 'The Magister would know how much we valued our new Corodel, what service his name and sword would have performed, in themselves and as a rallying force.'

'Rallying?' Aurilia had echoed, startled. 'Rallying whom? To what purpose?'

Phaedran had hesitated, then shook his head. 'Let that question wait till tomorrow, Aurilia. It grows late, and you will be weary from your journey. In the morning I will be meeting with a number of others, to hear reports of . . . our present circumstances. I would be glad if you both would attend as well, for you will have much to contribute. And there you will have your questions answered.'

So that brief conversation of the previous night had come to an end. And so Krost and Aurilia waited uneasily, the next morning, filled with curiosity about the meeting to which they had been invited, and filled also with tension, gloom and a shadow of foreboding that matched almost exactly the atmosphere pervading the palace and the city beyond it.

As it certainly pervaded the reception chamber, when a servant finally ushered them in. The room itself was spacious and high-ceilinged, designed to be bright and airy, yet somehow that morning seeming to hold pockets of shadow that clung to the draperies and lurked in corners, enhanced by the drizzling rain visible through the windows. And the same atmosphere seemed to have inscribed itself on the faces of the six men seated at the gleaming table that dominated one end of the chamber.

At least the chairs looked solid enough, Krost thought with relief as he and Aurilia were shown to seats at the table. And he looked around at the others with interest, while the prince made perfunctory introductions. Phaedran himself was at the head of the table, seated in an over-decorated chair that was almost a throne. On one side of him were three men in the blue-grey uniform of the royal militia, though wearing light, ceremonial body-armour. Krost vaguely knew one of them – the hawk-faced Marshal Trochain, new commander-in-chief of that force, flanked by two lesser officers as aides. Krost and the marshal exchanged nods that were friendly enough, but the responses of the two aides seemed more curt, almost resentful or suspicious. But Krost was used to such reactions. He had served Phaedran in many capacities at many times, and his special relationship with the prince had often annoyed the more pompous or ambitious members of the militia high command.

On the other side of the prince sat two quite differently garbed men, strangers to Krost, though he could guess at their profession. One of the two seemed fairly elderly, thin and stooped, his wispily bearded face deeply lined, his thin white hair trailing to his shoulders. Otherwise he wore a long shapeless cloak with hood thrown back in some unadorned material of dark blue, and in one bony hand held a twisted, delicately carved walking-stick. His companion, wearing a rich silk tunic over tailored silk trousers, was a tubby man with a shock of grey curls and a fleshy red face wearing an apparently cheery smile – although his small, deep-set eyes were hard, unblinking and quite devoid of humour.

Wizards, Krost said to himself, studying them. And if he

113

heard the names properly, the fat one was Farbanni while the old one with the stick was . . . Vallawn? Somehow that name sounded familiar. Certainly it did to Aurilia, by the look on her face.

'*Vallawn?*' Her eyes were wide with astonishment. 'I can hardly believe . . . I understood that you were . . .'

She caught herself then, but the old wizard merely smiled, eyes twinkling.

'Dead? Yes, I think the rumour was quite widespread. But I was merely in contemplative seclusion for some while. And now I have emerged, to participate how I can in these troubled times. Although I should be grateful for them, my lady, since they have brought me the pleasure of renewing our acquaintance.'

She inclined her white head. 'The pleasure is mine, Vallawn, to find you well. The Continent would be the poorer if we had lost an adept of your eminence.'

'Yet it is sad,' Vallawn went on gravely, 'that this meeting should be overshadowed by such dire events.'

'More and more dire,' Farbanni said almost with relish. 'Including, now, the regrettable death of the young Corodel.' He leaned forward, his face cherubic but his eyes filled with malice. 'I understand, Aurilia, that it was *your* summoning that brought the young man to this Sphere?'

Krost growled with anger at the taunt, but Aurilia showed only a glint of steeliness in her eyes. 'That's so, Farbanni. I brought him here, to his death, as you seem to need to remind me. And I will regret it for the rest of my days.'

As Farbanni, with a small smile, made an insincere gesture of denial, Phaedran's frosty voice cut into the exchange. 'You did not cause his death, Aurilia, and you need assume no blame. The one who is truly responsible is the one who threatens many more lives in our land. The death of Red Cordell is one more clear proof of that threat, to impel us to our purpose.' He gazed bleakly at Aurilia. 'But you will need no reminding, Aurilia, since you have as much knowledge of our enemy and his intentions as any of us. Perhaps more.'

She shook her head tiredly. 'Not *more*, Highness. The Circle

114

of Nine has been seeking to gather knowledge of Lebarran, but to little avail.'

That admission drew a faint, mocking chortle from Farbanni, which earned him a searing glare from Aurilia, and led Krost to try to divert the conversation.

'I can see the need for mages and Sisters here,' he rumbled. 'But what do you imagine *I* can bring to this council?'

To his surprise, it was Marshal Trochain who replied. 'In our view, Krost, you will before long have a great deal to contribute.' He glanced at Phaedran. 'If matters proceed as some of us believe they should.'

As Krost frowned, puzzled, the prince nodded sharply. 'Quite so – but let that wait awhile, Trochain.' He turned his frigid gaze on the two wizards. 'Gentlemen, before Aurilia and Krost joined us, you were about to report on some new development that you described as "dreadful". Please tell us all, now.'

'Willingly, your Highness,' Farbanni said quickly before Vallawn could speak. 'The fact is that all spells – ours, and those of other adepts co-operating with us – have so far failed to provide a direct sight of the Magister. As you know, Lebarran has been living in seclusion in what the old maps call the Clouded Valley. And its semi-permanent *natural* overcast has apparently been altered by his magic into a *barrier* – unlike the Dome erected by the late Talonimal, yet no less impermeable. It seems to *absorb* our seeking magics, to stifle and dissipate them. Even combined spells—'

'Yes, yes,' Phaedran broke in sharply. 'We are all aware of the difficulty, which it seems the Sisterhood too has encountered. What of this *new* development?'

Farbanni looked uncomfortable. 'That, Highness, concerns two younger adepts, Ephorte and Bellarek, who had been involved in this work. They apparently decided to take a different approach from the rest of us. You understand, they were young mages, gifted of course but young and proud, perhaps a trifle rash— '

'*Were?*' Aurilia interrupted, catching the past tense. 'What happened?'

Farbanni flung an unhappy glance at Phaedran. 'They chose their course of action entirely on their own, seeking no counsel . . . It clearly smacks of wilful ambition, even glory-seeking, though one does dislike speaking ill of the dead . . .'

'Get *on* with it!' Phaedran barked.

The wizard's fleshy face took on a sheen of sweat. 'It seems that Ephorte and Bellarek abandoned their attempts to probe the enemy from a distance. Instead, they transported themselves magically, in *person*, to Lebarran's valley, hoping to be able to observe him from closer range, while themselves remaining hidden by spells of veiling. But . . . their powers did not prove adequate.' He produced a large silk handkerchief, dabbing tensely at his forehead. 'Last night, when Vallawn and some other adepts were gathered in my home, to try yet another seeking conclave, Ephorte and Bellarek were magically . . . returned.'

'Dead?' Phaedran asked sharply. 'Lebarran sent back their corpses?'

'Yes,' Farbanni replied, looking slightly sick at the recollection. 'But . . . not entirely. They had been *emptied*. Though the clothing, skin and flesh were entirely unmarked, every internal organ including the brain, and every single drop of blood, had been extracted from the bodies.'

Phaedran sat back, his face stony. 'It is a mockery,' he snapped. 'Lebarran is showing his contempt, his scorn.'

'And demonstrating his power,' Aurilia added.

Phaedran frowned. 'Need we make too much of that? If these were just two young mages with foolishly inflated ideas of their own worth . . .'

'But there was also the case of poor Chedua,' Farbanni said warily. 'If you recall, he sought to open a window into the Void Beyond, to examine the entity that Lebarran calls the Unformed. But his protections also proved inadequate, and Chedua is now a mindless ruined husk, with most of his life-force drained from him.'

'And, Highness,' Vallawn said quietly, 'these were far from negligible adepts. All three have been gaining prominence in the city.'

Farbanni sniffed. 'Yet of course it *is* less difficult to gain prominence than it once was, since several of Quamarr's more notable mages have committed themselves to Lebarran's so-called Order of the Apotheosis.' His small eyes grew sly. 'Not to mention the three adepts who perished, your Highness, on your . . . expedition against Talonimal.'

Phaedran scowled at him bleakly. 'I know it all too well. Which is why we must consider even more seriously the enterprise that we have discussed. Before even *more* mages, and more warriors, are lost to us. Before the enemy gains even *more* advantage.'

Krost stirred restlessly, the sturdy chair groaning beneath him. 'Can you stop being mysterious, Phaedran?' he growled. The marshal's aides looked scandalized at the familiarity, but the prince, wholly accustomed to it, merely looked attentive as the dwarf-giant went on. 'Trochain mentions "matters proceeding", now you speak of an "enterprise". Are you planning some foolhardy *action*?'

The others looked nervously at the prince, while even Aurilia seemed startled by Krost's tone. But Phaedran merely nodded sombrely. 'It is so, old friend. I do not intend to sit still, to cower behind the walls of Quamarr, waiting for the enemy to come against us at his leisure.'

The marshal murmured his agreement, the wizards looked glum and tense, Aurilia looked even more startled. But Krost merely glowered.

'What do you intend, then?' he demanded. 'To declare *war*? To march on Lebarran's valley? By all the Realms and Spheres, Phaedran – he would send you *all* back with your insides missing!'

The two aides seemed even more scandalized, but the prince looked merely haunted. 'I do not overlook the dangers, Krost. But they will not grow less if we do nothing!' Abruptly he got to his feet, impelled by urgency. 'Krost, you were in the Dome, you know as well as anyone what Lebarran is planning – what ghastliness he hopes to create, with his creature from the Void – what plans he has for this world when his Apotheosis is complete. As we all know, now, from the contemptuous killing of the two young mages, and of our friend Cordell.'

117

'Which I would think should give you pause,' Krost rumbled.

Phaedran leaned over the table towards him, his face as pale and hard as marble. 'No, my friend. The time is past for pausing. I believe that we have now reached a crossroads, with only *two* choices open to us. We can remain as we are, trying to erect whatever dubious defences we can contrive, against the time when Lebarran and his Order move against us. At a time of *their* choosing, and in the fullness of their power.' His fist slammed on to the table, making everyone jump except Krost. 'Or *we* can do the choosing! We can take the initiative, control the time for that confrontation – while Lebarran is still in his valley, no doubt not yet ready to move, his preparations not yet complete. In that way we can fling back in his face the challenge he has offered, especially with the killing of the two mages and Red Cordell. We can march on Lebarran's valley, strike at him before he is fully ready, and if the fates will it we can *bring him down!*'

In the quivering silence that followed, Krost rose slowly to his feet to face his prince. 'If that is your decision,' he said, his hoarse voice rasping, 'then so be it. If you wish me to follow, to fight again at your side, then so be it. You are my prince, and I can do no other. To the death, if that is what awaits.' He too leaned forward, the table creaking as he rested his hands on it. 'And I most certainly believe it *will* await, prince. Even a non-mage like myself knows something of Lebarran's vast power. But we should also face those of his Order – and we know that he controls the half-demon Zhraike of the Highlands. What if he has other, unknown forces in reserve, to hurl at us?'

Phaedran straightened to his full height. 'He may well have, Krost. Which is why *we* must gather a force that can oppose him. As great a force as can be mustered, from the breadth of the Continent.'

Aurilia was nodding slowly. 'And you will call the Sisterhood to be part of this force.'

'I will,' Phaedran said firmly. 'The Earth-magic will reinforce the power of my wizards, as your women warriors will strengthen the militia.'

'I will have to consult the rest of the Nine,' Aurilia said numbly. 'But I have no doubt that they will have misgivings about this venture. Some may even feel that it may *hasten* the destruction of the Continent.'

'I disagree,' Phaedran said fiercely. 'Because I seek another addition to our force, to make it more powerful than our enemy might imagine.' He fixed his gaze once more on Krost. 'Krost il Hak, my faithful friend, I must look to you to provide that further addition. I must set you this task, difficult though I know it will be for you. I must ask you to return to your homeland, and seek to bring to our enterprise the aid of your people – the giants of the Highlands.'

ELEVEN

It was after midday before Aurilia was able to take herself back to her own suite, alone. After the meeting had wound down, following the revelation of the prince's plan and his impassioned plea, Aurilia had wanted to offer some words of comfort to Krost. She well knew the tormenting mixture of feelings that would be assailing him at the prospect of returning to the mountains that he loved, to confront the people, the giants, who regarded him as an inadequate dwarf.

But Phaedran took Krost aside, to offer some comforts and encouragements of his own. Aurilia, instead, was caught up in conversation with the older wizard, Vallawn, both of them ignoring the slightly snide intrusions of Farbanni. Eventually, then, servants appeared with a light but elegant lunch for them all, and Aurilia stayed out of necessary courtesy, to push the food around on her plate and eat a mouthful or two that seemed arid and tasteless, before excusing herself at the earliest possible moment.

Finally alone and in privacy, she sighed with relief as she drew the drapes to shut out the rain-dimmed light of the day. Then she began to bring carefully out from one of her satchels eight small, softly coloured ceramic cups, so delicately moulded as to be almost translucent. With them she took out a small stand of plain wood, with places carved in it to hold the cups. Setting the cups in place, she began to murmur a wordless song that seemed to rise and extend far beyond the range of her light voice – the song for distant gathering, of the Named Nine.

As the song swelled, eight tiny flames blossomed out of nothing in the heart of the eight cups, burning without fuel, steadier than any candle-flame, illuminating the warm colours of the cups. As they rose, each flame began to emit a sound barely above the threshold of hearing, a delicate humming like a distant choral background to Aurilia's song. But when the song trailed away to its end on a pure high note, the flames went silent and remained so while Aurilia swiftly related – in ordinary speech, and in full detail – what had happened in that morning's meeting, and what the prince was asking of the Sisterhood.

When she finished, all the flames began flaring and twisting in the cups and the room was filled with the sound of tiny whispering cries, like a hubbub in a faraway crowd, as all of the other Eight in the gathering tried to speak at once. They grew calm only slowly, as Aurilia exhorted them to orderly discussion, but even then emotions continued to run high in the ensuing debate. Some of them, including Inghilla, were adamantly opposed to what they saw as a futile, suicidal adventure. Some, including Aurilia herself, were deeply divided between loyalty and doubt. And a few, with the ancient Naemony among them, were merely full of troubled questioning and tended to withdraw into silence as the argument raged.

'I will say again,' Inghilla asserted, her voice small but strong from the cup that was hers. 'The idea is madness – the invention of a prince whose judgement is distorted by vengefulness and sorrow but above all by brutal male pride. Did you hear the word he used, as Aurilia reported? He sees Lebarran's threat to the Continent as a *challenge*! As if the Magister's evil ambition is no more than a gauntlet thrown at Phaedran's feet, some primitive trial of manhood! As if they are to do battle like a pair of rutting stags! Except that he wants *us* to be his antlers, my Sisters – to take the brunt of Lebarran's attack and perhaps be broken and destroyed!'

'But he *is* the prince,' the voice of Malavie ventured.

'Exactly,' Aurilia replied firmly. 'And all this talk of challenges and male pride is beside the point. We must carefully and rationally weigh up Phaedran's belief that we have only *two* choices – to try to strengthen our defences against Lebarran and his Order, or to turn defence into offence and strike at him, now, before he is entirely ready to meet us.'

'How can we be sure he isn't ready now?' asked Prelisse.

'If he were,' Aurilia said flatly, 'he would be battering at our gates this very moment.'

'We don't know that,' said the voice of Queminda. 'What is it that could delay or impede the power of a Magister? The fact is, we don't really *know* that he plans any violence against us or others. We have no real *proof*. He may merely be planning some huge private magical enterprise, which he chooses to call an Apotheosis.'

Aurilia snorted. 'That's wishful thinking, not a clear assessment. He might easily be delayed, waiting for some assembling of auspices or alignment of forces to do with his monster, the Unformed. But we can't imagine that he'll wait for ever. And certainly we *do* know what evil he is planning, which I promise you is *not* private. Those of us who faced the Unformed in the Lightless Dome know beyond doubt that Lebarran will seek nothing less than total mastery of this Sphere – and will destroy anyone who opposes him.'

'You seem now to be more clearly taking the prince's part, Aurilia,' said the sharp voice of Inghilla. 'And of course we cannot take issue with what you may have seen and heard in the Dome, since we were not there. But I wonder if my doubts about Phaedran could not also be applied to yourself. Like him, *your* judgement may be clouded, *you* may incline towards rashness and folly – because of your *own* sorrow and vengeful-ness, even perhaps guilt, over the death of your young Corodel!'

The other voices fell suddenly silent, save for a few sharp intakes of breath, while the anger that flared in Aurilia's eyes outshone the brightness of the eight flames.

'Inghilla,' she said through gritted teeth, 'you're taking an unwise position. You choose not to address the crucial questions but to belittle and disparage those who ask them. Listen, now, carefully. How I feel about the loss of Red Cordell has no bearing here. Just as Prince Phaedran's own feelings are his private concerns. But I know the prince, and I feel sure that at the heart of his wish to march on Lebarran, to strike the first blow, lies his selfless, all-consuming love and concern for this Continent. And in any case our duty here is to weigh up his *purposes*, not his reasons.'

The tiny whisper of Inghilla drawing breath to reply was the only sound in the vibrant silence that followed. But then Inghilla was forestalled – by the voice of the ancient Naemony, reedy and quavering at first, but gathering itself into firm clarity.

'My daughters,' Naemony said, 'our prince deserves better of us than this. And so does our emissary, our Auriflame, without whom we might be facing the threat of the sorcerer Talonimal as well as that of the Magister. Aurilia has presented the two choices as stated by Phaedran, and has asked us to consider if there might be another way to deal with the threat. Sadly, I feel there is not. I feel there is no doubt that Lebarran will launch his evil plan before long. I *know* Lebarran – I knew him when he was young, and even then his ambition and ruthlessness were as manifest as his immense power. If we do nothing, hoping that he may be diverted from his purpose, we would be deluding ourselves. If we merely raise defences, so letting him begin his onslaught when the aspects and alignments favour *him*, we would be fatefully relinquishing the advantage.'

'Mother,' Jhoranna's voice said anxiously, 'you're telling us we should go to war!'

'To ignore Lebarran would destroy us,' Naemony said. 'To wait for him would destroy us. But—'

'To attack him,' Inghilla broke in furiously, 'would destroy us more surely than anything!'

'Perhaps not,' Naemony replied. 'If we wait, he would attack us separately, and we would be unlikely to stand against him for long. But if we join Phaedran and launch an attack, we would be part of a powerful *united* force – Sisters, adepts, militiamen – made even more formidable by the addition of the giants. And also' – her voice lifted to counter another interruption from Inghilla – 'if we attack first, seizing the upper hand, gaining the momentum, we put ourselves in the best position to benefit from the vagaries of chance.'

'Fortune favours the bold,' Aurilia murmured.

'Exactly,' Naemony went on. 'It is a hard choice and a bleak outlook. It may seem indeed that we are simply choosing between different paths to destruction. But on Phaedran's path, where we strike the first blow, there can be seen small glimmerings of hope, of favourable chance. On the other paths, plainly, there are none.'

Silence fell again, until at last Inghilla sighed. 'Perhaps it is so.'

'It is,' Naemony said. 'And so, my beloved ones, we must marshal our forces and place them at Phaedran's behest. We must summon all our courage, our skill, our power, at their utmost, and carry them into battle. For let us have no illusions. There will be no second chance. If evil and horror are not to triumph over this entire Sphere, we can hold nothing back in the conflict. No sacrifice will be too great, if it can aid the victory.'

Her small flame blazed up strongly as she spoke. But around it all the other flames shrank and trembled, and a shudder swept through Aurilia, as foreboding seemed to fill the shadowed corners of the room.

That shudder stayed with her, reduced to a small inner quivering of unspecified dread, as she put away the materials of the gathering. Around her the shadows of the room retained the sense of menace, unrelieved when she flung the drapes aside to admit the watery afternoon light. It was with some relief that she left the suite, in her younger form, to convey to the prince the decision of the Nine.

When she was shown into the royal apartments she found Krost there with Phaedran, looking subdued. Her news was welcomed by them both, but since it made the prospect of war more real and immediate it did little to lighten the mood. So Aurilia and Krost both felt a twinge of dismay and reluctance when Phaedran invited them to join him in his regular daily visit to his daughter. But since they had both known and cared for Evelane since her childhood, they had to mask their uneasiness with a ready assent.

That they were right to feel uneasy became clear even before they entered the princess's private apartment, in a separate wing of the huge palace. They knew that Evelane was still deeply mentally disturbed, under the constant care of nurses provided by the Sisterhood. But that knowledge did not prepare them for the shrill stream of near-madness that they could hear along all the deserted length of the corridor that led to Evelane's rooms.

'Come now, come now, come to me, come to me ...' Evelane's girlish voice was lifted into a high falsetto, the words jerking rhythmically like a chant. 'Come, come to me ... Oh, will you come ... Come now, come now, come now ...'

Krost glanced at Aurilia, both of them certain that Evelane was maniacally calling to her dead lover, Talonimal, master of the Lightless Dome. But then Aurilia shivered and the hair on Krost's neck bristled as the weird chant changed.

'Mother, mother ... Ellemar, mother, cheat and betrayer, liar and thief ... Come to me, come to me ... Give me the gift, give it to me, give ... Thief, foul thief, cheating miser, why do you withhold it, why will you not come ... Ellemar, Ellemar, come to me, come to me ...'

'She often begins this chant when she comes out of a time of withdrawal,' Phaedran said. 'Her nurses let it run its course, unless for her own safety she has to be calmed. Thankfully it is usually brief.'

Aurilia could barely bring herself to look at the haggard expression that had come over his face. That his daughter should be so troubled was bad enough, she thought. But that in her madness she should be crying out to her dead mother, Phaedran's beloved wife Ellemar, with such anger and hatred and despair ...

'So she still bewails her lack of the magical gift,' Krost said.

'Endlessly,' Phaedran replied. 'It remains the root of her anguish and her illness – too deeply buried for any adept to reach and ease, just as Hallifort himself could not.'

'You sought the help of mages?' Aurilia asked.

'Of course,' the prince said. 'I would seek any help, go to any lengths. But they could not aid her. The resistances buried within her mind are too strong for them. And they all agree with Hallifort that if they sought to *force* those barriers they could wreck her mind entirely.'

With that Krost opened the door at the end of the corridor

and they went in to see Evelane. The room was large but comfortable, full of restful colours. And the woman seated at one side, the Sister in charge of the princess that day, seemed no less comfortable – round and homely and warm, with a gentle alertness in her eyes. She made only minimal acknowledgement as the others entered, before returning her attention to the dark-haired young woman, slim and pretty in a rich gown, who was jerkily pacing the floor near by, her eyes wide and staring, her hands twisting and flexing in constant motion as she continued her chilling litany.

'Mother, come, mother, come,' she chanted. 'Ellemar with your birthing gift ... Gift withheld, to leave your child weeping ... Come to me ... Mother, Ellemar, thief and miser, cheat and liar ...

'Evelane!' Phaedran's pain-filled voice cut through the terrible refrain. 'Please, my dear. See, you have visitors. Old friends ...'

The princess's voice trailed away in a tremulous whisper. Slowly she turned her blank gaze on to her father, then with a visible twitch looked at Krost. But her whole body tensed, taut as a bowstring, when she saw Aurilia. Her mouth writhed, and a shadow of remembered ugliness slithered deep within her eyes.

'*Whore!*' she shrieked. 'Oh, now, murderer, betrayer, thief! How you bared yourself, flaunted yourself, took him from me, stole him before he could remake me ...!' Flecks of foam gathered at the corners of her mouth, her fingers curved like claws. 'And now gone, Talonimal, where is he, gone, come to me, Talonimal, come to my bed, give me your strength, give me the gift ... He *would* have, he *would* have, but how you bared yourself, witch-whore, traitor-thief, how you clutched and took him with your lust, stole him, *killed him* ...'

The last two words stretched out and up into a frenzied shriek, before Evelane's eyes rolled up to leave only the whites exposed as she toppled to the floor, her body jerking spasmodically. And all around her, the room exploded into destruction.

Pictures and hangings were ripped from the walls, furniture was wrenched from the floor. The Sister-nurse was flung aside, along with her chair, into the midst of a heap of drapes torn from the windows. Delicate tables and the objects that they held were splintered into fragments against the walls, chandeliers and candelabra hurtled like missiles, a huge chest of drawers reaching halfway to the ceiling began to topple over towards Phaedran until Krost's mighty left arm heaved it upright again. By then Aurilia was fighting through the storm of flying objects to get to the fallen Evelane, but the other Sister struggled to her feet and got there first. Resting a hand on Evelane's brow, she murmured a quiet phrase, and suddenly the princess's eyes closed, her body went limp, and all the hurtling ruination of the room fell to the floor and was stilled.

Phaedran took a slow step forward, sorrow etched on his face. 'I have not seen that since the Dome,' he croaked.

'I should never have come,' Aurilia said. 'I should have expected her to blame me still.'

'It wasn't entirely you,' the other Sister said tiredly. 'It has begun a few times lately, but usually whichever of us is here can quiet her in time. I wasn't quick enough, today.'

'You did very well,' Phaedran said stiffly. 'No one can be blamed for this.'

The Sister nodded her thanks. 'She will sleep now, while the mind-cloud lasts. Then probably she will retreat to the withdrawn state.'

'Does it always follow the same pattern?' Aurilia asked.

'Mostly,' the other woman said, glancing hesitantly at Phaedran. 'These surges of uncontrolled, destructive mind-power usually come from hysterical young people who have infantile emotions in adult bodies. And who are filled with *frustrations* of different kinds, if you see.'

'And seeing me,' Aurilia said regretfully, 'triggered her feelings more intensely, reminding her of Talonimal and me, that struggle in the Dome . . .'

'Poor sad child,' Krost said with a sigh. 'If only she had been born with real magic, instead of this destructive thing . . .'

'I have been told,' the prince said, 'that in most such cases the young person grows out of it.'

The nurse gave him a reassuring smile. 'I'm sure, sir, that the princess will be a good deal better, in time.'

'Then pray that she *has* time,' Phaedran said hollowly. 'Pray that we all do.'

Shortly afterwards the prince retired to his private apartments – appearing, as Krost said, nearly as depressed as Evelane in her withdrawn state. In that atmosphere of misery and tension, Krost and Aurilia both felt disinclined to fall into any further brooding themselves. But when Aurilia suggested that they find a quiet corner and keep each other company over a drink, Krost demurred.

'I would welcome your company,' he said. 'But I have no desire for thin palace wine, or for lurking in the shadows of this place.'

Aurilia gave him a faint smile. 'You mean you want to go into the city, to some rowdy, smelly tavern, and pour down a gallon or so of ale.'

'Exactly,' Krost said. 'Good strong ale, in a place that is full of laughter and life.'

'And fleas and fights,' Aurilia added.

'Necessary parts of life,' Krost agreed. 'Will you not join me?'

'Indeed I will,' she told him, taking his arm. 'After what's been happening, I could do with a taste of ordinary, rowdy life. I might even start a fight myself.'

So they marched off – and while Krost collected his iron quarterstaff from his rooms, Aurilia went to hers to get a hooded rain-cape. Then, when a footman had organized a small covered carriage for them, they rolled away along the curving drive of the palace.

By then the drizzly afternoon was waning towards an early twilight, and Aurilia huddled into her cape, pulling the hood around her face against the dank breeze. Because she was half-muffled in that way, and because Krost was focused on his driving, neither of them paid much attention to the lone rider they saw approaching along the drive. When Krost slowed the carriage, giving room for the rider to pass, Aurilia had only a vague impression of a muddy-legged horse whose rider wore an oddly rough-looking short cloak over his head.

But then, with a jolt like a hammer-blow, she recognized the horse – and the voice of the rider.

'Amazing who you can run into at a royal palace,' said Red Cordell.

TWELVE

'It will never happen again,' Red said, lying back luxuriously, mopping with an edge of the sheet at a trickle of sweat across his naked chest.

But the sheet was plucked from his hand by Aurilia as she wriggled lithely on top of him, her own nakedness glistening from their exertions and the humidity of the night. 'What do you mean?' she demanded with an impish smile. 'Was it so unpleasant?'

Red laughed and pulled her close. 'Not *that*. I mean all the ... the miseries we got ourselves into, before, in the Fastness. It shouldn't have happened, and it won't again.'

'No,' Aurilia said, her smile vanishing. 'I've thought of little else since we parted. How I let myself get so absorbed in other things, and just let you ride away. To what I thought ...' She stopped, her eyes filling.

He tightened his arms around her. 'Don't. I didn't die, and we're here. And it was mostly my fault. You were concerned with important things, but I was mostly concerned with *me*. Not for the first time.'

Her fingers on his mouth stopped him. 'That's enough self-blame,' she said. 'What happened is past. And, as you say, it won't happen again.'

'Definitely. But ...' He let his hand trail down over the smooth firmness of her back, the curve of her waist, farther towards the rounded flesh beyond. 'There are *other* things that will keep happening over and over.'

She made a sound halfway between a laugh and a sigh, and moved up to kiss him fiercely.

Somewhat earlier, that first joyous reunion had created a wild scene in the palace drive, when Krost's hug had nearly cracked Red's ribs and Aurilia's tears had seemed as much of a downpour as the rain. When they had collected themselves, restraining their almost frantic demands to know how Red could be alive, unhurt and *there*, they returned to the palace where Red was welcomed with respectful pleasure by the servants and almost unreserved delight by Phaedran.

'I called your loss an ill omen, Red Cordell,' the prince told Red, gripping his hand, 'but your miraculous return is the most favourable omen we might have.'

They settled down then, in the prince's apartments, to hear the story of Red's survival. But to their surprise his account was terse and truncated. He told them of his confrontation with the demon, his injuries, the demon's flight from the dawn. But after that he said only that he had been saved, once again, by the intervention of Hallifort the Healer, who had later guided him out of the Wastelands. From that point he would say little more. Nothing about where Hallifort had come from, why he was there, where Red had been. Nothing except that Hallifort had regretfully said that he could not take part in the affairs of the Continent and could not – would not – reveal himself any further.

'I'm sorry,' Red said at last. 'I don't know much more about him myself, even now. But what I do know aren't my secrets to tell. They're his, and he wants them to stay secret. I gave him my word.'

'Red, no!' Aurilia protested. 'You can't leave it like that. He's as much of a mystery now as ever, and this is no time for us to be ignoring mysteries. Remember Inghilla's vision . . .'

Red held up his hands to stop her. 'Hallifort may be a mystery, but he's *not* a threat,' he said firmly. 'I'm completely sure of it. And I'm also sure that Inghilla's vision was wrong. I can't tell you how I know, but you can take my word for it.'

'Of course,' Phaedran said before Aurilia could speak. 'We must respect his wishes and your silence. We owe him that, at least.'

'We owe him a great deal more,' Krost rumbled.

Aurilia frowned as if ready to continue pressing the point, but then saw and recognized the determined stubbornness in Red's eyes. 'All right,' she said with a sigh and a smile. 'We'll leave Hallifort alone. Mystery or not, we *do* owe him.' Her smile softened as she gazed at Red. 'More than can ever be repaid.'

From there the conversation shifted as the others told Red of events in his absence, particularly Phaedran's decision to muster a remarkable force against Lebarran.

'And I would hope,' the prince said, 'that you and the sword of Corodel will be a part of that force.'

Red glanced around at his two friends, reading the disquiet in their expressions that mingled with loyalty and determination. 'Oh, I'll be there, sir,' he said, keeping his tone light. 'I wouldn't let you all go off to war without me.'

Phaedran gave him a wintry half-smile. 'I am grateful – to you all. It will be a great blessing to have you three beside me, as you were at the Dome.'

There was little more to be said after that, especially when the recollection of the Dome and its terrors put a considerable pall on the gathering. So they parted, with Krost returning to his suite while Aurilia took Red's hand and led him unresistingly to hers.

By mid-morning, pleasantly weary and heavy-eyed, they were lingering over a late breakfast in Aurilia's sitting-room when Krost burst in on the heels of a servant who had intended to announce him.

'Aurilia!' Krost said urgently – then halted, grinning despite his agitation to see Red there.

'Do come in, Krost,' she said with a laugh.

'What's up?' Red asked. 'Didn't you get any breakfast?'

Taking that as an invitation, Krost reached for a sweet roll. 'Aurilia,' he said again, his mouth full, 'Phaedran had a message early this morning – from the Sisterhood.'

She sat up, startled. 'They contacted *him*?' Then the faintest of blushes darkened the honey-bronze skin of her throat. 'No, I see – they may have tried to make mind-contact with me . . .'

'And found you otherwise engaged,' Red said innocently.

Krost chuckled, but his eyes were grave. 'The Nine apparently told Phaedran they were readying their warriors and themselves as quickly as possible to leave the Fastness and move south. They believe that Lebarran might find out about Phaedran's plan to attack, and might decide to strike the first blow.'

Aurilia nodded slowly. 'Of course. Lebarran might have spies, or just his own scrying power. He's *very* likely to find out.'

'So the Sisters want to be here,' Krost went on, 'to combine their powers with Phaedran's mages if Lebarran strikes.' He glanced uneasily at Red. 'And they want you to return to the Fastness, Aurilia, now. So the Nine will be united if they have to defend themselves on the way to Quamarr.'

Dismayed, Aurilia turned to Red. 'They're right about the importance of our unity from now on,' she said unhappily. 'I have to go.'

'Of course,' Red agreed. 'Do we leave right away?'

Krost coughed meaningfully. 'The fact is, the message said Aurilia should go *alone*. The others of the Nine will use their magic to lend you extra speed, as before – which would be hard to do over distance for more than one.'

'Maybe they also don't want you to bring any *distractions*,' Red said sourly. 'Like last time.'

Aurilia took his hand. 'It's a good point. I would serve the unity better if I knew that you were safe and untroubled.'

He sighed and nodded. 'I can't argue with that. I'll stay here and practise being patient till you come south again.'

'Thank you,' she said softly. 'It won't be long. But now' – she rose and made shooing motions – 'I have to get ready to leave. Without *distraction*.'

Red and Krost grinned and headed for the door, after arranging to make their farewells when she went to take leave of the prince. 'At least you and I can keep each other company, Krost,' Red said as they strolled along the corridor. 'You never did get that drink last night.'

'Nor will I yet awhile,' Krost growled glumly. 'Phaedran wants me also to leave at once. For my . . . for the Highlands.'

Looking at his friend's troubled expression, Red searched for some comforting words. 'I know it won't be easy for you . . .' he began.

'Far from it,' Krost agreed heavily. 'But it must be done, for the giants would be a mighty addition to Phaedran's army. If they agree to come.'

Red blinked. 'You think they mightn't?'

'Truly. My people are fiercely independent, and have always kept apart from human affairs. They do not even really recognize Phaedran as the Continent's ruler.'

Red shook his head disbelievingly. 'Once they know what's going on, how can they refuse? There can't be any neutrals in this fight.'

'I know that,' Krost said with a sigh. 'The difficulty will be to make *them* know it. Even setting aside the low regard they have for me, I am no ambassador.'

'You'll do fine,' Red told him encouragingly.

'Perhaps,' Krost grunted. 'In any case, it is my duty to go.' He smiled wanly. 'And the sooner I set off, the sooner I can return to the company of my friends.'

Red studied him thoughtfully. 'What would you say to having some company along the way?'

Krost looked both startled and pleased. 'Would you want to come with me, Red? I would welcome it – but you have only just barely survived the Wastelands. We might be riding into danger again . . .'

'That's the way life seems to go, around here,' Red replied lightly. 'Besides, if there's danger, you don't want to go riding into it alone.'

'True enough,' Krost agreed. 'But, Red, Aurilia will object. She has just said that she wants you to be somewhere safe, where she would not have to worry about you.'

Red moved a hand as if to brush the words aside. 'I don't see there's any need to *tell* her, Krost. It might just upset her – and distract her.' His grin was bright with a reckless eagerness. 'Anyway, whatever happens, there's *no* way I'm going to pass up a chance to meet *giants*.'

At about the same time, at a distance from Quamarr beyond all normal measuring, Lebarran Magister moved through the Void that exists beyond the Realms and Spheres, and was pursued.

It was not darkness that surrounded him there, nor was it light. It was not substance, nor was it vacuum. The colourlessness was no mere lack of pigment, no solid black or unrelieved white or even empty grey. It was simply a blankness, an *absence*, more cold and bleak and toneless than the depths of a polar sea. Yet the Void extends also beyond all reason and natural law – embracing contradictions, uniting impossibilities. To those with the power to discern, the emptiness of the Void can simultaneously exhibit fullness, the stillness can reveal movement – and the lifeless *absence* of it can contain presences. The Void is inhabited by things that lack material shape or form, that are without the true life essence, yet that are somehow alive, with a measure of the instinct to survive, a share of urges and hungers. Above all, a portion of preternatural *power*.

And a group of such things – amorphous, indefinite, not always fully visible, yet exuding an unmistakable aura of menace – were pursuing Lebarran where he moved.

Around him at least colour did exist in the Void. Colour from the furious brightness of his yellow eyes, from the phosphorescence of his hands, most especially from the green ovoid that trembled around him. A magical field of repulsion that shielded him from the Void-things even as their reachings and lungings caused it to quiver ominously.

Snarling, the glow of his hands growing even brighter, Lebarran spat a harsh word or two. The field's greenness grew more intense – but then wavered again, a portion of it bulging inward from some monstrous half-glimpsed pressure from outside. Lebarran jerked up a hand, and slowly, reluctantly, the bulge retracted – just as the green ovoid was rocked by a heavy impact on the opposite side.

'The Last Inferno take you!' Lebarran raged, shaping another magical reinforcement. Sweat was pouring from his skin, the tendons of his neck stood out like cables, small tremors juddered along his legs. 'I *will* find a way, by the blood of the Bestial Gods! I *will* bring you to heel! And when I do, you will taste my wrath!'

He staggered as the field was struck again, its colour dimming alarmingly for a moment before his power could restore

135

it. And as he fought, some part of his sorcery was also guiding the ovoid's slow drift through the blankness – seeking with growing desperation the opening through which he had made his way Beyond.

He had entered in order to test certain spells that he had discovered, which he hoped would give him the means to control and direct the supernatural power of the Void-beings. And he had set out, wisely as it had seemed, to use the spells first on lesser entities before trying their power against the most dominant, most dreadful being in the Void, that which Lebarran called the Unformed. But the spells had not proved strong enough. Worse, they had aroused in the Void-things a more terrible level of hunger than ever before. Although he had entered the Void with a protective spell shielding him, Lebarran had had then to armour himself as well with the full field of repulsion, before ignominiously fleeing.

Since then he had been searching for his entry-point – not of course the great Threshold which with the ghostly Bridge was the means of invoking the Unformed, but a smaller, less imposing entrance. So much less, in fact, that it had become agonizingly difficult to locate, having shifted as all things shift within the Void. Or having perhaps closed entirely and disappeared while his attention was focused on the pack of shapeless horrors harrying him.

And the danger was steadily growing that, before long, the Unformed itself might come to join the hunt, hurling its own immense might against the field. For Lebarran had no illusions about the ghastly Void-being. Although it seemed ready enough to enter some mindless sort of alliance with him – to achieve its impelling desire for a true form and true life-force – it was equally, ruthlessly capable of simply killing him, draining *his* life-force, because of the irresistible impulse of its monstrous hungers. So Lebarran had to find a way out before it arrived, or before the lesser things assailing him found some weakness in the field.

'Blast you!' he raged, gesturing again to strengthen the field against the pressures upon it. 'I will not be defeated here! I am the *Magister*! I am he who overcame the Distorted

Dimensions in the Realm of Glass! I *will* subdue these para-
doxes! I *will* prevail!'

And yet, despite his manic fury – or perhaps in part because
of it – Lebarran was aware of a wholly unfamiliar sensation.
He was indeed the Magister, the most powerful mage of the
Continent, perhaps of all time. His sorcerous strength was
legendary, his pre-eminence unchallengeable. And yet – there,
in the unknowable midst of the Void Beyond, he was for the
first time in his life being taken to the limits of his strength.

He was, in short, tiring.

The tremors that shook his stocky body were growing more
frequent. His legs were trembling more violently, threatening
his balance. Cramp gathered in the bunched muscles of his
thighs and shoulders. Small spots danced before his eyes, sweat
poured from his skin and soaked his heavy robe, his breathing
became laboured gasps, his glowing hands trembled, chills
flickered along his spine. Yet he fought on, thrusting his power
at the ovoid's inner surface, snarling and raging as he spoke
the words to stiffen its protection. While the monsters of the
Void, which knew nothing of weariness or pain or sensations
of any sort beyond basic instinctual fears and hungers, surged
and ravened around the field, driven endlessly by their craving
for the life-force within it.

Lebarran had no idea how many of the things were attacking
him. Dozens, hundreds . . . But such concepts held no meaning
in the Void. There might have been a countless host of them,
or perhaps just a few in constant alteration, dividing and shifting to gain the strength of many. And while they attacked,
while his search for the entry-point went on, he drew closer to
reaching his magical limits. Though he was beginning to droop,
head sagging forward, vision blurring, sometimes almost slum-
ping to his knees, his will and his fury held him up, kept him
making the shaky sorcerous gestures, panting the magical
syllables.

Until, on the edge of his awareness, he sensed another kind
of movement beyond the field. And the cold hand of dread,
as unfamiliar to him as exhaustion, took him by the throat.
Somewhere within the emptiness, the ultimate horror was

drawing near. The Unformed, in all its matchless, soulless might, was advancing upon him.

For an instant Lebarran was near to collapse, sensing how close that ghastliness was, how diminished his magical defences against it would be. But still he dragged himself upright again, foul curses streaming from his mouth as he perceived and fearfully accepted his only possible avenue of escape.

It was a narrow and grotesquely dangerous avenue. Yet Lebarran, who in his fury could not conceive of abandoning the struggle, did not hesitate. At once he shifted what frayed reserves of strength remained to him. The field of repulsion throbbed and lurched, under the pressure from the things outside, as layers of reinforcement were removed, but Lebarran ignored it. He knew that if his next spell was successful, it would not matter if the field collapsed. And if the spell failed – it still would not matter to him for long.

Raising his shaking hands, bracing his trembling legs, he began to croak the words in a harsh and guttural tongue. His hands glowed fiercely, patterns of unknown colours playing over the flesh. Sweating and agonized, he bared his teeth in a brutal snarl as he poured forth his power, risking everything in that final desperate surge, with the field of repulsion still swaying and buckling around him, and the dire menace of the Unformed drawing nearer.

As his voice began to fade into inaudibility, as he began to sag sideways like a tree under the axe, a glaring line of light appeared in the blankness of the Void before him. In that final moment, with the monstrosity of the Unformed looming into sight, the bright line became a gap, opening and spreading like a wound. At once the field of repulsion collapsed, without a sound. The Unformed and the lesser monsters reached out. The silent deathliness of the Void surrounded Lebarran, as if to cling and hold him.

But he flung himself forward, just before he was overwhelmed, bursting into and through the brightness of the gap he had created.

And as he went through he screamed a word. The sound

seemed to resonate hugely around him – not in the Void, but in a chamber at the heart of his massive dwelling whose walls were formed from petrified trees. And with the echo of that single word in the chamber, the shining gap in the air behind him closed and disappeared.

Lebarran stumbled, then fell, to lie crumpled on the cold earthen floor of his dwelling, his body heaving and shuddering as he fought for breath, as his overtaxed muscles spasmed. But while he lay there, he failed to perceive the new patch of unearthly brightness that was developing in the air behind him.

It began as another narrow, glowing opening, exactly where the gap had been through which Lebarran had escaped. But then it developed – unsteadily at first, though swiftly gaining more stability – into something far larger and grander. Within moments the new opening had expanded, and its borders had become defined by the hazy image of tall pillars with a pediment above them, forming a stately threshold. With, beyond it, the even more ethereal shape of an enormous bridge, extending into emptiness.

But around the perimeter of the threshold there could be seen no sign of a greenish glow from the protective barrier that had always, previously, been raised by whatever human sorcerer had invoked that entrance.

And on the bridge, towards the undefended threshold, glided the huge seething mass of the Unformed, implacable and malign.

THIRTEEN

Earlier, elsewhere in that same unnatural dwelling, five men had gathered in a group that was very nearly an anxious huddle. Their gathering was in a large chamber where the shadows of late afternoon were beginning to congeal around the motionless stony trees that formed the walls. The chamber was entirely bare and empty save where the five men had collected, where they sat on an oddly mismatched assortment of furniture – chairs, sofas, divans – with equally disparate tables or small sideboards around them. Now and then one of the pieces of furniture could be seen to waver, as if growing slightly rubbery or even insubstantial. And then one of the men would idly mutter a word, or lift a slightly glowing finger, and the furniture would be restored to motionless solidity.

The men themselves looked as distinctly assorted as their seats. Two of them, wearing long robes in rich heavy cloth, appeared quite aged – one with long grey hair descending to mingle with his longer grey beard, the other with only a few sparse tufts of white fuzz here and there on the parchment-pale skin of his head and face. By comparison, two more of the group seemed in the prime of life. One of that pair, a narrow-faced man with hair and beard trimmed severely short, wore a dark, high-collared tunic over plain trousers. The other, more heavily built with well-barbered hair and a ruddy complexion, wore a richly decorated frock-coat and tight-fitting trousers, and was more excessively beringed and bejewelled than any of the others.

The fifth of the group was younger, with pale wavy hair and a pinched waxy face. He seemed to be either ill or convalescent, for his short robe and dark leggings drooped and bagged as if originally made for a fleshier frame. Also, he had dark shadows under his eyes, a haunted expression on his face and a tendency to start wildly at any unexpected noise.

All five were hunched forward on their seats, leaning towards a bright fire blazing in a marble fireplace. The fire was giving off a considerable heat, without seeming to diminish its fuel, and the men were warmly clothed. Yet they hunched, some of them shivering now and then, pulling up collars and drawing together lapels, as a dank evening wind searched out the spaces among the petrified trees and whined plaintively through the chamber.

The ancient, almost hairless man sniffed, tugging forward the hood of his robe. 'I don't see why Lebarran can't contrive more comfortable quarters for us, if we *must* be here,' he complained.

'Contrive them yourself, Ostyril,' said the florid man in the frock-coat. 'And a juicy serving-maid with a flagon of mulled wine, while you're about it.'

The old one, Ostyril, glared. 'You may serve your own appetites, Zykiador.'

'Quite,' said the second old one, also raising his hood over his long straggling hair. 'It might be unwise to appear *too* sybaritic while we are here.'

The thin ascetic-looking man snorted. 'Come, Dhaminai. Lebarran knows our weaknesses well enough. And our strengths.'

Casually he extended a hand that acquired a surface phosphorescence. Against the far wall, from where the wind was blowing, a transparent barrier appeared, resembling a huge sheet of glass standing on edge across the breadth and height of the wall. At once the temperature of the chamber seemed to improve as the draught was blocked, and more so when the florid man, Zykiador, joined in to raise similar inner walls all around the room.

'Is that wise, Gul Ist?' asked the pale younger man jerkily. 'The Magister didn't say we could tamper with his dwelling . . .'

'He didn't say we could *not*,' Zykiador asserted, adjusting the lapels of his coat. 'Stop fretting, Yannahac. Lebarran won't punish anyone for this.'

141

'Nor for much else, I should think,' said the long-haired old one, Dhaminai. 'Not when he needs us more than ever – to help defend against this *attack* that is being launched.'

'Which should never have been allowed to happen,' quavered the other ancient, Ostyril. 'And *still* should not be allowed. I still say we should avoid the conflict – retreat, regroup, return to the original plan and achieve the Apotheosis before all else.'

'Retreat?' echoed the ascetic one, Gul Ist, with a sour laugh. 'Lebarran? As soon ask the sun to burn more coolly.'

'Anyway, it's too late,' agreed Zykiador. 'It has begun. We are fated to be dragged by Lebarran into whatever ill-conceived adventure he may have provoked.'

'Don't speak like that!' young Yannahac said desperately.

Zykiador sneered. 'I'll say it to his face, if I wish. *I* do not go in terror of him, Yannahac, even if you do.'

'But it's not so,' Yannahac insisted. 'The Magister isn't dragging us into anything. What's happening now is the fault of *Talonimal*, no one else. Talonimal, who broke from our Order, tried to pre-empt the Apotheosis, caused our plan to be exposed . . .'

'And reduced our collective power by his betrayal,' Dhaminai said testily. '*And* died horribly enough for his crimes. Leaving *us* to face this absurd attack that Phaedran is launching.'

'Absurd?' Gul Ist repeated darkly. 'I wonder. The prince has his own mages, who aren't without quality. And who knows what other forces he might bring against us?'

Old Ostyril nodded creakily. 'You are quite right to worry, Gul Ist.'

'I didn't say I'm *worried*,' Gul Ist snapped. 'Except in so far as our own magical strength, and perhaps even that of the Magister, will be greatly taxed by fighting a magical battle now. We might even be . . . permanently weakened. And then where would we find the power to gain mastery over the Unformed, and achieve the Apotheosis?'

Ostyril nodded again. 'Even our gaining the victory over Phaedran is itself not certain.'

'Gods and demons!' barked Zykiador, waving a meaty hand in which a golden goblet had appeared, steaming slightly. 'How

142

you old women fret and whine! Do you honestly believe, Ostyril, that the second-rate adepts in Phaedran's employ, even together with the Named Nine, can marshal anything to threaten Lebarran with us supporting him?'

'And the Magister has his other forces,' Yannahac put in quickly. 'While if his present enterprise succeeds . . .'

'Ah, yes, *that*.' Zykiador shivered, taking a gulp from his goblet. 'That fills me with unease, I don't mind telling you. It's remarkable that he should be able to range unharmed through the Void. But it's *folly*, no less, for him to go alone.'

'Although,' Dhaminai mused, 'if he *has* at last found spells that can control the Unformed . . . why, then, it will take more than a few minor wizards and that collection of witches to trouble us.'

'No doubt,' Gul Ist said coldly. 'But what a number of "ifs" we must call upon to raise our spirits. Zykiador is right – this present *enterprise* of his is ill-advised. And, come to that, has he not been about it for an undue length of time?'

'I told him,' Ostyril mumbled, half to himself. 'The Void Beyond is unknowable, I said, unpredictable. A mage should not enter there, however great he may be, except in the strength of a conclave . . .'

'Stop it,' Yannahac said worriedly. 'He is the Magister. He is stronger than any conclave.'

Zykiador laughed. 'He is *not*, young fool. Especially not against what the Void may hold. And all your fawning can't make him so . . .'

He stopped, jerking suddenly upright, liquid splashing from the goblet. As they all jerked, especially Yannahac, when from another portion of the weird dwelling they heard a sudden agonized cry. A single word, muffled but recognizable to them, screamed aloud. The sound seemed to carry and echo through the building, somehow exciting a resonance in the vast metal canopy that hung unsupported above it, producing a mighty deep-throated clang like a giant bell.

The five mages rushed from the room, Yannahac in the lead, the two eldest tottering in the rear. By the time they had hurried along the stony corridors to the chamber from which the

143

scream had come, the scene of horror confronting them was but a few seconds away from an ultimate disaster.

They saw Lebarran sprawled on the floor of the chamber, drenched in sweat, his ashen face contorted, the sorcerous glow around his hands more dim and fitful than the others could have believed possible. And on the far side of the room they saw the tall shape of the threshold, and the bridge beyond it. With no sign of any protective barrier at the opening. And with the looming shapeless mass that was the Unformed sweeping towards that entrance.

With a cry, Yannahac stumbled to Lebarran's side, trying to raise him up. But the others halted, staring, paralysed by the sheer volume of evil and terror pouring into the chamber from the presence at the threshold. Of them all, it was the ancient Ostyril who rallied first.

'Stop it, *stop* it!' he wheezed. 'Bar its way or it will destroy us *all*!'

He raised tremulous glowing hands, chanting jagged phrases. In front of the Unformed a faint greenish shimmer appeared, like the ghostly image of a grille or lattice. But the monstrosity at the threshold leaned its intolerable weight against that barrier, so that it began to tear. By then, however, old Dhaminai was also gasping and gesturing, creating the shape of a barred gate in the air, while Gul Ist's bright hands were contriving something like a huge curtain of crimson flame. But Zykiador was slower to recover, unable in his terror to focus his own powers, while Yannahac still crouched by the fallen Magister, crying out abjectly to him.

And, one at a time, the might of the Unformed thrust the sorcerous barriers aside as it fought its way into the chamber.

Then Gul Ist screamed, a nerve-shredding sound born of both fury and fear. 'Not like this, fools! *Conclave*! In *conclave*! Zykiador – Yannahac – *now*, or we die!'

The cry roused Zykiador from his panic like a blow, and even stirred Yannahac out of his cringing. As Gul Ist began chanting again, the others joined in, one after another, bright hands raised. The five voices grew in resonance and strength – and the shape that appeared in the air then was no screen or curtain but more like one wall of a massive cage, its interwoven

144

bars each as thick as a man's body, glittering with cold green light. It pressed against the mass of the Unformed, and as the ghastly presence heaved its weight against it, the cage wall did not yield. Instead – as the voices of the five mages grew to raucous cries, as their hands blazed painfully bright – it was the cage wall that began to move forward, the Unformed to give ground.

Slowly, jerkily, one hand's-breadth after another, the horror was pushed back. It made no sound as it retreated, yet somehow the room seemed filled with a torrential outburst of its hate and rage and evil craving. That torrent flooded over the mages, assaulting their will, lashing at their courage. Cold sweat burst from their every pore, their heartbeats raced, their legs trembled, their throats grew acid with bile. Yet their blazing hands remained unmoving and the chorus of their voices unwavering. And steadily, never pausing, the great glowing bars pressed the Unformed away, forcing its cloudy mass back across the threshold, back on to the bridge.

Until the moment when the last coiling portion of it passed beyond that boundary. At that precise portion of a second, in perfect unison as if rehearsed, the mages howled one word – the same word that had alerted them when shrieked, earlier, by their master. And with their howl, the columns and pediment shivered and faded, the spectral opening was sealed.

Reaction then swept punishingly over the mages. Yannahac and Gul Ist looked like men who had just finished a marathon, dripping with sweat, gasping, drooping on rubbery legs. Zykiador managed with a remaining scrap of power to conjure himself a cushioned chair, and sank into it moaning. The aged Dhaminai could only sink to the floor. And the frail Ostyril, eyes widening, clutched at his chest with a whimper and toppled sideways.

Gul Ist managed to intercept him as he fell, lowering him to the floor, almost absently resting a dimly glowing hand on the old man's thin chest. With his touch Ostyril seemed restored, breathing more easily, though still looking limp and enfeebled as Gul Ist's magic summoned a cushioned pallet beneath his skinny body.

'By the Silent Realms,' Gul Ist muttered, 'what would Phaedran not give to find us like this when he besieges us!'

'He won't,' Yannahac said stoutly. 'That was an accident. It could never happen again.'

'Accident?' gasped Dhaminai, who by then had found a fragment of strength enough to summon a chair. 'No – that was *folly*. The five of us in conclave were barely enough – yet Lebarran would go *alone* into the Void . . .'

The others nervously looked at their fallen master. By then Lebarran had begun to recover, managing to lift himself up to a sitting position against the wall. But with his eyes closed and his head drooping towards his drawn-up knees, he looked oddly small and crumpled, his force diminished.

'What I cannot understand,' quavered Ostyril from his pallet, 'is how the threshold could have *been* there. We all heard the Magister speak the word of closing. Somehow . . . the word must have *failed*!'

'It did not fail.'

The others jumped slightly. They had turned to Ostyril as he spoke, so had not seen Lebarran slowly raise his head and open his eyes. But at his unexpected words they turned back to him, striving not to show their dismay at the haggardness of his face, the dull film over his eyes.

'The word did not fail,' he repeated, his voice a rasping whisper. 'In the Void I was assailed . . . by the creatures, and by the Unformed itself at the end. I could not find the entry I had made . . . my protections were failing. So I took the risk . . . of opening a new point of crossing.'

Yannahac gasped. 'Opening a *new* one? Even while being attacked?'

'By then,' Lebarran went on, ignoring him, 'I had become . . . wearied. Once through the new opening . . . I was able to speak the word, to close it, but then . . . fatigue overcame me.'

'Indeed it did,' Gul Ist said grimly. 'And your Apotheosis, Lebarran, was only seconds away from becoming instead a final absorption!'

The others flinched, for normally such a remark would have ignited Lebarran's blazing rage. But although the Magister still seemed to be recovering – aided by a beaker of wine provided magically by Yannahac – his feral eyes did not flare with anger. They seemed instead somehow inward-looking, almost as if Lebarran was in the unfamiliar state of feeling subdued.

'But the threshold,' old Dhaminai said shakily. 'Who invoked *it*?'

Lebarran stared around at them. 'The Unformed,' he rasped. 'Somehow it contrived its own invocation, at the place where the opening I had made left the fabric of the Sphere weakened.'

Yannahac's hands fluttered as if to hold off the dire notion. 'Surely it was an accident,' he said again. 'Which couldn't happen again – not when the Magister has imposed his controls on the monster.'

'Yannahac,' Lebarran said wearily, 'I almost preferred you as the languid mocker you once were, rather than the cringing lickspittle you have become.' Yannahac, as if to prove the point, cringed. 'In truth,' Lebarran went on, 'I still have no clear idea how the Unformed might be controlled. Despite my perhaps ill-judged entry into the Void.'

The others glanced at one another, startled by the rare display of humility.

'But far more disturbing, now,' Lebarran continued, 'is the fact that the Unformed has become able to summon bridge and threshold from *that* side, without a barrier. I don't know how it acquired that knowledge, for no one knows how its mind works or even if it has any faculty that we would recognize as a mind. Certainly its hungers and strengths seem to have greatly increased, no doubt due to the foul magics of Talonimal in his Dome. In any case, beyond any question, it will now bend those enhanced powers to the task of trying to force its way again into this Sphere. Into this *chamber*, indeed, where the Sphere's fabric will remain frail some while yet.'

Everyone blanched and looked around as if expecting the horror to be looming among them at that instant. 'How can we hope to fight Phaedran,' asked Zykiador, looking sick, 'and defend against the Unformed all at once?'

'Especially,' quavered Ostyril, 'when opposing the Unformed so depletes us all. Even yourself, Magister, if I may say so.'

Again there was none of the explosive reaction that the

others would once have expected. 'Quite so,' Lebarran said coldly, 'though some of us have greater recuperative powers than others. But the task before us is entirely manageable. We have proved that we *can* bar the monster's path, and force it to retreat. Indeed . . .' He paused, frowning thoughtfully. 'The possibility occurs to me that the creature's powers may be in some way *diminished*, if it leaves the Void . . . which would be a most intriguing avenue of research.' Then he sat up more briskly, again staring around at them. 'In the mean time we must merely be vigilant. From now on, one of us must be always on watch in this chamber – with spells of sensing raised and ready – so we can be alerted in time if the Unformed tries to force an entry again.'

The others looked troubled. 'That will remove one of us from conclave,' Dhaminai said dubiously, 'if action is needed against Phaedran.'

Lebarran snorted. 'Phaedran's forces are still far away.'

'But they will advance,' Gul Ist pointed out. 'And even with your power, Lebarran, we would still be only *five* in conclave, against all of the prince's mages, and the witches, and the gods know what else.'

Lebarran's smile was wolfish. 'Have you let what happened here make you all faint-hearted? Let me remind you, you are the Order of the Apotheosis, chosen by me from among the most potent and learned sorcerers in the land. And I am still the Magister – who has just had a painful lesson in the value of conclave. Furthermore, we have a "what else" or two of our own. We have the Zhraike and the Stone People to rend and crush their bodies, to break their spirits. We may need nothing more. But if we *do* . . .' His raptor gaze held them as if hypnotized. 'You may know that I have unearthed a fragment of ancient lore, which even the eldest among us may not have known, concerning this valley. With it, we can summon a *multitude!*'

Ostyril raised a palsied hand in protest. 'You would not call up a demon horde from the Realms . . .'

'You think me a fool?' Lebarran snarled. 'Am I not aware of the chaotic, treacherous ways of demons? No – the host we can summon, if the need arises, will number as many as the trees in this forest, and will serve us single-mindedly, without fear or hesitation, to the death . . . and yet *beyond* it!'

FOURTEEN

As they reached the top of the incline, Red drew Grilena to a halt to give her a breather. But Krost, riding next to him, failed to notice at once, so that he and Wolle moved on almost blindly for several strides while Red watched with an uneasy frown. It's getting worse, Red thought. Krost had seemed quiet and inward-looking from the start, as they had left Quamarr. But as the journey had gone on, through all the days of riding south across the Grasslands and then climbing the rolling foothills, Krost's abstraction had deepened. And now that they were labouring over the far more demanding slopes of the Southern Highlands themselves, Krost had retreated even deeper into himself, rarely speaking, simply staring up at the high ridges and crags around them, his eyes bleak and haunted.

Red had remained mostly silent as well, unwilling to intrude on his friend's inner turmoil. And often during those days Red had tried to project himself into the same position, into Krost's simultaneous love and hate for his land and his people, his bitter yearning for that which had always hurt and rejected him. But Red could only go so far towards understanding that powerful mix of feelings. Red himself had enjoyed many places, even loved some of them, but had never been troubled by being absent from any of them. Indeed, he no longer felt the slightest unease at being away from his whole *world*. Equally, his independent spirit had never bonded too closely with any one group or community of people, certainly not in the town where he had been born or the city where he had lived.

Until perhaps now, he thought, with the small jolt that the realization often gave him. Here and now, in this Continent, with these people, I feel at home.

Which is just as well, he thought ironically, since I keep putting my neck on the line for them.

He had turned in the saddle, gazing back over the landscape that they had just crossed. That last long incline had brought them to an amazing vantage point, and the view was spectacular. The mountains rose up all around, rank upon rank, to overwhelming heights. Some were clothed with trees for much of their height and then with gleaming snow for the rest, some flaunted flanks and shoulders of naked blue-grey rock that was brightened near the peaks by small glaciers, glittering insolently in the summer sun that could not melt them.

'Anything wrong?' Krost called.

Red turned. Krost had stopped Wolle some distance farther on that almost level ridge-top, so that he and the huge dappled horse were silhouetted against the sky, looking to Red like some heroic, larger-than-life statue in a park. And around these parts he's a *dwarf*, Red thought incredulously.

'Just taking in the view,' he said, moving Grilena forward.

Krost smiled briefly. 'Come and see this one.'

As Red came up to him, he saw that on the farther side of the ridge-top the ground fell away again, far more steeply than the upward slope. Indeed, they might have been balked there entirely, if not for a narrow shelf or terrace that extended away to their right, dropping less steeply down across the face of the slope. But Red was mostly looking beyond that precarious trail – at a vast sweep of grassy tableland spread before him, looking sunlit and comfortable in the shelter of the towering rocky bastions around it.

'Beautiful,' he breathed. And then he finally realized what he was being shown. 'It's a plateau,' he added foolishly.

Krost's nod was tense. 'The Illan plateau. First and most beautiful of the plateaux of the Mykraladan.'

'The what?' Red asked.

'The Mykraladan. My people's name for themselves in the Old Tongue.'

'Will they all be speaking it?' Red wondered.

'It is used now mostly for special times,' Krost said shortly. 'Ceremonials, like weddings and funerals. Mostly funerals.'

There's a cheery note, Red thought, following silently as Krost turned Wolle towards the narrow trail on the shelf of rock. As the shelf inclined steadily down across the slope the trail became even narrower, requiring Red to be extra watchful and Grilena to be particularly careful about where she put her feet, although Wolle and Krost were moving along as easily as if on a broad highway.

But after more than an hour, their progress grew easier. The rocky shelf gradually gave way to a trail that was comfortable by comparison, where the lower reaches of the slope were increasingly clad in rich turf and scrub brush as it swept downwards. Relaxing then, Red let Grilena pick her own path along the trail, while he sat back to enjoy the warmth of the sun, the vivid butterflies amid the brush, the distant music of birds blending with the gurgle of a descending brook.

He was just idly thinking about the moments of unrivalled peace that the Continent had given him when, shockingly, the peace was shattered – by the totally unexpected sound of laughter. Over-loud, bellowing, *giant* laughter.

Grilena danced nervously as he reined her in, staring around. He saw that Krost had also stopped still, his broad face as blank and hard as the mountain rock. And then Red saw the source of the laughter, looming among the trees on the slope above.

In that moment he almost burst into nervous laughter himself. Because he was looking at three real, living giants – and his first, spontaneous, absurd thought was: they're not so big. He realized then that while Krost had described the giants more than once, he had been expecting – from some childhood leftover – a towering, overwhelming presence, a sort of humanoid King Kong that could scoop up Grilena and himself in the palm of one hand. Whereas the beings stamping down the hillside towards them, roaring with laughter, looked only a little more than twice Red's own height.

And me without a beanstalk to my name, he thought. Wonder if they say fee, fi, fo—

Then the thought broke off as the three giants reached the level of the trail and confronted them. And Red realized that someone more than twelve feet tall is still *giant* enough. Especially when they are correspondingly huge in bulk and

152

girth, with mountainous chests and shoulders, huge shaggy heads, and enormous hands that looked able to grasp Red's own head and crush it like an egg.

Still laughing, the three giants came to a halt in the middle of the trail, barring the way. Two of them, slightly smaller and perhaps younger than the third, were ranged on either side of their larger companion, as if deferring to him. All three wore thick shirts and trousers of rough-woven wool, with heavy hobnailed boots. And, Red noted, they seemed to have had no close recent acquaintance with a bath. But even more, he was aware of the heavy spears in their hands, like huge pikestaffs, with hafts that might have served as masts in the average sloop. And he was most aware of the edge of mockery in the three giants' laughter, and the tension in Krost's grim motionless silence.

'Short-legs Krost, back again,' said the biggest giant, his speaking voice becoming almost as loud as his laughter. 'I thought we had seen the last of your ugly face, dwarf.'

'Get out of the way, Lupyk,' Krost said impassively.

'And bringing along one of the little folk,' the giant named Lupyk continued, as if Krost had not spoken. 'Does he choose their company to make himself feel big? Or is he up to something with his little friend?'

'Up to no good,' said one of the other giants, on cue, and the third one chortled.

'Up to no good,' Lupyk repeated, grinning. 'Maybe they play games together. Dirty little games. And now the runt wants to bring his games back home, as if just the *sight* of him does not sicken us enough . . .'

'Move *aside*, Lupyk!' Krost growled, his knuckles white with his grip on the iron staff.

Lupyk reached out with his huge spear, holding the point unwaveringly in front of Krost's face. 'Come and move me, dwarf.'

Red twitched involuntarily, so that Grilena took a step forward, but none of the others even glanced at him. And Krost did not blink or flinch as he stared past the threatening spearpoint at his tormentor.

153

'Lupyk, I bear an important message for Ghiscral,' he said flatly. 'If you bar my path, I will fight you. And if that prevents the delivery of the message, Ghiscral will seek to know why.'

Lupyk sneered, still brandishing the spear, but Red could see that Krost's words had had some effect, while his companions were looking distinctly troubled. 'If we ever fight again, short-legs,' Lupyk boomed, 'nothing will keep me from killing you. Go your way, now, if you must – but remember what I say.'

He and the others stepped aside, and Krost rode forward, staring straight ahead. But as Red followed he could not keep from glancing up at Lupyk's huge face, looking past the sneering smile to see the brute savagery lurking deep in the eyes.

Shortly the trail curved farther down and away, taking the giants out of sight as Red moved Grilena up beside Wolle. 'Quite a welcoming committee,' he said, trying to be offhand.

To his surprise, Krost laughed, almost with relief. 'I had hoped to meet Lupyk later, or not at all. But now we have got it out of the way. His will probably be the most ill-natured welcome awaiting me.'

'*Did* you and he get into a fight, one time?' Red asked wonderingly.

'Many times,' Krost said, his smile fading. 'I have known Lupyk all my life – he is a distant cousin – and have known him to be cruel and bloodthirsty. We fought constantly as children, but less often as he gained his adult growth and . . . and I did not. The last time, some years ago, he might have killed me if the fight had not been stopped.'

Red felt awed at the thought of such a clash. 'He seems ready to start all over again.'

'He is always ready,' Krost growled. 'He especially enjoys tormenting those smaller than himself.'

'I know the type,' Red muttered.

But he said no more, letting the subject slide. By then they were moving downwards more swiftly, on to the majestic breadth of the plateau itself, and in the distance Red glimpsed tall buildings looming high among a scattering of trees.

As they drew nearer, the trail grew even broader and firmer, packed hard by countless weighty feet and hoofs. And soon Red could see some figures – very large figures – moving here and there among the buildings which were the size of mansions, made of enormous blocks of dressed stone with high mullioned windows and steeply pitched wooden roofs.

Krost pointed to one of the buildings standing near the trail. "My home," he said quietly. 'My family home.'

By then several of the figures visible around the buildings had begun to pause, shading their eyes, peering towards the two riders. In the next moment a number of them began moving towards the trail, towards Krost and Red. And then one of them broke into a run, with a flurry of skirts like tents and huge pigtails, shouting Krost's name.

Krost grinned. 'My baby sister, Aleka. You will like her, Red.'

Red smiled as the running figure bore down on Krost. She seemed noticeably smaller than Lupyk and the other two, Red thought, perhaps no more than eight and a half feet tall. So, being mounted, he did not feel too overshadowed as she came up to them, laughing delightedly, and flung her arms around Krost with unrestrained affection. Though he blinked when he saw that the embrace was quite effortlessly lifting Krost's vast weight slightly from his saddle.

When that first flurry of joyful reunion subsided, Krost managed to introduce Red. Aleka seemed a little shy, lowering her eyes demurely when Red smiled at her. 'Your sister's a lot prettier than you, Krost,' he said gallantly. And it was more or less true, he thought, in terms of Aleka's soft brown hair and eyes, creamy skin and winning smile. Even if those features did go with her height, bulging muscles and hips nearly as broad as Wolle's.

His remark made Aleka look slightly startled, as if she had not expected Red to speak normally. But then she giggled, an unsettling sound from a giant, and tilted her head to study Red more closely. Just as a group of far larger giants arrived, full of greetings and curiosity.

In their midst was a couple that seemed particularly affected by the sight of Krost, who, predictably, turned out to be his parents. They too were shorter than the norm, no more than ten feet tall by Red's guess, white-haired and wrinkled. But they were upright and fit, and when Krost dismounted to greet them they too each lifted him slightly, unconsciously, as they hugged him. Knowing the unusual weight of his friend, Red had a very clear and unnerving idea of the everyday strength of an average giant, and what they might be able to lift if they really tried.

Dismounting politely to be introduced, failing to take in most of the names except those of Krost's parents, Kulit and Orva, Red felt relieved that no one offered to hug him. This is how children feel, he realized, or remembered. Little kids, always surrounded by a forest of great big legs, getting cricks in their necks from having to look up all the time to see faces. Alarmingly huge faces, too, disturbing even when wearing friendly and interested smiles.

Watch it, he told himself. They won't like it if you seem afraid of them. And *you* won't like it if you spend all your time feeling overwhelmed and . . . belittled. Which is how Krost must feel, here, most of the time.

After some six-foot children had been directed to care for the horses, the gathering swung away towards the houses, heading for the one that was Krost's family home. It was, of course, immense – and the main room that they entered, with its mighty beamed ceiling, huge stone fireplace and oversized handmade furniture again made Red feel like a child in an adult world. Perched on what seemed to be a low footstool, he watched amazed as more and more giants crowded into the room, jostling and peering, to welcome Krost home – and, obviously, to join in the festivities. From elsewhere in the house enormous casks were being carried in – as if they were filled with feathers – and broached in foaming torrents of ale. And a table that filled one end of the room grew burdened with an incredible quantity of bread, fruit, assorted cakes and sweetmeats, all the variety that was available among the vegetarian giants.

Krost glanced ruefully at Red. 'They welcome any excuse for a party.'

'Good for them,' Red replied, looking around. He reckoned there were around forty adult giants in the room, divided more or less evenly between male and female. 'I suppose everyone else is at work.'

Krost looked puzzled, then understood. 'No, Red. Except for some who will be with the herds, as Lupyk and his friends probably were, there is no one else. Not in this tribe.'

'Just these?' Red asked, startled. 'Kind of a small tribe.'

Krost nodded. 'It is more like a large *family*, since most of us are at least distantly related. Giants do not breed easily or swiftly, so we remain few. This room now holds most of the Hak-illans, and we are the most numerous tribe on the plateaux.'

So, Red mused, the force of giants that Phaedran is hoping for won't be all that large. Though each of them would be something of an army on his own. Or her own . . .? But when he voiced that question, Krost shook his head.

'Among giants, the men do the fighting. It is tradition – and perhaps also they are more expendable, for a race that breeds slowly.' He glanced away, his brow furrowing. 'And now I must attend to my duty. There is Ghiscral ran Hak – the chieftain of the Hak-illans.'

Red looked over to see someone stooping to lumber in through the door. Someone who was a giant among giants, nearly fourteen feet tall with a breadth and bulk to match. You've heard of the brick outhouse, Red told himself, here's the brick apartment block.

Krost moved slowly away through the throng to join the immense Ghiscral, who patted him on the shoulder, making him stagger slightly, before bending over smilingly to hear what Krost had to say.

In the same moment Lupyk and his two friends swaggered into the room, staring at Krost with ugly, challenging grins.

But they turned away, grins vanishing, when Ghiscral looked up and glared at them. And in that moment Krost's father, old Kulit, loomed up at Red's side. In one hand he held a mug of ale that to Red looked the size of an oil drum. But in the other he held a far smaller cup – about a quart's worth, Red thought, probably used for giant babies. But it was brimming with ale, and when Kulit proffered it he took it thankfully.

'That's kind of you,' he said, getting to his feet to feel less towered over. 'I could do with a drink.'

The old giant's smile broadened. 'We get few visitors from outside, but those that do come always feel better for some good ale.'

'Helps us feel a little less overawed,' Red said candidly. And automatically he glanced over to where Lupyk and the other two were noisily filling their mugs.

Kulit's face went grave as he noted the direction of Red's gaze. 'I hear you and my son have already faced Lupyk today,' he said.

'On the trail coming in,' Red confirmed. 'Not a friendly sort.'

The old giant grunted. 'You would do well to keep Krost away from him.'

'It's not easy to *keep* Krost from things,' Red replied. 'But I'll do what I can.'

Kulit studied him. 'My son has not had an easy life,' he said at last. 'I am glad for him that he has found a friend.'

'Even if it's just a little one?' Red asked with a half-smile.

'Not so little in the heart, perhaps,' Kulit said. 'Krost tells me that you carry the sword and the name of Corodel.'

'In a way. But I'm not him.'

'Corodel visited the plateaux a few times,' Kulit went on. 'I remember him well. *He* certainly had a giant's heart.' His smile widened. 'Fearless and wild he was, almost to the point of folly. One time, he actually challenged and fought a young man of another tribe.'

'Fought a giant?' Red asked, wide-eyed.

'Oh, yes. And what is more, *beat* him. Though it is said that his opponent was drunk at the time.'

'So was Corodel, probably,' Krost said, joining them in time to pick up the story.

Red glanced down at his empty mug, then looked up with a merry grin. 'Personally, I wouldn't dream of being such an unmannerly guest.'

Kulit's laughter boomed. 'Among the Mykraladan, friend-of-my-son, the guest is *always* right, however poor his manners.' With a nod he moved away, pausing to glare briefly at Lupyk.

In that moment Red heard from outside a deep, sonorous reverberation, as if an enormous gong and vast bass drum

158

were being struck at the same time. The sound echoed across the plateau, reaching out to fill the mountains with its voice. And Krost nodded with grim satisfaction.

'That is the call to meeting,' he told Red. 'Ghiscral has agreed to assemble the tribes to hear Phaedran's message from me. They should all be here, gathered in the *tokirris*, the meeting-hall, by nightfall.'

'Are you ready for that?' Red asked carefully.

Krost lifted his shoulders in a stiff shrug. 'I will have to be. Though I have never spoken in the *tokirris*. It will . . .'

He stopped, scowling, as Lupyk appeared next to them, on his own, wearing his ugly grin again. 'I hear you plan to perform in the *tokirris*, dwarf. That should be a laugh.'

'Laugh if you will,' Krost growled. 'I will deliver my message.'

Lupyk's grin turned towards Red. 'And while you do that, your little playmate can sit on my knee, so he will not be bored.'

As Krost's face darkened, Red looked up at Lupyk with a flinty smile that did not reach his eyes. 'There's a saying where I come from that seems as true here. The bigger the mouth, the smaller the brain.'

Laughter rolled around him, and he saw that a number of giants – including Ghiscral – had gathered curiously. Glowering, Lupyk turned to stalk sullenly away. And Krost sighed heavily.

'Every time I come home,' he rumbled, 'I hope that things will be different. But they never are.'

Red nodded sympathetically. 'It's hard to get away from the Lupyks of the world. Any world.'

'But now I must forget him,' Krost went on. 'And hope that he does not speak against me in the *tokirris* tonight. It will be hard enough trying to convince the tribes.'

'Just tell them how things are,' Red said. 'You can't do any more.'

Krost sighed again. 'To them, it will all seem to do with the trivial, faraway affairs of "the little ones". Many of them will have little regard for such a message. And even less for the messenger.'

159

That night, in the *tokirris*, Red found that Krost's misgivings about the assembly had been fully justified.

All afternoon and evening the giants had been arriving, most of them mounted on taller and broader versions of Wolle, greeting each other uproariously, heading at once for the *tokirris* where more quantities of food and drink awaited them. The meeting-hall itself was a gigantic shell of a building, reminding Red of a fairly basic sports arena, with rough-hewn benches and trestle tables arranged in a U. There the giants gathered, ate, drank, exchanged jokes and gossip, and drank a great deal more. And as the noise level rose almost unbearably, Red glanced up at the vaulted, smoke-blackened ceiling and recalled the tale that Krost had told him – of the witch and seeress whom Krost had met, Silgid, and her disturbing vision of some huge ceiling crashing down. Maybe this is it, Red thought edgily as the *tokirris* seemed to quake with the giants' noise. Maybe Krost's speech will bring the house down . . .

But by then the giants were growing quieter, brought to order by Ghiscral's bellowing, settling at last to attend to the proceedings. And Red looked around at them with a sinking heart, while Krost strode into the centre of the U and began to address them with the message from his prince.

Most of the audience were grinning. Some were nudging each other, muttering comments, chuckling aloud, despite some half-hearted glares from Krost's father. It was all an amusement for them, Red saw, a diversion. A dwarf, pretending to be important. How could they take the message seriously, they seemed to feel, when it was delivered by such a comical little fellow?

Watching, Red's temper began to overheat. Krost was doing a good job, he thought – telling them quickly but effectively

160

what had been happening in the land beyond their mountains, what battles had already been fought. Red saw a few of the older giants frown briefly at the mention of their old enemy, the winged monsters called the Zhraike, but the rest of them seemed to dismiss that along with everything else. Certainly Krost explained the ambition and menace of Lebarran Magister with graphic clarity, but still the giants were unimpressed. And when he determinedly concluded by presenting Phaedran's appeal for help from the giants, he returned to his seat in the midst of an uproar of laughter and derision.

Ghiscral quieted them, however, insisting that they discuss the proposition. Which they did, dismissively. 'Let the little ones fight their own battles' was the general feeling, along with a vague disdain for Phaedran and his family's claim to 'rule' the Four-Cornered Continent. When old Kulit reminded them of the role of the Zhraike, that too was dismissed. Any Zhraike that might still exist were staying well away from the plateaux, it was pointed out, and in any case Krost admitted to having seen only a few.

The outcome, then, was without doubt. And Krost could only hunch his shoulders and stare gloomily at the floor when Ghiscral told him, not unkindly, that he must take back a negative answer to the prince.

That was when the half-drunken voice of Lupyk rang out from the midst of the crowd. 'Be on your way, short-legs, and take your little boyfriend with you!'

There was an instant of shocked silence, and then another uproar where remonstration mixed with callous laughter and the roaring fury of Krost rose above it all. Until Ghiscral, on his feet, hammered thunderously on the table with a fist like a pile-driver. Under the impact of his rage, the others quietened again.

'Lupyk!' the chieftain bellowed. 'The friend of Krost is a guest! Our guests are not to be insulted – above all, not in the *tokirris!*'

He turned towards Red, but then paused as if taken aback. All the giants, even Krost, had returned to their seats when

161

Ghiscral had imposed quiet on them. But Red was still standing, white-faced with anger.

Ghiscral peered at him. 'We offer you apology, friend-of-Krost,' he said formally. He paused again, frowning, as Red remained on his feet. 'Have you a wish to speak in the *tokirris*?'

Red did not hesitate. 'I have. If it's permitted.'

Lowering himself to his seat, Ghiscral gestured at the open space. 'Anyone may speak here. Especially a guest who has been insulted.'

With a slight nod, ignoring Krost's desperate signals trying to stop him, Red stepped forward – on to centre stage. Not the smallest tremor of an eyelid betrayed the sudden clench of his stomach, the dampness of sweat beneath his shirt. He looked around at the giants, watching them lean forward, many of them smiling as they had at Krost but many also looking interested. Ready for another clown act, he thought grimly, trying to control his anger, summoning all his actor's instincts and training to his aid. Listening to the low buzz from his audience that drifted through the huge arena, he heard within it over and over the familiar name being passed around. *Corodel*.

It was exactly the opening he needed. 'The name is Cordell,' he said, projecting his voice to the back of the hall. 'Just that. I'm not some dead hero come back to life. I'm not even from this world.' That, he saw, made most of them sit up. 'I just happen, by a magical accident, to be carrying the *sword* of Corodel.'

He slid the luminous sword from its sheath. And as the giants stared, fascinated, he lifted it and pointed it at Lupyk. Then, as the silence grew, he lowered it and sheathed it again with a crooked smile.

'Don't worry,' he said easily. 'I'm not here to wave my sword at Lupyk because of some insult. He can say what he likes. Strong ale always produces loud farts.' He paused, letting the laughter roll over him, grinning tightly at Lupyk's scowl. 'What *does* bother me,' he went on, 'is the *real* insult here tonight. Not just from Lupyk but from all of you. The insult to my friend Krost.'

They went still at that, many of them scowling, though a few older ones – not just Kulit – nodded as if in agreement.

162

Into that silence Red went on to tell them, again, about the events that he and Krost had lived through in the previous months. But he related them from another viewpoint. He told of Krost's central, vital role in those events – and of the courage, the strength, the unflinching resolve of the one whom the giants found so comical.

'In every other part of the Continent,' Red stated, his pale eyes intense, 'Krost il Hak is respected, admired, deferred to. By royalty, by wizards, by generals, by the leaders of the Sisterhood. Only here, among his own people, is he mocked and patronized. And I tell you – that is your failure, and your loss.'

They stirred and growled, but still the magnetism of his voice and his eyes gripped them. 'Soon Prince Phaedran will muster his forces, as best he can, to confront the threat of Lebarran and his Order. The Sisterhood with their women warriors will be there. The ordinary men of the militia will be part of that force. Leading adepts will be part of it. But where will the giants be?' He pitched his voice so that it rang around the huge space. 'They will be sitting on their giant behinds, full of ale and wind and ignorance!'

More rumblings and bristlings swept through his audience, but his voice overrode them. 'All except *one*. One of the giants will be there, risking his life with the rest of Phaedran's force, to try to avert the danger that overshadows this land. *Krost* will be there. Because he knows how dire is the need, how menacing the threat. Krost will be there because he knows what must be done – and because he has a giant's heart that wills him to do it!'

He held the pause until they were silent again. 'Let me tell you this. If the prince is defeated and the Continent falls to Lebarran, you will *regret* that you did not help. When the Magister and his monstrous forces come over the mountains against you, and you find – as you will – that you cannot oppose him alone. But even if Phaedran's army *wins* the victory, you will regret that you were not there. Because then the songs and legends will speak of only *one* giant who fought in that battle. They will speak of Krost il Hak – the only one of his entire race *not to be dishonoured*!'

That last word brought the speech and the silence to a

163

tumultuous end. Raging, roaring, the giants lunged to their feet – many waving fists and glaring at Red, many others arguing fiercely among themselves. Even Ghiscral's mighty thunderings could barely be heard above the din. But Red stood his ground, head high and eyes alight, as if daring his audience to prove him wrong. And finally, as the enormous centre table split with a resounding crack under the pounding of Ghiscral's fist, the giants began slowly once more to subside.

All except Lupyk, slack-mouthed and swaying, a huge flagon of ale in one hand, glaring at Red with his face mottled by rage. 'Why do we sit here,' he roared into the fading hubbub, 'to hear some puny catamite accuse us of dishonour?'

That reduced the noise level with startling abruptness. Some giants turned to stare at Lupyk, but most of them merely watched Red, awaiting his reaction. Yet he was no longer aware of their gaze. His temper had finally snapped, and cold fury boiled along with adrenalin through his veins as he bared his teeth and took a quick step forward.

'You're uncommonly concerned with catamites and things, Lupyk,' he snarled, his voice still easily carrying through the hall. 'Makes me wonder about *you*, when you're out with the herds. Do you screw the female beasts, or the males?'

For an instant the giants stared at him, open-mouthed. Then the hall shuddered and rocked with their titanic gales of laughter. Even Krost, who had risen from his seat trying to divert Red's anger, clutched his sides and roared. But Lupyk, his face purple with rage, hurled his empty flagon splinteringly to the floor and pointed an unsteady finger at Red.

'By the bones of my fathers!' he bellowed. 'Guest or no guest, whoever or whatever you are, you will *answer* to me for that!'

Again the crowd erupted, some still with disapproval but all with excitement. Even Ghiscral's thunderous demands for quiet went unheard, so for once Red's voice had no chance. But then another voice rose, incredibly, above the storm. Krost was still on his feet, all laughter fled.

'That will not be!' Krost roared. 'He is my guest and my friend! If you wish to fight, Lupyk, you will meet *me* in the square!'

164

That surprised the audience enough to quieten them a little, into many separate muttered discussions. And Red, belatedly grasping that a very formal challenge had been issued, saw Lupyk begin to smile his ugly smile and remembered what the giant had promised, on the mountainside earlier that day, if he and Krost ever fought again. His reckless anger then combined with desperate concern for his friend, and pushed him over an edge beyond all caution.

'Krost!' His yell cut across all other sounds in the hall. 'Shut up! He challenged *me!*'

The giants all stared at him with renewed interest and excitement, while Krost again tried to intervene. But it was too late.

'Do you accept the challenge, then?' Lupyk asked Red, almost amazedly.

Red's mouth twisted into the semblance of a grin that looked bitter and furious but also somehow strangely eager. 'I'm ready any time you say.'

'The essence lies in the *right* of challenge, as I say,' old Kulit asserted. 'A right that is grounded entirely in the nature of honour, and the need to protect honour from insult.'

Red sighed inwardly. It was later that night, he was sitting in the depths of an oversized chair in Kulit's home with an untasted mug of ale, and Krost's father was droning on about the finer points of the giants' code of honour and single combat. Red had no wish to be lectured on that subject, glumly expecting to learn a good deal the hard way, when he and Lupyk finally clashed. Meanwhile he could hear Aleka and old Orva weeping in another room, which was disturbing. And Krost was nowhere around, which was more disturbing.

Most disturbing of all, he had been told that in the fight – which would be at sun-up, in the open area at the village centre – he would not be able to use the sword. The traditional weapons for such duels were some kind of clubs that the giants called maces. I should have a look at a mace, he thought dully, practise with it a bit or just find out if I can *lift* it. Or maybe I should get some rest. But he doubted whether he could sleep,

165

even though in the wake of his earlier reckless fury he felt enervated, almost immobilized. And Kulit's not helping, he thought. I could be bored to death before Lupyk can get to me.

'In theory,' the old giant was saying, 'one could challenge a babe in arms if an insult had been offered. And then a member of the infant's family, for *their* honour, would accept on its behalf. As Krost wished to do for you . . .'

'But I'm not a baby,' Red said flatly. 'Where is Krost, by the way? He wouldn't be out squaring up to Lupyk, to protect me?'

Kulit looked shocked. 'No, no, he would not. Honour requires . . .'

'Right, the code of honour,' Red broke in with a weary gesture. 'Just the thing to help me paint myself into a corner.' Then he sighed, seeing Kulit's puzzled look. 'Sorry – I'm a little on edge for some reason. And all that crying doesn't help. I'm surprised your family is so upset for me.'

'Not for you,' Kulit said bluntly. 'Orva and Aleka weep because they know that when Lupyk overcomes you, Krost will seek to avenge your honour. And Lupyk has vowed to kill him.'

Thanks for the vote of confidence, Red thought. But coldness clawed at his insides as the truth of the statement struck home. Of course Krost would do that, he said to himself sickly. And what pointless stupidity. We're supposed to be recruiting for Phaedran's army – and instead we could both be killed here. And who knows, then, what Aurilia might do. Or what effect the whole shambles would have on the effort against Lebarran.

Maybe, he thought wildly as Kulit began to drone again, we should just grab the horses and run, and let the giants worry about their honour by themselves. But he knew beyond doubt that Krost would never agree to such a flight, and that he himself could never desert his friend. And as he huddled in the huge chair and faced the bitter fact that he had contrived his own inevitable fate, the door opened and Krost strode in, carrying a heavy object that just had to be a mace.

'I thought you would be resting, gathering your strength,' he said to Red, with a glower at Kulit, who looked abashed.

'No way I could gather as much as I need,' Red said dourly, eyeing the mace. 'Is that what I fight with?'

Krost handed the weapon to him. 'I have cut it down and trimmed it, to make it lighter.'

It still weighs enough, Red thought, hefting it. The mace was slightly longer than his sword, with a thick gnarled wooden handle firmly bonded to a lumpy head of rough iron. He stood and swung it back and forth, two-handed, finding that it was well enough balanced for all its crudeness. But then, he thought, Lupyk will be swinging one that's two or three times bigger.

Krost was watching him keenly. 'It suits you well enough. Just remember, never try to *block* his blows.'

Red's half-laugh was hollow. 'No chance. I'll be staying out of his way till he gets tired.'

'*No*, Red,' Krost said urgently. 'You must understand. Lupyk is a giant, with a giant's strength – and you have not truly grasped the nature of that strength. It can take *days*, of continuous full-scale effort, before a giant tires.'

Red stared at him, feeling slightly sick again. There had been times in his life when he had fought men much larger than himself, using his speed and his trained skills against them, invariably finding that they soon grew heavy-footed and clumsy with exhaustion. But now that wouldn't work. He had to remember that Lupyk wasn't just a twelve-foot man. He wasn't truly a man at all.

'But it might help,' Krost added, watching him, 'that Lupyk has been drinking all night. He is now sodden with ale, and will be in poor condition by sun-up.'

That's something, Red thought. Fighting a hungover giant might give him a small ghost of a chance. He thought of the story of Corodel's fight with a giant, how they had both been drunk. But not me, he thought. Grab any edge that's going. And something like a hazy plan of action began to form in his mind as he wandered off with his mace to the room he had been given, to try to find some belated rest. To his surprise, he managed to close his eyes and doze for a while during the rest of the night, though his sleep was troubled by mind-racking dreams. And he awoke with a jerk from the last of them to find Aleka entering the room, her eyes red and saddened, holding a small mug filled with a liquid that smelled spicily unusual.

167

'It is nearly sun-up,' she said mournfully. 'Krost said you would not want to eat, before ... But I – I have brought you *hanac*.'

Sitting up, Red took the cup with a word of thanks. It's like a kind of herbal tea, he thought, and took a polite sip, hoping to rinse the metallic taste from his mouth and ease the sour clench of his stomach. But he sipped again, and then gulped, as the spicy brew sent the most amazing sense of energy and vigour and well-being flooding through his body.

'*Hanac* is given to those weakened by illness, to help them recover.' Aleka was watching him, looking nervous. 'I should not really have given it to you, now. But ... I wanted to help you. Please tell no one.'

'I won't,' Red said gently. 'But thank you. Whatever happens, I'm grateful.'

Blushing slightly, she tilted her head as before, gazing at him as he drained the mug. What a buzz, he thought. Better than the brew he had once been given by Aurilia. Good stimulants in this place, he said to himself with an inner smile. What would the street value be back home? Then he turned his smile on to Aleka, deepening her blush, and sprang out of bed, glad that he had slept in his clothes. The mace felt almost light in his hand when he picked it up – just as his whole body felt light, fizzing with energy.

'Let's not keep Lupyk waiting,' he said.

But of course it was Krost, not Aleka, who kept him company as they went out of the house towards the square in the village centre. There Red saw as well as heard the booming combination of drum and gong being cheerfully beaten while the giants assembled, as noisily excited and curious as ever. Red ignored them as he made his way to the centre of the open space where Lupyk waited, looking bleary-eyed and faintly greenish, swaying slightly. But still his immense muscles rolled like boulders as he hefted in one hand a huge mace that looked bigger and heavier than Red himself.

Around the plateau the mountaintops were being dyed orange-red by the sunrise when Ghiscral stepped forward.

'Have you both prepared for what might befall you here?' he asked formally.

Lupyk sneered. 'It will befall *him*,' he growled, his voice slurred.

And as Ghiscral looked at Red, and Red began to reply, Lupyk lunged forward without warning and swung his mace.

Red's reflexes flung him in a wild flailing leap backwards, just out of reach of the blow, and then again leaping to evade the equally furious backswing. He could hear the crowd shouting, could hear Krost's roar of anger at Lupyk's premature attack, but the sounds came to him as if muted and distant, as his battle readiness poised itself. God help me, he was thinking, he may be big but he's *fast*. What chance would I have if he was sober . . .

But Lupyk was not sober, as was very plain in his next attack, another lurching stride and a mighty sweep of the mace that might have missed anyway – though Red dodged it – because the giant stumbled in a half-stagger as he swung. And Red nodded to himself, finding his balance, tightening up his alertness and his honed skills, fixing his concentration. He no longer heard any of the noise of the watching crowd, no longer felt concerned with the fact that his head rose little higher than his opponent's belt-line. He was utterly tuned and focused on the towering shape before him, weighing up Lupyk's lack of finesse and reliance on sheer power, assessing every nuance of his stance and approach, as the giant's vast mace struck down at him again.

His pale eyes bright, smiling a faintly eager smile, the *hanac* bubbling in his veins, Red drifted aside from the blow as if it was in slow motion. And as the giant mace whistled past, Red swung his own mace two-handed in a short flat arc, perfectly balanced and timed, and crashed its iron head against Lupyk's right hand, which was gripping his mace's haft.

Lupyk's eyes and mouth flew open at the unexpected shock as he jerked his hand and the mace away. Roaring, he kicked out at Red with a massive hob-nailed boot. But again he was off-balance, and the wild kick missed. And Red smoothly pivoted, bringing his mace around in a blurring half-circle with all

169

of his weight behind it, to smash it unerringly against the side of the giant's kneecap. Lupyk's roar of pain climbed up several octaves as he lurched sideways. Then he charged, bellowing, his mace sweeping back and forth in a series of maddened blows. And Red retreated, dodging and side-stepping, concentration unwavering, waiting for the moment when the giant's frenzy would run out of steam. Inevitably it came, the huge mace wavered as Lupyk again stumbled off-balance – and Red sprang forward to hammer another furious blow at his enemy's right hand.

As he spun smoothly away again, as the enraged Lupyk flailed at the space where he had been, the battle computer in his mind was weighing and assessing with cold judgement. Big trees can be brought down by little axes, he said to himself, one chop at a time. And he saw the bright glint of blood on Lupyk's right hand, and how he seemed to favour one knee very slightly as he lunged in pursuit.

But as Red slid aside, his battle awareness was reminding him of what Krost had said – how, despite the *hanac*, he would surely tire long before Lupyk. And then it would take only one blow from the giant mace to flatten and finish him. Get moving, he told himself. A *quick* tree-felling or none at all.

Again he picked his moment to sway and dodge and strike with savage precision once more at the giant hand. At that pitch of awareness, despite the crowd's noise and Lupyk's shout of pain, he could hear the unmistakable snap of broken bone. Recklessness gripped him then, so that almost in the same motion he pivoted once again to hammer not once but twice against the same spot on the giant's knee.

That extra blow almost finished him. Though Lupyk had almost dropped his mace from his damaged right hand, he swung the knotted fist of his left hand before Red could dodge away. The awkward punch struck only glancingly, but that was still enough to fling Red halfway across the square in a sliding, sprawling tumble. Half-stunned, the entire left side of his body afire with scraped skin and bruised flesh, Red barely managed to cling on to his mace, and had only begun to hoist himself up as the bellowing giant surged forward, mace raised high.

But as he charged, his damaged knee buckled slightly under him, so that he staggered and nearly fell. In that instant, Red gained his feet, the sight of the enemy's near-collapse acting on him like another draught of *hanac*. And while Lupyk was finding his balance, Red leaped forward, scrapes and bruises forgotten, swaying under another ill-directed sweep of the giant mace, slamming another savage blow against Lupyk's right hand.

The giant's roar rose almost to a howl, with a second audible crack of bone. As Red spun out of reach he saw the massive, bleeding hand – with two of its fingers jutting at ugly angles – fall helplessly half-open, the mace dangling. Again Red flashed forward, his rashness under control, his awareness at its peak – again Lupyk's left fist swung at him. But he drifted just far enough to one side so that it missed him. Then he feinted, a sharp flat swing at the giant's damaged knee, and as Lupyk lurched and tried to parry the blow Red smoothly shifted his feet and swung the mace in a compact reverse strike, with ferocious power, in an upward direction. The mace buried its iron head with a terrible muffled thud in the giant's unprotected groin.

Lupyk's face contorted and purpled as the breath left his lungs in a strangled burst. Dropping the mace, clutching himself and retching, he began to double up, then staggered and toppled over as his tormented knee gave way. And Red stopped and stood still, staring coldly down at his fallen enemy.

'Finish him!' roared a bloodthirsty voice from the crowd.

'It is permitted,' he heard Ghiscral say. 'The fight does not end until the victor declares it ended.'

Slowly Red reached out with the mace, letting its head almost touch the bony hollow behind Lupyk's ear where even an ordinary human blow might be fatal. But then, as if responding to an unheard call, he drew the mace back from the groaning giant and turned to look at Krost. Who gave him a small nod and a fierce, knowing smile.

Feeling suddenly weary to the depths of his being, Red flung the mace aside and faced Ghiscral. 'The fight is over,' he said emptily. 'You'll have need of all your warriors, Ghiscral, when

171

Lebarran Magister brings his power over the mountains against you.'

As the chieftain grimaced and lifted a hand as if to push away the words, Krost stepped up beside Red, sweeping his gaze across the crowd, resting it briefly and sadly upon his wide-eyed parents, before turning at last to Ghiscral.

'The Mykraladan do not emerge from this day with credit,' Krost said, his hoarse voice echoing in the sudden silence. 'Nor will there be credit for you in days to come. I know that you have felt shame that a *dwarf'* – he spat the word – 'should be born among you. But now it is *I* who feels shame, at what you have allowed to happen here, and what you are willing to allow to happen in the world outside. So I bid you farewell, my family, my tribe, my people. Whether I live or die in the conflict to come, you will not see me here again.'

He turned to Red. 'Come, my friend,' he growled, his voice steady despite the tears visible in his eyes. 'Let us be gone, and find ourselves more worthy battles.'

Armies are too slow and clumsy, Aurilia thought. And exposed, here under the open sky of the Grasslands. It mightn't matter if we were only going to face another slow-creeping army. But it's worrying, when we're probably being watched by the eye of a Magister – and when we might, even at this distance, feel the weight of his hand.

It was mid-afternoon, approaching the end of an exhausting and chaotic day. Aurilia was in her older form, the prairie breeze tugging at her hair as she sat on her gelding and gazed out over the Grasslands, a short way from the sprawl of tents and wagons where Phaedran's army had set up camp. The evening before, the company from the Sisterhood – more than a thousand well-armed warrior women, many also with some healing magic, led by the Circle of Nine – had come to the end of its high-speed march from the Fastness to join the prince's forces. By then Phaedran had taken his militia, along with a dozen or so mages led by Vallawn and Farbanni, out of the city southwards to a mustering point on the Grasslands. There they had been going through the final drills and preparations that would complete the militia's transformation from a fairly complacent city constabulary into a tougher, sharper, more mobile fighting force. And now, Aurilia knew, they were all mostly ready to set off. That evening the leaders of the militia and the mages, and representatives of the Nine, were to meet with Phaedran to assess overall readiness and probably to receive the order to march. Even though there was still no sign of Krost or Red.

Of course, she told herself, their stay in the Highlands would have been brief indeed if they had already got back. But even so she felt a tightening of the anxiety that had been her constant companion ever since she learned that Red had set off on another adventure. She had not been unduly angry – or even much surprised at the news, for she was all too familiar with Red's restless, reckless nature. Instead, it was simple anxiety that had burgeoned within her, where it had remained like a chronic, gnawing affliction. Don't let it happen again, she whispered silently, remembering too well the last time that Krost and Red had ridden off together. Don't let Lebarran send something else against him. I couldn't bear it if it happened again.

She had ridden out from the camp to find some peace and solitude, but most of all to watch across the land southward in the hope of seeing two riders. But the sweep of the Grasslands, at their most flat and featureless there in the heart of the Continent, showed an unbroken surface of bright turf without even a tree or a bush rising above it as far as she could see towards the horizon. So, as anxiety clenched around her heart, she turned again to regard the organized clutter of the army camp.

The long plain tents of the militia were arrayed in neat avenues – more than a hundred tents, with twenty-four men in each. Fairly near to them, also tidily arranged, was the collection of supply wagons, and beyond them the horses in their portable paddock of ropes and posts. The few dozen smaller tents of the militia officers stood to one side, near the far larger but still severely plain tent – more of a pavilion, with smaller tents linked to it – that housed the prince and his servants. The warriors of the Sisterhood had pitched their tents, light and airy hemispheres, on the other side of that central area as if to have the prince and the militia officers like a bulwark between the two main camps. Which was sensible, Aurilia knew, having noticed a good deal of glancing and smiling between militiamen and Sisters within even the first few moments. And there would still doubtless be a certain amount of coming and going between the two camps after dark, despite that bulwark, she thought amusedly. Nor would the army's effectiveness be any the worse for it.

Also within the central area near the prince's pavilion stood a number of wide, heavy carriages like good-sized rooms on wheels. Most of those were occupied by the mages, who did not care to experience the military life under canvas. But one carriage set apart from the others held a non-combatant who was a very unlikely adjunct to the army: the Princess Evelane, with her nurses.

Aurilia had been appalled to find that Phaedran was taking his daughter along on that perilous journey. But she had in the end reluctantly seen some point in the prince's decision.

'I cannot spare a sufficient number of wizards to protect her in the palace,' Phaedran had explained. 'But here, with us, she will be protected by the best of Quamarr's adepts. And by you and the Nine, Aurilia.'

'Do you expect us to divert our energies from any struggle with Lebarran to protect Evelane?' Aurilia had asked sternly.

'Not at all. In any battle she will be kept back with the supply wagons, out of the focus of danger. But if you and the mages raise a magical shielding or the like, it will protect her as well.' His face had taken on its bleakest expression. 'And also, practically speaking, with her here there is less chance of her being attacked or abducted, and used as a lever against me.'

Aurilia had seen the sense of that point even as she felt chilled by its cold pragmatism. But the feeling was swept away by Phaedran's next words.

'I cannot leave her, Aurilia,' he said miserably. 'Her hate-filled words in the Dome – I hear them still, in my mind, over and over, how I neglected and failed her. And I know that all the loneliness and anguish of her childhood have led to her condition now, as Hallifort indeed implied.'

Aurilia had rested a hand on his arm, striving to comfort him. 'Highness, you can't assume *all* the blame for what happened to her. The roots of her trouble lie in an accident of birth, when she inherited none of her mother's magic.'

Phaedran had sighed, his eyes haunted. 'Perhaps. And that is irreparable, so indeed she may be incurable. No matter. I will not leave her, I cannot abandon her to whatever might seek to assail her, alone, in a half-deserted palace. If we gain the victory in this conflict, she will remain unharmed. If we fail – why, then, she and I may at least die together.'

175

Remembering that as she stared back at the army camp, Aurilia shivered despite the warmth of the day. There had been a prophetic air about those words, she thought, or perhaps just a tempting of fate which was no less unsettling. But then she shook herself, gathering her purposeful will around her. The future will arrive in whatever form it chooses, she thought firmly, whether it is shunned or welcomed. Lifting her head, she gazed again across the sea of wind-rippled grass. And Red will arrive or not in *his* own time, she added, however long I sit out here drowning in apprehension.

She shook the reins and the gelding moved away, all too glad to return to the familiar bustle of the camp. Their shadows were growing longer, she noticed, as the sun slid downwards. Already the breeze bore cooking odours, as the first stages of preparation of the evening meal got under way. And after that, she thought, there will be the meeting in Phaedran's tent, with probably the decision to start the march in the morning.

At least, she told herself, we'll be moving south, towards the Highlands. Towards Red, if he's riding this way . . .

By the time the evening meal had been taken, twilight had deepened into darkness, and most of the militiamen were taking their ease around small fires. From the Sisterhood camp, a chorus of voices unexpectedly lifted in a song of lilting cadences and delicate harmonies. And Aurilia, still in her older form, walking with Inghilla towards Phaedran's pavilion, glanced up at the sky that was afire with a myriad stars. Yet as the song rose the starlight seemed to grow blurred, as if being seen through glass with water running across it. The two women studied the effect, seeing how the blurriness extended down and around the encampment as well as above it, and nodded with approval. Then, as a footman held canvas hangings aside for them, they stepped into the torchlit brightness of the pavilion.

The others had already gathered – Marshal Trochain and his aides seated next to Phaedran, across from Vallawn and Farbanni representing the wizards just as Aurilia and Inghilla represented the Nine. Vallawn turned to them at once with a smile, but there was the usual tinge of malice in Farbanni's apparent cheeriness.

'Ladies,' Farbanni said with an ironic half-bow. 'I thought you might be delayed, while exerting yourselves so graciously to protect us all.'

Inghilla gave him a disdainful look. 'Spare us your sarcasm, Farbanni.'

The portly mage grinned happily. 'We must assume, by your early arrival, that only *lesser* Sisters are being entrusted with raising this magical shield?'

Aurilia saw the militia officers begin to look worried, and her mouth tightened. 'A high adept should be aware,' she said acidly, 'that what has been raised is not a shield but a mere *alarm*. Which doesn't need the full unity of the Nine. The song has woven a web in the air that will alert the camp if any outside magical force touches it.'

'And then,' Inghilla added with an icy smile, 'you heroic wizards can leap out of your mansions on wheels and defend us.'

She turned away, but Farbanni was unwilling to let it go. 'Yet I understood, Inghilla, that you claim extensive *mental* powers in your portion of the Earth-magic. Are those powers not equal to the task of perceiving any sorcerous approach?'

Inghilla's smile grew even icier. 'They are. *If* I wished to weaken myself by staying awake all night to exert my awareness. Which would also diminish my contribution to the Nine, to the detriment of this expedition. Does that strike you as a good idea, Farbanni?'

As Farbanni scowled, the elderly Vallawn began to laugh. 'Give it up, Farbanni, you're overmatched. Be grateful for the Sisters' web, since without it *you* might have to stay up all night to keep magical watch.'

At that point the prince gestured to them sharply. 'Come,' he snapped. 'Let us begin before more time is wasted.'

As the meeting came to order and the militia officers began to detail their final organizations, Aurilia's attention began to wander, especially towards certain songs of seeking and how she might convince the others of the Nine to use them in a

177

search of the distant Highlands for news of Red. But she grew more attentive as it became Inghilla's turn to describe the warrior women's readiness, once fully rested from their journey to the Grasslands. In the midst of the discussion, then, they all heard the sound of shouts and a small disturbance near the perimeter of the camp, as if sentries had issued a challenge.

Phaedran looked pointedly at Trochain, who gestured to one of his aides. 'See what that is,' he ordered.

But as the other officer began to rise, the flaps of the pavilion doorway were flung aside. And Red stepped through with a jaunty grin.

That put an end to the meeting. Aurilia flung herself into his arms, shimmering into her younger form. But her and everyone's pleasure at seeing Red safely back was then overshadowed – when Krost shouldered his way through the door to give Phaedran a darkly regretful look that was almost as full a report as was needed.

Aurilia failed to notice, at first, being concerned with the widespread discoloured bruising on the left side of Red's face and his wince, favouring that side of his body, when she hugged him. But even her joy subsided to some extent when Krost announced that his mission to recruit the giants had failed. For a moment they all sat silent, shaken by the blow to their hopes. But at last, stiffening his back, Phaedran waved a hand as if to brush the problem aside.

'We shall have to do without them,' he said heavily. 'Their aid would have been invaluable, but we are not *lost* without them.'

'Indeed, Highness,' Farbanni said ingratiatingly. 'They would have served in any case only in *physical* conflict. Lebarran may oppose us entirely with sorcery.'

'Not likely,' Aurilia said. 'We know he has the Zhraike.'

'And he may command other forces as well,' Inghilla added. 'Human, demonic, anything . . .'

'Even so,' old Vallawn said soothingly, 'I don't doubt that the militia and the warrior Sisters, despite the absence of the giants, will distinguish themselves in battle.'

'They will have to,' Krost rumbled.

'My men will not be found wanting,' Trochain said quickly.

178

Then he glanced around glumly. 'Yet I fear a loss of morale. The men have heard the rumour that the giants might come, and it has been a useful means of rallying their spirits.'

'Then you must find another,' Phaedran said coldly. 'And the giants, meanwhile, must hope that they will not come to rue this inaction.'

'As Red told them, very eloquently,' Krost said with a half-smile. 'And there you might find something for morale, Trochain. Tell the men that the new Corodel has joined them, fresh from single combat with a Highland giant.'

'You tried to fight a *giant*?' Aurilia said with a gasp. 'Is that how you were hurt?'

'I just took a tumble,' Red said vaguely.

'Perhaps that is why they will not come,' Farbanni said snidely. 'It seems a poor way to win their support.'

'That is not why,' Krost growled. 'When they refused to help, Red . . . spoke to them, a challenge was issued and he accepted. And tell your men this, Trochain. Just like the first Corodel – he *won*.'

Phaedran acquired a wintry smile as Krost swiftly filled in the details of the fight, which discomfited Red but impressed the others, even Farbanni.

'It is sad,' the prince said when Krost was done, 'that those who should have been allies became enemies. But no doubt I would have shared your anger, Cordell, just as I am grateful for your loyalty.' He looked slowly around at them all. 'Cordell's victory over a stronger foe may indeed be aired about, as a foreshadowing of our own. It is an inexact omen, but it will serve to set the mood for tomorrow – when, now that our forces are complete, we shall break camp and begin the southward march.'

That announcement quickly sent everyone off to see to last-minute details of organization. Red went with Aurilia as she and Inghilla returned to help with the Sisterhood's arrangements. But later, as the camp finally settled into silence and sleep, Aurilia and Red commandeered a small tent set some way apart from the main camp. Previously, on the way to the Western Woodlands and the Dome, they had kept their relationship at least discreet if not secret. But there, Aurilia was determined not to let Red out of her sight again. In the tent, as they undressed by the light of a small taper, she examined the heavy bruising that covered the side of his face and extended down over his left arm and side, amid a number of abrasions just starting to heal.

'Lie down,' she said, eluding his grasp and moving away. 'We can't have Corodel the giant-killer riding to war in a damaged condition.'

'I didn't kill him,' Red said idly. 'Just sort of discouraged him.' But he obediently stretched out on the cot, watching as she bent over her satchels that she had brought to the tent. It was a sight he never tired of, the play of her supple muscles under the honey-bronze skin that the taper's light was turning to purest gold. She turned and saw him watching, but for once did not respond with one of her wicked grins. Her face remained sombre as she returned to him with a jar of ointment.

'I wondered if you'd be angry,' he said tentatively, 'at my going off with Krost without telling you.'

'Not angry,' she said, dabbing ointment on to his injuries, 'just terribly worried. So it may be as well I didn't know sooner.'

Gently he tilted her chin up, seeing the shadows that lay deep in her eyes. 'And now you're even more worried – because we're setting off.'

She bit her lip. 'More than worried, Red. Terrified. Because when we begin the march, we start a process we can't control, towards an outcome we can't predict.'

'That's war, I suppose,' Red said lightly.

'It's also . . . an end to alternatives. Especially with someone as determined and stubborn as Phaedran. From this moment there can be no turning aside or back— '

'It's been like that for a while,' Red broke in. 'Because of Lebarran more than Phaedran.'

'I know. But now . . .' Sudden tears glistened in her eyes. 'I'm filled with foreboding, Red. I can't rid myself of a premonition that we're setting off towards some monstrous, inescapable doom . . .'

He put his arms around her, pulling her close. 'That's war, too,' he murmured into the veil of her hair. 'Terrible things happen, good people die . . . But we can't run from it.'

'No,' she agreed. 'But, Red . . . twice now, since we returned from the Dome, you have ridden away. And twice I have died a thousand deaths, once believing you had been killed, the second time just waiting fearfully. So now, riding into war, I want us to stay *together*. Go together to meet whatever fate awaits us. Die together, if die we must.'

'Yes,' Red said at once. 'That's how it'll be. I won't leave you again, Aurilia.'

She sighed and nestled against him. And for a while they simply lay there side by side, clinging together motionless and silent, and if Red was aware of the tears on her face he did not speak of them. But gradually other urgencies began to be asserted, other joinings that brought them finally into the long, slow surge, familiar and unique, carrying them up to the nearly unbearable peak and flinging them over, falling away then into a rediscovered peace where they clung together no less closely than before.

An unguessable time later, Red awoke with a start to full alertness. The first grey tendrils of dawn were probing into the tent, a few sleepy birds were greeting the morning on the plain outside – and Aurilia was watching him, propped on one elbow, her tawny hair tumbled over them like a blanket. Idly he gathered a handful, inhaling its spicy perfume.

'Can't you sleep?' he asked.

She lifted a bare shoulder. 'I slept. But dawn's breaking, and I'll have to attend to my duties by sun-up . . . and this time is too precious to be wasted in unconsciousness.'

Smiling, he raised himself towards her. But she paused, pulling back with a frown, staring around. Red blinked, taken aback – then went quite still as he realized what had distracted her.

The dawn, weirdly, seemed to be retreating. The dim light in the tent was waning, fading, as darkness regathered around them. Red reached out, half-blind in the new blackness, to find Aurilia. 'What . . .' he began.

'Ssh,' she hissed, her voice coming from the tent-flap. 'Get dressed. There's a sorcerous dark all around the camp, drawing in towards us.'

He sprang up, fumbling to relight the taper, reaching for his clothes, watching Aurilia flicker through the double shape-shift that brought her back to her youthful form, but fully dressed in doeskin tunic and trousers. Reaching into her largest satchel, she drew out a slim sword in a plain sheath, which she buckled around her waist. Dragging on his boots and grabbing his own sword, Red followed as she stepped warily out.

Darkness prevailed all around them. A chill, dank darkness, with small eddying air currents. The light from the taper spilled from the tent but could not penetrate that blackness for more than a pace or two. When Red drew his sword, even its rainbow glow could not light up that uncanny night beyond the spot where they stood.

'It's . . .' Aurilia began. But her voice was drowned by a sudden piercing shrillness like the highest note of a flute amplified into a painful scream. As Red winced from the noise, Aurilia clutched his arm.

'The web,' she yelled above the shrillness. 'This magical darkness has drawn near enough to set off the alarm!'

He nodded, gratefully noting that the web's scream was settling into a steady high tone, sweet and pure and slowly fading. Above it he could hear all the sounds of a disturbed and frightened camp, many of them close by – the whinnying of horses, the thud of hundreds of running or stumbling feet, the clatter and clang of weapons being awkwardly readied by warriors who could not see, the harsh, nervy voices of officers trying to impose some control on the mêlée within that impenetrable dark.

'Come,' Aurilia said, still gripping Red's arm. 'We must get to the others. The wizards will oppose this darkness, and so must the Nine.'

But they had taken only two or three wary steps in the blackness when they were halted by the sudden shock of a very different sound. More piercing than the note of the web, far more raucous and discordant, it was a raw-throated screech of hate and menace, flung down from the invisible sky in a bestial chorus – which Red and Aurilia had heard before.

'*Zhraike!*' she cried, staring up. 'Here, on the Grasslands!'

Red looked up as well, tightening his grip on the sword, recalling the terrible winged half-demons that had been sent by their master to hunt in the western swamps.

'Here we go,' he said bitterly. 'Lebarran just declared war.'

PART TWO

THE MARCH

SEVENTEEN

They set off through the darkness, Red holding the sword high to make the most of its glow. Aurilia strode ahead unhesitatingly, seeming to know exactly where she was going, ignoring the pandemonium that they could hear spreading through the camp all around. But not panic, Red realized. Despite everything, the movements sounded mostly purposeful. And there were torches and braziers flaring up everywhere, with militiamen forming up swiftly, readying their crossbows – while beyond them Red could hear the unmistakable bass roar of Krost, who seemed to be organizing the defence of the horses.

But all the while, in the inky blackness above, the Zhraike were shrieking their battle-cries and no doubt wheeling and poising for the assault. Once, Red was sure that he glimpsed a huge winged shape with spear-sharp beak out-thrust, swooping down through the darkness directly above them. But it seemed to veer away, as if unwilling to face the luminous sword. And a moment later Aurilia was tearing open the flaps of a hemisphere of canvas looming almost invisibly before them, then pulling him with her into a soft glow of light that made him blink with its suddenness.

The rest of the Nine were gathered in that tent, grouped around the tiny wizened Naemony who looked as frail as ever but quite undaunted. They had already begun to sing, a low throaty music that was almost a chant, and Aurilia squeezed Red's arm and went to join them, weaving her voice into their chorus. Glancing around, Red saw a number of other Sisters in the tent with slim swords at their hips and short bows in their hands. Some of them had arrows already nocked and ready, and Red noticed a bright sheen like silver running along the edges of every arrowhead. The same silvering ran along the edges of the drawn sword held by the broad-shouldered leader of that troop of women – Brennia, who turned to smile at Red and beckon him to her.

'We'll do more good standing guard outside, while they sing,' she told him.

He nodded, falling in beside her as the warrior women moved to the door. By then the song had grown louder, more strident and higher pitched as if to counter the continuing, chilling screams of the unseen monsters in the sky. And as he and the women stepped back outside, Red had the idea that the darkness had begun to give way a little. His sword's brightness seemed to reach farther around him – and above him, as he again raised it at arm's length above his head.

In that instant he heard a fearsome Zhraike cry that seemed only another sword's length above the weapon's gleaming point. As he jerked his head up, seeing nothing, a nearby Sister whipped up her bow and fired a silvery arrow towards the sound. The demonic cry at once turned into a shriek of pain, and they heard the crash of great wings as the wounded monster flapped wildly away.

The other warrior women grinned, and some cheered softly, without lessening their watchful scrutiny of the darkness above. It was still diminishing, Red saw, growing thin and somehow frayed from ground level upwards. He could hear encouraged shouts from the militia as the men noticed as well, and could hear the irregular thrum of crossbows as some men also fired hopefully up towards the screeching Zhraike.

'Let's hope they can find their bolts, after,' one of the Sisters said mockingly. 'They'll need them when they can *see* the enemy.'

'Just hope those bolts don't come down on their heads, or ours,' Brennia snapped. 'They should hold fire till they're sure of a target.'

'But they're *men*,' said another laughing voice. 'Always in too much of a hurry.'

As all the women laughed, Red – still holding his sword high – began to feel both useless and slightly foolish. In the tent behind him the song of the Nine was still developing its eerie harmonies, and he guessed that the wizards of Quamarr would be working their own magics somewhere near by. Certainly the counter-magic was taking effect, forcing the darkness away more swiftly so that he found he could see Brennia and the others around him, and could dimly discern other people farther away like figures seen in a mist. He saw the horses' paddock come into view, then, and in the midst of the milling, frightened animals he saw Krost mounted bareback on Wolle, a huge torch in one hand and the iron quarterstaff in the other, roaring balefully up at the sky, a steady stream of the harsh language of the giants.

Brennia glanced over that way and grinned. 'The horses seem safe enough. What's he saying?'

'No idea,' Red replied. 'But his people and the Zhraike are old enemies, so it's probably a curse and a challenge, both.'

The words seemed almost to have summoned the reality. As he spoke, a single Zhraike suddenly burst through the retreating vault of blackness, above the paddock. It was like a man-sized bird, but scaly rather than feathered, its skin a sickly glistening greenish-grey, its neck long and mottled, with claws like metal hooks, beak like the curved blade of a sword and an immense spread of powerful wings. It plummeted down at Krost with a hate-filled scream, wings booming, beak poised to stab.

Krost stood up in his stirrups, eyes alight with battle-hunger, and hurled the torch up into the diving monster's face. And as it thrashed its wings to avoid the flame, Krost's other hand brought the great staff around in a whirling sweep. The snap of the neck could be heard above all the rest of the uproar of the camp. The body of the Zhraike was smashed out of the air, flung away beyond the rope barrier of the paddock, crashing to the ground in a motionless heap.

As Krost then brandished the quarterstaff and roared another furious challenge, the thinning, weakening darkness abruptly vanished like an image from a dream. Above them the sky was revealed in all the welcome fresh light of the dawn, its rosiness spreading a warm flush on the eastern horizon. The men and women on the ground stared up at the silhouettes of about a dozen Zhraike, receding as their broad wings carried them away. And around the camp, with the return of peace and brightness, small birds began hesitantly to resume their greetings to the new day.

Aurilia flung open the doorway of the tent and stepped out, followed by the rest of the Nine. Smiling, she moved to Red, watching with him as the last Zhraike vanished in the distance. Around them the noise of fear and battle had given way to shouts of joy and celebration, mixed with laughter. A crowd of militia ran exuberantly to surround the corpse of the fallen Zhraike, prodding it, marvelling at its size. As Krost came away from the paddock, Prince Phaedran stepped out of his pavilion and stared around. With him emerged old Vallawn, leaning on his crooked stick, looking placidly up at the sky as if it was just another pleasant summer morning – with Farbanni and the other mages edging more nervously out behind him.

An unspoken summons brought them all to gather in front of the royal pavilion, where Trochain and another officer joined them, looking pleased.

'A useful skirmish, Highness,' Trochain was saying as he came up. 'No losses or injuries among us – and our people have faced an unnatural threat with fortitude while our magic has repelled the attack.'

'Along with a certain strong right arm,' Red remarked, grinning at Krost.

The prince's nod was cool. 'It is too soon for self-congratulation, Marshal. We have not yet begun to be tested.'

'But, your Highness,' the other officer protested, 'whatever the enemy was trying to do, he surely has been thwarted!'

'Not at all,' Inghilla said sternly. 'The prince is quite right. This was probably only a minor probe by Lebarran, perhaps to unnerve us and weaken our will. We did not drive the Zhraike away – they were withdrawn. And we could thrust away the darkness with no great difficulty only because the spell was weakened by being imposed on us from some distance.'

'Quite so,' Vallawn agreed. 'And it was an impressive magic, even so, to send from so far away.'

Trochain looked unhappily over at the militia camp, still

190

echoing with merry shouts and laughter as some of the men paraded the dead Zhraike around like a trophy. 'However you view this skirmish, sir,' he said at last, 'the men are hailing it as a victory.'

'In which case, Trochain,' the prince said frostily, 'you must correct them. Over-confidence could be as dangerous as low morale.'

Krost growled deep in his throat. 'If we can fight off an attack from Lebarran while we are marching into his valley – *that* will be a time for cheering.'

As Lebarran's hand twitched, the image on the scrying-bowl pulled back from its focus on the group around the prince to show a broader view of the orderly furore in the army camp, as preparations began for the first day of the march. Around the bowl, in the variety of chairs that they had magically brought to the spell-chamber, the other sorcerers of the Order cast covert glances at one another, and at the brooding face of their leader. Only Gul Ist was absent, taking his turn to keep watch against any new assault by the Unformed.

But there had been no further attempted breakthrough by the monster. And for the four men around Lebarran, at that moment, there were more immediate concerns, prominent among which was the condition of the Magister himself. His desperate escape from the Void and the struggle with the Unformed had left the signs of fatigue and stress all too clearly visible upon him – chalkily pale skin, more deeply furrowed brow, sunken and dark-ringed eyes, even a faint tremor in the hands. All of which finally prompted old Ostyril to break the silence with a nervous clearing of his throat.

'I wonder, Magister,' he began, 'what could be said to have been the purpose of that . . . *intrusion* into the enemy camp.'

Lebarran said nothing for a moment, still staring fixedly at the shifting pictures in the bowl – the practised striking of the camp, the saddling of horses and loading of wagons, the prince and his officers poring over maps, Aurilia and the others of the Nine at work alongside the warrior women, Red and Krost watching the burial of the dead Zhraike . . .

191

Another twitch of his hand stilled the images, holding on a close-up of Red's face. Lebarran's yellow eyes hooded as he scowled at the image, recalling the purpose for which he had summoned the ape-like demon, recalling also the moment not so long before when his magic had sensed the distant banishment of the demon by some other power.

'No matter,' he muttered half-audibly to himself. 'When I put an end to this irksome conflict I can find another means to probe the mystery of the one called Hallifort.'

'Magister?' Ostyril said, bewildered.

The bowl's shiny-black surface went blank as Lebarran gestured, before turning his fatigue-dulled gaze on to the old man. 'What did you say?'

Ostyril again cleared his throat. 'I . . . we wondered if that thrust at Phaedran's camp was . . . entirely worthwhile.'

'Worthwhile?' Lebarran repeated harshly. 'Are you of the opinion that nothing was achieved?'

Ostyril glanced around at the others for support. 'You . . . you did not say what you *hoped* to achieve.'

'We assumed you wished to frighten them,' added old Dhaminai, twisting his straggly beard. 'To undermine their resolve . . .'

'Or perhaps,' Yannahac said quickly, noting the Magister's scowl, 'it was just an early foray to . . . to test . . . um . . .'

As his voice trailed away, Lebarran snorted wearily. 'If I had sought to test the perceptions of you all, they have been found wanting.'

'Come, Lebarran,' big Zykiador said fulsomely. 'You summoned us to conclave, directed us as to the spell, yet told us nothing of its purpose. What are we to surmise?'

'And in any case,' Dhaminai quavered, gesturing at the bowl's blank face, 'the prince's forces have *not* been unnerved or undermined. Instead, they have been emboldened! Their resolve has been strengthened by what they see as a victory!'

The others mumbled wary agreement, though Yannahac managed at the same time to look dubious. And he flinched slightly as Lebarran snorted again.

'Since you cannot see for yourselves,' he snarled, 'let me

instruct you. The effect of our *intrusion*, as Ostyril calls it, has been much as I hoped. Certainly I would have expected you to realize that these aren't cowards or incompetents marching against us but trained militiamen, along with adepts and witches of proven ability. Do you really believe that by hurling a mere spell of darkness and a few Zhraike at them we could undermine their *resolve*?'

The others glanced at one another again, looking crestfallen or puzzled or both.

'To afflict the courage and spirit of Phaedran's forces,' Lebarran went on, 'would have required a far more extensive array of spells. Can your limited wit not see that in sending that extent of power all the way to the Central Grasslands we would have expended an unacceptable amount of our strength?'

As some of the others slowly nodded, Zykiador still looked puzzled. 'Then why send anything at all?'

Lebarran rubbed his eyes wearily. 'Yannahac almost had the answer, but failed to grasp it. In fact we have achieved two purposes today. First, we've tested their power, revealingly. Remember, the entire group of wizards including Vallawn himself could only barely begin to affect our spell of darkness. Not until the Circle of Nine joined in as well did they begin to throw off the spell. Can you not see? *We* were acting from a great distance, only five of us in conclave, yet *they* required virtually their full strength to oppose us!'

Yannahac clapped his hands with obsequious delight. 'Oh, yes! You have defined their limits, Magister!'

'Precisely,' Lebarran rasped. 'So we may ask – how will they withstand us at close range? When also being assailed by my full complement of Zhraike, and the Stone People as well?'

The others were smiling and nodding, while Yannahac snickered.

'As for our second purpose,' Lebarran continued, 'it lies in the very effect that so worries Dhaminai – that they now believe they have won an early victory. So we may let them march south full of false confidence, which we can enhance by leaving them unmolested awhile. We may let those puffed-up wizards and the rest believe that they are strong enough to prevail.

193

Then, when they are closer to this valley, and less wary . . .'

'We will destroy them!' Yannahac cried, giggling.

'Precisely,' Lebarran said again, his voice sepulchral. 'Indeed, when our enemies are nearer, when we are rested and ready to attack, we might concentrate at first on some of their more important *leaders*. Once the army is headless, the rest of it can be effortlessly wiped out at our leisure.'

With that he lifted one slightly unsteady hand, gestured, and vanished from their midst, chair and all.

The other four blinked with mild surprise, and then Yannahac laughed merrily. 'See how your doubt was misplaced, Ostyril! His grasp is as sure as ever!'

Zykiador sneered. 'You would say so, Yannahac, if he was on his deathbed.'

Dhaminai shook his grey head worriedly. 'He speaks of the enemy's false confidence – but it does *my* confidence no good to see how the marks of his ordeal in the Void are still upon him.'

As Ostyril and Zykiador murmured agreement, Yannahac fluttered thin fingers dismissively. 'We are *all* tired,' he told them. 'Especially with having to maintain the watch against the Unformed. And the Magister himself is maintaining so *many* magics – the veiling clouds over the valley, the canopy above us, his scrying power . . . But you'll see, he'll recover himself fully as he always has and will crush those petty fools under his foot.'

'Perhaps not that simply,' Zykiador remarked, gazing into a brimming goblet that had appeared in his hand. 'But I do like his idea of singling out some of the leading figures.' He smiled maliciously. 'We might especially enjoy dealing with Vallawn. A most dangerous old viper.'

'I believe our first target should be the witches,' Ostyril declared with a death's-head smile. 'Old Naemony is already so feeble as to be nearly helpless. If we kill her, the unity of the Nine is broken – and one half of their magical force is then rendered ineffectual, at a stroke!'

EIGHTEEN

Red glared up at the nearest glacier as if it had affronted him. 'We might as well have stayed in the Highlands, Krost, and let the army come to us without all this retracing of steps.'

Krost winked at Aurilia. 'I thought you had some special reason to hurry back from the Highlands, Red.'

'Really?' Red pretended to look mystified. 'What could that have been?' Then he laughed and dodged as Aurilia, in her younger form, swung a mock-blow at him.

'For once you were sensible with your retracing of steps,' she told him. 'You and Krost could have easily been picked off if you'd been waiting around in the mountains alone.'

'Oh, I know the theory,' Red replied. 'If we all stay together, we stay protected. But do you call this *together*?'

He gestured at the slope below the crest where they had halted, and the other two looked down with glum expressions. It had too often been the same scene during all the days when the prince's force had wound its way through the foothills and up at last on to the higher levels of the mountains. On the slope that Red and his friends had just climbed, the whole company was stretched out, scattered and straggling along a lengthy and erratic line as it crawled up the dusty, gravelly steepness. The slope was the floor of a rock-strewn gorge that rose like a natural corridor through one of the great ranges of the Highlands. But it was proving a taxing path, its steepness and treacherous footing holding everyone back, especially the heavily laden pack animals and the many wagons and carriages. And everyone's progress was made more difficult by desiccating heat as the gorge trapped and amplified the blaze of the summer sun.

Red and Aurilia, keeping to their pledge to remain together whenever possible, had been riding with a troop of warrior women that had assumed the lead position for that day. But at the top of the slope they had all paused, dismounting to rest their horses and to watch the progress of the rest of the army behind them. There they had been joined by Krost, also concerned about the potentially dangerous straggling of the army's columns. As, of course, were others. Towards the middle of the slope, Marshall Trochain and his officers were sweating and red-faced in their furious attempts to bring the militia and the pack-animals into a tighter formation. And nearly everyone else was just as sweaty, and even more eloquently profane, as they fought the slope's unstable gravel. By far the most imaginative curses came from the drivers of the wagons and of the awkward, oversized carriages that were the wizards' homes on wheels. By then the mages themselves had taken to horseback, to avoid being heaved and tossed in the lurching vehicles as if in small boats in a storm. But amid all the struggling, creeping movement and clouds of dust Red spotted the more compact closed carriage of Evelane – and saw that the prince himself had taken the reins, trying to give his daughter the smoothest ride possible.

Krost saw that as well, and swung back up on to Wolle's broad back. 'Phaedran could do with some help, I think,' he growled, and trotted away down the slope.

'He'll probably unhitch the horses and pull the carriage up by himself,' Red remarked.

'Phaedran may wish he'd left Evelane home after all,' Aurilia said sadly.

'Stay together, stay protected,' Red reminded her. 'And you can't say the idea isn't working. We haven't heard anything from Lebarran since that first time on the Grasslands.'

She glanced around at the mountain crags to the south. 'That just makes me wonder what he's up to.'

'Very cheerful,' Red said with a grimace. 'Why don't we think positive thoughts? Maybe he's gone on holiday. Maybe he's got religion. Maybe his Unformed creature has . . .'

Her fingers on his mouth stopped him. 'Don't speak of it,' she said softly. 'Don't tempt the fates.'

'Whatever you say.' He smiled crookedly. 'What can we speak of?'

She remained silent, gazing down the slope into the rolling swirls of dust rising towards them. 'We might go back down and see if we can help – with Naemony and *her* carriage.'

Red sighed. 'Looks like being a long dusty day.'

They guided their horses down the slope along the side of the trail, letting them pick their own way over the rock and gravel, aiming for a carriage something like Evelane's but plainer and narrower. It was the one that had brought Naemony from the Fastness, since in her delicate old age she was unable to ride a horse for any length of time. Though Red wondered if she was any better off in the carriage, watching it pitch and sway over the rough ground.

Aurilia called a greeting to the muscular Sister driving the wagon, as she and Red rode up to keep pace beside the carriage. 'How is she?' Aurilia asked when they were near enough to speak quietly.

The driver shrugged. 'Seems to sleep a lot. Like a half-sleep, restless and twitchy.'

Aurilia nodded unhappily. 'It's not the gentlest ride.'

'Not easy for anyone,' the driver agreed. 'But you'd never hear her complain.' She gestured with a jerk of the head. 'Inghilla's in with her now.'

'I'll join them for a moment,' Aurilia said to Red.

Red took her reins as she slid from the saddle, climbed up on to the side of the carriage and disappeared through its narrow entrance covered by heavy hangings. With all the clamour of the army around them, Red could hear only a murmur of voices from within, but he had no wish to eavesdrop. As Grilena paced beside the carriage, he gazed relaxedly at the mountains rising all around the gorge, so sublimely beautiful, so forbiddingly indifferent, and tried to enjoy that brief moment despite the yelling and cursing soldiers around him, the neighing of unhappy horses, the squeaks and groans of wagon wheels, the shouts of officers, the crunch on gravel of boots and hoofs. But the contemplative lull ended when the hangings at the side of the carriage parted and Aurilia emerged with Inghilla. Not, it seemed, on the best of terms.

' . . . let some healers help,' Aurilia was saying as they stepped down to walk along beside the crawling carriage. 'If she could sleep properly at night, when we're stopped . . .'

'You can't heal old age, Aurilia,' Inghilla said loftily. 'I've told Naemony time and again, as I told her before we left – a journey such as this is simply *beyond* her. Even coming from the Fastness on level roads overtaxed her. As for these mountains . . .'

Aurilia's mouth tightened. 'Yet she's here, Inghilla. So we should be trying to make the journey easier.'

'No,' Inghilla interrupted. 'We could offer only short-lived, ineffective relief. What we *should* do . . .' She paused, frowning as she studied Aurilia. 'I've wanted to speak to you about this in private, my dear, as I have spoken to some others of the Nine . . .'

She was slowing her pace, drawing Aurilia back from the carriage so they would not be overheard. Curious, Red also slowed Grilena so that he could just make out their words.

'About what?' Aurilia was asking suspiciously.

'About Naemony,' the other woman said. 'And the likelihood that this journey will kill her, even before we confront Lebarran.'

Aurilia blanched at that, but her gaze remained wary. 'She knows the risks. Just as she knows that the Nine must be here in unity.'

'Quite so,' Inghilla said urgently. 'Which is what I've said to the others. My feeling is that we should relieve Naemony of her duties – let her return to the Fastness, put an end to her hardship.'

Aurilia looked astonished. 'But that would destroy the unity, and weaken us dangerously!'

'No, no.' Inghilla's smile was almost a smirk. 'Naemony could first designate her successor, as she must shortly do in any case. And then we can choose another to be Named into the Circle of Nine. Well before we reach Lebarran's valley.'

'That's ridiculous!' Aurilia snapped. 'A new leader and a new Name, to be introduced *here*, on the way to a war? How could we possibly manage the initiation, the rites of elevation and Naming . . .'

'We can find ways,' Inghilla said vaguely. 'Abbreviate the ceremonies . . .'

'If we do that, the new Name could reduce the united power of the Nine!' Aurilia almost shouted.

Inghilla's face closed. 'It will be more dangerously reduced when Naemony dies in these mountains.'

'*When?*' Aurilia repeated furiously. 'She's not dying yet, Inghilla!' Then her eyes narrowed. 'Do I detect *ambition* here? Are you trying to push Naemony aside so you can take her place?'

'I think *I* detect jealousy and rivalry in *your* words!' Inghilla replied, glaring. 'It's well known that I am likeliest to be chosen as successor!'

'Even if that's so,' Aurilia snapped, green eyes ablaze, 'you'll have to wait awhile yet! The absurdity that you propose would demand the unanimous agreement of the Nine – but you do *not* have mine, and you know very well that you would not have Naemony's!'

As her voice lifted, and a few heads turned with surprise at the sound of her anger, Red edged Grilena nearer to them, trying to think of a way to divert the quarrel. But Inghilla, her face suffused with rage, glanced in his direction and turned with a snort to stalk away. And Aurilia, looking just as stormy, flung herself up into her saddle and snatched the reins from Red.

'Let's ride on,' she snapped. 'I need some fresh air out of this dust.'

Great, Red thought dourly as she kicked her startled horse into a clattering rush up the slope. Now we have disharmony at the top. Let's hope Lebarran isn't listening.

By late afternoon, with the difficulties of the gorge behind them, the army's columns had tightened up into a more compact and steady formation, moving smoothly, remaining readily defensible. Their route had led them down into a shallow and sheltered vale, offering the grass of mountain meadows and fresh water from a bubbling spring. And by then, as it was decided to stop and make camp, Aurilia's anger had subsided –

199

though not her concern, as she collected two of the more capable healers from among the warrior women and took them to Naemony's carriage. As usual, Red went along, then idled restlessly outside the closed vehicle, watching the sunset brighten the mountain peaks, its colours echoed in the camp-fires that were springing up to push back the dusk shadowing the vale. A small warm breeze gently ruffled his hair, carrying with it the scent of the wildflowers that decorated the vale's meadows. Inhaling that perfume, he thought wistfully how good it would be if there was no dark violence and evil menacing them, if he and Aurilia might simply stroll across those twilit grasses in tranquillity, perhaps to find a private hidden nest for themselves among the fragrant flowers . . .

A heavy hand on his shoulder dispelled that train of thought. 'Did you enjoy the day?' Krost asked him jovially.

'It wasn't too bad,' Red said, 'up with the leaders. Not so much dust.'

Krost laughed. 'I think I have eaten most of a mountain, today, in those dust clouds. But this place makes up for it.'

'How's the princess?' Red enquired.

'Deep in her shell,' Krost said, his good humour fading. 'Not speaking, eating very little . . . Phaedran, though he would not say so, is fearful that one time she will withdraw too deeply ever to come out again.'

Red nodded sadly. 'It could happen. Meanwhile, poor old Naemony is having a rough time as well, and Aurilia's clashing with Inghilla over it . . . No one's having much fun on this trip, Krost.'

'No one does, on an army's march,' Krost rumbled. 'I only hope that Naemony is not too weak, for we are drawing close to our enemy.' He pointed southward with the iron staff. 'There is a high cleft there, Red, see, which will take us across another height of land. And then, if Trochain's old maps are true, there is a broken twisted trail down among some cliffs, leading to Lebarran's hideaway. The Clouded Valley.'

Red looked uneasily at the distant cleft, feeling slightly chilled by the awareness of their enemy's relative proximity. By then the sunset's colours had mostly faded and darkness was pouring down over the vale. Beyond the cleft he could see the first stars begin to show their icy glimmering – and as the breeze brushed by him again, somewhat cooler on his skin, he suddenly felt a yearning to be beside the warm reassurance of a fire, next to the comforting prospect of his and Aurilia's small cosy tent.

Behind him he heard her voice as the door to Naemony's carriage opened, and as Krost turned to greet her he began to turn as well, ready to draw her away towards the promise of that camp-fire. But he paused as a faraway movement caught his eye. Above the cleft that Krost had pointed out he saw a flicker of light, flashing across the darkened sky at an impressive speed. Catch a falling star, he said idly to himself, watching. But it was not like any meteorite he had ever seen. It seemed not to be falling, but *flying* – in a long, smooth curve, arching slightly downwards, as if . . .

As if heading for him.

And terrifyingly fast, he realized. And dipping down more steeply as it streaked forward, by then unmistakably heading for the camp-site, if not precisely for Red himself. 'Krost . . .?' he said hesitantly, hoping that the dwarf-giant would tell him that it was a natural phenomenon in the Highlands. But as Krost began to turn enquiringly towards him, the point of light came hurtling down.

Its flight was making a high-pitched sound like a breathy shriek as it came, extending itself into a shape like a huge glittering javelin, spearing towards a group of militia officers on the far side of the camp. And the breathy sound of it became a man's agonized scream as the bright javelin-shape struck, transfixing one of the men from neck to groin.

'*Mage-fire!*' Krost's great bellow was deafening. 'Get under cover! *Shield* yourselves!'

As his roar echoed across the vale, he seized Red and almost flung him towards the limited shelter of the carriage. Aurilia was already leaping back through the carriage door, shifting into her older form as she went. All around, Red heard the camp explode into uproar, panicky voices raised in enquiry, officers yelling, people running this way and that through the darkness. Near the prince's pavilion he saw a number of the mages hurrying into shelter, their hands aglow with magic. Others of the Nine were moving purposefully towards Naemony's carriage, where Aurilia's voice was already rising in an eerie song, joined by the quavery tones of her aged leader. And everyone else in the camp seemed, like Red, to be staring up at the starlit sky.

Where many more, dozens more, of the fiery points of light were visible, moving in blazing arcs down from the mountaintops towards the vale.

And where, among them, just visible in silhouette against the stars, storming towards the camp on huge wings, came wave upon wave of Zhraike.

NINETEEN

Red moved instinctively to the door of the carriage, sword in hand, watching the ghastly attack descend upon them. Aurilia and Naemony were still singing, inside, and Inghilla brushed past Red to join them while the rest of the Nine, unable to fit themselves into the narrow carriage, drew as close as possible to the doorway to form the unity of the song. By then Krost had bounded away to join the soldiery as they organized to face the Zhraike, and a troop of warrior women had appeared out of the darkness to surround the carriage, bows ready to protect their leaders.

Brennia, who had brought the troop, nodded to Red as she came to stand beside him, nocking an arrow. By then the flaming spears of mage-fire had begun their deadly fall on to the camp, while the Zhraike had swung away to attack from another angle out of darker portions of sky.

'We could do with more light,' Brennia said almost casually, 'to see where the Zhraike come.'

'More than this mage-fire?' Red asked tersely, watching one of the fiery javelins strike down into a tent, which erupted into flame. But then an idea came to him. 'Do you have anything like *flares*? Some kind of light or flame that you can shoot upwards?'

'Yes!' Brennia said quickly. Whirling, she flung orders at her troop, and three of them sprinted away into the shadows. 'A good idea, Red,' she said, turning back to him. 'No one fights well in the dark.' She glanced up and her smile vanished. 'Now guard yourself, my friend.'

Red braced himself, gripping the sword-hilt fiercely, as the mage-fire hurtled down and the darkened sky filled with the raucous battle-cry of Zhraike. It took a huge effort to keep standing there when his body and instincts wanted him to crouch and turn his back and burrow under cover. He heard the song within the carriage rise into a skin-crawling ululation, and from a short distance away he also heard the wizards' voices in a harsh muffled chant. And from nowhere, two enormous hazy shapes began to unfold in the air above the camp, like vast misshapen colourless umbrellas, with the stars and the falling mage-fire looking blurred and smeared through their transparency.

At once some of the mage-fire spears were deflected aside by the swelling strength of those shields, to fall harmlessly on empty ground. But some others of the blazing shapes broke through the protection, and those were no longer javelins but more compact shapes like malformed cylinders. And where they landed, they *exploded*, like small bombs. With each explosion, their flame flew in every direction, felling men and women, igniting tents and wagons. Suddenly the vale was alight with fire from a score or more spots, with militiamen and Sisters frantically trying to quench the blazes while also trying to elude the next murderous explosion.

Yet throughout it all the voices of the Nine rose in their song, and the incantation of the wizards struggled on, and the shielding above the camp strengthened, its two separate layers almost conjoining. As the layers steadied, more of the mage-fire was flung aside or exploded harmlessly against their surface, the flame flowing like liquid over the eerie translucency before vanishing entirely.

But in the wake of the mage-fire, unaffected by magical barriers raised against magical weapons, came the Zhraike.

They plunged down almost like spears themselves, before halting their dive at the last instant with great thunderous sweeps of wings, to slash and tear with talons as well as the stabbing beaks. Yet even as the first of the horrors began their dives, the warrior women responded. The Sisters dispatched by Brennia had done their work and spread their word, and all over the camp small pots of bright flame had been made ready. Nor was it ordinary fire, for as the silver-edged metal of the Sisters' arrowheads was dipped into the fire-pots it ignited at once in a white-hot blaze. Suddenly the sky was bright with the flaming arrows, exposing the Zhraike as they dived and finding targets as well, so that many of the winged monsters fell screaming with arrows embedded in their flesh and witch-fire enveloping their scaly bodies.

But as the militiamen hurried to make use as well of the pots of witch-fire, the Zhraike were also finding their targets in scores of deadly battles across the camp. Then it grew clear that many of the half-demon creatures were attacking special targets, the more important areas – and individuals – in the camp. One large Zhraike group hurled itself towards the cluster of wizards, another at a group of militia officers including Trochain, a larger one at the prince's pavilion where Krost's presence was obvious from the stream of enraged bellowing.

And yet another considerable band of Zhraike aimed itself at the light carriage of Naemony, and the Named Nine gathered in and around it. Brennia and her troop resisted heroically, igniting and firing a non-stop stream of bright arrows in a tireless outpouring. But though many Zhraike fell in flames, there always seemed to be more to replace them – while the defenders of the Nine were running out of arrows. Until at last Brennia fired her last shot, flung her bow aside and drew her silver-edged sword, glancing at Red with a grin.

'Time for another fencing lesson, Corodel.'

Red returned her grin. 'As long as this isn't the final exam.'

Then he spun away so that they were standing more or less back to back, as a dozen screaming Zhraike fell upon them.

He had never known a fight like it, being attacked by stabbing, slashing weapons from *above*, having to wield his sword over his head to parry and thrust and strike. His balance was threatened by the buffeting of huge Zhraike wings, he feared his arm would swiftly tire in that upraised position, yet he fought grimly, chopping and jabbing and dodging, while around him he could hear the clash of the warrior women's blades and a steady quiet flow of curses from Brennia. And beyond those sounds and the screeches of the Zhraike above him he could distantly hear other swords ringing, and the thrum of crossbows, and the cries of the wounded, punctuated by some continuing blasts of mage-fire. Yet, weirdly, the song of the Nine remained audible through all the bedlam of battle. As Red hacked at a flapping wing and blocked a beak-thrust in the same motion, he was vaguely aware that those of the Nine unable to get into Naemony's carriage had simply taken refuge beneath it, without missing a note of their shielding song.

But not too far away, the wizards were close to disaster. Many of their group, as the Zhraike fell upon them, had been unable to manage self-protection or counter-attack while also maintaining the spell of shielding over the whole camp. And the militiamen detailed to defend them had suffered grievous losses in the first moments of the attack. As the attack went on, five of the wizards were felled, dead or badly wounded, with Farbanni among them. And though old Vallawn stood firm, his hands bright and power crackling from his upraised stick, terror was taking effect on the others, breaking down their concentration. Two more fell then to Zhraike talons, while above the camp the wizards' portion of the sky-shield shook and wavered, which allowed a few more blazing bursts of mage-fire to break through and fall upon the battlefield.

And one of them struck and exploded only a few paces behind the carriage of Naemony and the Nine.

The carriage itself took most of the force of the explosion, though several of its women defenders were hurled to the ground by the blast. As Red risked a desperate glance, he saw that flame was engulfing its far side where the blast had struck. At a warning cry from Brennia he whirled back to the fray, chopping at a scaly neck, ducking away from a sweep of talons. But as he ducked a powerful wing crashed against him like a club and flung him to the ground.

He landed in a controlled fall, rolling instinctively. The Zhraike that had struck him, following him down, shrieked as it impaled itself on the upthrusting blade of his sword. The grisly corpse fell heavily on to him, briefly encumbering his sword-arm – but no Zhraike took advantage of that moment.

In that instant, the doorway of the blazing carriage was opened wide, and through it burst Aurilia and Inghilla, supporting Naemony between them, her frail body looking even tinier in a voluminous nightdress. Aurilia was in her younger form again, and had drawn the sword that she had carried since the Grasslands, its silvered edges gleaming. And as Red struggled up, as Brennia and the other women turned towards their leaders, all the remaining Zhraike attacking that group wheeled up as if at a signal – before flinging themselves down again, in a terrifying mass, at the emerging trio of women.

Before anyone could get to them, the flock of monsters broke away again, flapping powerfully up into the air, shrieking in demonic triumph. On the ground below them they left two of their number, felled by Aurilia's blade. But they also left Aurilia and Inghilla in a crumpled heap, blood pooling around their bodies.

And in the claws of two of the rising Zhraike who were flying in tandem, Red saw the tiny body of Naemony, nightdress in rags, dangling limp and unmoving in that taloned grip like a handful of broken twigs.

All over the camp-site the other Zhraike also abandoned the battle, swarming into the air in a wild gyrating pattern around the two who bore Naemony, celebrating their monstrous achievement. With that the rain of mage-fire also came to an end – and the defenders on the ground lowered their weapons and stared upwards in horror. The surviving Sisters were crying out in grief and despair, and their voices rose even higher as they saw Naemony's fragile limbs wriggle feebly for an instant, showing that although perhaps insensible in that cruel grasp she was being carried off alive.

But Red saw and heard none of those things. All he heard was the inward cry of his own private horror, all he saw was Aurilia beside Inghilla in that spreading pool of blood. He launched himself towards her – but despite his frenzy Brennia reached her first. Brennia, whose hands not only wielded deadly weapons but also magically staunched deadly wounds.

Dropping to his knees beside them, Red gasped with shock as Brennia half-raised Aurilia's head and shoulders. Aurilia looked beyond hope – motionless and unrecognizable, her face and one shoulder covered with blood like enshrouding scarlet

207

cloth. But Brennia placed her hands upon those veils of blood, and where her touch rested the bleeding miraculously stopped. Yet the cruel gashes in the flesh remained, the terrible furrows across Aurilia's brow and cheek that had somehow missed her eye before going on to rip through the cloth and skin of her shoulder. Sickness rose in Red's throat to see Aurilia so damaged. But with the sickness came relief as well, for clearly she was still alive, still breathing, though half-stunned with eyes closed. Calling her name, he reached to touch her, to waken her, and at his touch her eyes opened – her shocked gaze reaching past him to fix on the Zhraike high above, still all flocking and screeching around the pair carrying Naemony. Whose bony limbs still twitched, failingly.

'Mother,' Aurilia whispered. Then she turned her gaze on to the other survivors of the Nine, gathered near by, huddled and weeping.

'No!' Aurilia cried out in fury. 'Call her! *Call her back!*'

And she took a deep breath and screamed the Name at the top of her voice.

'*Naemosyne!*'

Trembling, the other women obeyed her order, lifting their faces and crying out as well. '*Naemosyne!*'

High in the air, within the frightful talons of the Zhraike, the tiny ancient figure stirred. Had the watchers on the ground been close enough to see her face, they would have seen her eyelids snap open. And might also have seen the mark of the Sisterhood on her narrow chest begin to blaze with the regeneration of her power.

In the next instant, as everyone saw, the glow from the mark seemed to spread like flowing fire. Her body was suddenly limned in brightness, an aura of dazzling silver. The Zhraike screamed with astonishment – but the two that clutched her screeched loudest, as if the aura burned their talons. Flapping frantically, they released their grip, and dropped her.

But she did not fall.

Instead, she came upright in mid-air, as she might have risen to her feet on firm ground. As she drew herself up, she seemed to throw off the enfeebling burden of her great age.

Standing straight-backed and regal, she shone as bright as a small moon above the camp, staring fearlessly around at the shrieking, wheeling Zhraike horde. Her hands reached out, somehow gathering and cupping a portion of the brightness that surrounded her, and the onlookers saw that her lips were moving as if she were speaking – or singing. Suddenly then the brightness in her hands enlarged, lengthening, acquiring shape. In the next instant, as its form became complete, Naemony was standing high in the empty air holding an immense broadsword made of silver flame – three times the length of her body, yet seeming weightless in her tiny hands.

And then she struck. Sweeping the blade with furious, effortless strokes from side to side, she hewed at her winged enemies. Swift and tireless, the uncanny sword carved through the horde like a scythe through grass, each sweep sending mutilated Zhraike corpses plummeting to the ground. Before the creatures could react, dozens of them had fallen victim to that terrible blade. And even when the screaming survivors began frantic attempts to escape, the sword merely lengthened itself further and scythed dozens more from the air.

The whole transformation and slaughter took no more than a few seconds. Yet at the end of that time only a handful of Zhraike remained alive, flapping away with desperate speed towards the night-clad mountain peaks. And with the battle won, the vast glittering sword vanished from Naemony's grasp. Still standing in the air, she began to sway and droop, strength visibly draining from her, her eyes starting to close.

Next to Red, Aurilia's voice was only a tortured whisper. 'Naemosyne . . .'

For a moment the old woman's hands lifted, reaching out to the empty air. But then they dropped again, her small body quivered, and she fell. Slowly, seeming as weightless as a late autumn leaf, she drifted downward to come softly and finally to rest on the ground.

Despite her own injuries, Aurilia was the first to reach her, with Red and the others at her heels. Naemony looked as still and pale as a corpse as Aurilia cradled her, speaking her Name. But the witchmark on Naemony's chest, visible through the claw-ripped nightdress, was still faintly glowing. And then the old woman's eyes opened, gazing almost serenely up at Aurilia.

'Daughter.' Naemony's whisper was only the smallest breath of sound, but everyone heard it in that motionless moment. 'Tell me . . . of Inghilla . . .'

'She is dead, Mother,' Brennia said tersely from behind Aurilia.

Deep sadness moved like a shadow across Naemony's eyes as she gazed around at the gathered women. Then she sighed, a tiny exhalation, and tremblingly raised one almost transparent hand.

'Daughter,' she said again. 'Aurilia . . .'

The witchmark on her chest glowed for an instant even more brightly, and as Aurilia continued to hold her she reached her upraised hand to Aurilia's face, drawing her fingers across the terrible open gashes of the wounds, trailing them then down to the other gaping cuts on her shoulder. And where the ancient fingers touched, the slashed flesh drew together, the open mouths of the wounds closed and sealed, to leave only the thinnest of lines across the smooth skin.

'Lead them, my Auriflamme,' Naemony whispered. 'Lead the Sisterhood, for whatever time remains . . .'

Then her eyes closed, her hand fell limply away, the witchmark's glow faded and went out on the frail chest where all breath at last was stilled.

TWENTY

'I'm glad everyone could see her like that,' Aurilia said softly. 'As she must have been in her youth – fearless and strong and glorious, a warrior queen.'

The other Sisters around her murmured their agreement as they went quietly on with their work. While Red, sitting silently near by, went on steeling himself against the sight of so much torn, broken, agonized flesh around him. They were in the outsize tent occupied by the Nine, to which most of the wounded – Sisters and militia, since the mages were tending their own – had been carried after the battle. There, as dawn arrived to begin sweeping the shadows from the vale, the tireless work of healing had nearly been completed, and the injured were at rest in peaceful hypnotic trances. In many cases, though, where gobbets of flesh had been clawed from the bone, where limbs had been torn from sockets, eyes gouged out, faces torn away, the Earth-magic could do little more than stop the bleeding and protect against infection. Even lesser stabs and slashes, when healed, remained visible in the ridged dark lines of the scars that those healers could never erase. Scars like those across Aurilia's face, which at that moment Brennia was covering with a salve that Red recognized.

Aurilia saw him watching and gave him a lopsided smile. 'The scars will mostly fade, you know. Naemony was among the greatest of our healers. I won't always look this terrible.'

'You're alive and in one piece,' Red told her, his voice roughened by emotion. 'That's all I care about.'

'And we fought them off,' Brennia said, stepping back from her completed task. 'That matters too. Your scars are battle honours, Aurilia. I saw you cut down those two Zhraike. Not bad – for our new Mother.'

Red twitched at that, having not quite come to terms with

211

Aurilia's sudden accession to the highest position in the Sister-hood. And Aurilia's smile faded as her face grew troubled.

'Not Mother yet, Brennia,' she said. 'Not without the cere-monies of elevation and installation. And I wonder if there will ever be a time for those rites – or anyone left to perform them . . .'

'Don't!' Red said sharply. 'Now you're tempting fate!'

But then he stopped and turned at the sound of a hoarse cough at the doorway. Krost was standing there, his left hand bandaged and the crusty line of a cut along one cheek, looking around with sorrow darkening his already sombre eyes.

'I wanted to see how you were all faring,' he said. 'Phaedran is much concerned.'

'He's all right?' Aurilia asked relievedly.

'He has a wound in one arm,' Krost replied. 'But he is recovering.'

'And Evelane?' Aurilia asked.

'Unharmed,' Krost told her. 'Fear may have made her with-draw even deeper, but she was safe inside her carriage. Phaed-ran and I were defending it.'

'At some cost, it seems,' Red remarked dourly, studying his friend's wounds. 'I must be the only person in the whole army who got off without a scratch.'

Krost gave him a half-smile. 'That is something of a change for you. Though Brennia also seems unhurt.'

Brennia nodded tightly. 'Red and I were together, with my troop, defending the Nine. The Zhraike moved away from us when Aurilia and Inghilla brought Naemony out . . .'

Her eyes suddenly filled with tears and she wheeled away with a small choking sound. Dismayed by that and by the sudden glistening in Aurilia's eyes, Krost stepped forward, reaching out a hand as if to soothe them.

'Forgive me,' he rumbled. 'I should not be reminding you of your great loss.'

Brushing at her eyes, Aurilia shook her head. 'Don't apolog-ize. We need no reminding. No one of the Sisterhood will ever forget how Naemony died.'

'We counted a hundred and more dead Zhraike, this morn-

212

ing,' Krost said with grim satisfaction. 'About two score brought down by fire-arrows, but more than half of the whole number slain at the last by Naemony. It was a glorious death, Aurilia, a hero's death.'

Aurilia looked away, remembering. 'Everything that remained of her life-force, summoned and expended in a final blazing moment... Many of us will wish for such a noble death in the days ahead.'

'God's *sake*!' Red snapped. 'Are we beaten before we start?'

Aurilia and Krost exchanged an unreadable look. 'What's your view, Krost?' she asked. 'Of our chances?'

Krost shook his great head. 'At least a third are dead, militia and Sisters, or wounded too badly to be useful. Many officers also fell, though Trochain is alive. Several wizards died and more were hurt when their magic gave way at the end. Vallawn is intact, but Farbanni may be too badly wounded even for the healers to help.'

'And add to that,' Aurilia said, 'the deep damage done to the power of the Nine, with the loss of Naemony and Inghilla.'

Red grimaced. 'All right, we're in poor shape. So do we turn and go home, wait for Lebarran to come after us?'

'That was Trochain's suggestion this morning,' Krost said solemnly. 'But Phaedran would not listen. He has become as he was in the Western Woodlands – single-minded, in a cold fury, determined to go forward and confront the enemy at any price, unwilling even to admit the possibility of retreat.'

Red remembered very well the prince's indomitable determination in the Woodlands, even though surrounded by enemies and unknown menaces. It had seemed then that Phaedran would go on *alone*, to challenge the Dome, if it had come to that. 'Will everyone follow him?' he asked.

'He is our prince,' Krost said simply.

'But it probably makes little difference,' Aurilia said, 'as Phaedran will know, whether we fight on or flee. The end will surely be the same, whenever and however we next confront Lebarran.'

'I don't believe this,' Red said, scowling. 'It's not like you to be so defeatist. We *won*, last night!'

213

'Against the Zhraike,' Aurilia said emptily. 'Not against Leb-arran. And when we next face him or some other of his forces, we'll do so with fewer soldiers and mages. And without the unity of the Nine.'

'Can't you fix that, at least?' Red demanded. 'Pick replace-ments so you're Nine again?'

She shook her head gloomily. 'They could never be passed through the processes in time, to be able to unite their powers fully with the others. And I myself haven't been properly installed, so I lack the preparation for my role in *centring* the unity.'

'And even without the other losses,' Krost growled, 'the loss of the Nine reduces the army's power nearly by half.'

Red took a deep breath. 'All right, it's bad news. But even so, I agree with the prince. If we're going to lose whether we go on or not, let's go on. Maybe we'll get lucky.' His pale eyes were bright with eagerness. 'More to the point, maybe we'll *make* our luck. We did it before, the three of us, in the Dome – because we kept on, even when that seemed suicidal. That's how it works. If you keep on, you give luck a chance to get into the game. Once you quit, the game's over.'

'This isn't a game,' Aurilia said.

He shrugged. 'All I'm saying is that we kept going before, in the west, and some unexpected stuff turned up to help us along the way. Just like last night. The Zhraike were all over us, until Naemony . . . did the unexpected.'

'She will not be there next time,' Krost rumbled. But he was watching Red with bright and interested eyes.

'No,' Red agreed, 'but *other* unexpected pieces of luck might fall our way. For all we know, Lebarran gave himself a coronary throwing all that mage-fire at us. But you don't find good luck if you turn away and refuse to go looking for it.'

'Perhaps,' Aurilia said with a weary nod. 'Perhaps retreat would be merely a postponement of death and destruction. Which may be the best we can hope for.' She was gazing at Red intently. 'Except for you, my love. You could hope for more. We seem to be in a lull, now, perhaps while the enemy sorcerers recover from last night's efforts. During this time,

Red, we could ask Vallawn and the wizards to return you to your own Sphere.'

'Send me *home*?' He stared at her, shocked, realizing how long it had been since he had thought about his own world at all, let alone about returning to it.

'I could face what is to come more easily,' she told him, 'if I knew you were safe.'

'But we promised to stay together,' he reminded her. 'To the end. We agreed.'

She lifted her hands in a helpless gesture. 'It was easy to make such a pledge when . . . when we seemed to have some hope. But now . . .'

'All right,' Red said quickly, his eyes bright with the idea that had just struck him. 'If that's how you feel, let's get the wizards to send you with me! Both of you!'

It was their turn to look shocked. 'I couldn't desert the Sisterhood,' Aurilia declared. 'My life is rooted in this Continent – and I must offer my life in its defence, if the fates require it.'

'And I,' Krost rumbled. 'But it was a kind thought, Red.'

'Maybe,' Red said acidly. 'But I don't think so much of *your* thought. You're both ready to die for your country, but you expect me to run off home. You won't desert your people, but you imagine that I could desert you.' Emotion was making his voice raw. 'You really think I could do that? You think I could face being alive, knowing I'd run out on you, let you die? I still say that we should keep going, together, and see if we get lucky. I'm sure as hell not letting you go on without me!'

As Aurilia reached out to him wordlessly, tears glinting in her eyes, Krost nodded heavily. 'Corodel used to say much the same thing – that if a man keeps going he can make his own luck.'

'Until it finally runs out,' Aurilia whispered.

Red managed a half-smile. 'Maybe we three can still find some. And if not – then we go down together, and make sure to take our share of the enemy with us.'

*

215

That same morning, on the farther side of the intervening mountain range, most of the Order of the Apotheosis were indeed resting from their exertions. On divans or sofas of their own devising, four of them sat in desultory conversation in the chamber that they had altered for themselves within Lebarran's dwelling. Yannahac was not with them, taking his turn elsewhere to stand guard against the Unformed, and Lebarran was keeping to himself in his spell-chamber.

The group of four all looked weary and drawn, with dark pouches under their eyes and occasional slight tremors twitching their faces. One of the two oldest ones, Dhaminai, raised a skinny hand and watched its palsied trembling with detached interest.

'If Yannahac should call to us *now*, for aid against the Unformed,' he muttered, 'we should have little to offer.'

The others glanced reflexively upwards, as if half-expecting the vast metal canopy above the dwelling to vibrate with another alarm. 'The Magister probably would,' Zykiador growled. 'He does have amazing powers of recovery, even after that barrage of mage-fire . . .'

'He will need them all and more,' wheezed old Ostyril from the divan where he lay like a sack of bones. 'To hurl such forces as we hurled last night, over such distance – another time, my friends, I will take myself out of conclave before he *kills* me!'

'He might then kill you anyway for doing so,' Gul Ist said coldly. 'Certainly he has grown more unstable, dangerously unpredictable, since his ordeal in the Void.'

'And since Phaedran began his march,' Zykiador added.

'Madness on *both* sides,' Dhaminai muttered. 'We may wonder which will kill us first.'

Ostyril snorted faintly. 'You overstate it, Dhaminai. Lebarran has always been unstable, but I doubt if he is *mad*. And you cannot truly believe that we are in any danger from the remnants of the prince's army.'

Zykiador's laugh was cruel. 'Hardly – especially now that the Nine have been broken.' He laughed again. 'Yet who would have dreamed that the old hag would have so much juice left in her?'

Dhaminai sighed. 'I might have foreseen it. I knew her, long ago. She was quite splendid in her youth . . .'

'Did you know her well?' Zykiador licked thick lips. 'In bed?'

'Oh, no.' Dhaminai wagged his head. 'I suppose she had lovers, but her first concern was always the Sisterhood. And she had little time for male adepts.'

Zykiador grunted. 'They're all like that, the witches. Most of them prefer other women . . .'

He stopped, as a small patch of cloudiness appeared suddenly before them in mid-air. Nervously the four mages braced themselves, hands glowing fitfully as they called on their wearied powers. But then they relaxed, their hands fading, as the cloudy patch before them resolved itself into a misty image of Lebarran's face, looking even more pale and lined.

'It's now certain,' he snapped without preamble, 'that Phaedran will not withdraw. My scrying reveals that Vallawn is unharmed and is rallying their remaining wizards, while seven of the Nine remain alive. And Phaedran is determined to advance.'

'Madness,' mumbled Dhaminai, almost inaudibly.

Gul Ist's thin face tightened. 'Then our efforts last night, which have so depleted us, seem to have been valueless.'

In the hazy image Lebarran's sunken eyes flared only minimally. 'Don't overstep yourself, Gul Ist. Last night's attack was useful enough.'

'Do you plan another, Magister, since they have not been halted?' Ostyril asked worriedly.

'Not at long range,' Lebarran rasped. 'I might myself send them some small surprises, later, in the night, when I have rested. Otherwise, we can simply let them come to us.'

'Will you summon that other force you mentioned, Magister?' Dhaminai asked. 'The invincible multitude?'

Lebarran's laugh was as fierce as his glare. 'We'll have no need of them against that ragged remnant of an army. If Phaedran is fool enough to lead them to my valley, into my forest' – his voice dropped to a sepulchral growl – 'you may be sure that none of them will emerge again, alive.'

TWENTY-ONE

The diminished army remained in that sheltered vale for all of the next day following the battle, resting, reorganizing and sorrowfully attending to the dead. While the militia proceeded with simple burials the women of the Sisterhood performed their traditional ceremonies – building pyres whose fierce heat was enhanced by witch-fire, singing their sad farewells around the flames, then carefully collecting the ashes. Some of the ashes would be returned to the Fastness, if any Sisters survived to return, while the rest would be scattered on the ground, on the wind and on natural water. So the dead Sisters, including Naemony, would be returned to the elements that their natural magic embraced.

Militiamen and Sisters not occupied with funeral needs spent their day at the normal routines of soldiers in the field, with particular care for horses and weaponry. But a sizeable squad was also detailed to rearrange the contents of those supply wagons which had escaped the mage-fire, along with the carriages that had belonged to wizards who had been slain. In that way a number of vehicles were made available, some to carry the more seriously wounded – who were to be left behind on the vale until they recovered enough to make their way home. They would be left unprotected, since the army had no resources to spare, but no one resented the harshness of that decision, believing that the enemy would undoubtedly aim his *own* resources at Phaedran's main force itself. Otherwise, some of the emptied vehicles would take the less seriously injured, especially mages, forward on the march, to provide what benefit they could. And among them, inevitably, would go the closed carriage of the princess Evelane.

During the day Red and Krost roamed here and there over the scarred campsite, lending a hand wherever they usefully could. And Phaedran also moved tirelessly among his people, helping and encouraging, his wounds bandaged and his face pale but looking as indomitable as ever. Usually Trochain accompanied him, but the other militia officers were as deeply involved with the day's labours as the men. Certainly they all knew that the time had passed for strategic planning and overviews. From then on, the army would simply go forward to find the Clouded Valley, then try to do what it had come to do.

More times than he could count, Red's gaze drifted up towards the cleft between two peaks above the vale to the south, where Krost had said was their route to Lebarran's valley. Nearly everyone else in the camp, except perhaps Phaedran, had been constantly doing the same. It looked like such a normal formation, Red thought, a simple little pass across a mountain range. But on the other side . . . I wonder what we'll see over there, he thought. I wonder if Lebarran will give us time to see anything at all.

He was fairly sure that most of the others were having similar thoughts that day. Certainly the warriors were unusually quiet and subdued at their work, aside from the mournful singing of the Sisters around their pyres. But even with those lamentations and the general mood of regret, the silence on the vale did not seem to grow out of despair, out of any paralysing hopelessness. While most of them may have shared Aurilia's bitter certainty that they were doomed whether they went on or turned back, they were also all seasoned warriors, tough and brave, and they were not crushed by that certainty. The risk of death had always been part of their profession, and if this was its time, they seemed silently to be saying, so be it. Instead of despair, the men and women evinced a stern and fatalistic acceptance, and with it a level of hard anger, showing that they would echo Red's words, wishing to do as much damage as possible to the enemy before they fell.

Throughout the day Aurilia remained with the others, the Seven that had been Nine, at the centre of the funeral rites. But when evening began to darken the vale again, Red went to

219

seek her out in the large tent that had housed the Nine. He found her deeply asleep, overcome by the after-effects of her wounds and her magical work of that day. So Red left her undisturbed, seeing that Brennia and her troop were still resolutely on guard, and wandered off – communing briefly with Grilena, then sitting awhile with Krost by the prince's pavilion where the dwarf-giant had chosen to stand sentry-duty. But at last Red drifted away to the little tent that he and Aurilia shared, stretching out on the bed fully dressed, convinced he would not sleep, then falling into a restless doze.

In the midst of a fragmented dream, a scrape and rustle at the door of the tent jerked him awake. Aurilia was standing in the opening looking at him. In her younger form, wearing a long flowing gown, she was indistinct in the darkness but seemed to be standing with an odd, hunched stiffness.

'Are you all right?' he asked, fumbling to light the stub of taper by the bed. As its flame rose, she stepped towards him, moving as stiffly as she had been standing. And he sat bolt upright, astonished, as the light fell on her face.

There was no sign of the smallest scar on her brow or cheek. The honey-bronze skin was as flawless as ever.

In that instant he might have smiled, thinking that some unexpected Sisterhood magic had completely restored her skin. But instinct saved him, triggered by her lack of response to his question and by her blank expression and unnatural posture as she came towards him. For an eerie moment, as he rose uneasily to his feet, the candle-light seemed to reflect from her eyes, a stark orange. And as he moved her lovely face suddenly contorted into an expression of evil savagery.

And she sprang at him, drawing a long-bladed dagger from the folds of her gown, plunging it at his chest.

Reflex whirled him away into a defensive crouch. But before either of them could move again, her orange-flecked eyes went wide, her body arched backwards, and the dagger dropped harmlessly from her hand. Her mouth gaping in a silent cry, she half-turned, hands flailing helplessly, before toppling forward across the foot of the bed, to show the shaft of an arrow jutting from her back.

220

Rigid with horror, Red stared at the doorway – where Brennia stood, bow in hand, a second arrow already nocked. And then he looked down again. For Aurilia's corpse had begun to move.

Without altering position, its flesh twitched and rippled. A foul vapour rose from the bloodless arrow wound, and a reeking, viscous fluid oozed from the open mouth and eyes. In the next seconds the corpse began to crumple and contract, as if some unseen force was compressing it. Finally its solidity gave way, and it collapsed into a pool of the tarry fluid, which in turn evaporated into more of the stinking vapour and then vanished utterly, leaving the bed and the ground unmarked.

'A sorcerous image,' Brennia said flatly. 'I saw it on its way here, yet I also could see Aurilia asleep in the tent of the Nine.'

Red fought to control the shuddering in the pit of his stomach. 'I owe you one, Brennia,' he said unsteadily.

She nodded with the ghost of a smile. 'You can return the favour sometime. But stay watchful. There may be others.'

'Others?' he repeated blankly. Then he went even paler, reaching for his sword. 'Maybe sent to other people!'

Brennia's eyes went wide. 'Gods!' she cried. 'Quick – I'll go to Aurilia and the Seven, you rouse the prince and Krost!'

They sprang away on their separate missions. Red sprinted towards the royal pavilion, hoping to find Krost still on guard. But there was no sign of him, and the militia sentries on duty had no idea where he had gone. For a moment Red hesitated between warning the prince and seeking his friend – and then, within the pavilion, he heard a muffled sound like a groan. Drawing his sword, he plunged through the doorway, with startled sentries stumbling along behind, and dashed towards the flickering gleam of a candle coming from the prince's sleeping quarters.

As he burst unceremoniously in, he saw the prince slowly rising from a chair, looking deathly pale with shock. While some paces away, walking stiffly towards him, was an elegant dark-haired woman whom Red had never seen before.

'Oh, my Ellemar,' Phaedran was saying in a choked voice. 'Is this another dream of you?'

The woman, the image of his dead wife Ellemar, continued her advance. And Red sprang forward, sword raised, as he saw her pluck a dagger from her gown. But he was stopped, as all their separate movements were halted, as if time itself had been suspended in that place. Red felt as if he had suddenly been embedded in glass, like a fly in amber. Helplessly he struggled against the unseen grip that held his every muscle motionless.

And in that frozen moment, with Phaedran and the image of Ellemar equally immobile, Red saw the princess Evelane move into the room.

Her eyes were wide in a frozen blank stare. Her face was expressionless, her upper body held rigid, and in the floor-length nightgown that she was wearing she seemed to glide across the floor as if floating. Unhesitatingly she moved to the sorcerous image of her dead mother, and slowly raised a hand to touch its cheek.

'Ellemar,' she said tonelessly. 'Mother. Have you come to my call? Do you bring me the gift? Will you beg my forgiveness and give me the powers that you denied me? Will you? *Will you?*'

Her voice lifted to shrillness on the last words, and with a feral snarl she moved her hand from the immobilized image's cheek to close it on its throat. 'But no,' she snarled, 'you have returned to *Father*, you have come to him, not to me, indifferent to me, withholding the gift, denying me what I yearn for, what is my right . . . *Denying me!*'

Still no one could move as Evelane's voice rose and her manic grip tightened. Yet despite that, the sorcerous simulacrum did not look at her, but kept its eyes – glittering orange in the torchlight – fixed on Phaedran, on its target, mindlessly focused on its sole purpose.

'You do not speak, mother,' Evelane said, her hysteria rising. 'You will not look at me. Why do you torment me? Why do you withhold my gift?' She shook the Ellemar-image with furious strength. '*Look*, mother, *listen*, mother, hear my plea, *give* me my magic, give it to me, give it . . .!'

Her face was smeared with tears, her lips flecked with foam, her body trembling like a grassblade in a wind. Yet her grip remained unshakable even as her other hand reached over to jerk the dagger from the image's grasp. 'You will deny me again . . . You must not, yet you will . . . You denied me before, by dying . . . If you will deny me now, you may *die again!*'

And she plunged the dagger into the image's breast.

As horrified as before, Red watched the simulacrum collapse into its foul dissolution, while Evelane turned blindly away to glide out of the room as eerily as she had entered it. As she left, the enveloping grip on Red abruptly vanished. He stumbled and caught himself, seeing the prince reel back as he too was freed, then whirling at a sound behind him. Krost was there, his face ashen, with the terrified sentries who had followed Red.

'It was a sort of magic image,' Red said unsteadily. 'One looking like Aurilia tried for me . . .'

'I have just destroyed one that came in the form of Aleka, my sister, to kill me,' Krost growled. 'I wondered if you were one when I saw you here. But *Ellemar . . .*'

They moved towards Phaedran, who was leaning on his chair looking stricken. 'I dream of her so often,' he said hollowly. 'I thought I was dreaming again. I still am not sure it is not a dream . . .'

'You are awake,' Krost said bluntly. 'And alive, thankfully.'

'It was weird,' Red said with a frown. 'Some sort of force held us all still. All except Evelane.'

'Perhaps she did it,' Krost suggested. 'She seemed in a kind of trance, as she seems when that other destructive power comes upon her . . .'

Phaedran was staring at the door where Evelane had left. 'Do you think this may be some power that Talonimal imparted to her? Some dire magical gift, after all?'

'No one can give anyone the gift of magic, except by birth,' Krost reminded him. 'It is all just as Hallifort said, back at the Dome. A mental outburst, from a damaged young mind.'

'It has to be that,' Red agreed. 'The poltergeist thing can happen even in *my* world, where there's no magic.'

The prince sighed gloomily. 'No doubt you are right. In any

case, what matters is that Lebarran's attempt failed – since we must assume the images came from him. We can take heart from that.'

As he spoke a number of others, including Trochain and Vallawn, burst in through the door, only to halt in bewilderment, seeing no enemies. And when everything was explained, Vallawn looked grimly thoughtful.

'It seems there were many images sent to do murder tonight,' he said. 'Yet none succeeded. Because, perhaps, they were not *perfect* replicas, as we might expect from a Magister.'

'Perhaps his power has grown less,' Krost rumbled.

'That would be a cheering thought,' said the prince, looking not at all cheered.

But Vallawn shook his head. 'He is still the greatest individual power that the Continent has ever known. More probably, the images were imperfect because he does not deem us worthy of more than a half-hearted effort.'

'I think I prefer *your* cheering thought,' Red said sourly as he and Krost left the pavilion.

Krost smiled bleakly. 'Vallawn is more sensible. Look for the most dire possibilities, and face them.'

'There's no shortage of them,' Red muttered.

Around them by then the camp had come to life, partly due to the spreading news of the sorcerous attacks, partly also to the first faint wash of light as dawn began reaching over the mountains. Krost then drifted off to see for himself if any other harm had come to the camp, while Red turned towards the tent of the Nine, or Seven, to be sure Aurilia was safe. He found her emerging from the tent, with the others of the Seven, surrounded protectively by Brennia and her troop.

'Are you all right?' he asked Aurilia, and was uncomfortably aware of echoing his words to the sorcerous image earlier.

'Well enough,' she said, reaching to take his hand. 'But I should have been with you. You might have been killed.'

'No chance,' he said, contriving a nonchalant tone. 'I knew it wasn't you.'

Even in the dimness her smile looked strained. 'Still, we

promised to stay together. And we must do so, especially from now on, as we move closer to the Clouded Valley.'

'Nowhere I'd rather be,' he agreed. 'Near you, I mean. I'm not so sure about the valley.'

'Come, then,' she said. 'We must get ready to march, soon after sun-up. All of the Seven will ride together, with Brennia's troop, to preserve what unity we can create.'

They moved away together, with the others, to begin their preparations. Around them the vale was in a military hubbub as everyone went about their morning duties. Together Red and Aurilia and the group of women snatched a few mouthfuls of breakfast, together they went to the paddock to prepare and saddle their horses. Grilena seemed less than co-operative, for once, dancing around nervously, jerking her head as if to throw the bridle off. But when Red at last stepped up into the saddle, leaning forward to stroke her neck, her mood abruptly changed, and she trotted away almost merrily, shaking her blonde mane.

'Good girl,' Red said to her privately. 'We'll show them how to ride into battle.'

To him it was a minor irony. Yet it seemed that people looked his way, at him and at the calm confident warrior women around him, seeking exactly that sort of inspiration. And he smiled inwardly, knowing that those who looked at him were seeing Corodel, the intrepid hero of song and story. Maybe I should wave the sword, he thought, and make a speech. But instead he merely rode quietly beside Aurilia to find their place in the army's formations, as they clattered and rushed in the final stages of their assembling. Then the militia troop detailed to take the lead that day set off at an easy walk, and as the first rosiness of the sunrise coloured the high peaks the rest of the army got under way. Red and the troop of women were tucked in about halfway along its columns, not far from the closed carriage of Evelane where Krost and the prince rode steadfastly, one on either side. And as the cavalcade clumped and jingled its way across the vale, Red looked up once again at the distant cleft.

'Aren't we going to be kind of exposed,' he asked Aurilia,

'while we climb up there and down the other side? Maybe we should have one of those magical shielding things . . .'

She shook her head. 'We have to conserve strength. Our hope is that Lebarran and his Order are weary from hurling mage-fire over a distance, so may not trouble us again awhile. If they do, we'll raise a shielding then.'

'Sort of risky,' Red remarked, 'waiting.'

She gave him a taut smile. 'That's war, as you said not so long ago.'

Steadily the army wound its way across the vale, then through a stretch of scrub brush growing like a fringe at the bottom of a slope leading up. That slope was far less steep than the one they had struggled up two days earlier – which to Red felt like the distant past – and the gentler incline also offered thick turf underfoot rather than bare rock and gravel. It was almost a pleasure, except perhaps for those in the jolting wagons and carriages, to make the ascent. As if the mountains have suspended hostilities, Red thought, along with the enemy. Maybe lulling us with a little peace, until we're closer. Until the next storm . . .

Before long, the leading squad of militia had attained the height of land on the cleft itself, the high mountain pass, and waited there while the rest of the army crawled slowly up after them, still all remaining creditably compact in their formations. By the time everyone was assembled on the summit, around midday, the leading squad had set off down the trail on the far side. It was an almost invisible track, winding among ominously looming slopes of dark rock and scree, the surface broken and pitted and strewn with rubble. Once or twice the main body of the army caught up with the leading troop, when the leaders paused to clear a better path through and over heaps of crumbling rock that had clearly fallen in small landslides. Most casual wanderers, Red guessed, would by then have grown discouraged and turned back.

Yet surprisingly the inhospitable track soon came to an end on the edge of a startling vista across a broad, grassy meadow, stretching for some distance ahead. As the main body of the army approached it, everyone looked delighted with the scene, the sweep of rich grass speckled with flowers as on the vale. But then they all saw what lay beyond the meadow.

In fact the expanse of grass seemed to cover the surface of a great *ledge*, for its farther side came to a sharply defined lip like the edge of a cliff. And there, below that lip, spreading over a vast distance beyond it, hung a dense, heaped, somehow unnatural fog or mist. Like a massive cloudbank that had been dragged down from the sky, unaffected by the sun that warmed the meadow, undisturbed by the small breeze that ruffled the meadow grass.

'Is that what I think it is?' Red asked Aurilia, as they and the army continued along the stony trail towards the meadow.

Her face was tight, her eyes shadowed. 'The Clouded Valley,' she said tonelessly. 'Or so I imagine. I've never seen it.'

'I wonder if anyone here has,' Red said, staring at the immense breadth of unmoving fog or cloud beyond the meadow's edge.

But then he stiffened as a sound reached his ears. A cry, almost a wail, from the leading squad of militia that had galloped on ahead, down on to the meadow. Red saw that they had halted on the grassy expanse, milling around in what looked like near panic, unslinging their crossbows.

Here we go again, Red thought dismally as he drew his sword, aware of Aurilia drawing hers, of Brennia's troop readying their bows, of tense shouts and movement all around him. He saw that the leading troop, on the meadow, were looking and pointing towards one distant end of the grassy expanse, where a substantial ridge formed a boundary that was dense with thickets of tall brush. And he could see shapes moving through those thickets – huge, looming, monstrous.

But as he stared, astounded, he recognized those shapes – in the same instant as, behind him, a mighty joyous roar burst out from Krost.

'By all the deathless Spheres! The *Mykraladan*!'

TWENTY-TWO

'Your army seems to have fought its war already, Phaedran,'
Ghiscral boomed jovially. 'And hard fighting it seems to have
been. I hope you have left some for us.'

They were all by that time gathered on the meadow. When
it became clear that it was not a new attack, the army had
surged down at breakneck speed to join the leading troop and
to gape at the towering figures that were marching towards
them, gripping huge pikestaffs and laden with other weapons
including iron maces and studded cudgels. Probably everyone
here has heard of the giants, Red thought, but few may have
seen them. And he knew how the others would be feeling,
being loomed over by beings twice their height and more than
three times their girth.

But if the people of the army were feeling overawed, they
were also looking decidedly thrilled at the arrival of such
impressive reinforcements. Or at least they had looked that
way at first. But from the moment that Ghiscral greeted the
prince, many of the people around Red had begun to look a
little askance and doubtful. Some because of the giant chieftain's overfamiliar disregard for the proper respect for royalty
– some because they had realized that for all their size the
new arrivals numbered no more than thirty. But others, more
significantly, had their delight diminished when they recognized the nature of the giants' smiles, and of their attitude
generally.

The word is patronizing, Red thought, having experienced
it. It's how adults smile at children who are trying to act grown-
up. He glanced at Krost, who would have had more experience
of such treatment, and saw regret and anger mingling in his
friend's scowl. Next to him, Aurilia and the warrior women
were also beginning to frown, as the giants smilingly bent their

heads to hear Phaedran's account of the battle that had so bitterly reduced his force.

'Zhraike, indeed!' Ghiscral grinned around at his men. 'Our old enemy! We should have been there!'

As the other giants rumbled amused assent, Phaedran nodded stiffly. 'You would have been welcome, then, Ghiscral.'

Nearby, leaning on his stick, old Vallawn snorted. 'What use they would have been against mage-fire is open to question.'

That made Red and many others smile, while Phaedran went on before Ghiscral's faint glower could darken further. 'But of course you are just as welcome now. Especially when we understood that you had . . . decided against joining us.'

The chieftain's brow cleared as his laugh boomed out. 'Our minds were changed, prince, after days and nights of argument – when we could not gainsay the truths spoken by the forceful emissaries that you sent.' He grinned over at Red. 'Your new Corodel fights as well as the old one, and is more eloquent.'

Red managed a crooked smile as everyone looked at him, and Ghiscral laughed again. 'Do you look for your friend Lupyk among us, Corodel? He is not here. After you overcame him, he left the plateaux – to hide his disgrace.'

'Too bad,' Red said shortly. 'We'll need every warrior we can get, where we're going.'

'That is so,' Krost said. 'Why have you brought so few, Ghiscral?'

The chieftain shrugged. 'I have brought only volunteers. Others were less convinced of the value of this fight, or more convinced of the need to tend their herds and look after their women and children.' His complacent smile reappeared. 'Or do you think, Krost, that we should have brought our women, as this company seems to have done?'

The other giants laughed, but Red saw a wave of anger sweep through the army as the warrior Sisters bristled. But before any protest could be voiced by them, Phaedran drew himself up at his iciest.

'These are not *our women*, Ghiscral, but warriors of the Sisterhood, who have proved themselves skilled and fearless fighters.'

Ghiscral looked mildly interested. 'Of course, the witches. We have heard something of their little magics.'

'Then hear *this*, as well!' That was Aurilia, striding forward with fury in her eyes, her hair beginning to loosen and crackle with power around her. 'In the battle two nights ago our leader faced the Zhraike alone. One aged woman with her *little magics*. And she slew half a hundred of them before she died!'

'Really?' Ghiscral said, smiling, while the other giants looked at each other and chuckled disbelievingly. 'She must have been a warrior indeed. But you need fear no more such battles, pretty one. Not now that we are here.'

Aurilia was about to flare up again, while the army stirred angrily around them. But once again Vallawn intervened, each word sharp as a whiplash.

'Beware rash promises, giant. We may find things in the Clouded Valley that can bring even you to your knees.'

'Quite so,' Phaedran snapped. 'And because of that, we have no further time to waste in talk. Our urgent task is to find a way down into the Valley.' He scowled up at Ghiscral. 'Unless you Highlanders know a way?'

The chieftain shook his huge head. 'We know little of this valley save some mentions of it in old tales. If anyone has explored it more recently, they did not return to tell about it.'

On that sombre note, the entire company moved to the edge of the meadow, the cliff-edge beyond which the mass of cloud hovered, thick and grey and motionless, extending into the distance towards mountain peaks that were its farther boundary. Ranged along the edge, they all peered down, noting that the cloud seemed to lap at the slope a short distance below their feet, so that it was like looking down from a slightly raised shoreline on to a strangely gaseous sea. Or, Red thought, like the view over LA in August. You'd think a high-powered sorcerer would fix himself some better weather.

But at least the slope below them looked promising. As far as Red could see, down to where the cloud began, it seemed a fairly manageable incline, its rocky surface split by plentiful cracks and fissures almost like crude steps.

'If it's no steeper the rest of the way,' he said to Aurilia, 'we'll climb down easily enough.'

Her shudder was almost undetectable. 'Leaving sun and warmth and life behind.'

Though I walk through the valley of death, Red thought. Except I can't say I fear no evil . . . Then he twitched with surprise, as the head and shoulders of Krost suddenly loomed up out of the cloud below, seeming for a moment to be floating there as if disembodied. But then the rest of his body followed as he clambered up on to the lip of the meadow, towards Phaedran. He went down for a look, Red realized, and no one saw him go. And he smiled to himself as he saw the giants regarding Krost with slightly puzzled frowns, as if amazed to find such boldness in a dwarf.

'The cloud is lying in a fairly thin layer above the valley,' Krost reported to the prince. 'Farther down, I could see well enough. And the slope is not hard to climb.' He paused uneasily. 'Except – it will be too much for horses and wagons, Phaedran.'

Red saw the prince's slight flinch before he nodded. 'Thank you, Krost. I suppose we should be glad we are not balked here entirely.' He turned to the marshal. 'Prepare to advance on foot, Trochain. And . . . and arrange the wagons and horses to be . . . left behind.'

Red and Aurilia looked at each other, both knowing why Phaedran had flinched, why his voice had caught. If wagons and carriages would be left behind, so would the prince's daughter. There would be no place on the final footslogging stage of the march for the half-crazed Evelane.

'And he thought if he brought Evelane she'd be protected,' Aurilia said sadly.

'She'll probably be as safe as any of us,' Red replied.

The preparations and regrouping seemed to go smoothly enough, in the short while that they took. Some of the wounded who had been brought along in the wagons were also to be left on the meadow, unable to manage climbing and walking. And they included several Sisters and a few mages, with Farbanni among them, somewhat restored, who might provide

231

some magical protection if it became necessary. Meanwhile everyone else, including any walking wounded who could still wield weapons, prepared light backpacks while also taking a much-delayed midday meal. Despite their imminent descent into a cloud-covered unknown, they all seemed remarkably calm – comforted by their familiar routines and also perhaps by the formidable addition to their force of the giants, with no sign of weakening in the solemn fatalism that had come to armour them.

Yet their calm was threatened a little when the time came to release the horses on to the meadow, also to be tended by the more mobile of those left behind. A tear or two shone in the eyes of the warriors, male and female alike, as they bade farewell to their mounts. Just as Red's eyes stung and his throat tightened when he put his arm around Grilena's neck in a last embrace.

'Wolle will look after her,' Krost said gruffly behind him, and Red turned to see his friend standing close to the big dappled horse, with a visible dampness in his eyes too.

The farewells then to the people remaining behind brought more sadness. Red saw the prince emerge stiffly from Evelane's carriage and stalk away with his back to everyone, staring out over the mountains. And then at last all partings and arrangings ended with a parade-ground shout from Trochain.

Forming up with the others, at Aurilia's side, Red noted that Krost chose to stay near the prince rather than join the giants – who were waiting restlessly at the cliff-edge, having insisted on taking the lead. Around Red the army adjusted and tidied its columns, regaining the appearance of untroubled calm as they waited for the order to advance. To Red's eye, it still looked to be a substantial force, even without the wagons and horses, even though its numbers had been reduced to little more than two thousand warriors. Yet Red wondered how relevant either numbers or composure would be, when they were entering the lair of an enemy who could hurl magic like bombs over mountain ranges. Still, as dread tried to clutch at him he drew his own fatalism around him like a cloak, and even found a crooked grin to offer to Aurilia as the giants hoisted their pikestaffs high and led the army over the lip of the meadow, towards the clouded, unguessable valley depths.

In other circumstances the descent would have been almost laughably easy. The stark granite of the slope was split and riven all the way down, offering ready footholds. The only drawback was the cloud or fog that wrapped itself cloyingly around them all, cutting off their vision, muffling their sounds. All around him Red could vaguely hear booted feet sliding and crunching over the stone, with laboured breathing and grunting and occasional muttered oaths. But the sounds were ghostly and remote, for he could *see* almost no one. Only Aurilia, immediately beside him, her tawny hair bright amid that greyness. And occasionally one or another of the Seven, or their bodyguards, would become briefly visible like an insubstantial wraith. But also, the impenetrable murk was clingingly damp, as if the cloud contained a steady drizzle. Moisture collected in small rivulets on Red's clothes, plastered down his hair, oozed into his eyes. Worse, it condensed on the rock underfoot, so that even those broken surfaces grew slippery as the army descended farther, making the oaths more vehement.

In that blind, groping progress it was easy to lose track of time, so that the sunlit meadow they had left above them began to seem an age and a universe away. It's like moving through a limbo, Red thought with a small shiver. And what if it *was* an actual, Lebarran-made limbo? A sorcerous non-place to which, unknowing, they had been magically transported, where they would slip and trudge interminably downwards, perhaps towards some ultimate abyss . . .

Think about something else, he told himself harshly, flicking wet hair out of his eyes. Think of happy times. But that avenue led his mind to recall images of riding Grilena through sun-bright fields, or lying with Aurilia between dry and fragrant sheets . . . And as he dragged his mind away from those yearnings, struggling to keep his inner balance, he almost lost the outer sort as his foot slipped on a glistening crevice.

One of Brennia's warriors, looming as if by magic from the

fog, grasped his shirt and hauled him upright. 'Don't break a leg here, Corodel,' she said calmly. 'The fun should start soon.'

Muttering his thanks, glancing around, he drew in his breath as he saw what she meant. They were almost all the way down. The slope was beginning to flatten out, with bare earth showing across the rocky surface as it continued down towards the valley floor. And around them the cloud that engulfed them was growing noticeably thinner. It was as if the cloud was sorcerously *shaped*, to fit like a cover over the valley, hovering some distance from the ground. And the thought of the power that could create and maintain such a covering made Red's skin ripple with another chill shiver. Though some of that also was caused by a thin misty drizzle that still surrounded them, not as blinding as the dense cloud but still slightly blurring outlines.

Yet they moved on unhesitatingly, with no signs of apprehension in their steadfast expressions as they maintained their formation and their pace over the bare uneven ground scattered with gravel and rock outcrops. The giants remained as the spearhead in that advance, forging well ahead – so that when they suddenly stopped, hunching with tension, it took the rest of the army several more moments of nerve-racking advance, readying their weapons, before they could make out through the drizzle what it was that confronted them.

Not an enemy, they saw, but not anything reassuring either. They had reached the outer fringes of a forest, which extended on before them as far as the visibility allowed them to see. It was by no means a dense forest, for the huge trees were spaced well apart and no other plants grew in among them – no saplings or shrubs, not even a weed on that sterile grey ground. But then, it was clear, nothing much was actually *growing* there. No leaves could be seen on the branches, no dry leaves on the ground. The forest was dead, and had been so for an unknowably long time. Such a long time that, as the army slowly realized, every bit of every tree – from knotted roots to spidery topmost twigs – had turned to stone.

Slowly the army crept forward among the trees. With their enormous trunks and sweeping, gnarled branches, they were not exactly beautiful, but imposing, monumental, almost stately. Like countless monoliths in an inhuman graveyard, Red thought – marvelling at how the trunks and branches had petrified without losing the outward appearance of trees, all the rough corrugations and cracks and knotholes of the bark, as if they were immensely skilful *carvings* of trees in coarse grey stone, cracked and scarred, chipped and flaked by time and weather. Many trees in fact had broken and fallen to the ground, or had half-fallen to lean against a neighbour like damaged columns in some ancient ruined temple, with stony fragments of branches littering the ground.

As they went forward, the pace slowed by tension and watchfulness, with still no clear indication through the sunless drizzle of how far the day had progressed, Red wondered uneasily what it was going to be like to spend the night in that forest. Or maybe more than one night. And as if the thought had communicated itself, Phaedran chose that moment to call a halt, for consultation, in the bleak gravel-strewn breadth of what passed there for a forest clearing.

'Do you know the best way through here?' Phaedran asked Ghiscral. 'I had no idea Lebarran's stronghold would be hidden in such a place.'

'Nor I,' the giant chieftain said, looking a little disconcerted. 'I have never heard of such a forest, anywhere.'

'It's probably Lebarran's idea of landscaping,' Red said sardonically.

One of the wizards, a bald man in a dishevelled robe, turned with a pompous glare. 'Lebarran is the Magister. His ways are not those of ordinary men.'

'Oh, I don't know,' Red replied. 'He seems to have his share of good old human cruelty, and power-hunger . . .'

The wizard blinked nervously. 'Have a care, Corodel. You should not speak of him too lightly in his own domain.'

'Why not?' Red asked innocently. 'You think he might get mad at us?'

That made most of the listeners laugh out loud, welcoming the brief easing of their tensions. But then Phaedran turned enquiringly to Vallawn.

'Can your magic help, here, to find a way?'

The old wizard shook his head. 'We have tried spells of seeing, Highness. But they are no more effective here *in* the valley than when we tried to use them before to look *at* the valley. As if the very air, or this drizzly mist, contains some power that blocks our vision.'

'Do you say that *all* your magics are useless here?' Phaedran asked.

Vallawn raised his crooked stick and muttered a resonant word. At the tip of the stick, a small blue flame appeared, dancing brightly. 'Not all, it seems, Highness,' he said.

'The Earth-magic still operates too, as far as we can tell,' Aurilia told the prince. 'But we also can't use any magical seeing or seeking.'

Phaedran's face tightened. 'Then we must search for the enemy's lair by physical means. Though I do not relish the idea of wandering endlessly around this unsavoury forest.'

'We could separate into smaller groups,' Trochain ventured, 'and search in different directions.'

'And make ourselves even more vulnerable,' the prince snapped. 'No, whatever else we do, we surely must stay together.'

Ghiscral grunted. 'We may not need to search for long, Phaedran. There may be a welcoming party coming for us soon enough.'

That made everyone peer anxiously around into the rain-blurred dimness. And Red noticed, as they all did, that the dimness looked a little worse. Either the rain-mist was thickening, he thought, or the forest's even more dismal twilight was gathering.

'We can go forward a while longer,' Phaedran said as the poorer light registered. 'For our camp, we must seek another clear area, larger than this, with defensible ground if such exists here. And instead of the usual sentries, Trochain, we will divide all of our number into three groups – so that fully *one-third* of us, with no exceptions, is on guard – in a ring around the camp – at every moment through the night.'

'And no fires,' Krost rumbled. 'Not even mage-fire on a stick. The sentries will need their night-vision.'

With that they moved on again, unconsciously huddling together in a more compact mass as they confronted the prospect of the night. But by then, for most of them, the unremitting tension – as they waited to see what their enemy would send against them next – was having a counter-effect. Red felt it in himself, and sensed it in the attitudes of the warriors around him. Let it begin, their eyes seemed to say as they studied the shadows among the stony trees. Let it come, whatever it may be, and put an end to waiting.

And yet they were waiting still by the time they were settling themselves for the night. They had found a suitable place, or at least a place that was less unsuitable, on a considerable expanse of mostly empty ground that angled slightly upwards in a flat shallow slope. When Phaedran pronounced it satisfactory, a basic camp was hastily set up at the top of the slope. But there were no tents raised that night, and no other comforts beyond a spare cold supper from their limited supplies and thin cloaks or blankets as meagre protection from the wetness. Still, they all knew that in any case there would be little sleep for anyone that night. Just more huddling together and perhaps a few whispered words for companionship, and an unwavering watch on the darkness for everyone whether on sentry duty or not.

Red joined those of the first watch, standing a pace or two away from Krost, unable to see him in the night's full darkness but somehow sensing the reassuring loom of his bulk. Silently, as he waited through those slow hours, he stretched and flexed all of his muscles in turn, trying to work the tension out of them, using familiar breathing exercises to find a measure of calm and to create a still centre within himself around which he could gather his resources. If I survive this war, he said to himself wryly as his tension receded slightly, I'll probably die from ulcers or some major stress-related disease. And the savouring of that irony helped him to untangle his nerve-ends as much as anything.

When his shift was relieved he crept quietly through the camp, avoiding the barely noticeable patches of deeper blackness where other people sat or lay, to find the place where

Aurilia and the rest of the Seven had settled with their body-guards. He was not surprised to find Aurilia wakeful and on her feet, standing a short distance from the others. His first awareness was of her spicy fragrance, which then enveloped him as she moved quietly against him, clutching him in a fierce embrace. For a time they stood silently like that, while Red wondered if she too was recalling previous times when they had waited together in a menacing darkness. At last she loosened her grip slightly, pulling his head down. Softly he kissed her, relishing the shape of her mouth, inhaling her scent, clasping the ripeness of her body, until at last she drew away with a small sigh.

'Part of me wishes you had gone back to your own world,' she whispered. 'But most of me is glad you're here.'

'There was never any chance that I'd leave you,' he said softly.

She raised her face to look at him, her eyes invisible in the darkness. 'Would you go back afterwards, when this battle is over? If I'm no longer here?'

'Why do you think I'll survive and not you?' he asked, frowning.

She shrugged. 'Perhaps because of what you said about luck, before. You have it, Red, in abundance – but I'm not sure the rest of us do . . .' She shivered faintly against him. 'This is a place of death, Red. Not just the trees but everything, steeped in death, in centuries and centuries of terror and torture and slaughter . . . We who have the Earth-magic can sense that dire history of death – and though the future can never be truly known, we also sense overpoweringly the approach of more death to come.'

Holding her, Red waited for the inevitable fear-reaction to overtake him at her words, and felt a distant surprise to find that he hardly reacted at all. I'm getting hardened to all this, he thought. Or numbed. And he had no idea if it was a good thing or not.

'I suppose we just have to let it come,' he told her vaguely. 'And see what happens. And try to survive.'

'And stay together,' she whispered.

'That most of all,' he said. 'Right to the end, and then some.'

So they did just that, finding a patch of clear ground where they wrapped themselves together in both their cloaks and lay quietly in each other's arms for the rest of the night. They even managed a brief time of shallow, fitful sleep. So they were jolted awake, hearts hammering, when they and the rest of the army heard the panicky yell from the surrounding ring of sentries.

And when they all leaped up, they found that some thin glimmers of early morning light were filtering down into the forest through the layer of cloud above it. Giving just enough illumination for them to see what it was that had come to confront them.

TWENTY-THREE

It looked as if a huge number of statues, figures sculpted in stone, had been placed among the trees around fully one-half of the clearing, facing the army. It seemed to Red, peering into the shadowy dimness, that the statues numbered at least as many as the army – at least two thousand of them, then, with perhaps more lurking unseen deeper in the forest. They were repellently ugly, like crude and ill-proportioned mockeries of the human form, slightly shorter than the average man but thick and powerful-looking with long heavy arms and stumpy legs. Their heads were small, their eyes invisible in shadowed sockets, their mouths lipless and wide, their jaws loose and brutal. Naked and hairless, they looked unfinished, with no indication of gender, and their flesh looked exactly as petrified as the trees – grey, rough and solid, often with hairline cracks on the surface and visible flaking at the joints.

Yet their resemblance to ill-fashioned statues was not complete, for in some incomprehensible way they were alive. They were moving, the whole great host of them, shuffling their wide feet, clenching their knuckly hands, shifting position in heavy lurches. Nearly every one gripped a knobbly, weighty length of broken tree branch as a club of solid stone. And a sense of savage malevolence poured from them with the force of a tidal wave.

Walking statues, Red thought dazedly. Just what you'd expect in a petrified forest. And what do you use to kill a stone?

But the question was about to be answered, he knew, if there was an answer. Phaedran's voice rang out and the army formed up for battle, militiamen and warrior women on either side of the giants. The prince was in the forefront of the militia, with the wizards around him and Krost looming watchfully at his side, while Red took his place beside Aurilia with the Seven.

240

But those formations were still gathering and settling, the warriors still readying weapons, when without any sound or other warning the entire mass of living statues lurched clumsily forward, as one, and attacked.

Yelling defiance, the army surged forward to meet the attack. But within seconds it became horribly clear that there was no easy way to resist the stone-fleshed beings. Arrows and crossbow bolts shattered against their bodies, sword-blades and even the giants' pikestaffs were blunted and broken by their rocklike flesh. Unharmed in that first clash, the stone people lumbered forward, spreading out in a crude crescent formation, swinging their heavy clubs.

The warriors and even the giants were forced to fall back from that awful charge. Trochain and his officers raged and roared in attempts to direct the withdrawal, which was rapidly becoming a tangled, milling mêlée as the helpless warriors tried to evade the clubs of the monsters they could not harm. In the midst of that spreading frenzy, Red ducked a swinging club and slashed at its wielder's face, but the sword's unbreakable blade bounced uselessly from the stony surface, ringing like a bell. As he dodged another blow, a fragment of broken stone gave way beneath his foot and threw him off balance. Half-falling, wide open to a further blow, he felt a sudden gust of heat – as a lance of blue fire scorched past him and blasted his attacker into rubble.

He spun around to see Vallawn grinning at him, holding up his crooked stick. Then from its tip more fire burst, and another stone monster exploded into fragments. Gathering his balance, with a salute to the old wizard, Red looked quickly around as he rejoined the continuing retreat.

A frightening number of human bodies lay scattered across the clearing, broken and crushed by the monstrous, relentless advance. Red saw that the other wizards were also trying to protect the retreat, but less effectively than Vallawn in their equal concern to stay well clear of the fray. Less effectively also than Krost – whom Red saw standing like a wall before his prince, moving back one balanced stride at a time, his iron quarterstaff clanging continuously as it battered at any of the stone people who moved within its range.

But the most potent rearguard action was being fought by the giants. They had flung aside their broken pikes and resorted to their huge maces, smashing at the stone people as Krost was, leaving trails of rubble as they drew back. Yet there were always more stone people, wave upon wave of them tramping unstoppably forward across the clearing, swinging their merciless clubs. They were hugely strong in their own right, and apparently felt no pain, so that glancing blows that failed to demolish their bodies had no visible effect. Even those who had lost entire limbs seemed undeterred, so that Red could watch with revulsion one stony monster whose arm had been snapped off at the shoulder simply pick it up with its other hand and wield it like a bludgeon. Just as he saw that for every creature beaten to the ground by the thunder of a giant's mace, two or three were lumbering in to attack that giant on either side. So giant bodies, too, were being scattered across the clearing among those of the human warriors.

Amid the seething, manic chaos of the retreat Red realized then that he had somehow been separated from Aurilia. Frantically he went searching, using his speed and combat skills to dodge any attacks, not trying to block or counter the whirling stone clubs. At last he saw her, clutching the broken stump of her sword, among the Seven who were being defended by Brennia's troop. The warrior women were using their sturdy bows as clubs, not doing much damage but at least fending off their share of stone-bodied attackers while they and the rest of the army continued to fall back. And the stone people continued steadily and inexorably to advance, clubs rising and falling. Until Red heard Aurilia cry out, a high urgent imperative.

'Run!' she cried. 'Get *away, quickly!*'

The command made little sense to Red, and as he continued to move towards her he thought he might have misheard in the midst of the crashing, clanging, shouting, screaming, deafening madness of the battle. But in the next moment neither he nor anyone else could mistake her words. She flickered through her shape-change, the white hair of her older form loosening around her like a silver aura. Raising a hand, she somehow

242

grasped the invisible fabric of the air itself to manipulate the transmission of sound. And her magically amplified voice blasted across the battlefield as if from a hundred megaphones.

'Get *back!*' she thundered. '*Run* – and leave them to us!'

The overwhelming power of her voice shook and stunned the army, and made even the stone beings hesitate fractionally. Then Phaedran's sharp voice reinforced the order, and at once all the warriors including the giants abandoned the battle and retreated at a half-run. And Aurilia's voice rang out again, no longer amplified but clear enough, aimed at those of the Seven who still stood with her – the seven women suddenly alone, in the midst of that expanse of bare ground, facing the remaining mass of stone people.

'The Mire!' Aurilia cried. 'Come, Sisters, sing it! *The Mire!*'

Impelled by the force of her, the Seven began to sing – shakily at first, more strongly as Aurilia's voice rose at the heart of the music. The stone people moved forward again, one ponderous step at a time, clubs raised – but the women stood unmoving and wove the song's weird harmonies as if offering themselves as sacrificial victims. Then Red leaped forward to offer some hopeless defence, aware of Krost moving at once to join him.

But they were still several strides away, with the stone people almost upon the Seven, and the song still rippling through the air, when the foremost monster took another step and *sank*, astoundingly, to mid-thigh in what had been solid ground. As, then, did the others around it, and the others behind them. As if the entire clearing where they were massed, just beyond where the Seven stood and sang, had turned into a soupy quagmire.

The creatures struggled with all their considerable might, but their struggling and their weight merely made them sink faster. Some at the rear of their massed throng hesitated and tried to turn away – but the oozy, bubbling mud spread swiftly in their direction and dragged them in. Silently, wildly, helplessly, they flailed and thrashed and steadily sank – one by one vanishing out of sight beneath the heaving, slimy surface. Until at the end only one huge stone head remained upthrust for a

243

moment, its mouth wide in a silent scream, before it was sucked under with all the rest.

With that the song trailed away to an end, and unbroken silence returned to the stony forest, the rain-mist swirling across the clearing as if to reclaim centre stage. In the silence the giants rumbled softly to one another, a sound that seemed to mingle disappointment with relief, while everyone in what was left of the army breathed a deep and grateful sigh, collectively, as if they had been holding their breath for a long time. And the Seven, with Aurilia again in her younger form, turned almost placidly to rejoin the others.

'That was admirably done, my lady,' Phaedran said with quiet formality to Aurilia.

'Most impressive,' Vallawn agreed. 'You seem no less redoubtable now, even though you are Seven.'

And Red, unable to resist it, grinned cheerily at the giant chieftain. 'What do you think of their "little magics" now, Ghiscral?'

Ghiscral bent his head, looking chastened. 'You are right to chide me, Corodel. I spoke unwisely, before.' He turned his gaze to Aurilia. 'I had no idea of the extent of your powers, lady. Without you, truly, we would have been overcome.'

'Forced out of the forest, anyway,' Krost growled. 'That was too much stone for even giants to break.'

'It was,' Ghiscral agreed. 'Though you broke more than your share, Krost il Hak.'

He reached down to pat Krost approvingly on the shoulder, staggering the dwarf-giant slightly. But at the same time Red saw how Krost's eyes lit up, how a grin spread over his face, at receiving praise from his chieftain that for once held no trace of patronage.

But Krost's delight and everyone's relief was necessarily short-lived in that place. Aside from the wholly bare strip of ground that had been turned into the mire – by then resolidified after the song ended – the rest of the clearing was littered with fragments of stone and equally crushed and broken bodies. Several hundred militiamen and Sisters had been killed or disabled, along with a number of wizards and more than a dozen giants, the rain-mist drifting over them like shrouds.

The prince stared broodingly around. 'We must do our duty by our dead, before we continue.'

Ghiscral rumbled assent, but looked troubled. 'Giants bury their dead – but I would not willingly bury anyone here. There may be other stone creatures in the forest. And if they descend from the ancient folk who are said, in the tales, to have dwelt in this valley . . .' He shook his head. 'The tales speak of those ancient ones as worshippers of demons – and devourers of corpses.'

That made everyone look sick. 'It must be fire, then,' Aurilia said calmly, 'in the Sisterhood way.'

Shortly, when the dead had been gathered, the Seven summoned their witch-fire, the wizards contributed their mage-fire, and the unfuelled white-hot blazes quickly did the work of cremation. After which the surviving Sisters carefully collected the ashes of their own dead, singing their small sweet song of mourning.

'I wonder,' Vallawn muttered gloomily, 'if those remains will ever be returned to rest in the Fastness.'

Aurilia shrugged, her eyes bleak. 'The ashes of our dead will somehow eventually find their own way to rejoin the elements, even in this place. Whatever happens to us.'

And everyone avoided the question that arose in all their minds: who would provide funeral rites for the last of them to die in the Leafless Forest?

Deeper in the forest, some distance from where the much-reduced army was bidding farewell to its dead, Gul Ist slumped on a narrow settee in the Magister's tree-walled dwelling. His normally gaunt face looked even more bony, his eyes were ringed with dark shadow, his narrow body seemed almost emaciated so that his severe tunic looked too big for him. Calmly he noted the tremor in his hands, the hollowness in his belly, the catch of his breathing, the gritty bleariness of his eyes.

During that assessment he was joined by Zykiador, looking pale, unsteady and somehow deflated, who waved a hand to call up an overstuffed divan and lowered himself on to it with a groan.

'Many more confrontations like this morning,' he complained, 'and we will end up like the old ones.'

Gul Ist gave him a weary scowl. 'We have not reached the limits of our strength, despite this fatigue. And this morning's struggle would never have happened if that senile fool Ostyril had not fallen asleep.'

'Let's hope that Lebarran can stay awake,' Zykiador said, 'now that *he's* on watch. With no more frenzies.'

They sat silent for a moment, thinking again of the events of that early morning. During the night before, after Lebarran had imposed his orders on the Stone People to marshal them for the dawn attack, the others of the Order had sought their rest in well-pleased anticipation of what should have been a final battle and, with the contribution of their own power, a decisive victory. Old Ostyril had taken his turn on duty, maintaining the watch in the spell-chamber against the Unformed, but he had been unable to stay awake. And now he would never wake again. For as the dawn broke through so did the Unformed, sweeping from its bridge in an assault of murderous speed and power. And it had overcome Ostyril and drained his life-force before the alarm could bring any of the others to his aid.

Astonishingly, then, while the conclave was still frantically trying to erect its counter-attacking spell, the monster had retreated across the misty threshold, back into the Void. Zykiador had wondered if it had left simply because its grisly hungers were sated – but for Lebarran, its retreat seemed to confirm his theory that the monster could not remain out of the Void for any length of time. As if the world of solidity and substance posed some kind of threat to a Void-thing's insubstantial existence.

But any consideration of that significant possibility had had to be postponed, for in the next moment old Dhaminai had collapsed with a seizure, brought on by fatigue, stress and the shock of Ostyril's death. More magical action had been needed to keep him alive – and when that had been accomplished, the wearied sorcerers found to their dismay that the dawn attack had gone ahead, in blind obedience, and the Stone People had not only been routed but virtually wiped out. When that news

flung Lebarran into a manic, incandescent fury that threatened
to become destructive, Gul Ist had tiredly and contemptuously
walked out.

'What are the others doing now?' Gul Ist asked Zykiador at
last, without great interest.

'Lebarran is on watch, as I say, while also staring morosely
at our enemies in his scrying bowl.' Zykiador gestured listlessly
and a full goblet appeared in his hand. 'Yannahac is hovering
and fawning around him as usual. And Dhaminai appears to
be rallying, with the Magister's treatment.'

'Drugs,' Gul Ist said distastefully. 'That false animation will
use him up faster than sorcery.'

'As long as he's alive when we need him,' Zykiador said
through a huge yawn.

Gul Ist clenched bony fists. 'It should never have come to
this,' he snarled. 'Lebarran should never have assumed that a
partial force – Zhraike one time, Stone People the next – would
crush the enemy. The sensible procedure would have been to
let them get close and then deploy *all* his force against them,
at once, together.'

Zykiador yawned again. 'Hindsight always sees clearly, Gul
Ist. And "sensible procedure" always loses out to human weakness, especially when magnified by vanity and high ambition.'

'It need not,' Gul Ist insisted, 'if such weakness can be overcome by self-mastery.'

'Oh, no doubt.' Zykiador settled deeper into his divan, closing his eyes. 'But few of us ever achieve that condition. The
weak cannot, for their selves are mastered by others. The strong
will not, for they prefer the mastery of others.'

'Then they are not truly strong,' Gul Ist snapped. 'Who can
hope to control others who cannot control himself? Consider
Lebarran . . .'

But then he stopped, because his words were being greeted
only by a low, fluttering snore from the depths of Zykiador's
divan. Gul Ist's mouth tightened, but then he sighed, wishing
he could set anxiety aside and sleep so easily. Bitterly he asked
himself when he was likely to sleep in peace again, before the
final sleep from which no one wakes . . . His thin lips writhed

247

in a vicious snarl. Lebarran has *wrecked* it, he thought furiously, he has laid *waste* to the plan. It should have brought us with effortless smoothness, secretly and without impediment, to the Apotheosis that would make us gods. But instead we are brought to this – only four of us left besides Lebarran, all of us exhausted, our leader grown more unbalanced, somehow unable to prevent an enemy force from marching almost to our very door . . .

'Gul Ist.'

Lebarran's strident voice speaking suddenly from empty air made Gul Ist leap with such violent shock that he nearly fell off his seat. But at once he gathered himself, realizing that Lebarran could not have perceived his stream of disloyal thoughts.

'Come to the spell-chamber,' Lebarran snapped. 'Bring Zykiador. Now.'

Hissing with anger at being so peremptorily summoned, Gul Ist woke the other sorcerer and both did as they were bidden. In the broad central chamber Lebarran sat in his high-backed chair with fatigue and tension as visibly etched on his face as on the others. Near by, Yannahac slumped in a lower chair, staring at the Magister with the troubled eyes of an insecure child.

'We will enter conclave—' Lebarran began without preliminary as the other two entered.

'Magister,' Gul Ist broke in, 'we are all greatly wearied. While Dhaminai . . .'

A furious yellow glare from Lebarran halted him. 'Dhaminai won't be needed. In conclave we four will be enough for what is to be done, and we will not be overtaxed.'

'Is it another attack?' Zykiador asked.

'Indirectly.' Lebarran raised his hand in a gesture of imperious command rather than sorcery, and Yannahac dragged himself to his feet. Trudging to one side of the chamber, he lifted up a small chest of dark wood inscribed with unreadable patterns. Struggling with its unwieldy weight, he staggered back to the group.

'Open it,' Lebarran ordered. 'Pour out the contents.'

Puzzled, the other men watched intently as Yannahac opened

the lid of the chest and tipped it over. From it poured a dusty stream of tiny objects, or fragments of objects – flakes and splinters and crumbs, mostly either a pallid white or a stained yellowish-brown.

'Magister?' Gul Ist could not quite hide the scepticism in his voice. 'What is this?'

Lebarran glowered at him. 'This, Gul Ist, is the means of destroying our enemies. Be silent and be instructed.' His glare moved to include them all. 'When this valley was young and its trees bore leaf and fruit, the ancient primitives who dwelt here – the Uthrylin – had some unlovely habits, including the worship of high-level demons and the eating of human flesh. Indeed, they fed on the flesh of their own dead, and often killed to acquire it, so that in time they would have wiped themselves out. But before then, an idle curse from one of their demons turned their forest and their own bodies into undead stone.'

'Changed their eating habits,' Zykiador muttered with a half-smile.

Lebarran's glare impaled him. 'In the time *before* that curse,' he went on, 'whatever portion the Uthrylin didn't eat of their own dead was usually buried with crude ritual in a secret communal tomb. And, a while ago, within a fragment of old lore that I mentioned to you before, I found the *place* of that tomb. And exhumed what remained within.' He indicated the heap of tiny fragments. 'The passing of centuries has left only these sparse remnants. But they will serve.'

Gul Ist bent over the heap, an unpleasant excitement on his thin face. '*Bone* fragments! I see! Hundreds, even thousands – just *waiting* to be embodied!'

'Exactly,' Lebarran said curtly. 'As you know, the embodying spell isn't difficult when some portion of the corpse, however small, remains to build it on. Even for this multitude – thousands indeed, Gul Ist – the spell will not be too strenuous for us in conclave.'

'To send the deathless dead into battle,' Gul Ist said avidly.

Zykiador chortled. 'And when these Uthrylin have done their work, we can enjoy a long rest.'

'With the forest free of enemies,' Lebarran agreed. 'And the

Continent free of serious opposition to our Apotheosis.' He raised his hands. 'Let us proceed.'

The others, all wearing nearly identical smiles full of evil triumph, raised glowing hands over the heap of bone fragments and began a guttural chant in unison. And the fragments instantly leaped into the air, hovering motionless for a moment before being whisked as if by a sudden wind out of the chamber, along the eerie corridors and away into the depths of the forest.

TWENTY-FOUR

'He is certainly no tactician, Lebarran,' Prince Phaedran said thoughtfully. 'Sending his forces against us as he has . . . Had he attacked us today with Zhraike, mage-fire and those stone beings all at once, we might not be here now.'

Around him the survivors of the army, preparing again to march, nodded with expressions of mild interest as if they were discussing military theory in a comfortable drawing-room.

'The Zhraike might have been less effective here,' Krost suggested, 'tangling their wings in these trees.'

'I wonder,' Vallawn said, 'if Lebarran has simply under-estimated us. After all, the attack on the vale would have done us far more harm if not for Naemony's . . . intervention, which the Magister could not have anticipated. As he may not have foreseen today's *inspired* defence by the Seven against the might of the stone people.'

'That may be so,' Aurilia said. 'But he is still the Magister. We, also, can't begin to foresee what he might throw at us next.'

Touch wood when you tempt fate, Red thought, and reached automatically for a nearby tree, only to jerk his fingers away from the cold and clammy stone.

Ghiscral grunted impatiently. 'Then before we meet whatever is next to come, we should move on. We can discuss tactics and such matters with our enemy when we meet him.'

Vallawn sighed. 'Can you maintain that giant-sized confidence even now, Ghiscral? I tell you, Lebarran may simply not have been giving us his full attention. As if we are no more than troublesome insects in his garden. He has expended a little effort, eradicated many of us, and may expect to expend only a little more to finish us off. Meanwhile, as mere insects, we are no real threat.'

251

'I don't know,' Red said idly. 'In my world, there are bugs that eat wood, and have been known to bring down whole houses.'

Ghiscral laughed boisterously. 'Well said, Corodel. Come, enough of this moaning of mages. Let us go and take a few bites out of Lebarran's house before we are done.'

Shortly they were on the move again, formed up as before with the militia and the warrior women flanking the giants. Not one of them made any acknowledgement, by word or even by sorrowful expression, of how reduced their numbers were. To Red it remained clear that despite their losses and grief, their awareness of the probable truth of Vallawn's ominous words, they were all keeping their nerve, marching smoothly and steadily, gazing around at the misty forest as if out for a country stroll. But that morning their calm readiness had a new element beyond the simple accepting fatalism of the previous days. There was also an awareness that they had fought bravely and well, and that they had been granted a share of good fortune to match their heroism. And although they all knew that good fortune tends to even out, pendulums to swing back the other way, still . . . who could know *when* such reverses might begin, when luck might run out? Meanwhile, they were alive. And the mere fact of being survivors, after such battles, led them all to relish every continuing moment of existence, with minimal thought for what the next moment might hold for them, step by step along that fearless advance.

After some while, for the first time since they had entered the forest, a small wind arose. An erratic, troubled wind that sighed and whimpered among the stony tree-trunks, its breath as chill and dank as the rain-mist that it could only disturb but not disperse. Above the marchers the wind drifted among the higher branches of the trees and stirred their spindly twigs with a muffled clatter.

'Sounds like old bones,' Red remarked to Aurilia. 'Like a lot of skeletons rattling around.'

And it was a measure of the company's almost serene state of mind that most of those who heard him responded, as

252

Aurilia did, not with a shiver but with an unforced smile, as they continued their steady progress.

If tension existed at that moment anywhere within the forest, it was to be found in Lebarran's spell-chamber. There he and the other four – for they had been joined by a somewhat restored Dhaminai, looking so shrivelled as to seem almost mummified – sat around the great scrying bowl. Yet they were not watching the advance of the much-reduced army. They were staring intently at an image of an almost treeless stretch of the forest, beyond the outer wall of the dwelling. To that clear space the mass of tiny bone fragments had been swept by their earlier spell, to be scattered widely over the bare grey earth.

But since then, as time had continued to wind steadily on, nothing had happened.

Until finally Yannahac, who had been furtively looking at Lebarran as much as at the bowl, could restrain himself no longer. 'Has the spell gone wrong, Magister? Should it take such a time?'

Lebarran flung him a brief fiery look, then wordlessly turned back to his brooding regard of the bowl's surface. But on Yannahac's other side, Gul Ist's sunken eyes had acquired their own share of anxiety and doubt.

'Perhaps the spell lacked sufficient power,' he said coldly. 'Perhaps we could not properly shape it, overtaxed as we have been . . .'

They all jumped as Lebarran's knotted fist crashed down on the arm of his chair. 'Be silent!' he barked. 'Gul Ist, your thinking is as pinched and ill-nourished as the rest of you! Overtaxed as we may be, though some of us far more than others, that has merely *delayed* the spell briefly! Hold your prattle and watch!'

He swung his yellow gaze back to the bowl. And at once a twisted smile of satisfaction began to appear on his face when – as if responding to a cue – the image on that shiny surface began to move. The others then also sat back, smiling their own gloating smiles, as they watched.

The tiny, widely scattered bone fragments had disappeared

from the expanse of empty ground, as if they had somehow sunk or been drawn down below the soil's blank surface. And all over that surface, at places that numbered many hundreds and more, the soil was moving. A slow upheaving, an ugly rippling and pulsing. As if something that lay beneath the surface, at each of those places, was struggling to come forth.

After some hours, the prince's warriors paused for a brief rest, a shedding of packs and easing of muscles. But still the mood of calm readiness remained unbroken, so that the various quiet conversations that sprang up were generally relaxed and casual. Red was enjoying himself, with Krost, listening to Aurilia and Vallawn who had begun chatting easily, about magic, but who were moving into something more like energetic debate.

'Consider other beings of power,' Vallawn said intently. 'The higher magic has a history of invoking and commanding assorted spirits, not to mention demons. But isn't the Earth-magic limited to a large extent? Unable or unwilling to reach beyond its natural roots here, to summon other beings?'

'It did a good job of summoning *me*,' Red pointed out.

As they all laughed, Aurilia was nodding firmly. 'Unwilling is the truth of it, Vallawn. Adepts and mages are drawn to other sources of power, in other Realms and Spheres, because *power* is so often their sole concern. Elements of egotism, ambition, pride, perhaps greed, run all too clearly through the history of the so-called higher magic. Whereas, no less clearly, the Earth-magic is more devoted to selfless beneficence, the nurturing arts of growth, healing, betterment . . .'

'And chopping Zhraike out of the sky with a sword of fire,' Vallawn interrupted with a small smile. 'But I do take your point to some extent, Aurilia. I could hardly do otherwise when we are here to do battle with a mage of the most ruthless ego and ambition . . .'

He paused, stiffening, his gaze going oddly blank and distant. The others peered at him worriedly, wondering if he had been taken ill, or worse. But slowly his eyes refocused, staring into the mist-veiled dimness among the surrounding trees.

254

'And battle may be about to resume,' he said hollowly. 'I had a momentary sense of a great inhuman host, chill and ghastly . . . I fear that some new vileness is being sent against us now.'

At once Krost sprang up to alert the prince and pass the word. Within moments the warriors had formed up again, weapons ready, needing scarcely a word from any officer or leader. And Phaedran took a slow, encompassing, approving look around at them all.

'My friends,' he said gravely, 'you have fought in this unequal struggle with matchless courage and prowess, and I am proud to have marched with you. Whatever is to befall us now, I know you will stand firm. And may the gods and the fates smile upon us.'

Three strikes and out, Red thought gloomily. But maybe this will be a different game.

As a small murmur of assent and acceptance rose from the army, Red looked around and caught Krost's eye. For a moment they held the look, in wordless mutual encouragement, tinged with the awareness of a possible farewell. Then Red grinned tightly and lifted the drawn sword in a salute, and Krost's eyes crinkled as he raised the quarterstaff in response.

Just as wordlessly, Red turned back to Aurilia and kissed her gently, oblivious to the others around them. And finally the army moved forward, calmly and steadily, their expressions appearing emptied of all emotion, like a pale blank sky after the passing of a storm.

Nor did those expressions change more than slightly when they saw the multitude of squat grey figures, bristling with weapons, stalking towards them among the trees.

At first they thought that it was another force of stone people coming to attack them. These creatures were also long-armed, short-legged and powerfully built, with the same small ugly heads and naked, strangely featureless bodies as the stone monsters. But as the distance narrowed the differences became clear. The skin of the new beings was not like pale rough stone but darker and smoother, more akin to the grey-black of the earth beneath the trees. And these beings moved more easily than the stone people, with more balanced strides, while their weapons – stone-tipped spears, stone-bladed axes – were far more advanced and menacing than makeshift clubs.

But most menacing of all was simply the number of them. They were a host, a multitude, too closely crowded for accurate estimation but without doubt many times larger than the force of stone people in the previous battle, vastly outnumbering Phaedran's army that had been reduced to little more than a thousand intact warriors.

As the army halted, silently and impassively watching the advancing host, their expressions revealing little tension even though the nature and certainty of their fate was clear, Vallawn glanced at Ghiscral with a small questioning frown.

'Could these be the original inhabitants of the valley?' he asked. 'I forget what they were called . . .'

'Uthrylin,' the chieftain said. 'These are something like, but the old tales say they were fur-covered. And they are supposed to have died out.'

'I see.' Vallawn nodded slowly as if at some partial answer to a minor academic query. 'These then will be *embodiments*. I do now begin to sense the sorcery that has re-animated them.'

Ghiscral spat on his hands and took a firm grip on his mace. 'Let them come and be *dis*-animated.'

'I wonder,' Vallawn murmured.

He took a step forward and pointed his stick at one of the nearest of the advancing multitude. A sudden azure bolt of force leaped from the stick – and as it struck, the being that was its target exploded into a cloud of matter that looked little more than dust and grit.

The blast acted like a signal. At once the vast horde of creatures, the re-animated Uthrylin, leaped forward with weapons raised. Though their mouths gaped open as if to utter battle-cries, they none the less charged in a total, macabre silence save for the thudding of their feet on the ground. And, almost as silently, the prince's warriors spread out slightly, planted their feet, and readied themselves.

For all their numbers, the Uthrylin attacked in an untidy,

256

disorganized mass, so that many in that first wave managed to get in one another's way as they sought to strike and stab. In any case, few of those first blows fell, for the line of defenders – moving with more military order and precision – struck first, and ferociously. Under mace and sword and other weapons, hundreds of that first wave of Uthrylin simply collapsed, not as dead or injured bodies but as instantly crumbling, disintegrating heaps of granular grey-black soil.

It's *dirt*, Red thought dazedly as he chopped at an onrushing Uthrylin, watching his sword slice its body almost in half and leave it in another powdery, shapeless pile. They're made of dirt. They're *nothing*.

But in the next moment he learned that he was wrong, as the monstrous reality became clear.

As that first wave of Uthrylin was struck down into so many heaps of dry soil, the heaps at once began to move – heaving, rippling, pulsing. Within seconds each being had become horribly reconstituted, rising again on newly formed legs, weapons again gripped in reshaped hands. Attacking again, no less savagely. Unharmed, unstoppable, undead.

Even worse, the prince's warriors had been drawn forward, charging gleefully and carelessly into the heart of the enemy multitude in what had seemed to be an effortlessly successful counter-attack, cutting the Uthrylin down like weeds. So the humans and giants found themselves like islands in the midst of a grey and overwhelming sea when the supposedly dead beings began to rise again all around.

By then the prince's army had also learned some other dire truths. Arrows, bolts and sword-thrusts had no effect on the creatures. Only being chopped or clubbed into fragments could stop them – and that only briefly, before their regenerating bodies rose again. And they were also uncannily strong and quick, so that men and women were falling in scores under their spears and axes, and even giants were being brought down by the weight of numbers or in hails of thrown spears.

Worst of all, as the battle went on, the Uthrylin attack began to show signs of a pattern, a directed purpose. The army's counter-charge that had taken them into the midst of the multitude had also managed, perilously, to scatter them. And the developing tactics of the Uthrylin seemed to be aimed at separating them even more from one another. Soon the militiamen were fighting in straggling groups, hewing manfully at their enemies but steadily being driven back or cut down by the throngs of horrors around them. Red could see and hear blasts of mage-fire from Vallawn and presumably the other mages, and could hear Krost's battle-roar, but those sounds were moving away from him as the overall battle became more and more split up into isolated pockets of conflict. Even more distant from Red was the furious bellowing of the giants, who had been the first to be cut off when they had led that wild initial charge. And the main force of warrior women were as widely dispersed as the militia, although Brennia had determinedly kept a handful of her troop around the Seven. But even so, there seemed little chance of magical relief this time from Aurilia and the others. Despite Brennia's efforts, two of the Seven, Jhoranna and Ulaminelle, had been felled by thrown spears, and the others found their unity and concentration disrupted by fright and by the sheer grisly chaos of the mêlée around them.

Aurilia herself had no time to gather and focus her magic, forced simply to defend herself without pause, wielding a sword taken from a fallen Sister. Next to her, Red was feeling as if he had been hacking and chopping at an endless supply of grey-black bodies for an equally endless time, watching them reshape themselves and rise from the ground even as he hacked at more. Clearly, he saw, the creatures not only would not stay dead but did not seem to grow tired. And even when his blade sheared through their spear-hafts and axe-handles, made of dry and often half-rotten wood, the weapons were restored just as swiftly as were the bodies of their wielders.

So, he thought bitterly, when we're too tired to swing our swords any more, it'll be all over.

That time seemed none too far away for Red and Aurilia, as they chopped their way through another line of Uthrylin that threatened to engulf them. But the line seemed somehow to close around them, while another group of the creatures drove like a wedge between them and the rest of the group, forcing Brennia and her women back and away. Red and Aurilia counter-attacked, desperately trying to cut their way back to the others of the Five who were still with Brennia's small band. But the two of them were held off, slowly forced away, and could do no more than stand shoulder to shoulder slashing and hacking at the swarming grey bodies. Until, almost shockingly, there were no more left standing to face them in that spot. Then they leaned briefly on tree-trunks, gasping for breath, resting their aching sword-arms, and looked around – to find, also shockingly, that they were quite alone.

The battle by then had spread so widely across the misty spaces of the forest that no other combatants could be seen in their vicinity. Even the noises of battle had diminished, with only a few shouts and crashes reaching them, from what seemed an alarming distance. In that brief lull Red and Aurilia moved away, peering through the dimness for a glimpse of any other survivors. While behind them, and here and there all around them, the grey piles of dirt that had been Uthrylin shifted and pulsed in their ghastly reshaping.

Red jabbed disgustedly at one pile with his sword. 'Don't you have some magic against them?' he asked Aurilia. 'They're *earth*, after all.'

She shook her head dismally. 'I can't undo the sorcery that went into embodying them. Although . . .' she bit her lip, thinking. 'If they're true embodiments as Vallawn thought, each of them should contain some remnant of the *original* Uthrylin, a scrap of skin or hair or bone or something. If there was a way to remove those bits and destroy them, the bodies would stay dead.'

'Great,' Red said, glancing around as those he had just felled rose to their feet again. 'How do we get them to lie still while we root through the dirt for a bit of bone?'

Somehow she managed a half-smile. 'I haven't worked that out yet.'

But then the momentary lull ended, as the renewed Uthrylin charged again. Turning to face that charge, Red and Aurilia began again to hack and dodge and parry and chop, swords slicing easily through the gruesome bodies, stony tree-trunks at their backs protecting them from thrown spears. But with each stroke Red could feel the muscles of his sword-arm growing more strained, and could see the strain on Aurilia's face as well. Slowly they began to back away through the trees, fighting as they retreated, moving in the direction of the other battle-noises that they could hear, by then more distant and even fewer.

But as they continued that slow, defensive withdrawal, some of the other sounds grew steadily more audible. And Red felt a surge of relief as he recognized Krost's voice not too far away, his roar by then reduced to a croak but still sounding indomitable.

Until abruptly that voice was cut off, as if a switch had been thrown.

Red and Aurilia glanced wildly at each other, then together launched a frenzied counter-attack against the group of Uthrylin, slashing and chopping in a reckless expenditure of energy. As their blades mowed the creatures down into squirming heaps of dust, they created another momentary lull, a small breathing-space. And in that instant Red and Aurilia whirled and ran. A spear or two clattered among the trees behind them, hurled by more advancing enemies, but their headlong sprint took them out of range of their heavy-footed pursuers. So they were momentarily alone and in the clear when they circled around a cluster of trees and found Krost.

He was on his hands and knees, like a great bear at bay, in the midst of mounds and drifts of soil where Uthrylin had fallen in droves. In front of him, so it seemed that Krost had been trying to use his own body as a shield, Prince Phaedran lay motionless and bloodstained. Huge smears of blood also showed on Krost's body and clothes, while a small crimson river was pouring from a gash on his temple. And though he still clutched the iron staff, he looked half-stunned, groggy and defenceless, while around him the heaps of dirt were stirring into new life, and a half-dozen intact Uthrylin were creeping towards him with spears poised.

Red and Aurilia sprang forward, swords flashing, and the

upright Uthrylin had no chance against their fury. Before long there were only several more piles of shifting, heaving soil that Red kicked hopelessly at, sickened, before joining Aurilia at Krost's side.

'We must get them away!' she gasped, stooping to take hold of Phaedran, who stirred and moaned. Red grasped Krost under the arms and heaved – but with the dwarf-giant's disproportionate weight it was as if the bulky body had become fixed to the ground. Gritting his teeth and straining, Red could only heave Krost along a slow inch or two at a time, in short agonized jerks, while Aurilia struggled to drag Phaedran away from the spot where so many of the enemy were beginning to rise again. Yet they persisted, wholly focused on the task, ignoring the pain of overstressed muscles just as they ignored the almost certain futility of any attempt to escape.

But then at last they were both forced to stop, to ready their swords once more for another desperate defence, possibly a final one – when another mass of Uthrylin stepped from the mist ahead of them, just as those felled by Krost rose to their feet, whole again, behind.

Aurilia looked around at Red, her green eyes momentarily filled with yearning. In that moment Red wanted very badly to be able to think of exactly the right thing to say to her, some perfect expression of his feelings and his farewell. But he had to content himself with a smile, and with her smile in turn.

Then they moved together, side by side but facing in opposite directions, ready for the attack that would surely overwhelm them. And as the lines of Uthrylin before and behind stalked slowly forward, it seemed to Red that the small wind that had been wafting around all day found a new strength, shaking the upper branches of the trees with a louder burst of hollow, skeletal rattling.

Until he heard Aurilia gasp, and felt his own heart almost stop beating. For he saw that the eerie rattling did not come from the trees at all, but from an enormous number of weirdly inhuman figures that seemed to be materializing from the mist, on every side.

261

TWENTY-FIVE

'My God,' Red said in an awed whisper. 'The Riodae.'

'The what?' Aurilia asked, staring at the new apparitions.

'The . . . ' He caught himself just in time, remembering his solemn pledge to Hallifort to keep the secret of the insect-people. 'They look like they're on our side.'

By then there was no doubt of that. The Riodae, their antennae rattling noisily as if in their own weird form of battle-cry, swept out of the forest in wave upon wave and fell upon the Uthrylin. In their mindless way the Uthrylin tried to stand and fight, but they had little chance of either victory or escape. The Riodae with their armoured bodies were impervious to axe or spear except for stray blows aimed to the head, and their uncanny insectile strength was far greater than that of the other creatures. Also, they had arrived in such numbers that there appeared to be two or three of them to every one of the Uthrylin. As Red and Aurilia looked on, astounded and elated, the insect-people simply took the Uthrylin in their four-handed grasps and tore them apart, scattering the crumbly soil that formed them.

And then, as each Uthrylin was destroyed, one of the Riodae would reach into the resulting pile of dirt with a small precise hand, deftly plucking something out of the midst of the heap. Something too tiny to be clearly visible, though Red and Aurilia had no doubt what it was.

In each case, the Rioda that had removed the tiny object would simply put it into its mouth. And at once the heap of soil that would before have re-integrated into a Uthrylin simply began to dwindle as if slowly dissolving into the ground, and finally disappeared.

'They *know*!' Aurilia breathed. 'They're finding the original fragments and destroying them!'

Red grimaced. 'I can think of tastier snacks.'

By then the one-sided battle had been surging and storming around them for some moments, but it was as if they stood in the calm eye of a hurricane. Not one of the Riodae even looked at them, let alone offering any sign of recognition to Red. Yet within that apparently chaotic mêlée the insect-people seemed always to be in the way to deflect the enemy away from the group of four humans. And the battle was clearly coming to a rapid end, at least in that part of the forest, when Krost groaned and stirred and tried to sit up. His head wound had mostly stopped bleeding, but he still seemed dazed as he struggled to raise himself. Yet even in that daze he was able still to lift the iron staff in battle-readiness when he saw Phaedran lying still and apparently defenceless next to him. Until he became aware of Red and Aurilia, no longer combatants but spectators, and of the slaughter that they were watching.

Staring, Krost struggled to his feet. By then the battle was mostly done, with a last small pocket of Uthrylin being summarily dealt with some distance away. Nor was there any trace at all remaining of the fallen Uthrylin. And the Riodae not involved in that final mopping-up were methodically collecting their few dead and injured who had suffered blows to the unarmoured head, still not giving the slightest sign that they had even registered the presence of the humans.

'What is this?' Krost growled. 'Bug-people fighting for us? Or am I delirious?'

'If you are, we all are,' Aurilia said. 'They just appeared, out of nowhere, and started destroying Uthrylin.' She looked speculatively at Red. 'But you seemed to recognize them, Red. Didn't you?'

'Me?' Red said with perfect innocence. 'What would I know about any of the creatures around here?'

'These beings are not from the Highlands,' Krost assured them. 'I have never seen their like anywhere in the Continent.'

'Nor I,' Aurilia said. 'Yet here they are, like an answer to a prayer.'

'Can we talk about it later?' Red asked pointedly, trying to divert their attention.

The others twitched and blinked, coming back to the present moment. 'Yes,' Krost said at once, 'we must find help for Phaedran!'

'And look for the others,' Aurilia added.

If there are any left, Red thought darkly. And while Krost, seeming more restored with every moment, bent to scoop up the unconscious prince as if he were weightless, Red looked around again at the Riodae that were completing the task of gathering their fallen, picking up those bodies as effortlessly as Krost had picked up Phaedran. For a fleeting instant, then, one of the insect-beings paused, with the mist floating around it like a pale cloak, and turned its oddly blank eyes towards Red. The long antennae quivered, rustling – and then the being turned away, along with all its swarm of companions, and melted silently into the forest.

Yet it seemed to Red – if his sense of direction was accurate – that they were not moving as if to leave the forest but to penetrate more deeply into its heart. I wonder if they're going after Lebarran himself, Red thought with a stir of excitement. And I wonder what made Hallifort change his mind about helping – if it *was* Hallifort who sent them.

Then he and the others moved away, warily following the vanished Riodae, seeing no sign of Uthrylin anywhere among the trees, hearing no sounds of continuing battle or indeed any sound at all beyond their own footsteps and the rustle of the breeze among the branches. At last Krost flung caution aside and raised his voice in a great bass shout that echoed through the forest. And all three of them laughed aloud to hear a gusty bellow of response from Ghiscral, not too far ahead.

But their gladness faded again when they reached the small misty glade where other survivors had gathered and saw how heartbreakingly few there were.

Only eight giants besides the chieftain himself were there, and none was free of some sort of wound. With them was only a few score of militiamen, looking worn out and almost witless with shock, and leaderless as well in the absence of Trochain and every other officer. Even fewer of the warrior women remained, with Brennia among them wounded in one side and a thigh. But with them were the other four survivors of the Nine, Wybrette and Malavie, Prelisse and Queminda, looking distraught and tearful as they moved among the wounded with whatever healing magic they could summon – and Vallawn was there as well, gloomily staring into the forest's mist, all alone, not one other wizard in evidence.

But the unexpected reappearance of Red and the others provided an immense lift to the spirits of those in the glade. Re-energized, some of the Sisters buzzed around Phaedran, plying their magic, while others tended Krost's hurts and some cuts and scrapes that Red and Aurilia had suffered without really noticing. Before long Phaedran was awake, his strength slowly returning to him, joining in the general discussion about the mysterious beings who had so astoundingly come to their rescue.

'They lacked magic,' Vallawn said, glancing at Aurilia for confirmation. 'I had no sense of the power within them.'

'Nor did I,' Aurilia agreed. 'Yet they knew just what they were doing, just how the Uthrylin could be destroyed.'

'I have heard tales,' Krost rumbled. 'Prospectors' tales, of things like oversized insects, glimpsed now and then in the Wastelands.'

'The Wastelands?' Aurilia frowned at Red. 'Where you ran into Hallifort again . . . Red, are you *sure* you don't know anything about those creatures?'

Red managed a convincingly easy laugh. 'Come on, Aurilia. I'm a stranger here, remember? Anyway, where I come from old prospectors are always seeing weird things in the desert. Because they're usually half-crazy with loneliness, sunstroke and drink.'

To his relief, Aurilia turned away to smile at Krost. 'Of course. These tales were no doubt told to you in the taverns of Quamarr, over plenty of strong ale.'

Krost laughed, and the others joined in. 'I admit it. Still, we have no other clue about where those beings came from.'

'Or who sent them,' Phaedran croaked, 'if they were sent. Or *why.*'

Ghiscral stirred restlessly. 'What does it matter, in the end?

265

Maybe they have some ancient feud with Uthrylin, and came merely to kill them.'

'Except,' Vallawn said thoughtfully, 'they seem now to have gone on, to do more. Perhaps to pit themselves against Lebarran and his Order, wherever they are.'

'Then we must follow them,' the prince said. 'With their aid we may still bring Lebarran down.'

Vallawn's small sigh combined regret and resolution. 'Indeed,' he said, rising stiffly to his feet. 'We must play out the drama to the end.'

A murmur of weary consent swept through the small company. Slowly they all stood up, reaching for their weapons, their eyes blank and distant, their faces expressionless.

'To the end,' Phaedran echoed grimly as he rose.

'And no battle ends,' Ghiscral added, 'till it is won or lost.'

It was clear that the embodying spell on the Uthrylin, and the effort of maintaining it while to some extent directing them in the chaos of combat, had taken a further toll on the sorcerers of Lebarran's Order. Old Dhaminai drooped limply in his seat, breathing only shallowly, looking even more like a disinterred corpse. Zykiador's face was a mottled purple, his clothing sweat-stained, his puffy flesh sagging. Gul Ist had turned a sickly grey, seeming even thinner and drier, while Yannahac slumped as if half-conscious, pallid and twitching. And even Lebarran himself – having briefly abandoned the watch against the Unformed for what he had thought would be a swift victory – looked shrunken and drained, the light in his eyes dulled and fitful.

Yet he stared unblinking into the scrying bowl, where the surface showed the great swarm of Riodae moving in meticulous formation. But that swarm was not the scene in the forest at that moment. Lebarran was scrying into the *past*, to see the Riodae as they had been while marching across the land towards the Clouded Valley.

'So they are not from another Sphere, not summoned by sorcery.' The Magister's mutterings were directed at himself, as if he were alone. 'From the Wastelands, indeed. Where they have lived all this while unknown even to me. Where the outlander escaped my demon, somehow, with the help of the mysterious Hallifort...' His eyes flared more brightly. 'By the powers, when this is over I will *find* this Hallifort and fling him for all time into the Realm of the Abyss!'

He gestured jerkily, moving his scrying sight back to the present, placing on the bowl's surface the image of the Riodae's relentless march through the forest at that moment, towards his dwelling. His hands flexed wildly on the chair arms and his face contorted in a terrible manic grimace as he whirled to face the others.

'Stir yourselves!' he barked. 'We must sweep these insects from the forest!'

Zykiador groaned. 'Magister, we have expended so much...'

'Weaklings!' Lebarran raged. 'Will you whimper and cower and be *overrun*? At once, now...'

'But, Lebarran,' Gul Ist protested, 'what of the watch that must be kept against the Unformed?'

Lebarran hesitated briefly. But then his feral glare fell again on the image of the Riodae in the bowl, and new fury grasped him. 'We have remained unthreatened this past while,' he snarled, 'and we will surely remain so awhile longer. These insects are our present concern. Come, now – use stimulants, if you must – but *prepare* yourselves!'

Under the lash of his fury they slowly responded. Their hands produced a faint unsteady glow as they summoned what they needed to energize themselves. A large foaming beaker of some potion for Zykiador, and the same for Yanna-hac, and for Gul Ist a vial from which a heavy yellow vapour rose. Gulping or inhaling, the three sorcerers at once exhibited a new vigour, though their eyes seemed feverish and their hands shook slightly even as their glow brightened. By then Lebarran, his own energies apparently refuelled entirely by rage, had surrounded Dhaminai with a cloud of force that had jolted him back into a febrile alertness. And then all five turned together to study the image in the scrying bowl, where the Riodae stalked through the forest, their eyes as chill and colour-less as the rain-mist swirling around them.

'Insects,' Lebarran hissed. 'We'll need no prolonged effort

against these. Nor will we require complex spells. And when they are all destroyed or driven away, we may use only the same undemanding magics against the helpless remnant of Phaedran's force.' His face was a mask of savagery. 'Also, indeed, we can bring them *to* us. They deserve a prolonged and anguished death, after plaguing us so.'

As he raised glowing hands to begin, Gul Ist intervened. 'Magister, you have not said ... What spell *do* you propose, against these insect-creatures?'

Lebarran smiled viciously. 'A spell to summon the familiar force that *all* insects fear, more than any other.'

If you go down to the woods today ... The words of the song repeated over and over in an endless loop in Red's mind. Maybe I'm cracking up, he thought. Maybe we all are. For why else would we be marching on through this gruesome forest on this terrible afternoon as if we knew where we were going and why? Which we surely don't. In fact, I'd bet that we're thoroughly *lost*. Though that may be the least of our problems ...

They had not caught up with the army of Riodae, had not indeed seen or heard anything of them since the defeat of the Uthrylin. The forest had shown them only the incessant rain-mist and the endless stony ranks of trees. And only once had the baleful silence around them been interrupted since they had set off. Just some moments before, they had heard a strange muffled thunder in the distance ahead – like the sweep of a mighty wind, although reminding Red somehow of the rushing roar of flame, like the sound of a forest fire that he had once experienced. But fire, in that forest? It would have to be mage-fire, he thought, his heart sinking. Yet they had felt no pressure from a wind, no breath of heat, no unusual phenomena at all to accompany the sound. Nor had the sound been repeated.

So they had not slowed or hesitated as they continued their advance. By then, the faces of the pitifully small company showed mostly only a numb emptiness, beyond their previous calm acceptance, almost beyond all feeling itself. Even those carrying quite severe wounds seemed indifferent to any pain or incapacity, stumbling along with the others as they all went forward in a mass that resembled no sort of military formation. Krost was, as always, at his prince's elbow just as Red was at Aurilia's, the four of them towards the centre of the company together with Brennia and her few warriors, the others of the Five in their midst. The remaining militia brought up the rear while ahead, in the lead as ever, marched Ghiscral and his few giants. And in an odd pairing Vallawn was at the giant chieftain's side, leaning on his stick as usual yet seeming to have no difficulty maintaining the pace. While around them the mist danced in eerie amorphous shapes and the waning breeze rattled the stony twigs as if in mocking imitation of the vanished Riodae.

Oh, Hallifort, Red thought dismally, if it was really you who sent them, have you taken them back now, too soon? But a stray wisp of logic reminded him that the Riodae had no magical power with which to confront sorcerers. They might have had no more chance against Lebarran, he thought, than . . . than we have.

And with that reminder of just how minuscule their present chances had become, he reached with his left hand towards Aurilia's arm, just for the momentary solace of the touch.

But his fingers never reached their goal. In that moment the forest around them was torn apart by an earth-rending explosion. And as the shockwave hurled them all in every direction like thistledown in a gale, Red was picked up as if by a giant unseen hand and flung crushingly against the unyielding trunk of a tree.

He ricocheted off the tree-trunk and fell to the ground, half-stunned by the impact, battered then by a second mighty explosion near by, and then a third. He flattened himself on the dank soil like a panicked beast, trying to find a place of safety. Around and above him, remorselessly, the blasts continued – a bombardment, there was no better word, of fiery magical force as murderous as mortar shells, or grenades, since each blast that fell among the petrified trees shattered them

269

into rubble and flung the sharp fragments in every direction like a deadly spray of shrapnel.

He had no idea how long he lay there, feeling the ground-shaking impact of the explosions around him, ducking while the stony shrapnel whistled above his head. Faintly, in the distance, between blasts, he could hear people screaming, and horror tore at his mind as he imagined that one of them might be Aurilia. Yet his body seemed immobile, his legs limp and unresponsive as if that first blast had crippled him. And every time he tried to fight the helplessness, tried to lift up his upper body at least in the hope that he could begin to crawl, another nearby eruption of flame flung him face-first on to the ground again.

I promised to stay with her, he reminded himself agonizedly. I have to *move* . . . And also, amid his concern for Aurilia, he was sharply aware of how much less hope any of them had if they let themselves be scattered through the forest again, waiting for Lebarran to pick them off one by one. *Move!* he raged silently at himself, struggling once more to activate his useless legs, and failing. Terror tore at him then as he struggled, with the awareness that his legs were not only unmoving but entirely without feeling. I'm *paralysed*, he thought in an inward cry – and then he caught himself, fending off the panic as his rational mind pointed out ironically that he probably would not have to live with paralysis, or with anything else, for much longer.

The touch of gallows humour cleared his head and strengthened his determination. As did the fact that the bombardment had moved away from him, focusing over towards his right, somewhere near the by then fading sounds of screams. Right, he snarled at himself. Go look for her, even if you have to slither.

At least his upper body was working fairly well, though aching almost everywhere from the bruising impact with the tree. Awkwardly he raised his torso enough so that he could reach down to his hip, feeling a brief gladness to find that his sword was still in its sheath. Heaving with arm and shoulder muscles alone, he dragged himself up against a tree-trunk,

270

staring around at the shattered trees around him – only to freeze as he heard a muffled exclamation coming from only a few feet away. Snatching wildly at the sword, he thrashed around to get into a position for some kind of defence. Until he heard the quiet old voice behind him.

'Calmly, young Red,' Vallawn said. 'It's me.'

Red twisted the rest of the way around and saw the old wizard, looking more or less intact save for some extensive rents in his cloak, crawling on hands and knees towards him. Or *hand* and knees, Red saw, for Vallawn's other hand was holding his crooked stick up over his head. From its glowing tip there seemed to radiate a hazy brightness that arched over and around the wizard in a protective hemisphere. A very unusual umbrella, Red thought, and had to bite back almost hysterical laughter.

'I'm glad you sat up,' Vallawn said. He seemed entirely calm and at ease, his breathing even, his gaze almost placid. 'I might have gone right past you.' He glanced along the length of Red's body. 'Are you very badly hurt?'

Red jerked slightly as a possibly random blast of magical force struck near by, and a few shards of stony shrapnel whistled past them. But the fragments all veered unnaturally away from the hazy hemisphere around the old wizard, who paid them no attention at all.

'I don't know,' Red said, answering the question at last. 'I can't move my legs.'

'Ah.' Vallawn crawled closer and prodded at his legs with a long finger. 'No bones broken,' he announced. 'You probably landed too hard and the nerves have gone dead with shock. They'll wake up soon.'

Even as he spoke, Red could feel the first faint tingling of pins and needles along his legs' overstressed nerve-ends. At once he tried to get to his feet, only to sink helplessly down again.

'Take your time,' Vallawn advised.

'There *is* no time,' Red growled. 'Do you know what happened to any of the others?'

'Aurilia's fine, I believe,' Vallawn said at once, smiling faintly

271

at Red's sigh of relief. 'As are Krost and some of the others who were near the front of our group, with the giants. The first blasts seemed to hit *behind* us – cut down some militia and threw everyone everywhere. When I got my wits together I heard a few shouts, from far away, that sounded like Krost and the giants. And I'm sure I heard some faint singing, which would be Aurilia and the others of the Five. But it faded as they probably moved away.'

'Where?' Red demanded.

Vallawn frowned. 'I have to say I was a bit turned around, in the trees, trying to get away from the blasts. And it's not always easy in this forest to know just where sounds are coming from. But I'm *fairly* sure' – he pointed – 'that they were over that way.'

'Then that's where I'm going,' Red said grimly. 'Can you help me, here? Get my legs working?'

'I have almost no healing power,' the wizard said. As he spoke he reached into his cloak with a small smile. 'But this works nearly as well.'

He brought out a narrow flat flask, opened it and took a swig, then handed it to Red. Warily, not knowing what to expect from a wizard, Red took a sip, to discover a cool, dry, light-textured liquid that tasted very familiar. It seemed to rush straight into his bloodstream, infusing every cell of his body with vigour and energy, managing even to reduce the electric sting of pain as life and feeling went on returning to his legs.

Slowly and carefully he got to his feet, passing the flask back to Vallawn with a grin. 'There's *hanac* in that, isn't there? The pick-me-up that the giants make?'

Vallawn nodded. 'Ghiscral very kindly gave me some, and I made a few magical improvements to it. To keep these old legs going.'

He began to tuck the flask away – but then both of them flinched reflexively at another magical blast, and then another. Until they realized that the blasts were not aimed at them but were striking into the region of forest that Vallawn had pointed to, a moment before.

'Lebarran is bearing down,' Vallawn muttered, peering into

the mist. 'If the Five are shaping some magical song – perhaps a form of shielding – the enemy will sense it, and will aim his fire at it.'

'Can they really put up a shield against those blasts?' Red asked tensely.

'If enough of the Five are still . . . operating,' Vallawn said.

Red clenched his jaw. 'Then we'd better move on while we can.' He hesitated, realizing the presumption. 'That is, if you're coming with me.'

'Certainly,' Vallawn replied. 'I've nowhere else to go. And at the moment, Lebarran seems to be focused on the Five, ignoring us.' As he spoke the shielding that emanated from his stick quivered once and vanished. 'So I will offer him no targets. He would sense my magics quite easily, but he may be too busy to seek for our mere selves. We'll go on without magic – if you don't mind the risk . . .?'

'If I minded risks,' Red said through his teeth, 'I'd be back in my own world by now. Come on – let's go find Aurilia.'

TWENTY-SIX

To his annoyance Krost could not keep from flinching, an
uncontrollable duck of his head, with each successive blast
of magical force and the attendant storm of hurtling stone
fragments. It made him feel only slightly better to see that
Ghiscral and the four remaining giants reacted with the same
reflexive recoils. Yet neither magical fire nor stony shrapnel
struck Krost or any of the others as they moved slowly forward.
And that was something of an astonishment, for the shielding
that had been raised around them by Aurilia and the rest of the
Five seemed no more than a delicate, nearly invisible tracery of
silver light, and apparently needed constant reinforcement, a
ceaseless repetition of the song-spell.

Meanwhile the Five themselves looked almost as fragile as
their shield. Aurilia's face was bloodless and she was staring
unseeingly ahead, moving like a sleepwalker as she poured
her energies into the song – so that Krost stayed at her side to
guide her, sometimes even to lift her, past obstacles. Just as the
giants were helping the others of the Five, actually carrying
Malavie and Queminda, whose physical strength had reached
its limits even though their tremulous voices kept up the song.

Once we were an army, Krost thought woefully. But now we
are a tiny doomed band in the midst of a kind of hell, with
fire raining down on us, waiting for the moment when our
magic will exhaust itself, long before our enemy's . . .

'No,' he growled aloud, the sound lost in the crash of another
mage-fire blast behind them. I wish I could shut off my mind,
he thought desperately. As Aurilia seems to have done, filling
her thoughts with only the shielding song, not letting herself
think about how few we are, how weary and weak. Even the
giants are weakened, from many wounds, and from meeting
an enemy they cannot fight. But Aurilia sees none of that,

Krost thought – she has closed her mind against it, against the numbers of our dead and wounded scattered in this hellish place. And is Phaedran one of the dead or lost? And Vallawn, and Brennia . . .? And Red, my young friend and comrade from a strange other place, is he now at last among the fallen in a war that was never his? But Aurilia must especially forbid that thought, for if she is distracted by grief and stops to weep our shield will surely fall . . .

Oh, gods, Krost thought, blinking furiously against the sting of tears, I wish I could shut off my mind.

And then he ducked his head again, for the hundredth or thousandth time, as another furious explosion near by deafened them with its roar and blinded them with its scarlet flame. As the splintered shrapnel stormed around them the shielding seemed to wobble and sag, when Prelisse stumbled over a stony tree-root and nearly fell. But a giant lifted her safely to her feet, Aurilia heightened her own voice for a moment without any effect on the unseeing blankness of her face, and the shield recovered. Just in time to resist the next blast.

They are coming more often, Krost thought. As if the enemy is gaining strength, even while the Five are nearing the end of theirs. But then, as the continuing blasts rained down, despite his inner turmoil of rage and despair, Krost dimly began to perceive that something odd was happening, had *been* happening throughout the whole bombardment.

Since the eleven of them had come together after the very first disruptive explosions – and since they had begun moving away through the forest together – every single one of the blasts that had since come down upon them had *missed*.

Either we have been impossibly lucky, time after countless time, every step of the way, Krost thought. Or Lebarran and his sorcerers have been just as impossibly inaccurate, every single time.

But as another huge blast erupted among the trees behind them, and then another in exactly the same place, the vague perception took firmer shape in his mind, and he guessed the truth.

They are missing us on purpose, he thought. The blasts strike behind us, or to one side or the other if we try to turn. So they are being very accurate, very controlled and exact. Because—

We are being *driven*.

Towards where Lebarran waits, in his lair.

His hand tightened on the iron quarterstaff, his face went hard and bleak as granite. No doubt, he thought, the Magister has some dire and loathsome plans for us when he has forced us into his presence. But if we do come face to face with him, let him in the arrogance of victory leave one tiny chink of an opening. That we might strike at least one blow before we meet our fate.

I wish Red was here, he thought irrelevantly, to make one of his wry jokes . . .

At that moment Ghiscral, slightly ahead of them all, raised a huge hand in a gesture of warning. The shield briefly wavered as they came to a halt, peering tensely ahead. They had come to the edge of a huge expanse of level, open ground, entirely free of trees except at its centre. And there the trees seemed to stand quite differently from all others in the forest. They were not widely spread but jammed tightly together, in an unnaturally straight line that extended for quite some distance. Like a wall.

And, dimly visible in the mist, another weirdly straight line of trees standing tightly together formed a right-angled corner with the first line. And in each of the lines, each wall, they could see a dark opening, like a cave-mouth or a doorway. It is a structure, Krost realized – a strange and terrible building. And the truth of it became more clear when they looked up through the mist to see the gigantic flattened cone of the canopy that formed the building's roof. A canopy that seemed to be made of dark metal, and that hung in the air high above the building without any visible form of support.

A small echo sounded distantly in the depths of Krost's memory, something that seemed familiar about the canopy. But as he tried to grasp the elusive trace, he saw a flicker of scarlet curve up over the building's unnatural wall, arching out between the tree-tops and the canopy above them, spearing down into the forest behind where the small group stood on

276

the clearing's edge. But as it struck and exploded, it flung a sweep of fire on either side of the blast – which rose and steadied into a fixed wall of red flame, blocking their retreat.

The Five, quaveringly maintaining their song, did not spare it a glance. But the giants stared around, exchanging looks of apprehension and uncertainty. And then all of them, including Ghiscral, turned to look at the eleventh member of the group.

'Krost?' Ghiscral rumbled.

Even at that moment, even standing on the edge of certain doom, Krost felt an inner surge of gladness and pride. *He*, the scorned and derided dwarf, was being asked for advice and leadership by the chieftain of his people. Yet nothing of his feelings showed in his face as he slowly shook his head.

'I see no choice for us,' he growled. 'We have been driven here by mage-fire, and now we are to be driven *in*. Unless we choose to stand here and be blasted or burned. For myself, I would go in – and see what chances the fates might offer us to fight before we die.'

'Well spoken,' Ghiscral rumbled approvingly, while the other giants nodded, squaring their shoulders, setting aside their doubts and qualms.

Aurilia turned her blank gaze towards Krost. 'The shielding will last a while yet,' she said tonelessly, before at once taking up her place in the song again.

Krost grinned fiercely. 'Then, my brothers,' he said to the giants, 'let us pay our visit to Lebarran in his den.'

Vallawn took a swig from his flask before passing it to Red. 'Aurilia and the others must have raised a potent shield,' he murmured, 'if they have risked entering there.'

Red took an automatic sip of the energizing liquid, staring tensely through the mist. Beyond the trees where they crouched he could see a huge swath of open ground leading to the weirdest-looking building he had ever seen, with walls made of close-packed petrified trees and a sort of roof like an enormous flattened metal pyramid hanging high above the trees with nothing holding it up. Shortly before he and the wizard had reached the edge of the clearing, the steady barrage of mage-

277

fire elsewhere in the forest – presumably aimed at Aurilia and the others – had come to a sudden stop. The ominous, weighty, unbroken silence that had followed had filled Red with even more dread than the preceding bombardment, for at first he believed it meant that the others had been overcome. But when they saw the uncanny building, Vallawn had said that he could still sense the Earth-magic operating near by. And he guessed that Aurilia and the other survivors had, unbelievably, entered the building.

So Red and Vallawn were going in as well. Although the thought of doing so was threatening to petrify Red as completely as the immobile trees around him.

'You think Lebarran still hasn't noticed us?' Red asked shakily, blinking at an opening in the building's nearest wall, a threatening gape of darkness.

'If he had,' the wizard said calmly, 'he would surely be attacking us. His attention must still be fixed on the Five. And perhaps he and his Order are growing weary from this prolonged assault.'

'What about Aurilia's weariness,' Red asked, his voice ragged, 'keeping up that shielding?'

'She is healthy and strong,' the old mage assured him. 'And as far as I can tell, their song-spell is being sustained. But we should proceed, Red, while we can.'

Red took a deep breath, gritting his teeth painfully, trying to call on whatever remained of his normally reckless spirit. 'Then let's go,' he snarled, and stepped forward at once before his blood and flesh could freeze completely over with fear. Come on, *Corodel*, he told himself bitterly, tightening his hand around the sword's hilt, it's time to go die like a man. And if you can get lucky enough to do Lebarran some harm, first, you might even keep Aurilia alive. Which is definitely worth dying for.

But what I wouldn't give, he thought as they strode swiftly across the open ground, if Vallawn could make us invisible or something. Because this is no place to feel as naked and exposed as I feel right now . . .

Even so, he and the wizard reached the outer wall of the building without incident, and edged along it towards the opening that yawned like a great dark doorway without a door. Slowly, warily, they stepped through – to find themselves in a shadowy corridor that stretched forward into darkness made more opaque by the rain-mist. Pulse-rate accelerating and neck-hairs bristling, Red lifted the luminous sword high to let its light reach out. The walls of the interior, he saw, were also formed from closely packed trees while the floor was simply bare earth. And as far as he could see, the corridor was bare and deserted all the way along to the narrow, darker opening at its far end. Deserted and entirely silent, an increasingly oppressive silence as if the air around them was too heavy with menace to carry sound.

'I don't like this,' Red muttered, his breathing laboured as he stared along the corridor. 'Where *is* everybody?'

Vallawn did not reply at once, standing with his head lifted and tilted. 'The Earth-magic is certainly here. And Lebarran and his Order as well. But . . .' He lowered his head, his eyes shadowed. 'I can sense something else,' he went on hollowly. 'Some other force, vast and terrible, gathering at the heart of this place. We must *hurry*, Red.'

And they set off, their way lit by the glowing sword, along the corridor.

'Pick him up! *Pick him up!*' Lebarran raged, leaping to his feet, sending his heavy chair flying backwards with a splintering crash, his face suffused and contorted with fury. Across from him, where the others had arranged their chairs in a loose circle at the centre of the spell-chamber, Zykiador and Yannahac were bending over their aged colleague Dhaminai – who had suddenly gasped, fallen sideways and then slid out of his chair on to the floor like a limp pile of rags.

'Put him in his *chair!*' Lebarran roared, his phosphorescent hands outstretched like claws. 'Help me revive him . . .'

'There's no point,' Zykiador grunted, straightening up tiredly, sweat streaming down his face. 'He's dead.'

'He *can't* be dead!' Lebarran raged. 'Pick him *up*, I tell you!'

'Leave him be!' Gul Ist suddenly yelled from his chair. 'You've killed him, Lebarran, with your drugs and your demands!'

The abrupt cessation of Lebarran's manic fury was even

more terrifying than the rage itself. His molten eyes fixed on Gul Ist, and his voice lowered into a cavernous rasp. 'I will kill you *all*, Gul Ist, if I have to, before I let one of those vermin out there elude me. In any case, the old fool was little use. We can gather them in ourselves. Continue, now, together . . .!'

He raised his hands, glaring around at them. By then Zykiador and the cringing Yannahac had resumed their seats, and with Gul Ist wearily lifted their glowing hands as well. And then they paused, looking cruelly pleased despite their fatigue as the magical awareness reached them.

'They're in the building,' Gul Ist snarled.

Lebarran's face twisted in a ghastly smile. 'Soon they will be here before us,' he grated. 'Grasp them, now, bring them, together . . .'

Hands raised again, they all tensed as if straining to move some invisible weight. But then Zykiador grunted and sagged in his seat as if suddenly deflated, Yannahac whimpered, Gul Ist hunched and gasped. And again in mounting fury Lebarran threw back his head and bellowed, fists clenched above him.

'How can it *be*?' he roared. 'How can their pathetic shield *resist* us?'

'Because we are *weary*, Magister!' Zykiador moaned. 'We are spent and weakened . . .'

He got no further. With another crazed howl, Lebarran gestured – and something invisible flashed across the chamber and struck Zykiador like a whip. Squealing, the other sorcerer toppled out of his chair, clutching at his face where a livid weal appeared along one jowl.

'Stop whining about weariness, you dribbling coward, and do my bidding, or . . .'

But then Lebarran too was interrupted. Not by a voice but by a far mightier and more frightful sound.

Above, where it hovered almost unseen in the rain-mist, the great metal canopy resounded, a deep sonorous clang.

And on the far side of the chamber, the air began to shiver and condense as a haziness appeared, growing and steadying – into the shape of tall columns that formed a threshold. With the image of a great bridge stretching endlessly beyond it.

Where something huge and shadowy and shapeless flowed towards the opening, the horrifying force of its hunger reaching out before it.

Lebarran threw back his head and howled maniacally again, a cry of uncontrollable fury and desperation. 'Not now! *Not now!*'

'Magister . . .!' Yannahac squeaked, as the others rose to their feet, staring at the monstrosity advancing upon them.

Abruptly, in another unpredictable shift, Lebarran was controlled again. 'Yannahac, to me!' he roared. 'Gul Ist, Zykiador, continue the attack!'

'But, Lebarran . . .!' Gul Ist cried.

'Do as I say!' Lebarran raged. 'We two will keep it at bay while you two kill the witches! Do you hear me? Kill them quickly, *kill them!*'

'Stop a minute,' Red whispered, his voice ragged with tension. 'This is getting us nowhere.'

They were creeping along another corridor, the fourth or maybe the fifth that they had traversed since entering the building. All of the corridors had been bare and deserted, as had the rooms that opened off them along the way – revealing nothing but the crude walls of the tree-trunks and the blank grey earth of the floor.

'No,' Vallawn replied, 'we're fairly near the centre, I believe. I can sense the currents of power more strongly.'

'But it's all so *empty*,' Red said. 'What if it's a maze or something, designed to trap intruders?'

'Then we might be trapped,' Vallawn said calmly. 'But more probably, Lebarran furnishes different areas as and when he uses them, as many high adepts do. I think we're still . . .'

He stopped, both of them jerking up their heads to listen. The sound that had penetrated the silence was not another magical explosion but something they had not heard before in that place. Another human voice, some distance away and muffled by the stony walls, but unmistakably raised in what sounded like an animal howl.

Instantly Red thought of a prisoner in torment and fought

281

against an image of Aurilia surrounded by torturers. 'Have they caught someone, do you think?' he asked Vallawn raggedly.

'No, no,' the wizard murmured. 'I'm sure that was Lebarran.'

Red stared at him. 'But it sounded like someone in trouble. Or out of his mind.'

'Very possibly,' Vallawn said. 'He always tended to be unstable, even in his youth. Though I doubt if an insane Magister would be any less dangerous.'

'Then let's hope he's in trouble,' Red said grimly, lifting the bright sword again as they moved on.

And then he was nearly driven to his knees with shock as the vast metal canopy above the building suddenly rang out with an earthshaking, clangorous note like the toll of a colossal bell.

Maybe something is going wrong for them, Krost thought, wondering if he dared break into Aurilia's near-trance to ask her. But their shielding, he knew, took precedence. Especially since the breath-stopping moment when they had dashed across the open stretch of ground and had entered the building. For a time then, inexplicably, the assault on them had paused. But even so, while they crept along a series of dim corridors where they could barely see, the Five had tremulously kept up their song and their shield. And that had proved wise, for the short lull had finally ended – when some invisible power had descended terrifyingly upon them as if to seize them in a monstrous grip. But the shield had resisted even that until the grasping force had suddenly vanished, as if swept away in the moment when the building's hovering metal roof clanged out its awesome note. Then Krost and the giants had huddled around the Five, certain that some ghastly new sorcery was about to be hurled at them.

But in fact all that was hurled was a resumption of the explosive mage-fire – showing that Lebarran was as willing to blow apart the walls of his dwelling as he had been to flatten the forest outside. Except that the new bombardment seemed noticeably weaker than before, the blasts more spasmodic and erratic, so that the shielding of the almost exhausted Five could still prevail against it. And between blasts, Krost could hear distant sounds like voices, coming from somewhere ahead of them in the network of corridors, sounding distorted with fury or with fright.

Cautiously but unhesitatingly they advanced towards the sounds, until before long they could hear more clearly. And then Krost felt even more certain that something was going wrong for the enemy. There was a roaring bass voice that sounded almost crazed with fury, a shrill voice that was a birdlike cry of abject terror, and now and then two other voices that seemed to be gasping and whimpering and groaning all at the same time. And when the small group within its shielding rounded a corner in that passage, to see a spill of pale light ahead from a doorway through which the voices came more clearly, they paused for a moment, readying themselves, with Krost and the giants exchanging grimly determined looks.

The end of the road, Krost thought. The goal that we marched from Quamarr to find. Now let us see what finally awaits, beyond that door.

Weapons ready, supporting or carrying the still faintly singing Five, Krost and the giants grinned briefly at each other and then went forward in a rush, surging through the doorway from which the light was spilling – into a scene of compelling horror and imminent destruction.

In the flashing instant as they burst into the bright chamber, Krost saw and recognized the monstrosity that he had seen once before, the huge shapeless presence that had received sacrificial offerings in the Lightless Dome. It was at its hazy threshold once again, but not just looming motionlessly as before. Its shadowy mass was thrusting against the threshold with unbelievable force, while hatred and fury and evil hunger poured from it in overwhelming waves.

Before it two men stood, their glowing hands trying to reinforce an enormous pattern in the air, a framework of huge vertical bars of lurid green energy like the door of a mighty cage, blocking the monstrosity's path. One of the men had to be Lebarran, short and bald and fur-robed, and it was his voice

283

that was bellowing the ugly spell-words in a towering, manic rage. The much younger mage beside him could barely manage to pronounce the syllables, in a high quivering shriek, through his crippling terror.

But the magical barrier seemed to be holding, in that fraction of an instant as Krost took in the scene within the chamber. And his attention then fixed on the other two men in that place – one narrow and gaunt, the other heavy and puffy, both looking half-dead with fatigue yet both rallying as Krost and the others entered. Rallying to raise their bright hands, to mould another crimson bolt of explosive magical force, and hurl it.

Krost had no time to do more than duck his head. The close-range blast struck at them with irresistible fiery power. The shielding of the Five wavered under that blow, sagging, and then finally, irretrievably, collapsed. And though the shield had deflected much of that fearsome blast, enough of its force broke through to strike the small group down and scatter them across the floor like discarded dolls.

The giants, in the lead as ever, had taken the brunt of the impact and lay stunned, portions of their clothing smouldering. But Krost, finding some reserves of strength and will, forced himself to his knees, forced away the darkness that sought to overpower his mind. Dimly he was aware that Ghiscral and one or two of the giants were also struggling to rise, and that Aurilia and the other women were also stirring. Mistily he could still see and hear the separate battle being waged by Lebarran and his companion against the horror at the threshold. But far more clearly he could see the two other sorcerers, grinning with triumph, raising their hands to launch another bolt that would not meet any remaining scrap of a shield to diminish its murderous force.

With a choked roar Krost lurched swaying to his feet and hurled the iron quarterstaff at the thin sorcerer. But the man dodged jerkily aside, and the staff clanged uselessly against the far wall. Then the man's gloating grin widened as he and the fat one shaped the blast that would surely be final. And Krost could only stand empty-handed and empty-eyed, knowing that he could not move quickly enough to reach them in time.

It seemed then like an impossible illusion, an edge-of-death hallucination, when he saw Red Cordell and Vallawn step into the chamber through another entrance, behind the two sorcerers.

At once the old wizard's stick swung up, and a flare of bright blue fire jetted from its tip towards the fat sorcerer. As the man shrieked and crumpled, the gaunt one whirled – but he was not swift enough.

Red was already moving, leaping forward with his lips drawn back in an animal snarl. As the sorcerer's bright hands came up to fashion a deadly spell, Red slowed, balanced himself and threw the sword like a spear. The luminous blade flashed through the air, flying straight and true across the short distance, and buried itself for half its length in the mage's bony chest.

Then Krost heard a small glad cry from Aurilia, who was regaining her feet, as were the other Sisters and the giants. And as Red jerked his sword free from the corpse of Gul Ist, the tiny remnant of the attacking force turned to confront Lebarran.

In the ominous stillness that had fallen upon the chamber they saw that the Magister had somehow won his battle against the huge besieging horror. The magical barrier was in place across the threshold, the vast shapeless mass of the Unformed was in retreat along its misty bridge, its emanations of hunger and hatred receding as it went. But the conflict had demanded a fearsome price. The younger mage lay at Lebarran's feet, in a foetal curl, barely conscious. And Lebarran himself was swaying, head drooping, drenched in sweat, the glow of his eyes and his hands almost extinguished. Yet even so he found a vestige of strength enough to draw himself up, with a bestial growl deep in his throat, as the others faced him.

Slowly, one steady pace at a time, Vallawn began to move forward, with Red at his shoulder. On the other side of the room Aurilia also moved forward, her eyes no longer blank but fierce and intent. And with her moved the rest of the Five, some tottering but still with heads high and eyes bright, and

285

all of them together beginning as they went to murmur the first notes of a song. Not the shielding song, Krost realized, but another – that seemed to be calling into being the hazy shimmering shape of a huge silver spear.

Lebarran curled his lip, glaring. 'Vallawn? Have you grown senile, thinking to challenge *me*?'

'Look to your own condition, Lebarran.' The wizard's voice was filled with distaste. 'You have nothing left but your madness to fight us with.'

Lebarran's growl was a hoarse bass rasp. 'Come closer, old fool, and learn how mistaken you are.'

Vallawn took another calm step forward, and another. 'You may strike at me, Lebarran, or at the new leader of the Sisterhood, yonder. Whichever one of us you choose, the other will in that instant strike at you. And I doubt if you have the strength left to strike and shield at the same time.'

Lebarran shifted his glare to the Five, also moving towards him, the great silver spear hovering ready in the air among them like a huge arrow poised on an unseen bow. And on the other side, Vallawn raised his stick again, the tip beginning to burn blue.

For an endless instant when no one moved or blinked or seemed to breathe, Lebarran swung his head back and forth like a beast at bay to regard the forces ranged against him. His hands twitched, half-lifting, but their sorcerous glow remained dull and weak. As his face contorted, the strangled sound in his throat was full of frustration and despair.

Until, with a sudden roar, in an unexpected burst of manic strength, he seized the crumpled Yannahac by the collar of his robe, lifted him – and flung him across the misty threshold that had not entirely faded from sight behind him. And before any of the others could react, Lebarran himself plunged through the opening as well.

On to the barely visible surface of the bridge – which then, along with the threshold and with both mages, faded and shivered and flickered. And vanished.

As it did so the enormous metal canopy high above the building boomed out its mighty, menacing knell once more.

Looking up through the misty dimness among the branches, Krost saw the vast shape's vibration – and at once a connection came together in his mind, so that he remembered what he had failed to recall before. The fateful vision described to him by Silgid.

'*Out!*' he roared. 'Get *out*! *Run!*'

And he scooped Aurilia up in one arm, leaped forward to pull Red along with the other hand, and hurtled towards the far doorway. The giants reacted instantly, gathering up the other Sisters and charging after him at full speed into the maze of corridors, while the stony walls around them trembled and the canopy boomed and reverberated high above. In the midst of that thunderous uproar no other sounds could be heard, not the mighty thumping of the giants' boots, not the shouts and cries that came unconsciously from them all as Krost's desperation infected and impelled them, filling their legs with frenzied strength as they fled. Krost was galloping as swiftly as any of the longer-legged giants, bearing Aurilia as if she were no weight at all, with Red in a flat-out sprint barely keeping pace. Yet, impossibly, old Vallawn had somehow managed to gain and hold the lead in that frantic race, lighting their path with the blaze from his upraised stick as he guided them unerringly through the labyrinth. While just as impossibly the volume of noise from the massive vibrating canopy kept on swelling and expanding, a colossal, intolerable assault, battering at them and driving them on as they ran.

And they were barely out of the building, no more than a few long strides into the open ground beyond its outer walls, when the gigantic metal shape – its magical support dispelled – came at last crashing thunderously down to crush and pulverize the stony trees of Lebarran's home.

CODA

'Tell me again I'm not dreaming,' Red said quietly.

When no reply came he turned his head, smiling to see Aurilia sound asleep next to him, sprawled and relaxed under the light covering, her hair outspread in tangled waves. If I *am* dreaming, he added silently to himself, looking at her, don't for pity's sake ever, ever wake me up.

Settling back, drifting in the peace of his own total relaxation, he looked up at the embroidered cloth of the canopy that stretched above the bed. At once he had a chilling recollection of that other canopy, the gigantic metal covering that had come crashing so destructively down on to Lebarran's dwelling. But then he slowly began to smile, thinking of it, remembering how Krost had led their escape, remembering how beyond the building they had all tumbled over in a gasping, exhausted heap as if the magnitude of that final destruction had flung them off their feet. And remembering how he had heard, lying there, a peculiar sound – and had recognized it just as the others had turned to stare at him. He had started to laugh. And then Krost started as well, and Aurilia, and the giants, and even the dazed and breathless Sisters, all lying on the bare dank earth beyond the ruined building and laughing until they cried.

But eventually, after that paroxysm of relief and release and astonished celebration had run its course, they had got to their feet and had begun the process that had ended, a long time later, with Red comfortable and at peace in bed with Aurilia in the palace at Quamarr, with nothing more ominous hanging over his head than a colourful piece of cloth.

It was a process, however, that had begun sorrowfully for that small band. They set out to scour the forest for survivors, which they hoped to find, and for the dead that they *knew* they would find. They had no idea how the few of them could manage that labour, or the funeral duties that would necessarily follow. Yet they set out unhesitatingly to do it, because it was what had to be done. And almost at once the surprises began, turning some of their sorrow to gladness.

First was the swift and startling return of full natural daylight, as the rain-mist drifting among the trees began to disappear like a stain being washed from the air. As it faded, the heavy layer of cloud enclosing the valley thinned and tore apart into evanescent streamers that drifted away to nothing. And the full splendour of a bright summer sun struck down into all the bare open spaces among the trees.

The brightness lifted their spirits just as it aided their search. And soon their spirits rose further as they came upon more survivors than they had dared to hope. They found Brennia and a handful of warrior women, half-crazed with despair at having been separated from the Five, then half-crazed with joy at being reunited. They found Prince Phaedran, weak with loss of blood from a new head-wound, being guarded by a few terrified militiamen. They came upon many others, militia and Sisters and several giants, dazed and lost, suffering from injury and concussion, but alive. All were gathered up and their wounds tended, to join in the enlarging company's jubilation at the miracle that any of them had lived to see the conflict end and the sun shine again. In such a state they could not wholly be brought to melancholy again even by the dolorous task of collecting up the dead, nor by the tragic numbers of them, nor by the keening of the Sisters over the witch-fire funeral pyres.

And finally they all set off on the journey back to the edge of the valley, to face the climb back up to the meadow from which they had descended. With all the wounded to assist or carry it had been a slow and tortuous ascent, but the survivors' elation had transcended pain and weariness just as it had overridden sorrow, and in the end the task was complete.

Red smiled as he remembered, thinking of the particularly wild joy of his reunion with Grilena, and Krost's with Wolle, which made them both wonder if the horses had some instinctive awareness of the danger that their masters had faced. By then, as a normal twilight fell on the meadow above the valley, the healing Sisters were still engaged in their work on the more seriously injured, leaving those like Red and Krost with comparatively minor cuts and bruises to wait their turn. So they spent the evening in a slow tranquil supper while telling the astonishing tale of their victory to those who had been left behind.

The only thing that marred the peace of that evening, Red recalled, was known to very few. Aurilia had told him that Phaedran, strengthened by the healers' skills, had gone to greet his daughter in her closed carriage, to take her the glad news. But she had merely gazed at him with empty eyes from the depths of her withdrawal before saying without emotion, 'I thought you would be killed. Why were you not killed?'After which she had turned away and would not look at him again.

But even the small shadow of Evelane's response had seemed of little consequence the following morning when the company prepared to depart. Then the giants had made their farewells before returning across the mountains to their plateaux. And Red smiled again, recalling the moment during that parting of high, bitter-sweet joy. The moment had come after the giants had been almost overcome by the gratitude and affection showered upon them by the other survivors, and after Ghiscral and Phaedran had exchanged respects that had gone far beyond formality. Then Ghiscral had turned at last to Krost, standing quietly to one side with Red.

'Krost il Hak,' the chieftain had said solemnly, 'I ask you now to reconsider your vow never to visit your home and your people again. Come back to the plateaux when you can, and bring Corodel with you.' He had glanced hopefully at Red before looking back at Krost. 'For you may be sure, Krost, that none of the Mykraladan will sneer or mock at you again. Instead there will be new songs sung about you and new tales told. And they will say what *we* have come to know, during this terrible fighting – that in your heart and your spirit and your will you are the biggest of us all.'

Then all the others had cheered, and most of them had wept,

with huge tears also rolling down Krost's craggy cheeks. And at last, the remnants of the prince's army set off from the mountain meadow to begin the long northward march back to Quamarr, and home.

Since arriving they had all been staying as the prince's guests in the palace, completing their recovery from wounds and weariness and the residual effects of violence and horror. But as the restful sunlit warmth of the Grasslands summer advanced, Red knew, the time was approaching when more partings would have to be faced. Soon, when all the surviving Sisters were fully restored, Aurilia would take her followers back to the Fastness – where she herself would begin all the complex ceremonial magic of being installed and confirmed as the new leader of the Circle of Nine. After which she would oversee the equally prolonged labour of selecting and preparing others to replace those four of the Nine who had not survived.

In other words, Aurilia would once again be extremely busy and preoccupied, leaving little chance that she and Red could continue the idyll they were currently having in the palace. That likelihood made Red less than eager to accompany her – especially when he would not even have Brennia as a fencing partner, in the Fastness, since she was one of those to be elevated to the Circle of Nine. He knew the prince would make him welcome, but it would be a comparatively idle and empty time. For even Krost was planning to leave the palace before long, to visit his new friend, Silgid, in her home on the edge of the Moorlands. And while Red was intensely curious about all that, he knew better than to invite himself along.

Maybe I'll ride east, he said to himself drowsily as sleep began to claim him. Go and visit Hallifort in the Wastelands, thank him properly for sending the Riodae. If that's really how it happened . . .

As his eyes closed, he thought briefly about how everyone still remained mystified by the Riodae and their near-miraculous intervention. But at least even Aurilia no longer suspected that he knew anything about them, although it could be hard sometimes to keep such an amazing secret from her. And then he was asleep, drifting down into the midst of a dream where he climbed up a sandy slope on to an expanse of flat bare land with a chill wind moaning around him. And in the midst of the expanse stood a pale figure like a living statue carved from alabaster, regarding him with the white-and-purple eyes of Hallifort.

'Forgive me,' Hallifort said softly, 'for intruding in this way.'

'I'm glad to see you,' Red said, peering around. 'Where is this?'

'It is a landscape of your mind,' Hallifort told him. 'But my presence in it is not an empty dream. This is the only way that I may speak to you.'

'Really?' Red replied, from within the untroubled floating calm that he often felt in his dreams. 'I was thinking of visiting you, in the Wastelands.'

'I beg you most urgently not to do so, Red,' Hallifort said. 'Indeed, I am here now in this way to urge you to remember your promise to me, to keep my secret and that of the Riodae.'

'I will,' Red assured him. 'I have. I'd hardly betray you after what you did . . . It *was* you, wasn't it, who sent the Riodae to the Forest?'

'It was – though I did not exactly *send* them. I merely conveyed to them that your enemies in the Clouded Valley would come to threaten the hive if they were victorious. So they marched to avert that threat. Sadly, they could not continue in the end to confront Lebarran. They have an ineradicable terror of fire.'

'No matter,' Red said easily. 'They turned the battle and helped us win.'

'Indeed. And that is precisely why it is even more urgent, now, for their secret to be preserved. The spell that protects the Riodae from discovery is more powerful than you could imagine, but it has never been tested against a destructive assault by a power like Lebarran's.'

'Lebarran?' Red said, shocked. 'But he's *gone*!'

Hallifort shook his head, his inhuman eyes sombre. 'He fled into the Void Beyond, where he has travelled before. It is a place where I may not travel or even see, but I doubt if he has been destroyed. And I doubt whether he took the other mage,

292

Yannahac, with him as an act of mercy. I suspect he seeks to use the other man as a form of offering, so that he himself may survive the voracity of the entity he calls the Unformed. And it is all too possible that he may succeed.'

Once again Red was amazed at the extent of Hallifort's knowledge of far-flung events. But he was much more overcome by the implications of his words. 'If he does succeed, you're saying he could come back.'

'Most certainly. And so the secret of the Riodae *must* not be exposed, Red. And I must remain indefinitely with them, behind the protection of the spell that conceals them. For if Lebarran returns, he will assuredly be vengeful – determined among other things to search the Continent for the Riodae and for me, to bring his wrath upon us.'

Red shivered as the wind howled to emphasize the words. 'I'll keep your secret, Hallifort. And of course I'll stay away from the hive. No one will discover the Riodae because of me, I promise you. But . . . can't we do anything about Lebarran? Can't he be stopped from returning?'

'If he survives the perils of the Void, he can re-enter this Sphere at any point and at any time,' Hallifort said. 'There is no hope of barring his path. Nothing can be done except maintaining vigilance.'

'Can you do that, Hallifort?' Red asked. 'You seem to know everything that goes on, all over the Continent.'

'I will keep watch, certainly, as best I can, and give warning if it is possible. But understand me, Red. I will do *nothing at all* that might expose myself and the Riodae to Lebarran's awareness. So the highest adepts of the land, and the Sisterhood as well, must also set a ceaseless watch, and maintain it at all costs.'

'I'll pass the message on,' Red said numbly. 'Aurilia and Vallawn can organize it . . .'

The uncanny statue leaned closer, its weird eyes intent. 'And remind them, Red, of another and potentially more dire threat. Remind them that, aside from Lebarran, the monstrous evil of the Unformed has discovered how to make *its* way into this world.'

The purple irises seemed to enlarge and quiver as if on the

verge of starting to spin. And Red awoke with a bone-wrenching jolt, shivering in the warmth of the summer night as if the wind from his dream was still blowing through the room.